Monday's Child

Monday's Child

MOLLIE HARDWICK

'Monday's child is fair of face . . .'
Traditional Rhyme of Birthdays

ST. MARTIN'S PRESS
NEW YORK

Copyright © 1982 by Mollie Hardwick
For information, write: St. Martin's Press
175 Fifth Avenue, New York, N.Y. 10010
Manufactured in the United States of America

First published in Great Britain by Macdonald & Co. Publishers Ltd.

Library of Congress Cataloging in Publication Data

Hardwick, Mollie.
Monday's child.

I. Title.
PR6058.A6732M6   1982   823'.914   81-21501
           ISBN 0-312-54408-1   AACR2

Laura Diamond, acclaimed by many as the most beautiful woman in Victorian England, encounters unsuspected trials and a surprising struggle in her quest for love and happiness.

THE WIND FROM THE RIVER sent Laura's hair flying out in a pale golden banner and tightened the fold of her skirt against long legs. She leaned against it, enjoying its force, feeling herself a piece of Nature with the shrieking, wheeling gulls. At the foot of the low wall the Thames lapped sluggishly, dull today because the sun was hidden. Once, in bright weather, it had been clear enough for darting fishes to be seen in its waters; but now pollution was creeping into Greenwich Reach from dirty London down-river. Laura held her straw hat tight with one hand, looking out towards the boats milling about or anchored, little craft under sail, barges, colliers and bigger merchant vessels. She thought of each as a small world, holding the excitement of strange places and unknown people within its wooden walls.

The man with the sketching-pad dared to breathe as he took pencils from his pocket and supported himself against the wall of the Trafalgar Tavern. She was posed so perfectly, a miracle of natural grace, vividly alive yet so still. He thought of the professional models he worked from, poor things whose chief qualification was their ability to remain unmoving for a long time. He could push and yank them into place, but they would never fall into the lovely natural lines of this girl. He began to rough in her outline, the thrown-back head, the jut of small breasts beneath the plain, high-buttoned frock, the tender oval of her face, the faintest suggestion of a hook to the bridge of the nose, giving her profile a delicate arrogance against the grey sky. Absorbed in his work, he did not notice that her head had turned towards him.

'Here! What d'you think you're doing?' Her voice was straightforward London, not rough but certainly not refined. He swept off his wide-brimmed hat.

'I beg your pardon, miss. I took the liberty of making a

5

sketch of you.'

'Liberty, I should just think so! You might have asked a person's leave first.' She was straightening her hat, preparing to go. He came forward, anxious, smiling.

'I'm really very sorry. But you made such a fine picture, I couldn't resist the temptation. You might have been the model for the figurehead of a ship, a Circe or a Bacchante.'

He had shocked her. 'What! Those stary-eyed old frights in the museum? Thank you very much. If that's what I look like I'd best go out at nights and stay in all day.'

'Well then let's say the model for the Britannia statue they want to put up in the park. Something elegant and classical – is that better? I say, please don't go. Won't you let me finish the sketch? It'll only take a minute or two. Just stand as you were, looking out towards the river.'

'All right. But be quick, mind.' Now she was like a ship restless on the tide, the fluid grace of her attitude lost in self-conscious stiffness, her expression as ungracious as her voice. Drawing rapidly, he guessed that she was perhaps fourteen or fifteen by the childishness of her dress, with its short skirt, and the gauche manner; a product of one of those unremarkable families which from time to time, for no obvious reason, breed a daughter of the gods, divinely tall and most divinely fair. He noticed that her eyes were dark, though what shade he could not see, and that the brows were strongly marked, for a blonde. He would very much have liked to see her smile, but it was evident that she was not going to. He hurriedly pencilled in some shading, and held out the drawing to her.

'There. It's not properly finished, but you didn't give me time.'

She was studying it with grudging admiration. 'It's very clever,' she said.

'Would you like it?'

'No. Thanks.' She was backing away from him..

'Wont't you sit for me seriously another time – come to my studio, perhaps? I live in Crooms Hill, not very far. It would be quite proper, of course, you could bring your mother or your sister, anyone you like – and I'd pay you.'

Just for an instant he caught a flicker of interest, then it was gone, scared away by the extremely improper suggestion he

6

had made. Everybody knew about artists and their goings-on; there were music hall songs about them.

'I oughtn't to be talking to you,' she said. 'Goodbye.'

'Won't you even tell me your name?'

She shook her head and turned away, walking rapidly up the narrow street that led from the river. Suddenly she stopped and gave him the benefit of her smile, warm, sunny, utterly charming. 'Thanks for drawing me.' Then she was gone, running from him, her boots clattering on the cobbles until the sound faded into the general noise of traffic from Trafalgar Road.

By God, he said to himself. Circe, Bacchante, Emma Hamilton. A natural-born enchantress. Probably attends a Board school, father pushes a pen and mother takes in washing. Yet they've turned out a young Venus – or she will be when she's older, at present she's a nymph. He was surprised, amused, to find himself filled with the remembered sensations of love at first sight and its bitter-sweetness in his student days, when he was a boy ready to fall at the feet of a stunning model, a pretty grisette, another fellow's handsome sister. But that was long ago. Now he was almost thirty and ought to be past such things. Yet he longed, despite all reason, to see the girl again; to watch her beauty grow, to immortalize her in pencil and paint. For a moment, perhaps five minutes, he would allow himself the painful pleasure of imagining a love as hopeless as it was innocent.

Laura slowed her pace as she reached the busy road that ran between the towering splendours of the Royal Hospital buildings and the jewel-like Queen's House set in green gardens. She had grown up alongside them and did not notice them any more. Her mind was full of the artist she had just left so hastily. She felt guilty towards her mother for having disobeyed her by talking, really talking, to a strange man; but guilty too because she had been rude to him, ruder than she need have been. He had spoken so gently, and his eyes had been kind and honest, not like the eyes of men who turned to watch her in the street, then whistled and chi-iked and called things after her. He had such a fine beard, too, dark brown and curly, a beard splendid as that of Lord Salisbury the

Prime Minister as he appeared in newspaper drawings. It was nice to be admired by a gentleman.

Admiration was not often welcome to Laura. In her fifteen and a half years she had had enough and to spare of it, for her beauty had brought so much trouble and bother in its train. To begin with, she had been no different from other children, just a pretty cherub with hair so fair that it was almost white, then a leggy little girl too thin for her height. It was when she was going on for twelve that the hair which was now like fine gold had begun to single her out from the other girls in her class at Roan's School. She had a complexion of milk and roses, too, whereas they had just skin; they decided to hate her. Roan's was a fee-paying school, its pupils above the level of those at the Board school, but from the day when Laura Diamond's beauty dawned the establishment virtually became an academy for the training of young fiends. Jealousy and spite followed her from the morning hymn to the dismissal of the last afternoon class. If she walked in the school yard, somebody running on silent feet would come up behind her and give her hair a vicious tug. Her arms and thighs were often stained green, blue and black with sly pinches from those who sat next to her. There was no end to the devices they used to get Laura into trouble with the teacher; her books and exercises were stolen, strange and sometimes horrible objects were put in her desk to frighten her. She began to hate school and long for the moment when she could go home.

A few of the girls, the plainer ones who could not possibly set themselves up as rivals, went to the other extreme and worshipped her. Little Polly Gilkes, undersized and having only one eye, the result of an accident in infancy, appointed herself Laura's devoted slave, always ready to carry books or sharpen pens. Her poor, grotesque face became an acute irritation, the worse for being mingled with pity. Minnie Dobbs, plain, pale and pious, who went to church three times every Sunday, associated Laura with the stained glass beauties of its windows; blonde angels, a Magdalen with streaming hair. Minnie mooned about after her idol, wearing a sentimental expression which provoked Laura to exasperated mockery, a retaliation which would end with Minnie in tears.

The boys were worse. Ugly boys, unwashed boys, spotty

boys, eyeing her up and down as if she were a joint of meat on a butcher's slab. Brutal boys, singling her out for cruel jokes because her looks tantalized them. The strap of her satchel would be cut slyly, so that both satchel and books fell in the mud when she set out to walk home. A slide along the pavement would be arranged so that a sliding boy could collide with her and knock her down; her hat, hanging on its peg, would be found wreathed with a rude message.

The spooney ones were easier to deal with, the ones who laboriously copied out verses and left them in her desk or between the pages of a book.

The rose is red, the violet's blue,
Sugar is sweet and so are you.

On 14 February there would be Valentine cards, stout cupids leering in a bower of pink roses, an elegant lady and gentleman being borne aloft in the basket of a balloon shaped like a heart. As she opened them Laura was conscious of anxious eyes fixed upon her by the anonymous scribes of Be Mine, Ever Thine Own, Your Unknown Lover. It was unfair that, this year, an acidulated teacher, Miss Postleby, should have hovered and pounced on Laura as she opened Valentines in the shelter of her desk-lid.

'Really, Laura Diamond! Are you not ashamed of yourself?'

'What for, Miss Postleby?' Laura turned wondering eyes on her, eyes that could seem the colour of old sherry or clear tarn water at times, and at other times the slate-grey of a stormy sky.

'These ridiculous, rubbishy cards. How can a decent, respectable girl from a good home touch such things? Give them to me.'

'But, Miss, please – they're not mine, I mean I didn't . . .'

The Valentines were already in the grate, flames and ashes, Cupid shot down. It was very unfair, just as unfair as Miss Postleby's quite unwarranted invasion of the playground to break up one of the round games that were played on fine days, Laura standing in the centre, half-shy, half-smiling, a ring of prancing lads encircling her:

Here comes a crowd of jolly sailor-boys, who lately come
 ashore,
They spend their time in drinking lager-wine, as they have
 done before.
As we go around, and around, and around, as we go round
 once more,
And this is a girl, and a very pretty girl,
A kiss for kneeling down.

The angry teacher, like an infuriated hen, scattered the boys
and shook Laura's shoulders.

'I will not have these improper games! Laura Diamond,
you will stay after school for an extra hour and write out
lines. Go along, all of you.'

'But Miss, it's not my fault! They *will* choose me . . .'

It had not been her fault. Yet she was always made to pay
for other people's silliness. If this was what one had to put up
with for being pretty, she wished she could be as plain as
Polly Gilkes, only with the usual number of eyes, for
preference. Or as plain as her own sister Ellaline, dear little
Ellie who had such a sweet nature and was liked by everybody. It would be nice to be plain and clever, one of the
young ladies who were causing such a sensation at Girton
College in Cambridge. Laura had seen pictures of them, tall,
stately and grave in their academic robes and mortarboards.
The only difficulty was that Laura knew she was not very
clever. Bright, the teachers admitted her to be, but no more.
Bright, lazy and dreamy, they said.

It must be possible to be pretty and not suffer the
indignities that were put on her at school. She found it hard to
imagine that the Princess of Wales, lovely Alexandra, had had
her hair pulled or her arms pinched by anybody, or that
people shook her for receiving Valentine cards. It must be
very pleasant to be royalty, to wear a crown and have
everything of the best. People would look at Princess Alexandra as the artist had looked at her, Laura.

She kicked a stone along in front of her, not seeing it, or the
street that led into her own. His eyes had been humble,
adoring, pleading with her for something – what? The
spooney boys wanted to kiss her, with damp unpleasant lips
and clumsy embraces that hurt. Polly and Minnie wanted her

10

to be nice to them, walk with them in the playground, arms entwined. None of that seemed to be what the man with the beautiful beard would want.

Suddenly she was at her own gate, the gate that led into the small, neat terraced house. Its windows looked right on to the lower slopes of Greenwich Park, a glorious piece of country-side dropped into an urban spread, growing ever more industrialized, a pleasance with trees and deer and long refreshing vistas of the River Thames and London in the distance.

The artist had been right in guessing that Laura's father might be a clerk. Daniel Diamond worked in Ponsford's, a firm of tea-shippers, on the edge where Greenwich met Deptford. But, far from taking in washing, Mrs Diamond prided herself on being almost a lady of leisure now that her two daughters were old enough to help her in the house, Ellie patient and naturally skilled in cleaning and cookery, Laura feckless and scatterbrained.

As Laura entered with a banging of the door and a slamming down of her satchel on the hall table her mother called from the sitting-room.

'You're late. Where have you been until this time?'

Laura strolled in, bracing herself for another inquisition. Her mother was sitting by the window, making the most of the summer afternoon light, a copy of *The Woman at Home* on her lap. She liked to keep in touch with a world outside her own, the world of the villa and the vicarage, catching glimpses of still higher life through the eyes of privileged female fashion correspondents. It was Alice Diamond's dream that some day one of her daughters would marry into such a world and transport her family to it, far away from the little three up, two down house whose only recommendation was that it stood on land which had been royal, hundreds of year ago, and looked out from its mean bay window on to a king's park and a house a queen had loved. Alice prided herself on knowing more than anyone about the noble past of Greenwich – the birth of Queen Elizabeth in the old palace, her dazzling of the natives in a dress ornamented with pearls as big as beans, her father King Henry going hunting, all in green, even to the shoes, the building of the great Royal Hospital and the founding of the Observatory on the hill.

11

Such things fascinated her. In the days of King Charles a ship called the *Diamond* had been launched at Greenwich; she thought of her daughters as two such ships, launched on the sea of life, and longed for their voyage to be as glorious.

Yet Ellaline was so plain, with her slightly protruding teeth and the shadow of a dark moustache above them, her only claim to beauty a pair of soft brown eyes. Ellie took after her father, whose Jewish grandfather had come to England from Germany. Alice preferred not to think about this. Her hopes were pinned on the daughter who was as fair as she herself had been before the gold faded to grey and the young face had fallen into lines, though her figure stayed trim in relentless corsets. She had lost two babies, both boys. Laura must make up for them, and for Ellie's teeth and the general drabness of Feathers Row, Laura who was so bright and beautiful, a daughter of Life, a girl born to be queen.

'I said, you're late. Ellie's been home half an hour.'

'I know, Ma. I'm sorry. I just went to look at the river. School was so stuffy today, you can't believe. Phoo!' Laura fanned herself. 'If those boys would only wash it would help.'

'Have you been with one of them?' her mother asked sharply.

'What, them? Ha! not likely. No, I just went for a stroll as far as the jetty. Is tea ready? I'm starving.' She went into the kitchen, warm and clean-smelling from recent baking and linen airing on the rack below the ceiling. Ellie's short sturdy figure was draped in the long pinafore which their mother insisted should be worn in the house. Laura hated hers and had to be nagged into wearing it. Now she hovered over the table, assessing the generously spread bread-and-butter, the warm, fresh-baked sponge cake with its dainty freckled top, the coconut biscuits and the sedate woollen hen which sat on the teapot to keep it warm. Her hand went to a biscuit.

'Don't,' Ellie whispered. 'Not until Ma comes. You know she doesn't like you starting first.'

'Oh, well. I think I deserve a bit of reward, though, after the day I've had.'

'Was it bad again?' Ellie's eyes, the brown of a bumblebee's fur, were alight with sympathy.

'Awful. I hate it. I hate them all. I wish I could leave. I'm

12

too old for school, I'd rather do anything.'

'Ask Ma again, perhaps she'll let you this time. Wait until after tea when she's in a good mood,' advised the wisdom of fourteen years.

'All right, I will.' Laura spun round to her sister, sparkling. 'Ellie, such a lark! I met a swell down on the wharf, and he drew my picture. It was ever so nice. He had a lovely brown beard and he talked like a real gent. I was as cool as cool, of course. I just said yes and no and kept my nose in the air . . .'

'Yes and not to what, may I ask?' Their mother was standing in the doorway, pale and baleful. There was a note in her voice that Laura dreaded. It might mean no tea and banishment to bed. She could have bitten off her tongue for talking so to Ellie, without making sure that her mother was out of hearing. The only thing to do was to treat it lightly.

'Oh, to nothing, Ma,' she said airily. 'There was this nice man doing a drawing of me before I even noticed. Then he showed it to me and asked if I'd like to have it, and of course I said no, and came away. That was all.'

'Haven't I always told you not to speak to strange men?'

'I didn't. he spoke to me and I hardly answered, really. You'd have been pleased if you'd been there.'

'If I'd been there you'd not have been talking to him. Who is this man? Have you seen him before? Where does he live?'

'How do *I* know? No, I haven't seen him before, and I don't suppose I will again. He said he lived in Crooms Hill, not that it matters. I wish you wouldn't make something out of nothing all the time, Ma.'

'Don't be cheeky with me, madam! Your mother knows what's best for you, and I don't like the sound of this at all. Strikes me you're not to be trusted out on your own.'

Laura's blood was up. 'So what are you going to do about it, Ma? Tie a string round me and Ellie so we never go out without each other, or come with me yourself? Perhaps you'd like to push me in a go-cart, even though I *am* nearly sixteen. You might have a bit more sense.'

Ellie was almost cowering, though she would not get the brunt of her mother's anger. She edged nearer to Laura, longing to take her hand and support her. But Laura was staring back at her mother defiantly, neither of them moving, like two cats about to start fighting. Then Alice Diamond

13

said, 'Go upstairs.'

'But Ma . . .'

'Go upstairs.'

'But I haven't had my tea!'

'You heard me. Those that disobey must do without.'

Laura's courage broke. She gave a loud sob and rushed from the room, her hurrying feet clattering on the stairs, her crying receding behind the slammed bedroom door. Ellie was crying too, tears of grief for her sister rolling down her cheeks. She tugged at her mother's skirt as she had done when a small child, begging for something for 'Lorla'.

'Please, please let her have her tea! Oh, do, Ma. You don't know how horrid the food is at school. And she didn't do anything wrong, truly she didn't, she never does, only people pick on her. Oh, Ma, please!'

'What do you know about it? Sit down and eat your tea.'

They sat at the table, Mrs Diamond determinedly eating and drinking, though her throat felt constricted with anger and distress: the anger partly with herself, for the uncontrollable harshness she had shown the daughter she jealously prized. Perhaps she should have been more reasonable, since nothing seemed to have happened. But it was a case of being cruel to be kind, and she would not let herself weaken.

Ellie swallowed a few crumbs of bread and butter. The tea was cold in her cup. She washed down the crumbs with it, but the taste was drowned in the salt of tears. After a moment she got up, muttering an excuse, and left her mother to the possession of the table and all its riches. Alice Diamond sat there, no longer eating, heavy-hearted with memory.

A memory that was shared by Laura, crying on her bed. For if the thing had not happened years ago she would not be suffering like this now.

She had never understood it. It had been to do with the sort of matters her mother had decreed were never to be talked about or even mentioned – things like the fact that she had 'become a woman', as her mother had put it, at the age of eleven, but that Ellie had only just attained that mysterious and uncomfortable state. Not being able to talk about the strange thing that had happened three summers ago made it all the more dark and sinister to look back on. She and Ellie had whispered about it, but Ellie understood even less than she did.

Her mind went back to it. A blue and gold May morning, Whit Monday, everyone on holiday, including her father, and the family was to enjoy a rare treat – a steamboat trip down-river to London. The two girls were put into their best clothes, Laura proud in a damson red holland frock which was new and slightly scratchy round the collar, but pleased her very much, a tam-o'-shanter perched rakishly on her head. Her father, usually so abstracted in his manner that it was hard to know whether he was even aware that people were talking to him, became quite lively at the prospect of a day's freedom from his dark office. Laura thought he even looked different, younger, in the brown Derby hat that hid his spreading bald patch, and his best black suit. He had polished his drooping moustache with Pomade Hongroise so that it gleamed. He looked quite foreign today, and Laura was rather proud of the difference between him and other, ordinary fathers.

She and Ellie ran about the deck, calling to each other to come and see this or that – a big ship with a Russian name on its bows, a riverside pub where people were drinking outside, waving and raising their glasses to the *Princess Beatrice* as she chugged by with her load of merrymakers. Down in the saloon there was everything one could possibly want to drink and eat – tea and ginger beer, shrimps, cockles and mussels, buns with sugar on top and jam in the middle. Laura and Ellie were given sixpence each to spend – 'and mind you don't make yourselves sick', their mother warned, though not very severely. She had been different, kinder, in those days.

Forests of masts and sails lined the riverbanks, sail and steam together. Laura scanned them eagerly: where had they been, where were they going, to what strange countries? Geography lessons were her favourites at school, rich in alluring names – Vladivostock, Rajputana, Mandalay, Carinthia and Styria, Lorraine and Missouri, Baltimore, Seville . . . She was not particularly good at remembering which rivers belonged to which, or what goods each country produced. When she went to them herself she would find out. A sailor, leaning on the rail of a Dutch vessel, pipe in mouth, caught her eye, took in the beauty of her laughing face and flying hair. He removed the pipe and blew her extravagant kisses.

She blew one back to him, then skipped out of his sight. The great landmarks were coming into view, one by one, as the bridges went past. The Tower, four-square, majestic in the sun, the Monument raising its crown of fire high above spires, towers, and chimneys, the twin peaks of Cannon Street Station, green Temple Gardens and, coming nearer every minute, the circular Shot Tower at Waterloo, and round the bend of the river the bulk of Westminster and the benevolent face of Big Ben.

'We're nearly there! Come on, Ellie, we're nearly there!' Hats were straightened and handkerchieves wiped sticky mouths as the Diamonds gathered to leave the boat at Charing Cross Pier. At last they were on land again, Laura skipping excitedly at her father's side, Ellie staying close by her mother, a shade timid of strange places and great buildings. It was agreed that they should move towards Piccadilly, where the Moore and Burgess Minstrels would be performing in St James's Hall, among other attractions, and Alice wanted to look in the windows of Swan and Edgar's, in Regent Circus, even though the shop would be closed. 'We ought to be in time to see the mail-coaches leave the White Horse,' Daniel said. 'It's a fine sight, something you girls don't get the chance of every day. And there's the Devonshire Gems on view at Devonshire House. I'd like to see 'em, if it's all right with you, Alice.' He glanced wistfully at his wife. His father had been a jeweller, and Daniel had grown up with a love for the sparkling objects, though his bad sight had prevented him from taking up the trade.

'I don't mind,' Alice replied, 'if the girls don't get too tired, walking all that way. But I daresay we'll find somewhere to sit down.'

It was in the Haymarket that Laura lost her parents. She had stopped in front of the Haymarket Theatre, transfixed by the photographs of divinely beautiful ladies and dramatically handsome gentlemen in situations whose details Laura could not even imagine, for she had never seen a play, only performances at Crowder's Music Hall. She stared and wondered, walking from one display case to the other, a new world of fascination before her, bearing her imagination outside even the thrill of the London streets.

She must have looked for a full five minutes before she

turned to see that crowds were milling up and down the Haymarket, but that her parents and Ellie were nowhere to be seen. They must have gone on ahead, and would be dawdling so that she could catch up with them. She hurried up the street, remembering that Pa had said something about a famous pipe and tobacco shop. Yes, there it was, the royal 'By Appointment' sign above its door. But her father was not looking in the windows; he was nowhere in the multitude of strangers.

Panic took hold of her. She stood stock-still in Fribourg and Treyer's doorway, her fist at her mouth, clutching the little reticule that held her spending money for the day against her. They had told her that if ever she was lost in London – how unlikely it had once seemed! – she should look for a policeman. She looked, and there was none to be seen, no reassuring helmet. She was alone in the crowds, her family vanished. She had never been so afraid.

'My dear, are you waiting for someone?' The voice was soft, foreign-accented, the speaker a slender woman of perhaps thirty, dressed from bonnet to boots in black, conveying great elegance with no suggestion of mourning. Beneath the neat bonnet there peeped out a Piccadilly fringe of auburn hair. Even in her distraction Laura registered that it was a very becoming style which she would like to wear when she was old enough.

'N-no, thank you,' she stammered. 'I'm lost. My mother and father . . . my sister . . . they've gone, I can't find them.'

'Oh, but that is sad. How did it come about?'

Laura embarked on rambling explanation, her eyes roaming in search of a familiar face among the crowds. 'And I want to find a policeman, but there – isn't one.'

The stranger nodded. 'There never is when one is needed. Don't be afraid, I shall take you to a police station and there you shall wait for your family. How old are you, my dear?'

'Twelve. Almost thirteen.'

'Ah. But you are tall, for twelve years. Amost as tall as me. Come, take my hand, don't be afraid. I know these streets very well.'

And indeed she wove her way in and out of the Bank Holiday mob as skilfully as a cat, seeming to know just what move those in front were going to make. As they walked she asked questions in her quick light voice: Laura's name, her home, her father's occupation. Laura answered abstractedly, not so afraid now, but very much wishing they could arrive at the police station. 'Is it far now?' she asked, more than once.

'Not far at all.'

Laura looked around at the narrow street they were in, much narrower then the Haymarket, a street of tall old houses and little shops, with a smell wafting up from the basements that was as foreign as her guide's voice, a blend of onions and rich cheeses and spices. 'Where are we?' she asked. 'Is this Piccadilly? Ma said we were to go there.'

'Not Piccadilly, no, but quite near. Ah!' She stopped in front of the fan-lighted doorway of a terraced house, a house like the others in the street, spear-pointed railings round its area, an ancient link-extinguisher at the corner of them, three steps up with a boot-scraper by the door. 'This is where I live, my dear. Now don't you think we should go inside and refresh outselves? I am very warm, and I can see that you are, also. A little lemonade, a little rest?' She smiled beguilingly, her head tilted. Laura wavered. She *was* hot, her new boots hurt, and her mouth was dry. But she was not to be turned aside too easily.

'The police station . . . ?'

'Very near now, just round the corner. We must not let your parents see you so pale and tired, must we, or they will say I have taken bad care of you. Come.' The lady produced a key and opened the door, ushering Laura into a dark narrow hallway. The stairs were dark too, and steep, leading to a landing off which another small landing led to a door which the lady opened, calling something in French.

The room had more furniture in it than any Laura had seen: a large chesterfield, two easy chairs and assorted small ones, a chiffonier loaded with objects, some pictures which looked un-English. It was not a cheerful room, or one in which Laura imagined resting very comfortably, in spite of the cushioned chesterfield. A man entered by another door, older than the woman, beginning to grow stout. He was clean-shaven and wore a clerical collar. He appeared surprised to see Laura.

'Ah, Philippe, we have a visitor, do you see? A young lady lost in the streets. I take her to the police, but first I think we rest for a moment. Her name is Laura – is that not pretty? My dear, this is my brother.'

The man came forward and shook Laura's hand limply, saying that he was pleased to meet her. It struck her as odd that he should sound perfectly English when his sister was so foreign, and also that, in spite of the collar, he spoke in a rather common way. He sat in a chair opposite Laura, studying her from head to foot, as though he'd never seen a girl before, she thought rather crossly. There was something about his eyes that reminded her of the more unpleasant boys at school. But, obedient to the lady's suggestion, she put her feet up on the chesterfield and accepted the glass of lemonade which appeared shortly. It was rather warm and not very refreshing.

'Now can we go?' she asked.

'But we have only been here five minutes, my dear. Philippe, don't you think our visitor is charming? Nearly thirteen years, imagine that, and so tall, so shapely.'

'Fine big gal,' agreed Philippe. Laura began to feel uncomfortable at hearing herself talked about so personally. She looked away from Philippe's appraising eyes, and so missed the eloquent exchange of glances between the two – a lifting of the brows, a nod, a jerk of the head towards the next room.

'We have something to attend to for a moment, dear Laura,' said the lady. 'Let me give you a little more lemonade – ah yes, and a very small drop of cordial, for you are so pale, child. Here.' She rapidly poured something from a small bottle into the lemonade glass and handed it to Laura, who said, 'It smells like medicine. I'm not ill, I'm not even tired now. Please, can we go?'

'If you will drink that good cordial.'

Unwillingly, Laura drank it. It tasted even more medicinal than it smelt. The couple went out, the woman casting a backward glance at her. Left alone, Laura looked uneasily round the room. She would have given anything to be out of it, somewhere her parents could find her. But it would seem rude simply to go when the woman had been so kind to her.

She became aware of a strange drowsiness creeping over her, though she had just told them she was not tired. Her legs felt heavy, and there was a buzzing in her ears. Not wanting to give way, she forced herself to notice details in the room. A

19

bird-cage hung in the window, empty. A large picture showed an over-fat naked woman lounging, it appeared, on a marble slab. On a small chair sat an elaborately dressed doll with a painted face. Then nothing more; she was asleep.

Had she but known it, the quantities of sticky buns and other refreshments she had eaten on the boat saved her from deep unconsciousness. The drug which affected hungry children so powerfully merely touched her, and then receded. The man and woman were back in the room, talking. Some instinct warned her to keep her eyes closed.

'But what could be better?' the woman was saying. 'I knew when I set eyes on her that she was for us. Such a beauty, and of just the right age.'

'That she ain't. Short of thirteen, she said, didn't she? Still protected by the law, then. We'd be fools to risk it, Cecile.'

'I tell you there is no risk! Who will find her? Why should they look here? And if they do search, it will be days before they come to us. She could be across the water by tomorrow. As to the age, she looks older and soon she will indeed be thirteen. And think, my dear, she is a *fresh* girl, no question of that, no need to have her examined.'

'Can't tell that,' the man muttered.

'I know, I tell you! Send for Madame if you will, but I know she would certify this one without examining. Come, Philippe, show some reason. It is the will of Fate – I am in the Haymarket, where the little ones promenade themselves for sale, when I see this pretty package waiting, but waiting for me to pass by. I speak to her, she is lost, and how can a child be more lost than in London? I lead her here, *et voilà, une trouvaille.*'

'All very fine, but she ain't one of your stupid ones. She'll talk, give people her name, then we'll be properly shown up.'

'She will not talk *afterwards*,' Cecile snapped. '*Elle serait trop honteuse*. She would not dare to go home. That sort fear their mamas, I know them. And she will be confused, she will not know where she is if we keep her well drunk.'

'You'll need to top her up now, then,' said the man. 'She's coming round.'

Alarm at the words she had heard, understanding not their sense but the threat they carried, caused Laura's eyelids to flicker uncontrollably. She opened her eyes. The two were surveying her as though she were indeed the package the woman had mentioned.

'Ah, *ma petite*,' said Cecile, smiling. 'You are awake. Now, see what pretty clothes I have brought you. How your papa and mama will rejoice to see you wear them. You must say they are a little gift from the lady who has rescued you.' She held up a purple dress, very low-cut in bodice and short in the skirts, trimmed with coarse lace. It had been mended in places, and smelt like the clothes sold second-hand on market barrows. Over Cecile's arm hung a yellowed petticoat with many frills. Laura recoiled.

'I don't want to wear those – they're horrid! My mother wouldn't let me wear them – and my own dress is quite new. Take them away!' Her voice was rising. 'I don't believe you mean to take me to the police at all. Let me go – I want to go!'

The man and woman exchanged a look. 'Very well, Philippe,' Cecile said quietly. 'Hold her.'

Laura screamed and struggled as the man caught her in a tight, painful grip. Cecile ripped at the buttons at the back of her frock, tearing them until it was open to the waist, then pulled it roughly down and off. Then her two petticoats were removed, and her camisole.

'See what a pretty little *poule*, Philippe. She will look fine in new feathers.' Laura gave up struggling and let Cecile put the purple frock and the petticoat on her. She was already bruised and scratched from the removal of her own clothes. Cecile stepped back to admire.

'So. How well it suits the golden hair and the pretty white *mammelles*. Not very large yet, but the old gentlemen like that. Would you not enjoy a bite of this cherry, Philippe?'

'Shut up,' Philippe growled. 'No call for that sort o' talk. Best get word to the old man to come and finish her off. I don't trust this one on the Dover packet. And get some more of the stuff down her.'

'Ah, yes, of course' The glass was refilled from the small bottle and put to Laura's lips. 'Drink it. You will drink.' A cruel pinch to her arm brought a cry, and as her lips parted the draught was tipped into her mouth. She swallowed, shaking her head with revulsion.

'*Bien.* Now sleep. You hear – sleep!' said Cecile fiercely, suddenly hard-faced and ugly. She pushed the man sharply in the back towards the inner door, and followed him through it.

Laura knew that if she let the draught take hold of her she would be finished, and whatever bad things they planned for her would happen. There was a remedy, a finger down the throat. It worked, as it always had done – the burning, nauseous liquid came back instantly. She hoped it would mark their carpet. She was free of it, clear-headed though frightened to death. A few moments ago it had seemed a bad dream from which she would wake to see the sunshine on her bedroom ceiling and know that it would be a fine day for the family outing. But that had happened, and this was all too true. What do they want of me? she wondered. To make me a servant – or what? One thing was clear, she must get out. There was no sound of conversation in the next room, they must have moved out of it, perhaps to 'get word to the old man', whoever he might be. She watched the door that led to the landing. Cecile had not locked it, Laura was sure. Stealthily she got up and stole towards it, stealthily turned the knob. No, mercifully it was unlocked. In a flash she was through it, remembering the way they had come, leaping down the stairs as fast as her long legs could move.

' 'Ere!' A woman, a servant in cap and apron, was standing at the end of the dark hall. Before she could move Laura was out of the front door and into the street, running, running, northwards, unconscious of the stares at her gaudy dress. A cabbie pulled his horse up sharply to avoid running her over as she raced across a street that crossed the main thorough-gare. She glanced upwards, taking in the letters high on a wall, DEAN STREET. A woman put out a hand to stop her, but she wrenched herself away and ran on. BOURCHIER STREET, MEARD STREET. There was an open space ahead, a square, where she could dodge her pursuers. She dared not look behind to see if they were behind her.

'Now, now, miss.' A deep voice, a large solid form in blue enfolding her. She was in the arms of a policeman.

The rest of that day seemed to last for years, as she sat in a large room at Great Marlborough Street Police Station, answering endless questions from a fatherly sergeant, the

22

answers being swiftly taken down by a young constable. She described the people and the house, remembered that a nearby window had displayed a notice saying Dancing Academy, and a small shop which sold various kinds of sausages had stood on the corner. The kindly sergeant and the big man who had rescued her exchanged meaningful glances and a few words.

'Looks like we've got 'em.'

'If we can only pin it on 'em.'

'There's the young lady's age, that'll count. They got the Dutchman that way.'

It all passed over Laura's head. Her violent trembling had stopped, and she had drunk a lot of hot sweet tea. She had been at the station for an hour, wrapped in somebody's greatcoat to conceal the horrible dress, when another constable came in and murmured to the sergeant, who turned to Laura, beaming.

'Your ma and pa's here, my dear. Seems they reported your loss at Scotland Yard, who telegraphed to B and C Divisions and were told you were here. So all's well that ends well, eh?'

But for Laura the adventure was by no means ended.

CHAPTER TWO

BECAUSE ALICE DIAMOND HAD BEEN badly frightened by the attempted abduction of Laura, she reacted like a mother whose child had just escaped being run down by a horse and trap. If the child had not been in the road in the first place there would never have been any danger. If, in the road, it had behaved properly, the horse's hooves would never have been anywhere near it. Therefore it followed that the child was in the wrong and must be slapped.

Laura's parents had listened in uncomprehending horror to the sergeant's explanation of what had lain behind it all. Knowing nothing of London vice, they could hardly take in the fact that virgins, and particularly child virgins, were highly popular with men who were prepared to pay for their pleasures. Every week young girls were shipped over to the Continent from London 'houses', where procurers and procuresses did a lively trade. Their livestock was often obtained from the streets, where crowds of young children and women paraded the fashionable pavements of the Haymarket and Regent Street. Sometimes the innocent were lured in – nursemaids in the parks, young servants – ready enough to exchange their virtue for hard cash. Worse, they might be decoyed into a 'house', then sold to an interested client for a quick turnover of money or shipped over the Channel to waiting flesh merchants, for the price of something like £1 per girl.

'And we can't touch 'em, you see, sir and ma'am, unless someone at the top takes action. There was a committee set up in '80, that looked into the Belgian trade and caught three of 'em over there. We know all about that house in Dean Street, your daughter having been sharp enough to spot whereabouts it was, and we're watching like cats at a mouse-hole for just such a thing as this, unlawful kidnapping of a young person.

'Now I reckon that with your daughter's evidence in court we could bring a good case against these two beauties, Madame Cecile and her pal Phil Gabbit, which is only one of his names. There'd be an outcry when it was made public, and most likely a new bye-law would be brought in. So . . .'

'I won't allow it,' Alice said.

'But it's quite straightforward, ma'am. The young lady's entitled to testify, being aged over eight, and under the age of consent, thirteen, so there's no reason why she shouldn't.'

'I won't hear of it. Nor will her father. Dragging our disgrace out in public – why, we'd have to move, and as for Laura, it would be enough to take her character away for life. Nonsense!'

The sergeant looked baffled, and Daniel shifted uneasily. 'Alice,' he said, 'if it brought about a change in the law, don't you think . . .'

'I won't have Laura dragged through the courts. She's not to be told any of this, mind, only that bad people wanted to make her their servant, which is what she thinks.'

'But ma'am, where's the disgrace you talk about? As far as I can make out, the young lady was behaving quite properly when Madame Cec picked her up. She's got nothing to be ashamed of.'

'How do we know how she was behaving?' Alice snapped back. 'Flaunting herself, carrying on like a peacock to show London how fine she was. That woman didn't take notice of her for nothing.'

'If you'll pardon me, such persons as Madame Cec have got eyes all round their heads for likely girls. It's good looks they go for, and you daughter's remarkably pretty, if I may say so.'

'Too pretty for her own good,' Alice said darkly.

And she treated Laura as such in the years that followed, blocking every path that might lead her to temptation and destruction. Yet Laura was never told the reason; the mysterious goings-on at the house in Dean Street remained a mystery to her. It was simply made quite clear to her that looks like hers were dangerous and must be guarded like treasure. Thus it remained, until the day she saw something else in the eyes of a bearded artist, something which seemed

25

to say that her beauty was not wicked or a cross she had to bear. She looked for him again and again, searching the river frontage where she had seen him, the park with its famous view where many artists painted; strolling as if casually up Crooms Hill, with its handsome houses. But he was never there to answer her questions: What did you see in me and why do they think it wrong? Am I beautiful now, more beautiful than you thought I was then?

At sixteen she was at last allowed to leave school, where she had not very satisfactorily been teaching the little ones their letters. It was a tremendous relief to be away from the spite and the sentimental yearnings alike.

'Think of it, Ellie – long frocks at last, and my hair up!' She sighed. 'Ma won't let me wear a fringe, though – no fear.'

'You'll look lovely without one, dear.' And she did, the hair gathered to the top of her head like sheaved corn, curling wisps clustering on her neck. She was a little plumper and rounder than she would be when she was fully grown, but her waist was taper-slender, set off by the bustle which refined ladies referred to as a dress-improver. Alice saw her daughter growing up and away from her, out of her control, no longer a baby in leading-strings or a coltish schoolgirl, but a young woman, uncertain of herself as April weather.

Ellie was growing up, too, but not flowering into beauty. Her skin was still as sallow as ever, her hair as lifeless, her figure unfashionably flat. Laura worried about Ellie's looks, and pored over Hints to Our Girls in magazines. If they worked for some, they failed signally for poor Ellie. The peroxide of hydrogen applied to her moustachioed upper lip merely lightened some hairs and not others, and did nothing to lessen the growth.

'Oh well, never mind,' sighed Laura. 'I'm sure it will go away when you're older. I'm going to try the very littlest touch of colour for your face, just a suspicion.'

'Lorla! Not rouge? Oh, I couldn't.'

'Not exactly rouge. It's this.' She produced a tiny round box labelled Angel's Blush. 'I said it was for my mother.' They giggled. 'Let's try it.' Laura positioned Ellie before a mirror and delicately touched her cheeks with the fluffy pad. The effect was painfully artificial. Laura shook her head.

'No, it won't do. It makes you look like an actress. What a

pity.'

'I don't mind, truly, dear. You're the beauty of the family, it doesn't matter about me.'

'Stuff! Everybody can improve themselves,' said Laura confidently, having no need to do so herself. 'Now remember to keep your shoulders straight and brush your hair a hundred times every single night, and you'll soon see a difference.'

Now that they were young women, it was time they helped with the family budget. Alice set out to find respectable work for them, and managed to place Laura in a haberdasher's shop in Church Street, where a pleasing young person was wanted to sell ribbons and laces and other fancy goods. Laura enjoyed handling them, enjoyed even more the variety of customers, from wharfingers' wives to ladies from the great houses up the hill, Chesterfield House, Macartney House, The Grange. Her chatty manner and warm smile encouraged them to linger in the shop and buy more than they had intended, a fact much appreciated by Miss Plum, the proprietor, whose age and stoutness made her prefer a comfortable chair behind the counter to standing behind it serving. 'Not to mention bobbing about and running up the steps to top drawers, which is for young legs.'

Miss Plum's reminiscenses of her youth entertained Laura greatly. As a girl, she had sailed round the Horn five times with her skipper father, had been introduced to cannibals in the South Seas and seen live Red Indians wearing feathers and warpaint in the plains of North America. None of this experience lessened her enjoyment of the local gossip, of which she was an active centre, or the smalltalk of the newspapers. The Queen, like Miss Plum herself, was suffering from bad legs and a bad back, and there was said to be something very rum about her grandson, young Prince Albert Edward Victor; was he really a bit barmy, and was it true that Her Majesty had kept John Brown's bedroom just as it was when he was alive, like Prince Albert's? Laura, who was not a great reader, listened with delight to Miss Plum's impressive readings-aloud from the paper.

'I see that Stead's out,' observed the old lady one winter morning when trade was slack and they were warming themselves by the back-room fire. 'Two months and seven days he did, in Coldbath Fields, and says he enjoyed every minute. More like a palace than a prison, he says. Funny, that is, but then he seems to be a funny sort of man.'

'Why?' Laura asked. 'I never heard of him.'

'Never heard of Mr W.T. Stead, the editor, my dear? Well, where have you been? It was him who got into trouble with his Maiden Tribute nonsense – leastways a lot of people say there was something in it, only he went about it the wrong way, pretending to buy that little girl and then telling as it was all a put-up job to get publicity for the trade in 'em.'

Laura stared. 'Buy a little girl? Whatever for? Who'd want to do such a thing?'

'Why, a lot of wicked people, people as live off poor innocents by selling 'em abroad, and such.'

Laura's mind was working. 'That's funny. I was once . . .' She remembered that she had been enjoined by her mother never to speak a word about her experience in the Dean Street house. 'I was once told of something like that. But I never understood what it was about. Do tell, Miss Plum.'

Her employer studied the eager, lovely face. It occurred to her that young Miss Diamond was possibly a complete innocent, unusually so for a girl of no very high station in life. The thought came to her that such innocence, combined with such beauty, might well be a dangerous thing. But she was not the child's mother (who struck her as a bit of a Tartar) and it was not for her to draw back the veil from this particular mystery. Time enough to find out for herself.

'Well,' she temporized, 'it's a sort of selling into slavery, which is against the law here and pretty well everywhere else, though it wasn't when I was a gal. Nasty practice. I shouldn't talk of such things to you. Let's make some toast, eh, and tell me how that dear sister of yours is doing.'

'Oh, a treat,' said Laura, busying herself with breadknife and toasting fork. 'Pa's got her into Ponsford's as a lady clerk. She writes the most beautiful hand and has *such* a good head for figures, not like me, I can't add two and two. She's ever so happy and the pay's not bad, for a girl. Butter or dripping? Have you seen Ellie lately? She's really quite . . .' she stopped herself saying 'improved in looks' and turned it into ' . . . quite blooming.' I expect it's being out in the world. I always think Ponsford's is like a foreign place, all those India and China names – Bohea and Hyson and Assam and Souchong – and the smell . . . mmm!' She luxuriously sniffed the imagined savours. 'You can almost see the ships, big ships with white sails on very blue sea, not like the river – and little brown and yellow people dressed in bright colours. Oh, how I should like to go *Abroad*. Tell me ·about your father's voyages again, Miss Plum, if you please.'

Though Laura did not know it, Ellie's new bloom had very little to do with Ponsford's. Except that Adolphus Duffin worked there. He had taught her most of what she knew about the work she did, patiently instructing her in copying, filing, and the keeping of accounts, Adolphus was only twenty, but had the ways of a much older person, a serious manner and a habit of listening carefully to what was being said to him, his head slightly on one side, as though it were the most important matter in the world. He was neither short nor tall, his dark hair lank, his complexion sallow like Ellie's, badly marked with the pits of adolescent spots. His dark eyes beamed behind a pince-nez which gave him a studious look, and his voice was gentle, mildly Cockneyfied.

Ellie worshipped him. Ever since the evening he had asked her 'May I walk you home, Miss Diamond?' and she had looked up in wonder that anyone should want to do such a thing, he had increasingly brought into her life what it had never known before. She, the plain quiet one, eclipsed by her sister's light, was admired, listened to, complimented. It didn't matter that Adolphus was plain and quiet too – he was all the more easy to talk to. Their times of companionship were few, a shared dinner-bundle, the walk home, and later the walk to work, for he began to pick her up every morning at the corner of Trafalgar Road.

She had never taken him home. For one thing, she was in awe of her mother's sharp eye and sharper tongue. It would be so shaming if Ma were to laugh at Adolphus, or at both of them. And for another thing, to take a young man home was such a very pointed thing to do, as if one assumed that he had Intentions and must be properly inspected by the family to see if he would suit. Adolphus never suggested it himself. He was a shade in awe of Mr Diamond, who had a remote air suggesting aloofness to the young and timid, and he was feeling his way very cautiously with Ellie herself, unused as he was, a sisterless boy, to girls' company and conversation.

'Won't you call me Adolphus?' he asked her, greatly daring. 'They all call me Dolphin. Well, it's natural, I suppose, with a name like mine, and better than Dolly. But I'd like it if you would . . .'

'I think Adolphus is a fine name,' she said, blushing because first names were such intimate things, especially when they had known each other so short a time. 'But Dolphin is nice too. Dolphins are the sailors' friends, you know, and the Greeks and Romans admired them very much for their cleverness.'

'I say! And not the only clever ones, either.' At his warm tone she blushed again, and the blush suited her, bringing a glow to the cheeks that were not so pale nowadays. She was slightly plumper, too, enjoying her picnic dinners by the river with Adolphus as she had not enjoyed food before. And, perhaps from the determined brushing recommended by Laura, her hair appeared shinier, more luxuriant. One night at bedtime, in a fit of daring as she sat before the mirror, she pulled a bunch of it at the front and cut it off with scissors, then started back appalled at the effect. She rushed into Laura's room.

'Oh, look! Isn't it awful? I thought I would be in the fashion, and now look at it – like a brush! Lorla, what *shall* I do? Ma will kill me when she sees.'

Laura, sitting up in bed, studied the spiky effect. 'It *is* a bit sticky-out . . .' She slipped from the bed, a slender figure in a voluminous flannelette nightdress which would have hung like a sack on most women, but turned her into a benevolent young angel from a fashionable cemetery. Her thick plaits, chains of bright gold, swung forward as she laid a comforting arm round Ellie's shoulders.

'Don't cry, pet. There must be something we can do. I know – curl-papers.'

'But we don't *use* curl-papers!' Tears were welling, falling.

'That's not to say we can't, is it? Here, this will do. It's one of Ma's magazines that she's finished with, she'd put it out to light the fire and I saw some interesting fashions in it. Here we go, then, and nobody's going to miss it.' She tore out page after page, halved each one neatly, Ellie watching her wonderingly, then wetted a hairbrush in the washstand ewer.

'Now. We get all this nice and wet. Then we twist each bit round a piece of paper, so.' For ten minutes she worked intently, knowledgeably. One day she would have a fringe herself – it was as well to know how to do it. At the end of the operation Ellie's brow was covered with a mass of curious spirals, dark twisted with white, like a formal wig for a Greek play. Laura stood back to admire her work.

'Well, that's not bad, for a beginner. I've had to fasten them off very tight, dear, so they may be a little uncomfortable, but try to lie on your back in bed as much as you can, and come in very early tomorrow so that I can take them out for you before Ma sees. There, go along, and don't worry.'

They kissed. 'Good night, dear, and thank you.' But Ellie did worry, lying awake waiting for the things to dry, trying not to turn her head against the pillow. It was not Ma's angry face she saw in her mind, but Adolphus's, surprised, disappointed, thinking how ugly she was.

Alice spared her befringed daughter nothing in the way of disapproval. Never, she said, had she expected to see a girl of hers cheapen herself so. Such a common style, and to go and cut it without asking! She'd have got a good spanking a year or two ago, and she should thank her stars she was too old for one now. So, through breakfast by lamplight, with the dark still outside, the diatribe went on. Yet Alice was not really as angry as she sounded. It was only Ellie, after all, plain-faced Ellie – not her golden treasure, Laura, who was to be kept inviolate until the right time and the right man came along to make her a princess, and redeem Alice's wasted youth.

Daniel, tired of his wife's voice, pushed his plate away and said, 'Come on, Ellie, Don't want to be late.' Thankfully, she put on her dolman and bonnet, horrified to find that it didn't fit now that her hair was different. Laura whispered to her in the lobby. 'Never mind. Go along as you are. I'll see about it.'

That morning she said to Miss Plum 'You know that bonnet Mrs Evans brought in to sell – can I buy it, please?'

'But it wouldn't fit you, my dear.'

'It's not for me, it's a present. And can I buy some trimmings, seeing it's rather plain?'

'Why not? there's some here reduced from last summer. Take your pick.'

31

Amused, she watched the lovely intent face bend over the alluring contents of the tray – shiny cherries, soft silk and velvet roses, yellow wheatears, tiny forget-me-nots. All so pretty, but most too bright for the winter season, and for Ellie's looks. One after another was tried against the dark green of the bonnet, a slight thing meant to cover only the front part of the head, its peak designed to be embellished with trimmings. Some ladies carried a whole botanical garden round on their bonnets or, even worse, stuffed birds. That wouldn't do in this case. Laura pinned the trimmings she had chosen against the bonnet.

'There. What do you think of that?' The colours were all muted: dark damask rosebuds, green leaves, purple-brown anemones, a few violets.

'Very nice, very tasteful. Neat but not gaudy, as they say. Don't you want a bit of something to lighten it up, though?'

'Of course – how clever. These daisies, I think. Yes. That's quite charming, just the effect I wanted. Oh!' A daunting thought had struck her. 'How much will all that be? Because . . .' Because Ma will notice if there's too much missing from my wages, Miss Plum read in her eyes.

'That'll be nothing at all,' the old lady said firmly. 'They're only reduced to other people, free to you, dear. Now don't say anything, for I won't listen. Don't I get more than I bargained for out of you? Errands run, my tea and toast got, and the shop kept when my legs is particular bad? Your heart's bigger than your eyes, gal, so don't argue with me over a few bits of frippery. Take 'em, do. Just give me what Mrs E's asking.'

Laura hugged her. 'Oh, you are good to me! You don't know how grateful I am, or how much it means to the person . . . well, I might as well tell you, it's Ellie.' She described the cutting of the fringe and its results. 'So as she can't go out looking like a guy, I thought I'd get her another bonnet somehow. Won't she just be pleased with this!'

Ellie was delighted, the more so because Adolphus immediately noticed her improved appearance – the becoming pussycat bow the ribbons made under her chin and the fetching crop of ringlets framed in the bonnet's peak, hiding a slightly bulging brow. He complimented her, stammering at his own temerity, and Ellie's heart soared up among the clouds. Even so, she hesitated to tell Laura that she had an admirer, and who it was. This was partly because she could still hardly believe her own luck. What else held her back she couldn't have said. They had always shared secrets; this was the first she had kept to herself. It was her treasure, too precious yet to be revealed.

Not long after the bestowing of the bonnet the sisters received an invitation. A few doors away from them, in one of the larger and older houses in Feathers Row, their friend Florence Taberer's brother Dick was about to become twenty-one. In celebration there was to be a musical evening on the Saturday of his birthday. At school Laura and Florence had been Best Friends, Florence, darkly pretty, sparklingly attractive, too busy flirting with her beaux to be jealous. She was engaged, as the whole of Greenwich must have known by now, to one Georgie, who worked in a bank and was as solemn as his fiancée was lively.

When Ellie heard of the invitation she turned pale, then flushed and went out of the room. When she came back she wore an unusual air of resolution.

'I should like to invite someone else,' she told Laura, managing not to let her voice tremble. Laura, laying the table for tea, looked up in surprise.

'Oh – who?'

'A young gentleman at Ponsford's.'

'Goodness, how thrilling. Tell all about him.'

'There's nothing, really. Just one of the clerks. He – I don't think he has many friends. I thought it would be nice . . . if Florence doesn't mind.'

'Why should she? Run round and ask her.'

Ellie literally ran, anxious to get there before her courage gave out. Well, well, Laura thought, what a new bonnet will do . . .

Mrs Taberer prided herself on having a drawing-room, not a mere front parlour like commoner people. It was not even a front room, but a double one, running the length of the house with doors in the middle which could be closed to make it two rooms. On this Saturday night the doors were open, a fire lit in both fireplaces. Everywhere was bright – Mrs Taberer's artistic but cheerful draped curtains, her flower-crammed carpet, the walls with their busy pattern of ribbon

33

swags and cabbage roses, fashionable Japanese screens. Young people filled the room, the girls as bright as flowers themselves, the young men darkly clad but wearing their best collars and such colourful waistcoats as they possessed, or could borrow from their fathers.

They were chattering and clapping the end of a piano solo when Laura entered, and the noise stopped suddenly. She wore a dress that had not been new for two years, of a plain schoolgirlish cut, high in the neck and long-sleeved, the fashionable bustle only faintly suggested by gathers at the back. A deep frill tacked on to the hem had been added to make the dress long enough. Laura's hair, new-washed and shining, was looped and coiled on her neck, neither up nor down, altogether beautiful.

She sensed waves of feeling directed towards her from the company. Envy from some of the girls, a swift picking-up of any points about her that they could criticize. Stunned admiration from boys who had not seen her before. She knew all the feelings well, too well, from school days, and rebelled against them. How nice it would be to be just ordinary and be liked for oneself, not for one's looks. Either plain and popular, or gorgeous and able to dress up to it. She could imagine sweeping into the room wearing a daring, splendid gown of the kind Mrs Langtry wore, low-cut and extravagantly bustled, with jewels round her neck and one of the new transparent fans. But there was nothing for it, she must make the best of her dreary frock. Smiling, she advanced, to be embraced by Florence and greeted by the others, put into a chair near the piano.

Ellie touched her sleeve. 'This is my friend – the one I told you about. Adolphus, this is my sister.'

Laura turned to the thin young man in a collar too big for him. He was more or less what she had expected. He looked nervous and out of place among these loud, hearty young people. His hand, when she shook it, was limp and bony, and he seemed unable to speak. Ellie led him away to an inconspicuous corner, and Laura soon forgot about him as she chattered with the others, in between paying obedient attention to musical fireworks on the piano, sentimental duets, comic songs, and the appearance of Mr Taberer from downstairs to sing his party piece, 'The Bogey Man'. She felt a good deal more cheerful than when she had first arrived, enjoying the company and the compliments, no longer feeling that her mother had somehow contrived to get into the next room and had an ear pressed to the wall.

It was during a rendering of 'Maid of Athens' by a youth with a reedy tenor voice that she became aware of eyes fixed on her. Ellie's friend had left his corner and was perched uncomfortably, it seemed, on a round 'sociable' couch, jammed between two other people.. And he was staring, not at the singer, but at Laura, an intense, almost hypnotised stare. She looked away, but the next time she glanced in his direction the stare had not wavered. Slightly irritated, she looked round for Ellie, and discovered her crouched on a footstool near the fire. She would speak to her at the supper interval. A gentle hint about manners would do the young man no harm.

But as a rousing Gilbert and Sullivan chorus came to an end and Florence clapped her hands to command everyone to follow her and Georgie downstairs to supper, Laura found Ellie's friend at her side, gazing dumbly at her.

'Yes?' she said sharply. 'If you're looking for Ellie, she's over there.'

His voice was almost a whisper. 'No. For you, Miss Laura.'

'Me? Nonsense. Go and partner Ellie.' She turned to tall Dick Taberer, hovering near with an arm crooked to receive hers, and smiled at him radiantly. They moved towards the stairs, Laura noting out of the corner of her eye that the young man from Ponsford's was standing where she had left him, his eyes still on her, and that Ellie was close to him, hesitating: Ellie who was too timid to knock very loudly on a door, certainly too timid to claim an unwilling partner.

'What's the matter?' Dick asked. 'What clouds thy brow, fair maiden?'

'Oh, nothing, just a vexation.'

The vexation remained throughout supper. As Laura ate her way through chicken and cold ham and a delicious sweet, she was aware of the intent yearning gaze fixed upon her. Ellie was nowhere to be seen. As the move upstairs began she went up to the lingering Adolphus, who visibly paled as he saw her approaching.

'Where's my sister?' she demanded, 'Aren't you supposed to be with her?'

He opened and shut his mouth, then said 'She was here . . . I don't know . . .'

'Then you jolly well ought to know, seeing she was kind enough to bring you. And would you mind telling me why you've been staring at me all evening?'

Adolphus gulped. 'I . . . I couldn't help it. You're so beautiful. You're the most beautiful girl I've ever s-seen.'

'Then you can't have seen very many. I don't like it, and I'll be obliged if you'll stop it at once, do you understand?'

He nodded, looking so miserable that she felt a pang of remorse, but she was determined not to weaken. 'I'm going to find Ellie now, and *you're* going to be very nice to her, mind.' She marched off.

She learned from Florence that Ellie had gone upstairs with a headache. There Laura found her, lying on a bed, drowned in tears. There was no need for explanation. Laura patted her shoulders and murmured inadequate comfort.

'Never mind, dear. It was all silliness. That young man doesn't know how to behave. I don't suppose he goes into company much, does he? There you are, then. Don't cry any more.'

Ellie choked out that she wanted to go home. Laura took her downstairs, leaving her to hide her blotched face in the hall while she made excuses to Florence.

'Funny friends you have,' Florence commented. 'That boy, Muffin or Puffin, went off as if we'd set the dog on him, without a thank you to me or Mother.'

'No friend of mine,' said Laura tersely. As she went downstairs to join Ellie the reedy tenor was in full song again. ' "Why," ' he trilled, ' "should we wait till tomorrow, when you're Queen of my Heart tonight?" '

It seemed to sum up the evening.

CHAPTER THREE

As if things were not bad enough, their mother was waiting up for them, ready with a lecture on the lateness of the hour. Ellie's obvious state of distress turned it into an inquisition, during which Ellie burst into fresh tears and ran up to bed. Laura tried to explain.

'It was her friend, Mr Duffin. I think she felt he should have paid more attention to her, instead of paying so much to . . . to someone else.'

'You I suppose?'

'Yes,' Laura admitted reluctantly.

'And what sort of encouragement had you given this young man – whoever he may be?'

'He's a clerk at Ponsford's – Pa knows him. And I hadn't given him any encouragement, Ma. I'd only just been introduced to him, we hadn't exchanged above two words.'

'Don't try to fob me off, Laura. I can tell you've been making yourself cheap again – ogling and smirking at men. I wonder you're not ashamed!'

Laura flushed. 'I have *not*, Ma. I never do. How can you have such ideas?'

'Ideas? Ideas? What about that business at school, those two boys fighting over you, your teacher coming to me to complain? I suppose that was one of my "ideas", was it?' Alice was working herself up into a temper. 'Goodness only knows what you do to make them think you're That Sort of Girl, but it must be fast behaviour of some sort. Giving this man the come-hither – *I've* seen how they look at you. You watch out that you don't get your head turned, my girl.'

Laura got to her feet abruptly. 'I'm very tired, Ma. I'm going to bed. Goodnight.' There was no more to say, no way of communicating with her mother.

'Go along, do – and mind you don't wake your father.'

Both knew there was little chance of that. Daniel had long since opted out of his wife's running battle with their eldest daughter. He was only too glad of his nightly rest from a colourless life.

Left alone, Alice went over the grievances she had built up and nurtured. The slut, setting out to charm the first young man to pay any attention to poor Ellie. The sideways look, and the smile . . . Heaven knew how many other males at that party had been stricken. How unfair it was that the girl should just sit there, doing nothing – for Alice knew in her heart that Laura made no effort to attract, it was all Nature's doing. From that night there was added to her ambition for Laura an eating jealousy, as she saw the girl's beauty increase while her own hair turned greyer and her once-pretty face sagged into folds and wrinkles. Where had that face of Laura's come from? Certainly not from Daniel's side of the family, remembering his mother Miriam, a small dark monkey of a woman with melancholy eyes like his, and his father, sandy-haired but large-featured and quite foreign-looking. As for Alice's people, they were North Kent merchant folk and looked it, as plain as their own sugar-bags and butter-tubs. Only Alice herself had been different, and now that was gone, wasted away in twenty-five years of Feathers Row.

Alice went to bed in bitterness, as the laughter and footsteps of the Taberers' last departing guests rang in the street outside.

Laura told the whole story to Miss Plum, unable to keep the injustice to herself. 'I didn't mean to take that silly, creature from Ellie. How could I have done anything like that to her?' Miss Plum, remembering the bonnet, agreed that it was unlikely.

'My guess is,' Laura said, 'that he'd hardly seen a girl in his life until he met Ellie, and hardly knew there were any such things as girls. Then he got to know her, and found himself attracted, as was only natural, such a pet as she is. And after that he saw me, and wondered whether he didn't like me better after all – what a donkey, to take fancies to people without so much as knowing them to speak to. I might have had a – cleft palate, or been half-witted, or something. All because of having yellow hair, if that's what they see in me. I tell you, Miss P., I sometimes think I'll dye it black and put berry-juice on my face to make it dark, like the gipsies do in tales to disguise dukes' children.'

Miss Plum heaved with silent laughter, imagining the result of this treatment. 'I shouldn't go as far as that, my dear. You be glad of a bit of admiration while you're young, for when you're my age it won't come your way no more. Gather ye rosebuds, Laura. And if Ellie holds any of that party nonsense against you, she's not the girl I took her for.'

Nor, indeed, did Ellie bear the slightest grudge, or say a word of reproach or complaint. She knew that Laura was quite innocent of any intention to steal Adolphus; knew too that she had taken a bad scolding from her mother. And her pain was too great to talk about. At work, she gave Adolphus only the most brief greeting, and the shadow of a smile. He was glad of it, confusedly ashamed of himself and at the same time still dreamily infatuated with Ellie's sister. It was as though he and Ellie had never been friends. Daniel, who had watched without interfering, saw it all and shook his head sadly. It had been his hope that the young daughter who was so like him would find happiness; but not this time. Not this time.

In the weeks that followed Laura was uneasily conscious that the silly episode of the party had changed her life, and not for the better. Her guilt towards Ellie, baseless though it was, made her impatient at times with her sister's quiet meekness. Why couldn't the girl have stood up for herself and told Adolphus to mind his manners and pay attention to her, and nobody else? As for Adolphus, his habit of appearing suddenly in her path, pale, wistful and yearning, began to annoy her beyond measure. She had no idea how he discovered where she was likely to be at any given time, but she grew heartily tired of seeing his stricken face in the street. The limit of her patience was reached on the morning when she saw it pressed against the glass of the shop window. Miss Plum was upstairs; Laura saw her opportunity to settle her score. She went smartly outside and confronted Adolphus.

'What do you think you're doing here?'

He began to stammer, looking, if possible, paler than before. 'Come in,' she said, 'I can't stand here arguing in the street.' In the shop, the bell's jangle silenced, she faced him, her back to the counter.

'A nice sort of young man *you* are, I don't think. What do you mean by following me about like this? Do you want to get me a bad name? Because you're going the right way about it. Now, then!'

He hung his head. 'I'm sorry, Miss Diamond. I know I shouldn't. But I . . . I love you so much. I absolutely worship and adore you. I've thought about nothing else since that night . . .'

'When you treated my sister so badly. What about *her*, poor girl? I think she had the idea it was her you were in love with – and then to behave like that to her, in public.'

'I'm sorry. I didn't mean . . .'

'No use to keep saying you're sorry. If you're as sorry as that, tell her so and be nice to her. And you're to stop following me – for if you don't, I'll give you in charge, and what's more I'll tell my father and get him to report you to Mr Ponsford.' She felt cruel to speak so harshly to this poor creature, fancying she saw tears gathering in the eyes behind the thick glasses. An unreasonable impulse to comfort him came over her, and she fought it.

As though he saw a gleam of sympathy, he said, 'Miss Diamond, you're so beautiful. I've never seen anyone, not even a picture, to come up to you. That was why I followed you. Just to look. But if it makes you unhappy I won't do it again.'

'No, don't. And you're certainly not to come here any more.' For a moment she thought he was going to advance on her, so despairing was his look. But he turned away, gazing back at her as he opened the door, then vanishing for ever, she hoped, from her life.

It was on a bright morning in April, one of those mornings when spring seems to quiver in the new air like the singing of violins, that the errand-boy Miss Plum employed to take goods to her customers failed to appear. Laura volunteered to take his place. Restlessness filled her, a suppressed excitement; the craft in Greenwich Reach suddenly seemed laden with romantic possibility, their goods and the people they carried touched with the allure and suspense of a story thrillingly begun. The shop, compared with the bright scene outside, was dark and stuffy, smelling of the well-worn drugget on its floor and Miss Plum's favourite peppermints.

She gladly put on her coat and hat again, and prepared to set out with her basket of small neat packages.

'Mind you go to Mrs Reide's first with the ribbon,' Miss Plum said. 'Placentia House, Crooms Hill, near the top. She's a lady as likes what she wants when she wants it.'

'Who doesn't?' said Laura.

Crooms Hill was a stately incline of old, graceful houses, each one different from its neighbour. Statesmen, artists, architects, courtiers, men of letters had lived in them in former times, and grand people still did. Climbing its gentle slope gave Laura a feeling of going up in the world, becoming grand herself. In her present euphoric, soaring mood she felt she could turn aside and walk into one of the houses, into the hall beyond the pillared portico, and become the mistress of it, as natural as life, with nobody noticing any difference, even the snobbish servants.

'My carriage, James,' she murmured to herself. 'Tea at the Ranger's House at four o'clock. It may be only a step, but one can't be seen *walking*.' She smiled, and a passing baker's boy narrowly escaped dropping his tray of loaves in the gutter.

This was it – Placentia House. Funny name, like a patent medicine, but everyone knew that the old kings and queens had lived in the Palace of Placentia, where the Naval College stood now. Mrs Reide, or whoever named the house, must have thought it a pity to waste such a royal name.

The house was detached, a cobbled courtyard in front of it, a gate framed by an arch at each side, a coach-house down a drive. Laura pulled the bell and waited. In the silence that followed it suddenly occurred to her that she might be breaking a social rule by applying at the front door instead of the servants' or tradesmen's entrance. It was hard to imagine young Dick the errand-boy having the cheek to ring such an imposing bell at such an imposing door. Shocked at her own temerity, Laura scuttled round to one of the side gates leading to the back of the house.

To her relief, the gate was unlocked. She found herself on a path which took her past the end of the house, with no sign of what might be the right door – only a side entrance almost as handsome as the front one. Then she was in the garden – a large formal garden, from which steps bordered by yew

41

bushes led down to a terrace. A harsh cry alarmed her, nervous as she already was; she spun round to see a peacock regarding her critically a few yards away. As she watched, admiring the iridiscent sheen of its neck and the proud carriage of the small crested head, it slowly unfurled its tail into a many-eyed fan of glorious colour. Laura had only seen peacocks once before, in the Zoological Gardens. It amazed her that people actually kept such gorgeous creatures.

'Aren't you a beauty!' she said to it. 'And don't you just know it.' Tentatively she stretched out a hand. The bird put its head on one side, then took a few stately paces towards her, as if it expected food.

'No, I've nothing for you. And I've got to find the way in.' Reluctantly, she turned away from it. At the back of the house were French doors, and beside them extended a long building that was mainly glass, like a miniature Crystal Palace. Laura approached it and looked in.

A man, in a long holland smock, his back towards her, palette and paintbrush in hand, was standing before an easel which supported a canvas. On a small dais, reclining in a chair, sat a young woman as nearly naked as anybody Laura had ever seen, her plump pink charms fortuitously draped here and there with a gauzy scarf, her elaborately-curled head resting on her hand.

Laura's gasp of astonishment was loud enough to be heard inside. The man turned, and their eyes met. He strode to the glass door and opened it.

'Britannia,' he said. 'Britannia, by God.'

She knew him at once, though the beard he had sported when she had last seen him had been replaced by luxuriant curling side-whiskers. In the three years that had passed since their brief meeting by the river, she had thought of him many times, yet had somehow never expected to see him again. But he had said he lived in Crooms Hill.

'It's you,' she said inadequately.

He smiled, the same warm kind smile she remembered. 'It is, indeed. And you're my young lady of the Trafalgar, grown up. Well, well. What a surprise, to say the least. Good of you to bring her to me, Solomon.' Laura turned to see the peacock standing behind her. The artist's eye of Maurice Reide had just recorded a picture which would stay with him

42

for ever: a vision seen through glass, the lovely startled face of the girl, her plain street-dress the colour of pale lilacs, the peacock behind her like a goddess's symbol. He drew her in, seeing her cast a nervous glance at the model.

'Thank you, Miss Liebert,' he said. 'Take a rest, will you?' The young woman stood up with great composure, stretched and retired behind a Japanese screen, followed by Laura's scandalized gaze.

'I can't stay,' she told him. 'I was really looking for the tradesmen's entrance.' She explained about the parcel of ribbon and the unanswered front door. Maurice laughed. 'You should see how far the servants' quarters are from the hall – and they're a lazy lot, anyway. You came round the wrong side of the house.'

'Then I must go now, please.'

'No, of course you musn't. She can't want her haberdashery this minute, whatever she needs it for. Sit down. How do you like my studio?'

She gazed round, fascinated by the trappings of art. Lay figures, faceless, standing in attitudes like people turned to wood, classic busts in plaster, a Diana, an Apollo, a Roman torso in armour with no head. Canvases stacked round the walls, all portraits, some groups of people in abandoned attitudes, as nude as Miss Liebert, some formally dressed or disguised in costume. There was a pleasant smell of oil paint.

'I think it's awfully nice,' she said. 'I've never seen an artist's studio before. I didn't think they were . . . I didn't think houses like this had them.'

'A good many have, up here. You've seen the painted hall in the Naval College? Old Thornhill lived on the hill while he was designing it. And others have settled here for the views, the park, the river. I don't paint views, I paint people, but it suits me.' Miss Liebert emerged from behind the screen, a respectably clad, ordinary young woman.

'Will that be all today, Mr Reide?'

For a moment he looked puzzled. He had meant to spend the morning painting. But the girl the peacock had brought to him had got in the way of it, and he would never climb back into the mood. 'Thank you, Miss Liebert. Tomorrow, same time?'

Laura summoned up the courage to ask, 'Why are you

painting her – like that?' She knew about artists' models, everyone did, but had never thought of them posing in quiet pleasant rooms with an affluent look, in grand houses. And the painter was no wild Frenchman, but her artist, a gentleman every inch but for his paint-smeared smock.

'I'm painting her as a nymph, something allegorical.'

'I don't know what that means,' Laura said frankly.

'It doesn't matter. Only that allegories don't wear clothes. Never mind. Tell me about you. Why haven't I set eyes on you since that afternoon?'

She talked about her life, school, leaving school, the shop, aware that there was nothing to say, that nothing had happened to her until this morning, when she had opened the wrong gate and entered this new, exciting world. Her words sounded childish and silly to her own ears. Only in herself she no longer felt a child, but the woman she had seen herself to be in his eyes, three years ago; the brown eyes and the look in them were the same.

'I haven't asked your name,' he said. 'How remiss of me.'

'Laura Diamond.'

' "Laura. Rose-cheeked Laura, come, Sing thou smoothly with thy beauty's silent music . . . Heaven is music, and thy beauty's Birth is heavenly." '

She was wide-eyed. 'What?'

'Nothing – poetic nonsense. Forgive me. The disadvantages of education. Since we are introducing ourselves, I'm Maurice Reide. Come and look at my pictures.' He conducted her round the studio, pausing before his own favourites among the canvases. 'Which do you like – if any?'

Laura meditated. 'That.' It was a portrait of a woman in today's dress, a sombre gown, deep dark eyes, a fine-boned face. 'She looks as if she were going to speak – and I'd like to know what she would say.'

'Bravo! A perfect insight. I wish the judges on hanging day had your perception.' He knew that he was talking above her head and longed to be able to meet her at her own level, or lift her to his. She was youth and springtime and a vision he had seen twice, once by the river, with the wind blowing the gold hair now bundled under a cheap little hat, once in his own garden, just now. It was like being haunted by a beautiful recurrent dream which could never become reality, for she

44

was only a shopgirl, someone looking for the tradesmen's entrance.

'I could have painted you a hundred times by now,' he said, 'if you hadn't chosen to vanish like Cinderella.'

'I know I was rude to you, and I'm sorry. But Ma – my mother said . . .'

'You were not to speak to strange men. Quite right.'

'Later I might have changed my mind. But I never saw you again.'

'I've been away, abroad. Two years in Paris, and sometimes at my rooms in town.'

'Rooms? Besides this?'

He smiled down at her. 'Yes. This is not exactly the centre of the art world. I have to have a place of my own.'

This, of course, was not just his own, she remembered. 'I must go. Mrs Reide – your wife – will be expecting the ribbon.'

'My wife? My dear child, she's my mother, not my wife. What made you think that?'

'I don't know, I just thought it.' Laura felt silly, the more so for a curious sensation of lightness that had come over her when he spoke, as though what he had said mattered. 'But I must go, truly – I've more errands to do. Please.'

'At least you'll have some refreshment. Heavens, what do people have at this time of the morning? Tea, a glass of sherry?' He could see by her half-puzzled, half-amused look that he was making no sense to her. He was afraid of seeming to mock her, just as afraid that she would vanish from his life again, and the words to keep her would not come to him. Suddenly, he said '*Verweile doch, du bist so schön.*' Damn it, he was bedevilled with quotations, could he say nothing in plain language? But she had not turned her back on him, prattling fellow that he was; there was wonder in her face, and a charmed look that charmed him in turn.

'What does that mean?' He was to find that she never pretended to know anything that was beyond her. 'It sounded pretty, but I've never heard the words before. Is it English?'

'No, my dear.' (Damn it again, he was being patronizing.) 'It's German. And it means "Stay awhile, thou art so fair." It's what Dr Faustus said to the fleeting moment . . . oh, never mind. Don't go, that's all.'

'I . . .' The sound of an opening door drew their eyes away from each other. In the doorway that led to the house stood a woman, a tall slim woman, clad in something that managed to be both informal and elegant, a composition in cloudy purple and grey. On her still-brown hair, once as rich as her son's, her widow's cap was the daintiest, most un-funereal wisp of lace. She could have been painted where she stood without further posing.

'Oh,' she said, her voice as elegant as her appearance, and very youthful, 'you've company. Do introduce me.' She glided into the room, the most graceful movement Laura had ever seen. Clumsily Laura rose from her chair, unaware of etiquette's rule that no lady rises for the entrance of anyone less than royalty.

'Madeline, this is Miss Diamond,' Maurice said, uncomfortable, and to Laura, 'my mother.'

His mother? Madeline? Confused, Laura said, 'Pleased to meet you,' and failed to interpret the gleam of amusement in the brown eyes that were so like, yet unlike, Maurice's. Madeline Reide inclined her head, smiling.

'Another of your charming models, Maurice?'

'No.' He glanced helplessly at Laura. She understood, and rescued him. 'I came on an errand and missed my way. It was to bring you some ribbon, from Miss Plum. Here you are.' Delving into the basket, she produced the package and handed it over without bobbing a curtsey, something an errand-girl would have done. Madeline continued to smile.

'Good Miss Plum. How is she – her poor legs? She suffers dreadfully, I know.' She was untying the parcel.

'Not bad, now the weather's turned, thank you.' Linked serpents of silver-blue were emerging from the wrapping coils of ruched ribbon.

'Ah, the exact colour, how clever of her.' Madeline re-wrapped the trimming, with a movement final enough to suggest that the audience was over. 'You weren't expecting to be paid, my dear? Everything goes on my account.'

Laura blushed. 'No. I know that. It's all right.' She was aware that the blush was noticed, and blushed all the more for it. Her hands felt large and she wished she had worn newer shoes. There was nothing for it but to go quickly. She backed towards the door, Maurice anticipating her to open it.

'Goodbye, thank you,' she said, not hearing his answer in her rush to be gone. Her last sight of mother and son was of them standing side by side, Madeline's arm linked in Maurice's. They looked well together, remarkably alike, and not very unequal in age.

'What a pretty creature,' Madeline was saying. 'Gauche, though. May I ask just how she missed her way and arrived in here?' Maurice explained.

'I see. Well, you should take advantage of Fate and ask her to sit for you. Just your type – very like that blonde Italian girl, Julia something. Why don't you, now?' She was smiling, teasing.

'I don't know where she lives – don't know anything about her.' Maurice was not going to fall into the trap this time. He well remembered Julia Something, a professional model from Soho whose beauty had fascinated him. Her foreign quality had made her seem better-born that she was. He had been on the verge of starting a serious courtship when his mother had drifted down to the studio one day and stayed, though she knew he disliked an audience when he was painting. After Julia had gone she picked up some preliminary sketches he had made, then stood thoughtfully in front of the canvas.

'You're in love with that girl, my dear,' she said. 'Oh, don't bother to protest – I always know. How sweet. The little fiorella, so pretty – I don't blame you. Such a pity looks don't last. How old is she – twenty? And by the time she's thirty she'll be fat. It shows already round the chin, and the arms. They eat so much oil, of course. That, and garlic.' Madeline sniffed. 'It is a bit obvious, isn't it?'

'I hadn't noticed,' Maurice said, though he had, slightly.

'You would if you got really close, my dear. Imagine it in bed – phoo!' Maurice flushed. He had not kissed Julia yet. He reluctantly let the picture form in his mind of her at thirty, twice her present size, three chins under her delicious mouth, above it a pronounced moustache instead of the faint, attractive line of down that shadowed it now. He had travelled in Latin countries and knew what slender girls turned into after a few years of cooking and babies. The knowledge had been there, but it had taken his mother's gentle ridicule to bring it home to him. She was adept at destroying any illusion of his that threatened to take him away from her; even make him laugh at himself about it.

They had always been closer than mother and son, closer than many brothers and sisters. Married at eighteen, Madeline lost her husband in a carriage accident two years later, when Maurice was a baby of one. The rich, pretty widow attracted suitors by the score, but though she flirted madly she would be serious about none of them. Her short experience of marriage had not been remarkably enjoyable; like many natural flirts she was cold. Her son filled all her requirements. He was male, he adored her, he obeyed her and presented no threat to her independence. When he went to Westminster School his pretty, elegant mother was the envy of other boys and roused much interest in their fathers; he was as proud of her as she of him. They went everywhere together, until he decided to make painting his life and travelled to study in Paris.

Not even Madeline (as he always called her, at her request) could share his carefree student life. She had no wish to – it was good for him, she said, to play about and find his feet. What she did do was to take an elegant apartment in one of Haussman's Grands Boulevards. There she entertained *tout Paris*, the best of Parisian society, and was in turn entertained by them; living in high style, driving out in her hired equipage, always drawn by white horses, an admirer by her side. Maurice could never be sure that he would not meet her in the Bois, at the opera, even dining amid romantic squalor in Montmartre, or that she would not suddenly descend on him at the rooms he shared with two other students, a gay, expensively-scented vision dressed by Worth. It was very inhibiting to a young man trying to experience Life and discover women; and yet he was pleased to see her, glad to occasionally take refuge in her lovely blue and gold drawing-room and talk and laugh with her. There were girls, of course, pretty grisettes, ravishing models; he was never tempted to get serious about any of them as his fellow-students frequently did – they would sooner or later come under the appraising eye of his mother, and she would pounce on their faults and ask him if he didn't think he was being rather silly.

He came back to England with a sound training in portraiture and a good reputation among those who knew. He was a man, now, bearded, taller than herself; they made a handsome couple, people said. The presence of a young and beautiful mother continually at his side put an invisible barrier around him in the eyes of girls. It had been so when he was twenty-one, it was so now that he was thirty-two. In the past ten years he had had two mistresses, both English, both sophisticated, both married. Madeline had known all about the affairs and had not said a word until they were over, when a few shrewd remarks dropped casually, as if she knew nothing, had helped him to see the end of love, or what he had thought love, as less than a tragedy and even something of a comedy.

She encouraged him to find sitters among the fashionable set. She would like to see him a Millais (not that J.E.M.'s pictures were more than money-spinners now), sought-after, revered, knighted perhaps, a Great Man independent of commercial models and scenes from mythology or Shakespeare. She had no need of snobbery, she just wanted the best for Maurice. And for him to be still hers.

He understood her, partially agreed with her, enjoying all that she gave him. And he was a bachelor, lonely, discontented with everything but his painting, despising himself for something he found it hard to define. When she left him in the studio, staring at the half-finished portrait of Miss Liebert, he felt curiously uncomfortable and dissatisfied. There was a niggling unease in his mind about Laura Diamond. Had he joined Madeline in laughing at her? Something had been said about her being gauche. He had seen no gaucherie in her, only a sweet freshness. He had no wish to paint her in his studio, exposing her to comment and light laughter; but he very much wanted to paint her in his own way. She had gone away blushing and unhappy, her poor little basket of finery on her arm; he was ashamed of himself, resentful of Madeline. For once he almost saw her as the tyrant she was – almost, but not quite.

The next morning, as they were finishing breakfast and Madeline was absorbed in her correspondence, he said, 'I'm going out for the whole of the day. Will you tell cook I shan't be in to luncheon?'

She looked up. 'Of course, darling. Are you going to

49

town?'

'No. I have a great urge to sketch types – people, anyone. Thought I'd go down on the wharf and take in some of the lightermen, the uniformed ones and the others.' He was explaining too much, but she seemed not to notice.

'What a good idea. I have some perfectly exhausting people coming to tea so I shall take a very sketchy luncheon, and then rest. Have a nice rewarding day.' She returned to the letter she was reading, and he knew that she had believed him.

Laura was setting out the counter when he entered the shop. He saw the shock on her face and swiftly said, 'I came to say I was sorry about yesterday. I'd meant to ask you to stay – my mother didn't quite understand. Will you forgive me for letting you go so abruptly?'

She said softly, 'Nothing to forgive. I'd have had to go, anyway. I knew she didn't like me being there. You shouldn't have bothered.'

'I wanted to see you. Can you . . . can you come out with me? Today, I mean. Oh, it sounds very odd, I know, but . . .' He was floundering. 'I could do some sketches of you in the park, by the river, and we could eat some food.' He sounded ridiculous to himself, and prayed she would understand. Miraculously, she did, sensing his troubled state, the warmth that had been engendered between them alight once again. She gave him her radiant smile.

'It would be lovely, really lovely. But I work, you see. I'm here until seven, and I can't ask off.'

'Can't you?' asked a wheezy voice. Miss Plum had hobbled in from the back room, where she had been unashamedly listening. 'What's all this?' She knew Maurice well by sight and had done so since he was a schoolboy. The gossip of Greenwich was only too informed about Mrs Reide and her possessive attitude towards her son, which was generally regarded as unnatural and very unbecoming to a matron of her years. Miss Plum had summed up Mrs Reide long ago and had despised the son for putting up with such nonsense. Now that she saw him close, and took note of his eyes (she set much store by eyes) and the look in them for Laura, she decided that he was not the nancy-boy she had taken him for. The agreeable thought came to her that she could be the means of knocking the fetters off the poor man, if only for one day.

'I heard what you said, sir, and seeing it's you I don't see no harm in Miss Diamond going out with you for a bit of drawing practice. It's a beautiful blue day and she's been looking pale., I don't mind, not a bit.'

'But you'll have to manage on your own . . .' Laura began.

'I managed before you were here, didn't I, miss? I shall just sit here and let 'em come to me, and what I can't reach from my chair they must get for themselves. Don't you fret about me.'

'I do thank you very much,' Maurice said in the deep warm voice that appealed to feminine ears. Laura's face, startled, joyful, told its own story. Miss Plum waved them out. 'Be off, now. And see she gets home safe.'

'I will, be sure of that.' Laura snatched up her hat and went out before him, casting a last grateful look and word to her employer. Miss Plum watched them out in the sunny street, the man proudly linking her arm in his, hoisting his sketching-bag on to his other shoulder. Had she been foolish, agreeing so quickly? But there again, if a girl with looks like that was going to get into trouble – as she was bound to do, sooner or later it might as well be with a gentleman.

Chapter Four

THE SAME DOUBTS WERE IN LAURA'S MIND as she walked beside Maurice. To accept such a sudden invitation from a man she'd only seen twice and knew nothing about, no more than he knew about her – to be taking a day off from work with him, and Miss Plum agreeing as though she had arranged the whole thing . . . perhaps all three of them had gone pleasantly mad. But she was determined not to throw all caution to the winds. 'Would you mind,' she said, 'not holding on to my arm? It's very kind of you, but I'd rather not. Where are we going?'

'Anywhere. Everywhere. Let's sample all the pleasures of the town. I'll tell you what – I could do with a change from my own works. What about the Royal Hospital and its paintings, if that wouldn't bore you?'

'No, I'd like that.' Particularly as her mother would be most unlikely to be doing the same. She shrank from the thought of an encounter in the street, the awful embarrassment and lame explanations. This was her day, not to be spoiled.

The old seamen who had once lived out their lives in the magnificent building, London's noblest sight from the river, were long since gone, like the monarchs who had given their names to the place, King Charles, King William, Queen Mary, Queen Anne. The splendours remained, and Laura, a stranger since a childhood visit (for if you lived in a place you didn't keep going to inspect its attractions), gaped in wonder at them. Painted centuries before photography, these were more real than sun-shadows; fluted pilasters standing out, fully dimensional, from the walls, a tumbling mass of bodies, gods and heroes, Virtues, nymphs, the deities of great rivers and their tributary streams, rosy flesh and streaming hair, bare buxom breasts and the black rippling muscles of slaves, a man-o'-war with her gunports opened, laden with treasure and the spoils of war, mortal worthies, unconcerned among the immortals, Tycho Brahe and Flamsteed, Newton and Galileo. And, centred in that huge framed oval, the ceiling, the calm faces of the rulers, Dutch William and Stuart Mary, framed in their heavy curls, cherub-encompassed, ignoring the plump blond Hanoverians who were to come after them, sitting complacent on the wall of the upper hall.

Maurice studied Laura's upturned face. She said little, and he liked that. As they passed through the ranks of naval portraits, beards and ruffs, telescopes and sharp far-seeing blue eyes, she hardly spoke; he sensed that she was in the same state as himself, a pleasant trance induced by happiness.

In the Nelson Room she paused before Abbott's portrait of the admiral.

'You admire him?' Maurice asked.

'I don't know much about him. They told us at school about the funeral procession that set off from here, where we are, and about his blind eye. I never took much notice. He looks very gentle.'

'For a fighting man, he was. Also the fool of love.'

Laura's gaze questioned him. He saw in it the same simplicity, the natural allure without coquetry, the flower-like grace, that Romney had seen in the young girl who was to enslave Nelson. And look what happened to Nelson, he thought wryly. His fetters must have been so light at first, mere chains of blossoms binding him to her beckoning hands; yet in the end she and his country were equal in his heart, and he died for them both.

'Never mind,' he said. 'Just a story I might tell you some time. Have we had enough of pictures? *I* have. Let's go out in the fresh air and create some that aren't of old sailors. What did Miss Plum call it – drawing practice? And so it is.'

They strolled up through King William Walk to the slopes of the park, Laura keeping a nervous eye in the direction of her home on the farther side. The clustered trees, Spanish chestnuts, gnarled with age, younger elm, oak and lime, were emerald-spangled with new leaf, the grass damp, fresh and green as it would never be again that year once the feet of trippers had trampled it. They climbed the hill to the Observatory and the house of old John Flamsteed, whose scanning of the heavens had given the world Greenwich Mean Time, and sat there looking down to the Queen's House and its flanking colonnades, like an ivory toy made from a child's building bricks, framed precisely by the twin domed pavilions of the Hospital, which framed in their turn the vessel-crowded Reach and the trees and chimneys of the Isle of Dogs.

'Perfect perspective,' Maurice murmured, 'the eye of genius.' He saw that she understood him no more than the docile Miss Liebert of Wapping would have done. It mattered not at all. He got out his sketching-pad and pencils, and began to draw her. There was no need to tell her to keep still. She fell into poses as naturally as a child before it grows old enough to be self-conscious, holding them until he told her to change. Drawing her profile, silhouetted against the soft varied greens of the park slopes, he remembered that Lady Frances Stewart, the one beauty whose heart and bed amorous King Charles failed to win, had also had what Pepys called a sweet little Roman nose. On a whim, he adapted her attitude, sitting on the grass, to that of a woman seated on a shield. In one hand he stetched a trident, on her head a crested helmet. In place of the river he roughed in an outline of waves and ships, then passed the sketch to her.

'But that isn't me. It's . . .'

'Britannia. Well, both of you. The likeness is strong.'

'I remember, you called me that when I walked into your studio.' She handed it back with a small rueful smile. 'I think you only like me because you can make fancies up about me.'

'Nonsense!' But she had said something unexpectedly shrewd, and he wondered uneasily whether it might be true.

'Talk to me,' she said. 'It's very quiet, just sitting.'

'Very well. What shall I talk to you about?'

'Things you've seen, places you've been to. I do like to hear about places.'

Remembering at random, he told her of Paris, the great sweeps of the boulevards, the romantic river, Notre Dame enthroned on its island among a warren of medieval streets, the wild students and the pretty girls, the café life, the promenading fashionables in the Bois. Then he took her to the vineyards and chateaux of the Loire, to Switzerland of the smiling lakes and towering mountains ever under snow, to the steep terraces of Capri and the pure blue water of its grotto, where one might drink wine under trees that bore living oranges and lemons. And as he talked he watched the changing expressions of her face: delight and longing and wonder, and a great wistfulness.

'I've never been anywhere,' she said. 'Nowhere at all. Well, we did once take the boat down to Richmond, and that was very pretty, but not a bit like the places you talked about. I don't suppose I'll ever go to any of them. Ever.'

'Of course you will.'

'Will I? How?'

He wanted to say, Because I shall take you, my lovely girl, and show the world off to you and you to the world. I shall dress you in clothes that will make you the envy of Paris and the desire of Rome. You shall sail between the palaces and churches of Venice in a jewelled dress with your hair spread on purple cushions like a great courtesan . . . As he framed the words in his mind he knew that he must say none of these things to her. Instead he said, awkwardly, 'Oh, I expect you'll find yourself in all sorts of places. Everybody travels these days. Cook's Tours . . . that sort of thing.' It sounded a silly, inadequate answer to him, and probably meant nothing to her. When he looked at the sketch he had been almost automatically making, of her face turned three-quarter-ways towards him, he saw that it was of a tragic mask, Eurydice, Persephone snatched from happiness.

Suddenly she drew in a deep breath of the fresh air and said, 'I'm awfully hungry – aren't you?'

'By Jove, I am – now you mention it. I thought – there's the Trafalgar, and the Ship, or Goddard's Eel and Pie if you care for that sort of food – but I did pack a few bits in case you'd enjoy a picnic. The grass is quite dry, we could have a nice little spread . . .'

Laura, who had never been taken to a restaurant or a tavern in her life, or anything grander than a tea-garden, would have liked nothing better than to dine in the stately Trafalgar or the ancient Ship, where members of parliament gathered. There were stories of wonderful fish dinners and suppers; things had been written in books about them. But as Mr Reide had gone to the trouble of packing a picnic, she gave him a heavenly smile, saying, 'Oh, I'd like that. It's too fine for indoors, isn't it.'

From the depths of his sketching-bag he produced half a veal pie, tomatoes from the greenhouse, a wedge of brown bread, two kinds of cheese and two peaches, which Madeline bought in and out of season from Fortnum's, and a round metal flask of wine. He had collected them all from the kitchen under the benevolent eye of cook, who spoiled him.

'Ooh,' said Laura, and forgot tavern richnesses. Maurice watched her eating with a child's eagerness, almost greed, yet still graceful, a nymph polishing off mead and nectar. He knew she could not be used to wine, yet in that fresh air it only brought a brighter colour to her cheek and made her a little livelier than she had been. 'This is nice,' she said, 'not like what we had at Christmas – I don't know where Pa got it, but it was really sour. Ellie, that's my sister, said she'd rather have lemonade. Ma doesn't really like us having wine, but *I* think it's tea that spoils the complexion, don't you? Because they always draw old maids with red noses and cats, and they drink an awful lot of tea, don't they? Old maids, I mean, not cats.' He noticed how white her teeth were when she laughed, like peeled almonds, so unlike the decayed and blackened teeth one saw everywhere. He hardly listened to her chatter about her family. He was simply not interested in them; if they were all presented to him in a row he would have nothing to say to them. They were the barrier that separated her from him. They had put the Cockney into her voice, had placed her in a haberdasher's shop. He smiled faintly as she told him about her Uncle Sidney who was a ship's chandler and lived in Deptford and always sang a low song about a spinnaker boom when he came to visit, however often Ma told him not to.

His interest was only roused when she mentioned her Aunt Gerti in Whitechapel. 'My great-aunt she is, really, such a tiny little thing hardly up to my shoulder. Sometimes she and Pa talk German together – not that he knows much, but they manage to chat quite a bit. I wish I could speak it . . .'

'German? Why German?'

'Well, because Pa's mother came from Germany, a town called Linz. There were laws against Jews in those days, so they came to England, Aunt Gerti and Grandmother Miriam and their parents, and grandmother met my grandpa. He was a jeweller, after his father and grandfather. I expect that's why they were called Diamond.'

Maurice was interested. So that was the explanation for the exotic quality she had, the aquiline bone-structure and the dark eyes. Perhaps it also explained her longing for foreign travel.

'You said something in German to me the other day,' she said. 'Do you remember?'

'I remember. It meant "Stay awhile, thou art so fair." Their eyes met, and he saw her blush, comprehensively, and turn her head away.

So this is what it comes to, she thought. Just as Ma said, gentlemen always want to get you to themselves so that they can work their wicked way with you. Exactly what form the wickedness would take she hadn't the faintest idea; Mrs Diamond had brought the girls up in complete ignorance of the processes of sex, and the furtive whispers and gigglings of schoolmates had fallen upon deaf ears. To listen to such things was almost as bad as saying them. One boy's repeated attempts to enlighten his class about what he imagined to be the facts of life had been reported to the teacher, and rewarded with a severe caning on the hands in front of the assembled school. She was not afraid, only pleasantly excited by a feeling of strange, strong attraction which she failed to comprehend, knowing that Maurice Reide's presence filled her with a tremulous joy that had never visited her before.

But in all that sweet, lazy afternoon he said and did nothing that could not have been witnessed placidly by a synod of clergy. His touch, as he turned her head this way and that, or arranged a fold of skirt, was gentle and respectful, as she supposed it must be if he had occasion to touch the scandalously bare Miss Liebert. Sometimes he talked of things he knew would interest her, and she listened, wide-eyed, not interrupting with comments as so many girls would have done. The sun was warm and the sky cloudless, like high summer. Drowsiness stole over Laura.

'I'm sorry, I'm so sleepy. Will it bother you if I shut my eyes for a little?'

'Not at all. Pray do. I shall sketch you as a sleeping nymph.' As gracefully and unself-consciously as a kitten, she lay back against the grassy bank and curled up in a lovely relaxed pose, one hand under her cheek, one knee above the other, so still that she hardly seemed to breathe. Maurice watched her, marvelling at her innocent trustfulness, then began to draw her, first as she was, then fancifully, as a nude sleeping Venus watched by gleeful Cupids. As he undressed her with eye and pencil, revealing the woman's form and flesh beneath the stiff dress, he who was so used to stripped-down models felt an excited emotion not one of them had ever aroused in him. And he knew that he must control it.

Because he realized it would shock her if she saw it, he put the finished sketch in his portfolio. When she woke, flushed, yawning and stretching like a child, he showed her the first sketch and she exclaimed delightedly at it.

'Keep it,' he said. She put out her hand, then drew it back.

'I'd like to. Thank you. But I couldn't . . . Ma would think . . . Well, it would be awkward, explaining. I shan't tell her I've been away from the shop, you see. I think I ought to go back now.'

'Of course.' They spoke little as they walked down through the park. A young deer sidled out from a thicket and hovered near them, all huge eyes and quivering nose. 'Oh, can I feed it?' Laura cried. 'Is there anything left from the picnic?'

Maurice rummaged in the bag and produced half an apple. Laura held it out. The creature approached nervously, step by step on delicate hooves, then with a sudden dart took the apple from her palm with soft lips, and began to munch it.

'They're ever so tame,' she said. 'Except at the fair when all the rowdies come and rampage all over the place with donkeys, and frighten them.' She watched the deer scurry away, and added, 'I've never been to the fair myself. We aren't allowed.'

Not even to Greenwich Fair, she who dreamed of far places and foreign skies? Maurice felt anger and an urge to make some grand chivalrous gesture towards this Andromeda, chained to the rock of convention and prudery – a stronger emotion than he had ever felt in the whole of his selfish life. He was just about to make some wild proposal – of what, he hardly knew – when they found themselves in the street, with people about them. Laura cast a nervous glance in the direction of her home. 'Don't come any further,' she said.

'Of course I must.' He put his hand on her arm, feeling her response, as though she wanted to draw close to him. Then she pulled away, and they walked to the shop in silence. At the door he looked down at her, not knowing how to say farewell, conscious of the mute appeal in her eyes.

'Well,' he said. 'Thank you for your charming company.'

'It was a lovely day out. I did enjoy it so much. I . . . will I . . . ?'

'Of course. I shall see you again very soon.' It would have been right and proper to kiss her hand, but hardly a gesture that would have gone unnoticed in Greenwich Church Street. Instead he made her a little bow.

'Goodbye, Miss Diamond.'

'Goodbye, Mr Reide.'

Miss Plum was there, sitting behind the counter with her knitting.

'Well, my dear, you're back nice and early. Had a good day, have you – plenty of sketching?'

'Yes, lots. Mr Reide drew some lovely pictures of me. Only I couldn't take any, because . . . Thank you very much for letting me go, Miss Plum, it was very kind of you.'

'Not a bit. I like to know folk are enjoying themselves, having a bit of fun.' But she knew from the dreaming look on the girl's face and the sleepwalking way in which she took off her hat and coat that it had been more than a bit of fun. Guilt assailed her. She should have known that Young Laura was not the girl for thoughtless slap-and-tickle, not yet for selling herself for a few presents and compliments from a gentleman. Not that Maurice Reide, little as she knew of him, had ever struck her as anything but a gentleman in the best sense; but there, men were all the same. Whatever he'd done or not done, it had put stars in Laura's eyes.

Maurice walked home slowly, his mind in turmoil. Laura's wraith walked beside him, her beauty, her sweet childishness, the inexperience he cherished, thinking how he might make up to her for all she had missed. He would be Pygmalion to her Galatea. In his hands she should be moulded into a lady. He would improve her voice, her manners; not that they mattered, he told himself impatiently. And all this could only be done by marriage, for he would never soil her innocence. Plenty of painters had married their models. There had been a disastrous case, of course . . . the aristocratic François and the pretty grisette who had scandalized even the society of the Left Bank, but Laura could never behave like that. Millais had married Effie Ruskin after her sensational divorce, and made a faultless baronet's wife of her, as she had made a rich commercial artist of him, once a Pre-Raphaelite dealer in dream and legend. The Queen had refused to receive her, but everyone else did. As for Laura's family, he preferred not to think about them, at the moment. Or about his mother.

Madeline's eyes were no less sharp than Miss Plum's, and she had a nice little piece of evidence to explain the reason for her son's abstracted air. They took a quiet dinner together, Maurice saying very little and often not answering her remarks very intelligently. Afterwards, as they sat in the drawing-room, Madeline engaged on a panel of needlework, Maurice reading. The glances she stole at him told her that he seldom turned over a page. His eyes were seeing something other than the print before them.

She laid the piece of canvas down on top of her workbox, needle neatly impaled in it, and removed the spectacles she disliked wearing.

'Did you have a pleasant day's sketching, darling?'

He looked up, bemused. 'What?'

'I said, you haven't shown me any of your sketches – you know how I like to see them. Especially when you had such a pretty model.'

This time he heard her, his face a picture of mild shock. 'How . . .?'

'Elise saw you. I sent her into town on an errand, and she came back with this story of seeing you with the girl from Miss Plum's. So you've decided to engage her as a model? How wise of you. I thought she looked ideal.' Madeline went back to her sewing, her eyes on it, not watching him but listening to the nuances of his voice.

'Not at all. I mean, I haven't engaged her. I just happened to meet her in the street, and walked back with her. I don't need another model at the moment, until I've finished the Psyche.' He flipped over a page, trying to seem intent on his book. Madeline bit off a thread and selected another reel of

60

silk, comparing its colour carefully.

'Would you turn the lamp up, pet? Just listen to the rain. What a *triste* evening, the day quite gone to bed, as Nanny used to say, after such a promising start.' She knotted the end of the thread and began a line of chainstitch. 'Did you enjoy your al fresco luncheon? Cook told me you took half a pie, greedy child. But then food tastes twice as good in the open air – I always think that's the only saving grace about shooting parties, boring, boring things. Maurice, this young woman – I don't know her name . . .'

'Diamond.' He wished heartily that he could get out of the room on some pretext and end the conversation.

'How pretty. Her surname, I take it? As a Christian name it would be – well, hardly Christian, would it. What are her people, do you know?'

'Her father's employed in a China house, India house, whatever they call it. She has a younger sister, and apart from that I know nothing about them. Why should I?'

'Oh, no reason, darling, except that you *are* very much attracted to her, aren't you? Now don't give me that putting-off look – I can always tell. And I thoroughly approve. Oh yes, I do. She has quite remarkable looks – a bit of a hybrid, I would guess?'

'Part Jewish,' Maurice said shortly.

'Ah, yes. Refugee Jewish. Mixed blood often produces these striking results. I can just imagine the parents. Father a little dark fox-terrier type, Mama pale and pinched. I might be quite wrong, but that's how I see them. The eyes, and that light hair . . . Local born, of course – there's no mistaking the Grinidge accent. A pity to hear it coming from such a charming mouth.'

'Madeline –'

She put down her sewing and leaned forward, her hands prettily clasped.

'My darling boy, don't be cross. I know, I can see it, Miss Diamond has dazzled you with her rays, and never mind the voice and whatever the rest of it may be. Now, you take my advice – have a fling with her.'

'What?'

'You heard me. Have a fling with her, get her out of your blood. A very little of that kind of young person goes a long

61

way. Don't look at me as though I were making an immoral suggestion, darling.'

'But you are.'

'Not a bit. She'll be taken up by some man or other, don't you see? It would be a kindness to the girl to break her in gently – dear me, that sounds faintly indelicate. You'll find she's quite charmed to be the little friend of a handsome artist, proud to tell her friends about it – or make a lovely big secret of it, and just *hint*. They adore this kind of situation . . .'

'*They*? Who do you think Miss Diamond is – a scullery maid?'

Madeline laughed lightly. 'I suppose it did sound a bit like what *Punch* would call servantgalism, and I didn't mean that.'

Maruice got up and slammed his book shut. 'I don't know what you meant, Mother, but I'd rather not talk about it any more, if you don't mind. I'm going down to the studio.'

She looked pensively after his retreating back. So she was 'Mother' tonight, and that meant he was really angry. She guessed, rightly, that some of the anger was directed at himself.

When he came back an hour or so later, she was sitting as he had left her, the needlework laid aside, the lamp low and the fire burnt down; she had not rung for more coal. She looked a picture of gentle dejection. Maurice tilted up her chin.

'You've been crying.'

'No. Well, only a little. I'm sorry I said what I did and made you cross. It was nothing to do with me – I shouldn't have spoken. It upsets me so when anything comes between us, dearest.'

He knelt at her side, taking her hand and laying it against his cheek.

'Nothing can, you know that. We understand each other so well, you and I. Don't worry any more about it.' Now he felt guilty towards Madeline as well as towards Laura, and hastened to compensate her. 'It gets very dull for you here, I know, and for me, too. Why don't we go and see a play tomorrow, and have dinner somewhere? That would cheer us both up.'

Madeline clapped her hands. 'Oh, but delightful! What shall it be – the Italian Opera, or the Lyceum? No, not that, I don't feel like dreary old Shakespeare. *You* choose, though – whatever you like. Oh, and I've got an even better idea – we could stay at your rooms for longer, a week perhaps, and do lots of lovely things. There's Emily Huntingdon's soirée – and I can indulge in an orgy of shopping while you see your friends – you could look in at the Hogarth Club and have a bachelor evening with Charles . . . what fun it will be.'

Dining fashionably late on the following night, among the architectural splendours of the Langham Hotel's famous dining-room, Maurice agreed that it *was* proving fun. They had laughed themselves helpless at a farce and shared a bottle of champagne in their theatre box. Now they faced each other across a small, intimate table. A narrow silver vase held a single rose, exquisite, forced, its stem tortured with the wire that bound it in a sheaf of maidenhair fern. The head waiter had presented it personally to Madame with a most discreet compliment. Madame was glowing with pleasure, jewels sparkling on her very white shoulders and a jewelled comb in her hair, which tonight was a slightly richer shade of brown than usual; she had an excellent coiffeuse in Bond Street. As she smiled and twinkled at her handsome escort, they could have been mistaken for lovers, and were treated as such by the waiters. Madeline was happy: my son, my darling son, will be with me always if I'm clever.

And Maurice, for the time being, was also happy. It was impossible to imagine life without Madeline. The shared jokes, their eyes caught when something ridiculous happened, the private language they had, the cachet her elegance and her wit gained him: these were things that were displayed at their best in such a situation, just as Madeline had intended when she suggested the interlude in London. The image of a younger and fairer face which haunted him was pushed to the back of his mind, and a door slammed on it.

At the end of their London week the spring sunshine lured them to Paris, where they stayed until Madeline decided to return in time for Ascot.

Laura waited. A day, two days passed, and she was not anxious. 'I shall see you again very soon,' he had said. That might mean a week at least – he had his painting, and a social life of which she knew nothing. She imagined him in various situations, always thinking of her, planning when he could meet her next. She made excuses for him. He would not like to send one of his mother's maids with a letter. She hadn't told him exactly where she lived, so he would not be able to intercept her on her way to and from the shop, as the dreadful Duffin had done. Would he come to the shop one day, when she least expected him? Yes, that was it. She would look up from sorting laces or counting money and there he would be, smiling, and he would say . . .

'Dreaming again?' her mother asked sharply. 'You're going to burn that dress with the iron any minute now, and it's new.'

'Sorry, Ma.' She replaced the flatiron on its stand.

'What's the matter? Have you something on your mind?'

'No. Of course not.'

'Well, it seems to me funny how quiet you've gone, never hearing what one says the first time and always staring at nothing. I think I'll get the doctor to have a look at you.'

'Oh, don't go on at me, Ma. I'm not ill, I'm quite all right. People have moods sometimes, that's all.'

Ellie guessed the truth, having been through the same experience. She didn't believe that Laura had been hurt as she had, only that she was in love and could think of nothing else. It would have been easy to manufacture situations in which they would have been alone and confidences natural, but she held back from them. Laura would tell her in her own time.

Daniel Diamond, who had seen his younger daughter's humiliation, feared that the same thing was happening to his elder girl, and worried. But the habit of silence was too strong in him to talk to her, or to his wife, even when he saw Laura's face grow thinner and her mouth begin to take a downward droop, after two weeks had passed and no word had come to her.

Only Miss Plum knew and tried to help. 'Mr Reide's got things to do that keep him away, most likely. No use worrying about nothing and making yourself ill. Laura, child – you've no *reason* to worry, have you?'

Laura looked blank. 'Reason? Well, he said "soon", and it's over a fortnight.'

'I know that, love. I mean, you're not in any sort of

trouble, are you?' That was as near as she could get to it. But Laura looked blanker still, and the old lady gave up. The child was not only too pretty for her own good, but too innocent besides. 'There's one thing I could do,' she said, 'send you up to Placentia House with a note. I'll make something up – ask Mrs R. if she's likely to want a repeat of the ribbon. Then you'll have the chance to slip round to the back and see what's doing in the studio. He'll be glad to see you, most like.' It was a flimsy solution, and might prove not to be a solution at all.

Laura's eyes were bright. 'Oh, you dear! I never thought of that. I can't just walk up and down the Hill, but if I've a note it will be all right. How do I look? I'd never have put this old thing on if I'd thought . . . oh, well . . .'

'You look as pretty as a daisy. Wait, now, while I write the note.'

The day was grey and cool, dust blowing in little storms from the dry road and pavement. There was the house she had visited just once before; how long ago it seemed. There was no sign of life at the windows, and the coach-house doors were shut. This time she went to the right side, where the tradesmen's entrance was, and pulled the bell nervously, her heart beating violently. A uniformed elderly maid answered.

'Yes?'

'I . . . I've come from Miss Plum. With a note for Mrs Reide, if you'd be so kind as to . . .'

No hand was outstretched. 'Mrs Reide's not at home. She and Mr Maurice are abroad.'

'Abroad?' The pretty face had suddenly turned the colour of a bleached bone. 'How long for?'

'How should I know?' (And what's it to do with you, the maid's tone implied.) 'The house is to be redecorated before Madam comes back, so I expect it will be some time.' She became human. 'Are you all right, miss? They'll make you a cup of tea downstairs if you want to sit down.'

Laura managed a smile. 'No, thanks.' She could not have borne to go into the house where Maurice should have been. 'I'm just a little tired, that's all. Thank you very much though.'

Thank you very much for telling me what I ought to have known, that he was just paying me the sort of silly compliments I bet he pays any girl who doesn't look like the back of an omnibus. What a fool he'd think me if he knew I'd believed him – the things he said. At least, he didn't say anything very much, it was more the way he talked as if I was a lady. And the way he looked. I believed *that* . . .

Instead of going straight back to the shop, she turned aside into the park and found the spot where they had spent that afternoon. Because of the weather there were few people about, and none near her. She sat down, her back against a tree, and gave way to a flood of tears. She cried until her eyes were swollen up and her throat sore, until she could cry no more. Then she mopped her face with a sodden ball of handkerchief and set off towards the shop, looking at nobody, however curiously they looked at her.

Miss Plum needed no explanation. 'I see,' she said. 'that's what men are like, my dear. Swine, if you'll excuse the expression.'

'It was my fault,' Laura answered curtly. 'It was a mistake.'

'We all make mistakes. Now you go and wash that face in cold water, and I'll put some cologne on a clean hanky for you. Nobody will know, by the time you get home.'

But Laura's father knew when, unexpectedly, she called on him at Ponsford's on her way home. He asked no questions, but chatted of trivia, not looking at her too often, missing nothing of the still-swollen eyelids and blotchy complexion.

'What a rum thing you should have looked in today, seeing what's just come.' He waved a large gold-edged card 'One on every desk in the place.'

'What is it, Pa? The light's awful in here – I don't know how you see to work.'

'An invitation, that's what, my dear. "Mr and Mrs George Ponsford are happy to invite all members of their staff to a Supper Dance at Evelyn Towers, Deptford, on Friday 18 May, in celebration of their Silver Wedding.' And so forth, and so forth. Handsome, I call it, when you think how many of us there are, and families too. "Mr and Mrs Daniel Diamond and Family." I think we can run to new frocks for my three ladies, don't you? Now *there's* something to look forward to, wouldn't you say?'

'Yes, Pa,' Laura replied indifferently.

But it was at Evelyn Towers that her life was changed – when she met Fred.

Chapter Five

AMONG THE GENERALLY PALE, BESPECTACLED and stooping employees of Ponsford's, Fred Mares stood out like a maypole. He was all of six feet tall, broad-shouldered and slim-hipped, a boxer's build, his smallish head with its thatch of thick blond curls set on a strong muscular neck, giving him a resemblance to a young bull. His face was plump and country-fresh, his eyes china blue, his expression innocent as a child's. He came of a family of Devonshire farmers, but disease had killed his father and forced his mother to sell up and move to London to join households with a widower brother. There, growing up among the masts and funnels of the busy river, Fred had lazily considered the possibility of becoming a sailor, and rejected it because the life was too unsettled. Farming was in his blood – or that part of farming which involved leaning on a gate watching the crops grow, as his mother often said tartly, slaving all hours was not for him. But farming was impossible now, so he had drifted amiably towards Ponsford's where, at an early age for responsibility, he was put in charge of stores.

Female eyes settled on him like wasps on a jam-jar. Even the mistress of Evelyn Towers and its plushy grandeurs, Mrs George Ponsford, lifted the lorgnettes she didn't need to survey her husband's sensational employee, while the daughters of other employees giggled and whispered to each other. Laura asked Ellie 'Who on earth's that?'

'Who? Oh, that's Mr Mares. He looks after stores.'

Laura had seen, without knowing what they were, reproductions of the tiles designed by William Morris depicting sturdy aproned young blacksmiths and Saxon peasants of godlike aspect. Fred might have been one of them come to life. It seemed strange to her that a young man of such an appearance should do such a mundane job. Again and again her eyes went back to him, as she danced with assorted middle-aged gentlemen or sat out with her mother, who sharply told her, 'Don't stare.'

'I wasn't.'

'Yes, you were. It's not ladylike.'

Laura continued to glance in Fred Mares' direction. He seemed not to be dancing at all, but to prefer leaning against a massive mantelpiece, watching the company with an expression which might have been rapt contemplation, or merely boredom – which, in fact, it was.

'Isn't that young Mr Ponsford over there?' Mrs Diamond was asking Ellie, indicating an impressively dressed gentleman with an equally impressive black moustache. Ellie nodded. She had just caught Adolphus Duffin's eye and hastily looked away. Her mother surveyed George Ponsford, Junior, critically. He might not be titled, but his father was rich; titles sometimes came with riches, in later life. Laura might do worse. She was about to tell her daughter to sit up straight and look pleasant when Laura rose and drifted away across the floor of the ballroom. Possessed by she knew not what whim, she strolled in the direction of Fred Mares, and positioned herself on the edge of a group waiting for the next dance to begin, fanning herself languidly. The simple ruse worked. After a moment of contemplation, he detached himself from his support and strolled over to her.

'Care to dance?' His voice was light-toned and slow, with a marked Devonshire accent which Laura found attractively exotic. She gave him a dazzling smile, and moved off on his arm as the quartet of musicians ranged behind a row of expensive potted plants broke into a waltz.

Fred knew the steps, but seemed to execute them more slowly than anyone else on the floor, with the result that he and Laura constantly bumped into other couples. It was vexing to have to keep murmuring apologies, but she minded less than she would have done because she knew they were attracting envious stares as well as angry ones. It was agreeable to be the prettiest girl in the room, dancing with the handsomest man. Since the defection of Maurice she had made the most of her looks, courting attention instead of avoiding it, for her pride was bruised and sore. Tonight she wore a low-cut dress of deep harebell blue; her colour was high and her hair shone like tinsel in the bright lights of the ballroom.

None of it was lost on Fred. If she had been a prize cow he would have walked all round her slowly, sizing up her points, before setting the coveted white rosette between her horns. As it was, he congratulated himself on having picked a jolly pretty girl to set off his own good looks, of which he was perfectly aware. Their steps began to match better. Laura noted with approval that he wore a scented pomade on his hair and his small fair moustache. It was a considerable improvement on the blend of sweat and clothes cleaned in petroleum which surrounded most partners. The feel of his strong arm around her was reassuring. He said very little, and she liked that, better than meaningless chatter. When the dance ended he asked her for the next one.

It was time for the speech-making, an address of congratulation to Mr and Mrs Ponsford, Mr Ponsford's dignified and lengthy reply, the presentation of a silver box subscribed to by all members of staff, a chorus of 'For he's a jolly good fellow'. During the ceremony Laura and Fred sat side by side, silent but very much aware of each other, and her mother, on the opposite side of the room, never took her eyes off them.

The evening ended decently early – no West End hours for Ponsford's.

'I must go,' Laura said. 'It's been very nice.'

'Ar, yes. Very nice. I'd like to call on you, if I might, Miss Diamond.'

Laura thought quickly. 'Well. Why not? It's 19 Feathers Row. come on – on Sunday afternoon. Half-past three. Goodnight.' Her hand lingered in his huge one.

Alice Diamond scolded her all the way home, Ellie and her father trailing uncomfortably behind. 'To make such a spectacle of yourself, practically asking that man to dance with you, and then dancing with nobody else! Young Mr Ponsford would have asked you, if you'd been free.'

'He could have asked me before, but he didn't, did he?'

Her mother snorted. 'That's neither here nor there. The way you went on tonight, you'll be talked about tomorrow, and don't say you don't care, because I do. It wouldn't have been so bad if you'd picked somebody proper – a storekeeper, indeed!'

'He isn't a storekeeper, in the way you mean it, Ma. He's in charge – that's a different thing. And he's perfectly proper. He didn't say a word to me he couldn't have said before you. Anyway,' Laura's voice sounded braver than she felt, 'he's coming to tea on Sunday, so you can find out what he's like for yourself.'

The storm raged on until Daniel intervened. 'Draw it mild, my dear, people are looking. It'll keep until we get home.'

'That's right, you stop me having my say and give that girl her own way as you always do! If you'd been as firm as you ought to've been she wouldn't defy me like this. I'm sick of the lot of you.' She broke away from them and began running, like a wild woman, towards her home.

'Oh dear,' Ellie said. 'That means she'll be sitting up.'

They knew only too well what she meant. Alice's way of registering strong protest at offences committed against her by her family was to march up to her bedroom, draw a chair up to the window and sit, bolt upright, staring out expressionlessly. She had been known to sit there all night, or part of it, fully dressed; while Daniel dozed uneasily, conscious of the resentment flowing out from her, the wife to whom he had somehow never been able to give what she wanted: whatever that might be. Tonight she would be there, a grim outline against the window, storing up bitter things to say to him, quelling things to say to Laura and her unacceptable suitor.

But whatever angry disapproval Alice might feel, there was no way in which she could decently prevent Fred Mares coming to tea. He had been invited, and he came, resplendent in a well-kept black suit and a very stiff, very clean collar. Alice had thoughts of Sitting Up instead of playing hostess, but that would have been rather too drastic a flouting of the social conventions, and would also have left Laura and the young man insufficiently chaperoned – for she considered Daniel and Ellie quite soft enough to leave them together. She would content herself with putting on her chilliest manner and flattening Fred.

But Fred seemed not to notice the chill, and offered no opportunities for flattening. He sat four-square, knees comfortably apart, accepting something from every plate handed to him (for this was a genteel afternoon tea with plates tiered on a cake-stand and the teapot and best service on a tray at Alice's side). Demonstrating obvious appreciation and a young man's appetite, he munched away at thin bread and butter, meat paste sandwiches, Ellie's home-made rock buns and a Madeira cake, saying 'Thanks, very nice', to everything offered. He emptied cup after cup of tea from the dainty china cup which looked inadequate in his large hand, so that Ellie had to brew more.

The conversation was not easy. Daniel tried to help by introducing topics concerning Ponsford's and drawing Ellie into the discussion, but she was too shy to take up the leads he threw her. Alice conveyed the unmistakable message that Shop was not suitable for the tea-table, maintaining a stony silence while father and daughter struggled and Fred answered in his amiable monosyllabic way. Dumb and stupid, thought Alice savagely. It was Laura who got him to produce whole sentences, as she questioned him about his boyhood and his Devon home, and how the death of his father ('moi fäther', was his pronunciation) had led to his coming up to London with his mother to live with his uncle, a nautical instrument maker, in Deptford.

'My Uncle Sid's a ship's chandler,' Laura said. 'I wonder if they know each other?' Alice shot her a repressive look. Sid was no subject for boasting.

'Oi dunno,' replied Fred. 'Reckon he know most folk, Uncle Jabez.'

'Miss the countryside, do you?' Daniel asked.

'Not to notice,' Fred said indistinctly through a rock bun. 'Done nicely for meself up here.' Laura thought the way he talked was amusing, fascinating. She noticed the deep dimple in his round chin and the way his bushy gold eyebrows went up in the middle, giving him a surprised look. He was astonishingly good-looking, his affable manner put her mother's to shame; and he was as different from Maurice as a man could be.

He began to take her out regularly. On the next Bank Holiday they went to Blackheath Fair, Laura feeling perfectly safe among the milling crowds of dubious-looking revellers because Fred's strong arm was linked with hers; she admired the careless skill with which he threw quoits at a range of prizes, winning her a tawdry necklace of glass beads and a bottle of cheap rose perfume. She put on the beads, and dabbed some of the perfume on to her skin, to please him. They were stared at, the two young people of sensational looks, a blond god and goddess among crowds whose appearance ranged from the plain to the frankly ugly or deformed. They were stared at when he took her to Crowder's Music Hall, where he laughed at all the jokes, watched the jugglers and the magician with the unswerving attention of a child, and bought Laura lemonade at the interval. They even attracted attention among the absorbed eaters at Goddard's Famous Eel and Pie Shop, where Fred displayed a gargantuan and indiscriminate appetite, alarming to watch. Laura remembered that Maurice had suggested Goddard's as one of the places where they might eat; but of course he wouldn't have risked being seen with her. As they came out she flaunted herself a little on Fred's arm.

A Sunday came when he took her home to Deptford. His mother was surprisingly small to have produced a child the size of Fred, prematurely lined and worn with the hard life of a farmer's wife. She greeted Laura with wan pleasure, and chatted dutifully over tea about the price of food, the shocking case of Mr Parnell, and the latest murders. 'I do like the newspapers,' she said wistfully, 'they tell you such a lot about what's going on. I was never a one for lessons and learning, but my Mam saw to it I learned to read, and a blessing it is to me now I can't get about much.' Otherwise she seemed quite uneducated, almost simple. She spoke to Fred quite flatly, without emotion, as he did to her. Laura supposed she must be proud of him, but if so she failed to show it.

Uncle Jabez, when he appeared, proved to be a sharp-featured bald man with a thin voice in which Devon was overlaid by East London. He seemed fascinated by Laura's looks, staring at her so pointedly that she began to be annoyed. When he offered to show her his workshop she went with him meekly if mistrustfully, and examined sextants, compasses and chronometers with assumed interest, Jabez hovering behind her, administering sundry strokes, pats and pinches strong enough to be felt through her bustle. Her face was flaming and her heart beating fast, but she dared make no protest. This was Fred's home, she must not make trouble in it. They returned to the parlour, Jabez pressing closely against her as they reached the door, and nothing was said.

'Why *do* you, Lorla?' Ellie asked, that night.
    'Why do I what?'
    'You know. Fred.'
    'What about him?'
    'Ma doesn't think he's good enough for you.'
    'Ma wouldn't think the Prince of Wales was.'
    'But Pa doesn't either, dear, and . . . I don't. I know he's very handsome, but looks aren't everything, are they? I don't think you really like him.'
    'Of course I like him, or I wouldn't go out with him, would I, silly?'
    Ellie's eyes were big and pleading. She was trying very hard, before it was too late. 'You only do it because of something else, don't you – something you wouldn't tell me about. I think somebody, a man, disappointed you or hurt you somehow. I *do* know how it feels and it isn't nice, but taking up with the wrong person isn't the way to solve things. It goes in the end, that feeling really does, if you only wait long enough. Now you're laughing at me – I suppose I do sound like a granny. But I can't bear it, somebody who doesn't understand you and won't treat you well.'
    'He treats me very well indeed!'
    'Oh, I know, presents and all that. But it's something different – something here.' She laid her hand over her heart. 'Fred's quite cold inside. Don't you feel it?'
    'No, I don't.' Laura snatched a dress from her wardrobe and began to change. 'Now that's enough. I get it from Ma all the time and I don't want it from you, Ellie. I'm old enough to look after my own affairs, thank you.'
    That Saturday evening she came home late. Ellie had gone to bed, but her parents were downstairs, as she half-hoped, half-feared, they would be. Alice looked up at her entrance from a pile of mending.
    'This is a nice time to come in.'
    'Is it?' Laura replied pertly. 'I hadn't noticed.'
    'Your supper's spoiled.'

'I've had my supper, thanks.' She was busy unpinning her hat, taking off her jacket with its fashionable frilled edging and velvet bow at the waist. She saw her father's eyes on her, so like Ellie's, melancholy and reproachful. She decided to strike the blow and get it over.

'I'm going to marry Fred. He's asked me and I've said yes.'

Alice jumped up from her chair. 'You can't! We'll forbid it.'

'How, Ma? Have me put in prison? Or just lock me in my bedroom? There isn't anything you can do about it. He's coming to speak to Pa tomorrow, and if you don't say yes I'll run away, that's what I'll do. You don't want a scandal, do you?'

Alice's lips were trembling, her face white. 'Laura, you can't.' Daniel put his arm round his wife. 'Your mother's very upset, Laura. We'd better all go to bed and talk about this in the morning.'

'No, Pa. We'll talk about it now. Ma, you've been awful to me all my life – awful. You've treated me as if I was a bad woman always chasing men, and you know quite well I've hardly even talked to any, until . . . until Fred. I've put up with it and never complained, I've been your good obedient little girl, and now I'm eighteen and I've had an honest offer and I'm going to accept it, if it's only to get away from here.'

'Laura, that's not enough,' Daniel said. 'You've got to love the man, and we don't think you do.'

'Who says I don't? And Ma ought to be very pleased with Fred. He's the best-looking chap that's ever been seen round here, and she's gone on about my looks as long as I remember, so now she's got another beauty for the other end of the mantelpiece.' Laura heard her voice, strident, unable to stop. 'Lucky for Ellie she takes after you, Pa, or she'd have her life made a misery like mine. The times I've wished I'd been born plain you wouldn't believe. Well, I'm sorry Fred can't make a lady out of me, as Ma wanted, but perhaps he'll rise to be Lord Mayor yet, who knows? And anyway I don't care, just so long as I get away. Goodnight.'

She went out quickly before her father's stricken face melted her; they heard her running upstairs and the key turn in the lock of her bedroom door.

There was a shocked silence in the room. Then Alice said

bleakly, 'I only wanted the best for her. Only the best.'

Laura and Fred were married not at the ancient church of St Alphege, which the Diamonds attended, but at the humbler modern one in Deptford patronized by Fred's family. The day was cold and blustery, English summer greyness under a heavy cloud-cover. Miss Plum, in a back pew, turned her head to watch the bride enter on her father's arm, tall and slender in the gown of cream silk for which she herself had given the material as a wedding present. She had not said a great deal in the way of congratulations when Laura gave in her notice, only that she was sorry to be losing her and hoped she would be very happy. The church was half-empty. On the bride's side there was Alice, frozen-faced, her asthmatic sister Jane whose husband was the reprehensible Sidney, at present mercifully sober, small wizened Aunt Gerti, a few neighbours, Florence Taberer, her family, and her fiancé Georgie. On the bridegroom's, his mother and uncle, a high-coloured heavily pregnant young woman who was Fred's sister from Tavistock, and her farmer husband, a few Deptford faces. Nobody else.

Fred looked magnificent in his best suit with a pearl-grey waistcoat and top hat to match, a white carnation in his buttonhole. Ellie was Laura's only bridesmaid, wearing a modest dark blue dress and a bonnet with a small bunch of forget-me-nots as trimming. In the echoing church the couple's responses were barely audible. The ceremony, with no singing, only an organ voluntary during the signing of the register and the wedded pair's return down the aisle, seemed to be over very quickly. The company then repaired to the church hall next door where the wedding breakfast was to be held. Alice had refused to prepare anything for it; the whole thing had been turned over to a caterer.

The guests made a great deal of noise for a fairly small assembly, ravenously demolishing the spread of cold meats and the fancy dishes set before them, and the quantities of tea. To the dismay of the caterers and the disgust of Uncle Sidney, the bride's mother had ordered no champagne, only two bottles of inexpensive wine. Fred ate steadily, replying to congratulations in between munches. Laura, her veil thrown back, was flushed and radiant. Alice ate and drank almost nothing, while Daniel sat at her side, watching his daughter and her bridegroom. A speech was made by the best man, and another, facetiously near the knuckle, by Uncle Jabez, replied to by Fred in the shortest one on record. 'Thanks,' he said, 'me and my wife's very pleased to see you all – main pleased, ain't we, midear?' On which he sat down.

The food was almost gone, the last drop of tea being drained. Daniel went to Laura's side and took her arm.

'Come in here a minute.' He led her away from the chatter into a small quiet ante-room. 'I expect you've wondered why I've not given you a present.'

'No, Pa.'

'Well, I've got one. I just wanted us to be on our own when I gave it you. It's this.' He took a small jeweller's box from his pocket. Laura opened it. From a bed of black velvet a single diamond winked up at her, a tiny star flashing colour from its facets as she turned it this way and that in the light. A thin delicate gold chain was coiled round it. A very curious feeling went through Laura, as though she had seen the jewel before, or knew what her father was about to say.

'It's a good one, though it's so small. A gem of purest ray serene, Laura. Like you've been to me, girl. Now that your name's not Diamond any more I want you to keep this as a . . . a sign.' He struggled for words. 'I'm not good at saying things. But this is what *you* are, the real you, the best of you. If your life gets hard, look at this and you'll feel better. If you meet someone and you aren't sure whether they're all right or not, look at this and it'll tell you. It'll keep you safe, if you'll let it.'

'Oh, Pa.' The first tears of her married life flowed down Laura's cheeks as she clung to her father. 'It's beautiful. I'll do what you say, and . . . and think of you. Will you put it on for me, now?'

Gravely he unfastened the high lace collar of her dress and put the chain round her neck. The diamond glittered and shone against the white skin just below the hollow at the base of her throat.

The time had come for the happy couple to leave, not for a honeymoon, which Fred considered a waste of time, but for the small terraced house he had rented in one of the streets

76

which had sprung up recently near Ponsford's. It would save him a long walk to his work and back, he said.

The cab deposited them at the door: one of many doors all looking the same, with a tiny patch of uncultivated garden in front between it and the pavement. Fred unlocked it. Laura waited for him to pick her up and carry her over the threshold, but he went straight in and looked round with satisfaction.

'Very neat, very cosy, eh? I reckon we picked this stuff properly.' He slapped an armchair familiarly on its back. 'I tell you what, Laura . . .'

'What?'

'I didn't get anythin' like enough to eat at that place, what with all the talk. What say you do us a nice little meal, midear?'

'*Meal*? After all that . . . What do you want?'

'Nice bit of ham, couple of eggs – there's plenty in the pantry.'

'But . . .' Laura looked down at the cream silk. 'I can't cook in my wedding dress.'

'Go and take it off, then.' He settled himself in the armchair and picked up the morning paper, humming tunelessly as he scanned the front page. For a long moment Laura looked at him, then turned and went up the narrow stairs. Fred did not look up to watch her go.

Chapter Six

WAS IT ONLY AN EVENING, that string of hours in the house in Miller Street? To Laura it seemed like several long days compressed together. She had never been alone with Fred before, always in company, usually in public where there were things to do and watch. Now there was nothing to do, nothing to watch but Fred.

After the meal, which Laura couldn't touch, he settled himself back in the armchair and fell asleep. She was to discover that he had an immense capacity for daytime sleeping, instant and profound. He slept and slept, snoring slightly. Laura tiptoed out, though there was no need, and roamed all over the house that was now her home. The tiny kitchen, almost filled by an ugly cooking range. What could all those ovens be wanted for? Laura wondered. At Feathers Row there were only two. The copper, its lid open, waiting to receive a boiling of clothes; her mother put out the linen to a washerwoman who called every week. Outside the scullery was a tiny walled yard and an outside privy.

Laura wandered upstairs. Two bedrooms, the larger one at the front, containing a brass bed, a washstand, a dressing-chest and a chair. She remembered buying these things with Fred, but they looked very different in place. The wallpaper, the choice of previous tenants, was a busy complicated riot of greens, dark reds and black. The smaller bedroom was unfurnished as yet.

She returned to the parlour and sat, bored and low-spirited, watching Fred until he woke with a slight start, yawned and stretched. At his lazy smile she thought, Good, now we're going to talk. But he only glanced at the clock, picked up the paper again and began to read, with intense slowness, as though every word mattered. Political news, local events, editor's comments; court cases, hatches, matches

78

and dispatches, sports results, property for sale and to let, advertisements, stop press. It seemed that all these were of equal interest to Fred, or lack of interest, judging by his unmoved expression. Obviously, he took after his mother.

'*I*'ve nothing to read,' Laura said desperately.

'Eh?'

'Is there a book or a magazine? Anything I can look at?'

He looked round vacantly, shook his head, and returned to his paper. Laura got up suddenly. 'Then I'm going to bed,' she announced.

'Ar. I'll be up.'

There was only one consoling thought in Alice Diamond's mind about her daughter on that wedding day: at least I've kept her pure for marriage.

It was only too true. Laura's ignorance of the physiology of the sexes, and its relation to life, was as profound as the most idealistic of Victorians could wish. As she removed the extra-pretty chemise, corset, bloomers and petticoats gloomily bought by Alice for her trousseau, and put on the extra-pretty nightie, its bishop sleeves and high-necked bodice lavishly trimmed with cotton lace, there was no thought in her mind that they were anything but a celebration of her wedded state: certainly not that they were meant to have any kind of effect on Fred. She got into the large bed which she knew she would have to share with him, as she had once shared with Ellie, whispering confidences and giggling into the night, sometimes consoling each other with embraces when Ma had been difficult or a kitten had died. Presumably that was what would happen now, though it was not easy to imagine what confidences Fred might have to impart, since he seemed practically speechless at home. Laura was not frightened, having not the least idea that there was anything frightening to come. She didn't connect marriage with the alleged wicked ways of gentlemen. Marriage was, as far as she had allowed herself to give it any thought, something to do with kisses, and spooning, the sort that went on at parties over ice-cream. Eventually it ended in babies; perhaps they turned up under gooseberry bushes or, in the absence of a vegetable garden, suddenly appeared in one's bed. There was a sepia print in her Aunt Jane's house called 'Maternity', representing a well-coiffured young woman reclining amongst pillows with a heavily-frilled infant in her arm, being admired by an older one on tiptoe and a cat with a bell round its neck. It must be rather fun to wake up and find something dressed prettily in pink or blue kicking beside one . . .

Fred ambled in, loosening his collar. 'Well, then,' he said.

Laura was completely unready for what happened next. It was not so much that Fred's approach was unsubtle as that he had no approach at all. He was not inexperienced, but his only experiences had been with country girls, usually well topped up with cider at harvest home suppers, in barns and hayricks. Whether or not they enjoyed themselves meant nothing to him - girls were not supposed to, anyway. He was not all that interested himself; it was something chaps did to prove they were grown men. Laura's struggles and screams surprised him greatly. 'What's wrong, then?' he asked, letting go of her enough for her to roll out of his reach and on to the floor, crying hysterically with fright and pain and humiliation. Before he could stop her she was out of the room and down the stairs. He heard the parlour door slammed and locked from the inside. 'Well, Oi be damned,' he said. Within five minutes he was asleep again.

When he came down to breakfast she was in the kitchen, frying the breakfast, an outdoor jacket over her nightdress. She was pale and swollen-eyed, and would not look at him.

'This is a nice turn-up, all right,' he said. 'What've I done, old girl?'

'I don't want to talk. Here,' she slapped the plate down in front of him.

And they never did talk again, except for the exchange of commonplaces. Laura dragged out her days in the terraced house, lonely because she knew no neighbours and would not go near her mother or Ellie, except when duty indicated a social call, and everybody was stiff and awkward. Let them think what they liked. She came to understand that Fred was a big simpleton, bone-idle with just enough skills to keep him employed, as near to being without mind or emotion as any human being could be. He was, as Ellie had said, cold inside. Not cruel or bad in any way, just cold. His handsome outside was all there was to him - and that would soon change, for he lived for his food.

At home Ellie had been the domesticated daughter, the one allowed to cook and copy Alice's recipes, while Laura had been relegated to laying the table and washing up, rather to her relief. Now she spent much of her time in the small cramped kitchen, wrestling with the pies and dumplings and stews Fred demanded. He came home for midday dinner, as well as supper. It saved money, he said, and their house was so handy for Ponsford's. What temper he had was aroused by Laura's ineffectual touch with cooking, resulting in lumpy gravy, half-boiled potatoes, stringy meat, heavy cakes.

'What d'you call this? Didn't your ma teach you nothing?'

'Nawthen,' she mocked.'Oi didn't have no teachin'. Likely you should've married one as had.' But mockery was beyond him.

Apart from the unwelcome cooking and the washing of Fred's tent-like shirts and underwear, and her own, there was nothing to do. The neighbours barely passed the time of day with her, the women distrusting her looks and the men too much afraid of their wives. As the summer days passed she began to feel like an old woman, a very old woman, as old as Gagool in the new novel about King Solomon's Mines which she had taken out of the library. Not over-fond of reading, she now resorted to losing herself in novels; if their romantic sillinesses were not very life like, they were a good deal more entertaining, telling of far places and fortunate people. Nothing about life was what she had expected it to be. Especially marriage. She had hesitatingly tried to ask her mother whether what Fred had tried to impose on her was natural, and had been sharply told, 'It's what women have to endure, and duty's duty. You made your bed, my girl, and now you must lie on it.' If lying on it were all! Laura thought, but the next time Fred attempted to exert his rights she let him, degraded though she felt. Novels were all lies.

One morning in early September she rose in better spirits than usual. The heavy grey weather of August had given way to bright sunshine, a fresh wind was blowing off the river. She looked out through the poky kitchen window at the sky, and her mind was made up - she was going out. She had a whole ten shillings for spending money, saved up during three weeks out of the allowance Fred gave her for housekeeping, less than she had earned at Miss Plum's. Very well, she would spend it - not in the local shops she knew too well, but in London.

She wore her best street dress, her going-away costume (only they had not gone away) of pale lilac, with a little hat of green trimmed with velvet violets, tipped forward on the Piccadilly fringe she had given herself now that her mother could no longer say what she must and must not wear. It was very becoming, seen in the long thin pier-glass fixed inside the wardrobe that showed only a ghostly image of oneself.

The tram-ride from Trafalgar Road cost her twopence. As he took the money, the conductor pressed her hand and remarked that it was a finer day for seeing her. A man on the opposite seat stared at her so hard that she turned away and looked determinedly out of the window, clearing some of the grime from it with a corner of her handkerchief. The journey could not by any stretch of imagination have been called a pretty one, but the novelty lent it charm, as the tramcar lurched and clanked its way through crowded commercial streets. New Cross Road, Old Kent Road, New Kent Road. Lucky tram, securely perched on its rails, away from the running war fought between the drivers of carts and cabs for road space. Travelling on it was like being on a tall ship with a sea-fight going on around her. Here was the Elephant and Castle, and its new theatre, and in Westminster Bridge Road it was possible to look across to the domed bulk of Bethlehem Hospital, and think of the poor lunatics inside. Now the tram was passing Astley's, where horses, more fortunate than the struggling creatures between shafts, had once danced and even acted. Every time the Diamonds had taken a tram to London in Laura's childhood her father had pointed the building out, so that when she saw it now a vision of fantastically intelligent horses prancing in spangled costumes and exchanging dialogue in refined human voices rose in her mind.

But the tram had reached its destination, the terminus at the side of St Thomas's Hospital. From now on passengers had to walk, unless they cared to wait for an omnibus. Laura chose to walk. The air was exhilaratingly fresh, the river sparkling and dimpling in a myriad points of light, the sunlight which drew beauty from smoke-caked stone and brick and flattered London into her best looks. Laura's spirits rose with every step of the way. She smiled without knowing it, making heads turn as she passed. Free for a day, free from the little brick prison in Miller Street and the big stupid youth who would be her gaoler for the rest of her life.

At the foot of the Haymarket she paused and looked up it, remembering her childhood experience. At last she realized something of what it had been about, and a chill passed over her, forgotten when she turned into Lower Regent Street and found herself at the gateway of Paradise; the shopping centre of the West End began here.

The curving mile of Regent Street lay before Laura, and Piccadilly and Bond Street, and Oxford Street beyond. Temples of fashion offered a bewildering array of fine clothes. Ball-gowns, mantles, hats and bonnets, fans and shawls, Irish linens and French laces, delicious shoes and cobweb handkerchieves, silks and satins draped in shining lengths, frozen waterfalls of colour; and above the great plate-glass windows imposing names shouted of quality – Lewis and Allenby, Marshall and Snelgrove, Redmayne, Debenham and Freebody, Sykes, Josephine & Co, Corse-tières to the Courts of Europe, Box, Court Bootmaker; those happy enough to be By Appointment to the royal household proudly flaunting the lion and unicorn and crown.

It was dazzling, it was intoxicating to the senses of a young woman starved of colour and luxury. She paused at every window, gazing, filling her eyes with richness. There was no question of going in. She couldn't imagine facing those haughty assistants behind their mahogany counters with only ten shillings to offer – or rather nine shillings and eightpence, counting out the tram fare. Only one of the great emporia tempted her in, since she saw people moving freely through its doors. Inside there was a heady air worth breathing deeply, an utterly feminine compound of perfumes, leather, and what Laura could only think of as newness – an ineffable distillation of perfect things with no taint of use on them, no stain of benzolene cleaner or green soft soap. Another scent mingled with it, as she moved from one level to the next across the deep-piled green carpet – food. The store had a famous grocery department, as beautiful to the eye as its fabrics and jewellery. Cheeses red and white smiled on spotless boards, bread-crumbed hams pinkly beckoned, shell fish bottled in exotic jars offered nameless pleasures of taste and sea-tang.

And Laura realized that she was hungry. She had walked the length of Regent Street and back again, with a long diversion westwards, and was back at Piccadilly Circus. Her feet were hot and aching, her throat dry, but most of all she longed to eat.

Where? Names leapt out at her – the Piccadilly Restaurant, the Criterion, St James's Hall and Restaurant. Huge, grand places. If only there had been somewhere small and modest, but there was not. She had never eaten by herself in public in her life; such a thing was simply not considered, even in eel-and-pie circles. How did one go about it, and was it even allowed? There might be some law that would bring a heavy hand down on her shoulder if she crossed one of these impressive portals. She stood outside Swan and Edgar's emporium, nervously aware that she was attracting attention, though there were others standing there, glancing expectantly around them, for this was a favourite place to meet.

Suddenly she panicked, aware of the censorious gaze of a monumental matron followed by two cowed daughters emerging from the shop, a footman toiling behind them loaded down with parcels and bandboxes. With some vague fear of being given in charge, Laura darted round the corner and set off northwards round the Quadrant. A lull came in the stream of cabs, carriages and omnibuses, and she impulsively crossed the road and found herself outside a decorated façade with a name that was familiar to her above its doors. The Café Royal – she had read or heard of the name, and it had some sort of cheerful association. Hardly caring by this time what that might be, she went boldly in, to find herself confronted by an awesomely tall waiter, or manager, whatever he might be.

'Yes, madam? Can I assist madam?'

'I, er. Could I have dinner here?'

'Luncheon is now being served, madam.' Icicles dripped from the syllables.

Laura glanced desperately round, taking in a swift impression of crimson plush, tall pillars, crystal chandeliers, a lot of men clustered at tables, laughing and drinking, waiters hovering round them. She had certainly come to the wrong place. But the terrifying being was saying, 'If madam would care to follow me upstairs . . .?'

Meekly she followed him up the imposing broad staircase . . . The thought of flight crossed her mind, but that would be too horribly undignified. The stiff tail-coated back preceded her to a table well away from the balcony which overlooked the ground floor and the male drinkers, eaters and smokers. Ladies were not encouraged to sit where they could exchange signals with gentlemen down there – above all ladies by themselves. Innocent Laura had not the least idea of the reason for the waiter's obvious disapproval of her, though she noticed that she was the only unescorted woman among the few already lunching.

He pulled back a chair for her and handed her a menu. 'If madam would care to order . . .'

Laura looked at it with horror. It was a four-page jumble of words she didn't understand, dishes she had never heard of, terrifying French words. She had thought of asking for a poached egg on toast and a pot of tea. Obviously such things were not served here. She cast a wild look towards the staircase.

The waiter was enjoying her discomfiture, and decided to prolong it. 'Perhaps madam would care to consider.' He laid the dreadful menu ceremoniously before her and stalked away. She saw him confer with two other waiters, and their smiles, though fortunately their words failed to reach her. 'On the game, you reckon?'

'No powder nor paint, but her mane's dyed all right.'

'A *poule*, certainly.'

The plaster caryatids which surmounted the pillars of gold and jewel colours were no more petrified than Laura. At the foot of one page, one which a complete meal seemed to be set out, she saw the unbelievable price: five shillings. Five whole shillings! Her mother could feed the family for days on that, with careful management. It was an unheard-of price (and, indeed, was steep for the West End in those days. Three shillings was nearer the usual amount). It would take half her money, the money she had meant to spend in a shop.

Another waiter was at her elbow, flourishing another menu. 'Would madam care for some wine?'

'Oh no! I mean . . . thank you.' She felt that even the back of her neck was blushing. Two ladies at a nearby table were eyeing her pointedly. She recognized the music the orchestra downstairs was playing, a selection from *The Mikado*, and thought that whenever she heard it in after-life it would always remind her of this awful moment. The flowers that bloom in the spring, tra-la. Her distraught gaze, roaming the huge, ornate, frightening room, met that of a man sitting alone three tables away. He smiled, and the smile was friendly, even sympathetic. Her lips trembled in an attempt to smile back. It was immodest and bold to smile at strange men, but any port in a storm . . .

He laid down his sherry glass and napkin, rose, and came over to her table.

'Would you think me very improper if I asked if I might join you?' His voice was as friendly as his smile, warm and deep, tinged with North Country. 'We're both alone, after all.'

Laura knew she should say No, but she said Yes. As he brought his glass over and settled himself opposite her, her spirits began to lighten. He didn't look like a dangerous character; in his forties, perhaps, sturdily build, expensively suited, a face more pleasant than handsome, brown hair thinning a little, clean-shaven, hands beautifully manicured, a gold signet ring with a crest on it. He passed a visiting card across the table.

'Mr Broadbent,' Laura said.

'That's right. James Broadbent of Broadbent's Mills, Blackburn. You know that part of the world?' He was sizing her up, as the waiters had done. Alone, not a lady, scared out of her wits, and beautiful as a picture. Might be just setting out on the primrose path, might not.

'No,' Laura answered, 'I live in Greenwich.'

James Broadbent leaned towards her. 'Look here, you can slap my face for saying this if you like, but I saw the way those waiters treated you and I didn't like it. Now, if you've a man for company they won't dare to do it again, cheeky swine – pardon the expression.'

'But why *do* they? I'm not used to places like this, but they needn't be rude . . .'

Not a pro, then. He was curiously pleased to hear it, man

86

of the world though he was.

'Well, my dear young lady, as you live out of town you may not know that not all restaurants welcome ladies on their own. Stuffy of 'em, but old ways die hard, more's the pity. One day they'll find out what year it is. Now this place, they allow female patrons upstairs though not down, because a very Bohemian lot come here, artists and writers and chaps that don't mind their manners much. But it's usual for a lady to have company.'

'I see. I knew I shouldn't have come in here. I wish I never had.' Tears glinted in her eyes.

'Well, I'm not! I'm delighted to have a charming guest instead of lunching alone. You will be my guest? I know this place pretty well, and I promise I'll order you a luncheon you'll enjoy, with decent service, too, if you'll give me the pleasure of your company. Is it a bargain?'

'It's a bargain.' Laura gave him the full benefit of her smile, sunshine after a shower, and James Broadbent's susceptible heart was enslaved as it had not been for years. The waiters, about to leap obsequiously forward, exchanged cynical glances. The young tart had brought off a pick-up already.

The sherry was drier than any Laura had tasted before, and reminded her of cough medicine, but its effect was instantaneously exhilarating.

'This is nice, it really is,' she said. 'Do you know, before you spoke to me I felt like throwing myself over that balcony, and now I'm really enjoying everything. Isn't that strange. I don't care about *them* any more.'

'Nor you should, Miss . . .' Her hands were still gloved.

'Mrs. Mrs Mares.' What a silly name, she thought, saying it, but he seemed not to think so. She ate her way through the meal with a schoolgirl's appetite, a meal grander than any food that had come her way before, chosen not from the *table d'hôte* but from the *à la carte*, and costing more than five shillings. *Crème aux truffles, rougets grillés à la maitre d'hôtel, minion-fillets de poularde à la parisienne, soufflé aux framboises.* Rich and rare, rich and strange. He saw that she had never heard of the obligatory small helping of each course suitable to a lady's supposedly delicate appetite; and why should she, owner of an eighteen-inch waist? The uses of the Café Royal's array of cutlery were quite unknown to her. He watched her, gently amused, as she picked up knives, forks and spoons at random, not correcting her but letting her eat as she chose. As she ate she talked, often with her mouth full, the sort of commonplaces she thought appropriate, giving away more than she realized.

Jim Broadbent was hardly listening, absorbed as he was in falling into a state somewhere between passion and compassion. It was not his practice to seduce the innocent, but he knew he was not going to be able to help himself. He adored women, collecting them as other rich men collected antiquities. He told her something of himself, not too much: his father had been a self-made man, he had inherited the mills and the grey stone manor house on the moors outside a manufacturing town, he came to London often on a round of the 'Manchester houses' that sold cotton wares. 'I like to think of myself as a man of both worlds, Mrs Mares – North and South. When I'm there, I work – when I'm down here, I play. I'm a man that loves towns, and London's the best and biggest town there is.'

'Yes, oh yes.' Her eyes were stars, the brighter for the glass of wine he had insisted on her taking on top of the sherry. 'I've never seen much of it, not enough. Not until today. It's as though it was all meant, meeting you like this.'

They sat on, when the last of the raspberry soufflé was finished, and the tables were thinning around them. He ordered liqueur brandy, which she sipped, though protesting that she would be drunk. The moment had come, though in one part of his mind he wished it need not. Yet he would not be hurting her . . . He put his hand lightly over hers as it lay on the table-edge, the hand that wore the wedding ring.

'I'm going to speak boldly to you, Laura. Aye, it's bold enough, calling you by your name, I know that all right, but it's a grand name, and it suits you. Will you come away with me – now?'

'Come away?' The hand slipped from his and her eyes widened.

'That's what I said. I'm running down to Brighton for a few days, sea-breezes and a bit of a change. Come with me and I'll give you the time of your life. There's nothing to stop you, is there? Nobody who needs you?'

Laura stared at him. It was quite true. Fred was the only

person who might be concerned, and Fred didn't need her. He would simply move to his mother's until she came home. The night before they had had their first real quarrel. His mother and uncle had spent the evening with them, and Laura had let them see her boredom and impatience. Afterwards Fred had shown himself as she had never seen him before, surly, then darkly angry, saying ugly words to her that made her feel fouled all over, then possessing her roughly. Afterwards she had rolled to the extreme edge of the bed and lain there afraid to move, wondering how she could bear to live with Fred, deciding at last that the next morning she would go somewhere and do something that would take her right away from him and from Miller Street, just to give her time to think. That was why she had felt curiously light-hearted at breakfast time, and had decided to spend the day in London. And so here she was, sitting opposite this kindly, attractive stranger, who had offered her something quite unthinkable, quite impossible.

'Can I . . . is there . . .' she began, looking round. Broadbent leapt to his feet and raised her gallantly from her chair.

'There's a ladies' retiring room in the corner, over there, behind those curtains. You'll find somebody in attendance.' He watched her go, remembering his own and other men's experiences of girls who had used just such an excuse to vanish from their escorts' lives. He turned away, half-smiling, resigned. He would not look at the curtained door, or glance towards the staircase head to see her slip away without a farewell. Let her play it as she would.

In less than five minutes she rejoined him, a waft of cologne about her, and sat down. 'I should have to let my husband know,' she said.

Broadbent showed nothing of the exultation that leaped in him. 'Nothing easier.' He snapped his fingers to a hovering waiter. 'Paper and envelope.' Almost instantly it appeared, expensive writing paper bearing the Café's address and the characteristic capital N encircled with a bay wreath which inevitably suggested Napoleon Buonaparte but was, in fact, the emblem of Mr Nicholl, founder of the establishment. Broadbent produced something she had never seen before, a slim gold Waterman fountain pen.

'Try that. It suits most hands.'

'Oh, it's lovely . . . What shall I put?'

'Say you've met a friend and you're going away for a few days, and there's no need for worry.'

Frowning with concentration, she wrote slowly, carefully, in her large unformed script. His guess had been right, he thought, watching her; the husband was nothing to her, someone she had married on impulse or by arrangement. He was not spoiling a perfect match, only presenting her with a pleasant interlude in a dull life; no more than taking a mill-girl to Blackpool, he thought. Suddenly she looked up, aghast.

'But I can't go! I've nothing to wear – only this. I'll have to go home and get . . . no, I couldn't. Oh.'

He was touched by her disappointment. 'Rubbish. We'll see to that.'

Unbelievably, they were in the lingerie department of Messrs. Swan and Edgar, a scented hushed place where sweetly smiling, high-coiffeured lay figures stood about like stone nymphs in a grove, draped in lace as fine as cobwebs, snowy cottons, sinuous silks, garments more suited to a ballroom than a bedroom. It was a salon dedicated to femininity, yet Jim Broadbent the charmer managed to enter it as a customer without the faintest suggestion of rough masculine intrusion. He wanted, he said, a nightdress and negligée of the best quality, of course, for his niece. If Laura's startled look at being so described was noticed by the elegant, obsequious lady assistant, she was too well-trained to give any sign. Nieces, daughters, and cousins, all beautiful, were frequently the companions of male customers. The best quality only, of course, was required. Various articles were produced and displayed against an undraped lay figure. He rejected out of hand batiste smothered in frills of Valenciennes, finest Indian cotton with a fussy waterfall front, a heavily embroidered creation in pearl-grey. 'Much too old for you, my dear. What about that one?' He indicated another model wearing a filmy chiffon nightdress, simply cut, almost like a Greek robe, with a flowing sleeved overdress which camouflaged its scantness, a deep soft rose-pink in colour.

'That is certainly madam's size, sir, if she has no objection to the rather, er, strong shade.'

'Have you, my dear?'

Laura shook her head. She was almost sure the whole thing was a dream, and had no desire to break it.

'We don't want any of those wishywashy baby pinks,' Broadbent said. 'That will do nicely. Will you wrap it up, please?' Laura saw how much money passed across the counter, and was horrified. From lingerie they went to footwear, and bought a pair of enchanting slippers, pink and silver, the trying on of which made Laura ashamed of her black cotton stockings.

'Now all we need is a travelling case.' He bought her one, an elegant slim thing of pale gold pigskin. Outside the store he hailed a cab to take them to Victoria Station, where he claimed two handsome leather bags from Left Luggage. Then they were on the train, in a first-class carriage with white linen head-protectors on the backs of the seats and a small bouquet of flowers in a glass vase, and the whistle had blown. The Brighton train began to move.

The haunting guilt which had hung over Laura and threatened to spoil her dream vanished. She had burnt her boats – there was no turning back now. She was going for a holiday with a gentleman who was like no other she had ever met, and the worst that could happen was that Fred would be cross. She lay back in the deliciously comfortable seat, settled herself, and lazily watched the flickering scenery, until her eyelids grew heavy and she slept. Broadbent was charmed to see that she even did that beautifully.

Chapter Seven

WHAT SHE HAD EXPECTED TO FIND at the end of the journey, Laura could not have said. Her only experience of the seaside had been at Southend, where the family had spent a few holiday weeks. The weather had either been stiflingly hot or depressingly wet, and they had always gone to the same boarding house, with a view of sea if you slept in the attic and used binoculars. There had been a powerful smell of fish everywhere, and Ellie had been frightened of paddling in the sea after cutting her foot on a stone. Laura's memories of Southend were not, on the whole, pleasant.

She was not prepared for the intoxicating fresh air which waited for her outside the station. It might have a tinge of fish in it, but the rest was pure ozone, as Pa called it. It did something amazing to the spirits, at first breath.

Of course they would stay at a superior boarding house – that was why Mr Broadbent had bought her the nightdress and robe, so that the landlady wouldn't think her a fly-by-night with no luggage. But their cab drove straight down a long street to the seafront, and there was the sea itself, a shining expanse mirroring the sunshine of late afternoon, bathing huts fringing its edge, seagulls wheeling and crying above it and shouting shrilly from the roofs of what appeared to be palaces lining the promenade. The cab stopped outside one of them; the horse must have gone lame, thought Laura. It was the most imposing of them all, a stately building of columns and wrought-iron balconies and tall windows, six storeys high as far as could be seen from the road.

A flunkey in uniform stalked out and helped open the cab door. 'Come along,' Broadbent said, 'this is our destination.'

'This?'

'The Bedford Hotel.' A hand under her elbow, he piloted her through the portico of iron and glass, into the most magnificent hall imaginable – pillars soaring to the roof from a gallery on each level, giving a wonderful effect of light and space. 'The Grecian Hall,' Broadbent said. 'They're rather proud of it. Go with the page, my dear, he'll show you your room.'

'This way if you please, madam!' The man preceded her towards a tall gate of black and gilded metal and pressed a button at the side. It slid open, to reveal a sentry-box-like room with painted panels. Laura hesitated, but there seemed no choice but to enter it. The page followed with her ludicrously small bag, closed the door, and the whole room began to move upwards with a whirring sound. Laura gave a small shriek, and the page smirked. A lot of visitors were startled by the new electric elevator, as used in America. Fortunately for Laura's nerves it stopped at the second floor, and she was led along a corridor of doors numbered in gold. The page paused at Number 237, inserted a key, and let her into a room of such splendour that she gasped, affording him another silent laugh. A huge bed with draped net curtains surmounted by the Prince of Wales's feathers was its centre, the counterpane matching window curtains of sea-green silk. The carpet was cream-coloured, worked with a shadowy flower design, the chairs, dressing-table and escritoire of fragile gilded wood. Over the fireplace hung a painting of a woman in the costume of an earlier time, reminding Laura of the portraits in the Queen's House. But one didn't expect to sleep in the Queen's house, and this was just as grand.

'It's very pretty,' she said, knowing somehow that it was the wrong thing to say.

'Mr Broadbent's suite. 'E always 'as it.' The page placed her case on a luggage-table and waited expectantly. Laura looked blank, and he abandoned hope – Mr Broadbent's ladies were sometimes slow on the uptake, and this one struck him as a real country cousin.

Left alone, she stared round the wonderful room, touched the soft springiness of the bed, and looked from the window at the sea, only a few yards away across the promenade; near enough to see its colours change from deep green to darkest blue and grey-brown. It had never looked like that at Southend. A vivid memory came to her of the poky little room she and Ellie had shared in the back street lodging, the smell of greasy food and the miasma of other lodgers. Suddenly she laughed out loud and gave a childish skip of pleasure.

A tap at the door, and Jim Broadbent entered. 'Settled in? Like it?' Her face told him the answer. 'Good. Did the page show you where everything is? No? Lazy skunk.' He demonstrated the capacity of the huge wardrobe, the bathroom, with its primrose and brown tiling and wonderful fitments adorned with porcelain lilies. 'If you ring for the chambermaid – there's the bell – she'll light the geyser for you. I expect you'd enjoy a bath before dinner.'

A bath? In Feathers Row it meant standing in a large tin bowl and washing all over with water from a can. And dinner? 'But we've had dinner,' she said, 'at least, that man said luncheon, but we did eat a lot. Just a cup of tea . . .'

He laughed. 'You shall have some tea, of course. But later on you'll find you're hungry again. Doctor Brighton's mixture never fails. I'll call for you at half-past eight.'

'But . . .' she gestured towards her dress, so out of place in the Café Royal, whose splendours had quite paled besides those of the Bedford.

'Don't worry about that. Dinner will be served up here. Oh – and your new things will do very well.'

Laura stared at the door that had shut behind him. Wear her new *nightdress* and its wrapper for eating in? It sounded faintly improper. She supposed the chambermaid would serve the meal to her – that was why there was a table, and chairs – but why had Mr Broadbent said he would call for her? It made no sense at all. Perhaps they did things a funny way round in Brighton, or – not a comforting thought – perhaps her new friend was a bit strange in the head.

She gave up. There was the room to discover and enjoy, and there was lying on the sofa in front of one of the long windows gazing out at the sea with its little boats and the promenade with its carriages and omnibuses and riders; and then the chambermaid appeared with a dainty tray of refreshing tea, and lit the bathroom geyser so that madam could take a bath. Yes, madam could be quite sure that the geyser would not blow up.

Washing-down in a tin basin had been nothing to this, Laura thought, wallowing in hot water scented with the musk

94

rose bath powder thoughtfully left for her use, soaping herself lavishly with the creamy pink ball which also smelt of roses, and afterwards splashing herself with Florida Water from the inviting flask on the small marble table. The towels were large and fluffy and miraculously warm from the electrically-heated rail, and now that dusk had fallen the apartment was even more miraculously lit by electric light, serenely diffused from pearly globes. Laura went round switching it off and on: the central chandelier, lamps on each side of the bed. How marvellous it was, how different from pungent gas and messy matches. She put on her underclothes, and over them the nightdress and negligée, relishing the airy softness of the chiffon, admiring her own reflection in the tall pier-glass, spreading her arms like wings, watching the changing gleam of her diamond on its chain.

It had told her this adventure would be happy, when she had taken it from her neck in the ladies' cloakroom at the Café Royal, and thought hard of what her father had said. 'If you meet someone and you're not sure whether they're all right or not, look at this and it'll tell you.' She had looked at it, and it had glittered up at her, though the colours had not seemed so lustrous or so many as when she had first held it. If what she was going to do had been wrong, surely the stone would have been dull.

A tap at the door. 'Come in,' she called. To her astonishment it was not the door to the corridor that opened, but the one next to the bathroom, which she had tried earlier and found locked.

'You look like the Rose Fairy from the pantomime,' he said. 'I'm afraid I startled you. My room's next door – this is half of my suite.'

'Oh. I didn't understand.' It was embarrassing to her that he should see her like this, but not, apparently, to him, for he smilingly held open the door and motioned her through it.

'I thought we'd dine in my room. It's a bit more spacious.'

It was certainly larger, and even grander, with a stately masculinity about it, a massive half-tester bed, mahogany furniture upholstered in dark blue and silver. By the table, which was laid for a meal, stood a dumb-waiter bearing two fat dark green bottles topped with gold foil, and two wine glasses.

'I hope you like fizz. Perfect drink for any time of day, in my opinion. Don't bother to cover your ears, I'm an expert.' He was tackling one of the bottles with a large, elaborate corkscrew. Laura had not been about to cover her ears, for she had no idea what fizz might be. The cork came out with only the mildest of pops, a surge of white bubbles rose and susbsided.

'Is it . . . champagne?' she ventured.

'That's right.'

'I've never had it. Never seen any before, 's a matter of fact.'

'Never too late to learn.' He handed her a glass and raised his own to her. 'To your bright eyes.' She drank, almost choking on the cold sweet effervescence of it, and made a wry face.

'I'm not sure I like it . . . yes, I do, Thanks.'

'Good. Let me fill you up.' They usually said the bubbles tickled their noses, and put on an act, but he could see that this was no act; she had probably drunk more alcohol that day than ever before in her life. The effect of it began to show in her heightened colour and her ready laugh. Not wishing her to be overcome, he left the second bottle unopened and took her out through the French window to the balcony which their rooms shared. They stood watching the lights that clustered thickly over Brighton, more scattered along the coast, the moving stars that were fishing boats out on the dark water. Broadbent said very little, relishing her rapt enjoyment and her closeness, and the gleam of her beauty in the pale glow from distant street-lamps.

Before they moved out he had pressed a bell for the removal of the champagne. It had been taken away, and in its place the table was laid with food no healthy girl could have refused, even after a hearty luncheon. There was chilled cucumber soup, served in tiny bowls, a dish of fish in delicate velouté sauce, a pâté that was something between sweet and savoury, served with hot wafer-thin toast wrapped in warmed napkins. The wine was German, a golden-green nectar of which Broadbent drank sparingly and Laura only one glass. When a waiter appeared to clear the table and silently disappeared she no longer worried that he should see her so dressed, for Broadbent had casually remarked that ladies received informally wearing tea-gowns, which were a kind of negligée.

Outside the air of the September night had been crisp, but the room was warm from the fire discreetly re-fuelled by the waiter, and softly lit by the bedside lamps. Broadbent sat himself down in the armchair by the fireside, and held out a hand to her.

'Come over here, lass.'

She went to him, confidingly, and perched herself on his knee as she had often done on her father's.

Of course she should have guessed. Even a simpleton would have known what his invitation had meant, that he wanted the same thing from her that Fred wanted. But that was what only married people did, she had thought in her abysmal ignorance. Lying alone in her own beautiful bed, to which he had carried her after midnight had struck from a nearby church clock, she thought you're green, Laura, green as grass, and that's a fact. Eighteen years old, and stupid . . .

Yet when the first shock and recoil was over, she had learned in Jim Broadbent's arms what pleasure an experienced lover of women could give them, as his gentle skill woke in her feelings she had never guessed could exist. They seemed so natural that they surely couldn't be wrong; yet they must be, or why had she been brought up under a blanket of ignorance? Perhaps because love-making, as Jim had taught her to call it, could be repulsive, shaming, as it was with Fred. Now she knew about tenderness, and passion, and her thoughts went back, with a pang, to a day in Greenwich Park and what she had read in Maurice Reide's eyes. If only it could have happened then, if only . . .

Long after she slept, the man in the next room lay awake. He had had as much of a shock as she, in a very different way. At the Café Royal he had thought her a naïve young thing looking for a good time without much idea of how to go about it. There was her willing acceptance of his company, something a respectable girl would have rejected indignantly. She had come away with him without demurring too much – what young woman could possibly not know what an invitation to Brighton meant? Yet now he knew he had been utterly wrong; he had seduced someone who was as near virgin as was possible in a married woman. His thoughts about Fred were uncomplimentary. The oaf had taught her nothing, had not even aroused affection or loyalty in her, he guessed.

And she was so lovely and so sweet, deserving the best a man could give her. He would do that, at least.

She woke next morning to the gentle swish of the curtains being drawn by a chambermaid, and a flood of sunshine.

'Good morning, a beautiful day. Madam's breakfast.' The elderly chambermaid's manner was respectful. The Bedford had in its long history entertained the highest in the land and several other lands, dukes and duchesses, King Louis-Philippe of France, Prince Metternich, and close relatives of the Queen. Highly respectable beyond doubt it might be, yet it did not turn from its doors those who had money and standing and distributed lavish tips, even though they were accompanied from time to time by charming surrogate daughters, nieces or cousins, about whose accommodation the strictest propriety would be observed. Only the most flagrant flaunting of convention would draw a reproachful query from the management. An hotel celebrated in the late Charles Dickens's *Dombey and Son*, and proud of his own patronage of it, had a reputation to keep up.

Madam's breakfast consisted of a pot of coffee whose taste was as good as its fragrance, a silver rack of toast, boiled eggs under tiny quilted cosies, and Keiller's Scotch Marmalade. She found it delicious. Then there was another luxurious bath, because the chambermaid drew it for her as a matter of course, and a message that Mr Broadbent would await her in the Palm Lounge in half an hour.

He greeted her with an avuncular kiss on the brow. 'You slept well, my dear?'

'Wonderfully.' Laura was a shade surprised not to meet him with embarrassment. Somehow it all seemed very natural. 'And I had the most . . . a very good breakfast.' She was beginning to learn not to enthuse too much about things which were everyday commonplaces to him. It was part of the grown-upness that she felt this morning, as though some ceremony of initiation had taken place the previous night.

'I thought we might take the air,' he said. 'It's a bright

breezy day, and there's plenty to see. Unles you'd prefer to ride? I walk a lot myself down here, for the benefit of this,' he patted his well-filled waistcoat, 'but there are plenty of nice little trotters for hire, quiet enough for a lady, if you fancy that.'

Laura replied frankly that the quietest of trotters would be useless to her, since she had never sat a horse in her life. 'In that case we'll walk, and you shall see all the sights and all the shops.'

He was an astonishingly patient and understanding man when it came to shops. Wherever Laura paused he paused, lingering good-humouredly while she feasted her eyes on chocolate-boxes and French bonbons, animals and birds cunningly made from marzipan, antique shops full of quaint bric-a-brac and furniture from other ages, the celebrated lace shop of Chillmaid and Tinkler. They strolled on the Steine and in the grounds of the Royal Pavilion, the stupendous onion-domed Oriental palace born of a prince's fantastic dream. Laura the untravelled felt she was living in another world from her own. Even the people looked different. Ultra-fashionable, ultra-smart, dressed to kill, they were there to be seen rather than to see. There was a holiday air about Brighton, something quite different from the opulent streets of London's West End, a feeling of excitement and promise.

Broadbent glanced down at her absorbed, glowing face. 'We'll take luncheon at Mutton's,' he said. 'Something light, oysters and a glass of sherry. Tonight we'll go to the Theatre Royal. There's a farce on with a London company – you'll like that, won't you? Then dinner at the Bedford. But first we're going in here.'

They were outside Brighton's biggest and most fashionable store, Hannington's. 'Run along in. Buy yourself all the fancies you want, stockings, petticoats, that sort of thing. When you get round to frocks and bonnets tell one of the assistants to come and find me. I'll be in the bookshop next door. You're to pay for nothing, mind – that'll all be taken care of.'

'But I can't.'

'And why not?'

She shook her head, bewildered. 'It wouldn't be right, to

let you pay for my things. The . . . the nightdress was different.' She coloured, remembering why it had been bought and how it had been first worn. He patted her arm.

'You just do as I say, there's a good girl. The Greenwich fashions are all very well, but in Brighton you're on parade. Now mind you get all you need.' He was gone before she could argue.

She did as he had told her, avoiding the most expensive garments out of consideration for his pocket, though there was obviously no need to worry about that. Going from department to department, buying pretty things she had never dreamed of owning, she wondered if all this meant that she was now that half-understood thing, a Kept Woman. Yes, that must be it. Now she knew her own value. Her life had taken a new turn. Marriage to Fred had been an awful mistake (but she had known that from the first) and this was what she was really meant to be, the companion of a man who adored her: something beyond any dream she could ever have dreamed, even when . . . she put out of her mind a once-cherished hope, a broken promise. She would never think of him again.

'That's more like it.' Jim surveyed with approval the dress of subtle mushroom-pink, gathered into fashionable folds at the back, tiny-waisted, high-necked. 'And that's the one we'll take for the evenings.' It was a lovely thing of shot silk, its colours changing as she moved from deep green to turquoise, from golden-grey to rose, its low square neck bordered with tiny chiffon flowers worked with metallic thread. But you'll want something a bit grander than that round your neck.'

Laura's hand went protectively to the diamond on its thin gilt chain.

'I always wear it. I don't want anything else.'

'A cheap little thing like that?'

'It's not cheap. It's a real diamond – and my father gave it to me.'

He shrugged. 'As you like. Nobody's going to notice it when they look at the rest of you.' Surveying herself in the mirror, Laura agreed with him. For the first time she saw herself as a beautiful woman, and gazed and gazed, beguiled by her own reflection – a princess, a mermaid, an enchantress.

Maurice Reide pulled the cord of the Venetian blind of the long studio window. It shot up to the top, showing him the blank unused room, dust on the floor and furniture, an unoccupied easel, stacked paintings with their faces turned to the wall like punished children. The servants left on board wages hadn't bothered with this part of the house during the months it had been empty. He unlocked the window and went out into the garden, tidy and ordered, the last roses of the summer out on their bushes, the grass close and neat. Solomon the peacock sat on the low wall where, beside geranium-filled urns, steps went down to a lower lawn. At Maurice's approach the bird looked up from its reverie, stepped down and moved towards him, jewelled head on one side.

'Hello, old boy. What's the matter? Your hens not been keeping you company?' Maurice touched the small proud head, aware of a response from the lonely bird, his pet since it had been a dingy chick. Together they paced round the gardens. Looking back at the house, Maurice saw curtains drawn back, windows opened, now that he, the master, had returned, alone.

All through the arid August heat of Paris, empty of its fashionable society, he had thought of Placentia House and the gardens. Madeline's apartment only had a balcony which looked down on the busy boulevard. No birds sang at dawn or evening, though one might see them in the windows of patisseries, stuffed and glass-eyed, sitting on nests of chocolate: might buy pâté made from thrush or blackbird. Heat, dust and inactivity oppressed him. His so-called studio contained only sketches and roughed-in paintings, begun, never to be finished.

'Why don't you paint?' Madeline had asked him. 'I thought that was why you wanted to come to Paris.'

'*You* wanted to come to Paris. I don't know that I did.' He stared moodily out of the window. It was true. He was too old for Paris now, or not old enough. His student friends were long gone and Madeline's cronies seemed elderly, rackety, artificial to him. His life seemed to have flown past like slides in a magic lantern, stopping now at a picture of apathy, an idle man in his thirties staring out at a street in a country not his own. Madeline shrugged impatiently.

'Why don't you come with me to the château, then? The D'Arlignys invited us both. There'll be fishing and tennis, and the grape harvest, and . . . oh, all sorts of amusing things.'

'I don't know that I want to be amused – at any rate by the D'Arlignys.'

'What *do* you want, then? How very dull you are these days.'

'Thank you. I know it.'

'Well, do something about it! It's no fun for me having you mooning about the place, I can assure you. I might as well be married – to a bore.'

'Why don't you marry Louis, in that case? He might be slightly less of a bore than me.'

Then the fight had broken out, ostensibly about the young count who hung round Madeline like a bee round a flower; but in fact about the deterioration in the relationship between mother and son which had begun after they left England. Though Maurice had resisted recognition of it, his day of freedom with Laura had been a turning-point. Weakness and the temptation to do the easiest thing had seduced him into letting her go, since when she had haunted him day and night; not only her looks, but something that had shone out of her, a radiance no other woman had ever had for him. He passionately wished that he had kept his promise and seen her again, faced up to her family, however awful they might be, made Madeline accept that he was a grown man. It would have been so easy to mould Laura gently into the kind of girl his circle would accept, so that they would not be able to patronize or insult her. In his mind's eye he saw her as he could have made her, just as he mentally visualized a picture before he began to paint it. Coward, coward and snob, mamma's boy. Nature's lay idiot, I taught thee to love, some old poet had said, and there had been something in her eyes and her voice that had told him she could love him. And he had let her go.

He interrupted Madeline's tantrum. 'I'm not going to the château. I'm going back to England.'

'. . . as if I hadn't enough to put up with, hardly a friend left in Paris . . . *what* did you say?'

'I said I'm going back to England.'

'Le Comte de St Étienne,' announced Madeline's maid from the door.

Madeline's outraged expression gave way to smiling charm as she extended her hand to be kissed by the man who entered. He was older than Maurice, but not much, boyish-faced and amiable, with a dark round shining head and the neatest of moustaches. Englishmen thought him a remarkably good fellow, for a Frenchman.

'My dear Louis, how providential that you should call. I was just at that moment thinking of you.'

'But how happy you make me, Madeline! Make me even happier, tell me your thoughts.' He made a face of comical melancholy. 'Unless they were bad ones, in which case I shall leave at once in order to shoot myself outside . . .' he bowed, 'La Madeleine.'

'How ridiculous you are. I was merely thinking of asking you whether you'd like to escort me to the Château d'Arligny. Jeanne and François have asked me to stay with them, and – well, they're charming, but one needs other company.'

'What could be more delightful? But . . .' he gestured towards Maurice. So far in his ardent courtship of Madeline, he had been quite unable to break through the barrier she put between herself and the rest of the world, her son. Maurice was always there at her side, being flirted with, appealed to, teased, used as a woman uses a favoured suitor, called for when others threatened to become too pressing. There had certainly been a cooling-off recently, a suggestion of pettishness on her part and boredom on his, but it was too much to believe that La Veuve was actually soliciting his, Louis's, company, instead of Maurice's.

She shrugged. 'Oh, Maurice is tired of us all. He intends to go back to London and paint. Corpses being pulled out of the dirty river, I expect. Something thrilling, like that.'

'There is always the morgue,' suggested Louis, who had a literal mind. He saw that her eyes were on Maurice, waiting for him to deny her nonsense now that she had openly offered another his place. But Maurice said politely, 'I hadn't corpses in mind, but I feel I'm rather wasting time here. By all means go with Madeline, Louis. The Loire should be delightful at this time of year. Madeline will be able to practise her shooting skill and provide us with game for the winter.' He read the anger in her eyes, and the frustration, and a question: Why are you deserting me? What's behind it, this return to England? He was quite satisfied that she had no idea of the reason.

The heavy grey pall that had lain over Paris was behind him; clear blue skies and scudding clouds met him as he stepped from the train at Victoria. His rooms were stuffy, smelling of gathered dust. He paused for a shave, then took a cab to Greenwich. At Placentia House he would change completely, freshen himself up, restore himself to the man he had been on the day he had last seen Laura.

It was strange to wander about the house and not to meet Madeline. Half-guilty, he went almost furtively past the door of her bedroom as though she might come out of it. Her favourite chair in the drawing-room looked as though nobody had ever sat in it, the cushions plumped and smoothed. He felt something almost akin to the ecstasy of freedom he had once had on breaking-up day at boarding-school; only now the freedom was from Madeline, his sweet tyrant for so long.

'You shall see Laura again soon,' he told the peacock. 'I shall paint her with you, in a rainbow dress, and call it *The Rivals*, and it will be the academy picture of the year.' Unimpressed, Solomon stalked away, back to his wall, tail drooping, and gave his long eldritch cry.

Laura had told Maurice that she lived in Feathers Row, but not the number of the house. He would have felt too much of a fool going from door to door – even more of one if confronted unexpectedly by her mother. No, he must prepare himself and go ready to say exactly the right thing. In any case, she would almost certainly be at the shop. He made his way there, surprised to find himself so nervous. She might be angry, cold, distant; he had deserved that.

Four or five customers were inside, but only Miss Plum was serving. He waited, conscious that he was being eyed, a man in so feminine an establishment. Finally, to his relief, the last customer paid and left. His moment had come.

'You're quite a stranger, Mr Reide,' Miss Plum said, sounding not overwhelmingly glad at the reunion.

'I . . . yes, I've been abroad for the summer. My mother's still in France, as a matter of fact.'

'Is she?' The old lady was arranging small bundles of laces and tapes in a tray, not looking at him. 'And what can I do for you, sir?'

'Well. I came to see Miss Diamond, really.'

This time she did look at him, fair and square. 'She's not here. And she's not Miss Diamond.'

'I don't understand.'

'She got married in July. She's Mrs Mares now.' And, her tone implied, you can put that in your pipe and smoke it. She saw with satisfaction that her words affected him like a blow between the eyes. He was taking it badly, and serve him right, selfish pig, assuming he could walk in after all this time and flatter that poor girl into expecting him to do the honourable thing, when he'd almost broken her heart before, *and* driven her into tying herself up to that great stupid nincompoop. Yes, he looked even more disappointed than she had hoped.

'I'm surprised to hear it,' he managed to say. 'She didn't mention anything . . . anyone.'

'No, it was arranged quite sudden, just a short engagement.'

'Mares,' he said, thinking a wildly silly name it was. 'Who . . .'

'Young man works at Ponsford's. They're living near there. Do you want the address, sir?'

'No. No, thank you. I'm sorry – to have troubled you.'

'Good day, sir.'

Watching him go, she felt a twinge of pity. He looked more stricken than a gay deceiver had any right to look, and the whole sorry business was very probably the fault of that mother of his.

Maurice leaned on the wall by the Trafalgar where he had first seen the girl who would haunt him now wherever he went, whatever he did. River and sky were a dull vapid grey, the gulls' cries mocked him with idiotic laughter.

Chapter Eight

'GOOD MORNING, ANOTHER BEAUTIFUL DAY. Madam's breakfast.'

Laura stretched and stirred. On the fourth morning of her holiday the chambermaid's voice was as bright as the sun streaming in. The yolk of the eggs would be as golden, the toast as delicately crisp. The pink nightdress was as insidiously scanty and comfortable, the daily-changed linen as cool and scented. Nothing was different.

Except that beside the teacup and saucer was an envelope, addressed to Mrs Laura Mares. Somehow she disliked the look of it, and took her first invigorating sip of tea and bite of toast before opening it. She had never yet seen Jim's writing, large firm copperplate, broad strokes, a businessman's hand.

My dear little Laura,

I'm sure you're a sensible enough girl to realize that I had to go back to my family sooner or later. I thought it best to let it be like this, with no goodbyes said. I hope you had a good time, I certainly did. What luck our meeting, eh? You'll keep everything I bought you and think nothing of it. Just a few trifles an old man fancied giving you. There's a week's stay at the Bedford paid for, so enjoy yourself, and may you come across some other lucky chap. Thanks for everything, old girl.

Your affte.
JIM.

The letter drifted on to the coverlet, then the floor. So she had been fooled again, taken for a dream-trip by a man who knew all the rules, while she knew none. 'My family'. Of course he had a middle-aged wife and children up North, children older than herself, probably. She had thought he was charmed by her, charmed enough to make her the woman in his life, even his wife, one day, just as she had once thought of another man. Green, green, Laura, oh so green! He had only been playing, as that other had. She had not been in love with him, nowhere near it, only very admiring and grateful. 'Your affte.' So that was what they said, when they finished with you . . .

The worst shock was that, for this excursion, she had lost her respectability, her Good Name. Somehow she had to get back to where she had been, explain away her four days of absence; she, who was such an untrained liar and hardly knew herself, never mind the thoughts and hearts of others. Because Jim had chosen to write to her, she pondered on writing to them, Fred and her parents, making clever excuses. But she had hardly written a letter in her life, beyond thanks for a present. She was simply not clever enough for that. She would have to go and tell them something they would believe.

The wardrobe, full of new delightful clothes, shocked her all over again. Of course she couldn't face her family in anything Jim had bought for her. She put on the lilac street-dress she had travelled down in, and the little green hat. She had money given to her by Jim, notes and silver carelessly piled on her dressing-table, or handed to her to be stored in her handbag. More money than she had ever seen in her life. The clothes could stay where they were for the moment; after all, he had paid the Bedford for a week.

From Brighton Station she took a day excursion to Victoria. By late morning she was in Greenwich, turning her key in the lock of the Miller Street front door.

Everything in the little house was tidy. No dirty dishes in the kitchen, no ashes in the parlour grate. Upstairs, the bed neatly made, and in the middle of the floor the basket trunk she had brought with her from home. She opened it. Inside were underclothes from the chest of drawers, her dressing-table set, mirror, brush and comb, a framed certificate that Laura Diamond had passed her senior examination in the scriptures, a childhood photograph of herself and Ellie. No sign of Fred's things, no feeling of him in the house.

In all her life she had never been as afraid as when she stood outside the front door in Feathers Row, hearing the reverberation of the knocker inside. Then she was face to face with her mother, being looked up and down by cold, hard eyes.

'Well?'

'I thought I ought to come and explain.'

'Explain what? Why you left your husband?'

'I didn't. I mean, I went out for the day on Monday. And somehow I felt I wanted a bit of a change, so I went to Brighton.'

'Yes?'

'Well. It was very nice there, and I felt better, so I stayed on for a day or two.'

'Alone?'

'Of course.'

'Liar.'

'Ma!'

'Liar. You've been with a man. Oh, I can tell, even if I didn't know you. It was just what I said to poor Fred when he came round here and said you were missing, gone off with a friend. She's gone off with a man, I said, like you might have expected, and if you'll take my advice you'll go to your mother's, because if she comes back she'll only be off again, that's the sort she is.'

'I never behaved like that, in all my life!' Laura was caught between tears and temper. They were still standing at the door, the next-door neighbour shaking a rug and listening. 'You've always been unfair to me, Ma, and I'm sure I don't know why. I've told you the truth, whether you believe it or not.'

'So you can look me in the eye and tell me again you weren't with a man?'

Laura shook her head violently. 'I'm not saying anything, because you wouldn't believe me anyway. Aren't you going to ask me in?'

'No, I'm not. I'm finished with you. And so is Fred, so there's no need to go round there telling your lies. He's packed your trunk and left it for you to pick up, and gone to his mother's. It's not that I ever thought he was the right husband for you, but he didn't deserve such treatment, and only two months after you were married! We're all downright ashamed of you, and you might as well know it.'

'Pa? And Ellie?'

Alice stared her down. 'What do you expect?'

Laura looked beyond her to the little dingy hall, the coatrack and umbrella stand, the dismal sepia print of *The Stag at Bay* that she had known all her life and would now never see again. With a farewell word she turned and went out through the iron gate that always needed oiling, and without a farewell word Alice shut the door.

Useless to go to Ponsford's and see her two dear ones look at her with reproachful eyes. There was nothing for it but to go back to Brighton. No London tramcar was yet at the farestage. She turned down towards the riverfront, and stood in a kind of daze where the Trafalgar Tavern looked out towards the Isle of Dogs: where, ten minutes earlier, Maurice had stood, thinking of her.

Ellie ran into the house ahead of her father. 'Is there any news, Ma?' she called.

Alice came out of the kitchen, fastening one of the cuffs she wore over her sleeves for cooking, confronting the two of them.

'News?'

'Have you heard anything of Laura?' Daniel asked. There were lines of worry and sleeplessness etched on his face which had not been there four days earlier.

Alice straightened her lace-edged apron unnecessarily, and said with elaborate casualness, 'Oh yes – she called today.'

'She – what? Called? She didn't stay?'

'She wasn't invited.'

Daniel sat down heavily at the table, Ellie standing protectively beside him, her hand on his shoulder. 'I don't understand,' he said.

'It's quite simple. She turned up here, bold as brass, to inform us that on Monday she fancied a day out, and it turned into a nice little holiday, *not* on her own, that was very plain to see.'

'You mean there was someone with her?'

'Well, she didn't bring him here, of course, but you should have seen her colour up as red as fire when I faced her with it that she'd been with a man. So I told her Fred had worked that out already and gone off to his mother's, and her trunk was there packed for her to take away, and that she might pack herself off too. Which she did, without more ado.'

Daniel said, 'I can't believe it – even of you, Alice – that you'd send her away and not give her a chance to explain. I can't believe you wouldn't keep her here and let her talk to me.' He looked round the room, as though he expected to see his daughter appear.

'Keep her here? A fallen woman?'

'Don't you say that of our Laura!' Daniel was angry, angrier than his wife had ever seen him. She took a step back, towards the safety of the kitchen. 'There may have been a hundred explanations. She may have been ill, or Fred upset her, or anything, if you'd only let her explain. Whatever she's done there must have been a good reason for it. And what have you driven her to now, if it's not too much to ask? How's she feeling, when her own mother turned her away from her doorstep?'

Ellie, who had been looking in horror from one to the other, asked, 'Did she say where she'd been?'

'I believe she mentioned something about Brighton. Well, that was enough for me . . .'

'Never mind you.' Daniel's usually soft voice was rough. 'I'm going to find her, and when I do she's coming back with me, whether you like it or not. I shall go round to the Mares and see if she's there, not that it's likely, and if not I'll ask Mr Ponsford for a day off and go to Brighton to look for her.'

'I'll come too,' Ellie said. 'With two of us there'll be more chance.'

'Brighton's a big place,' Alice said spitefully. 'I wish you luck with it.' She tore off her apron and cuffs, threw them down, and marched out of the room. They heard her go upstairs and slam the bedroom door. When Daniel set out for Deptford he glanced up at the window. She was there, staring out between the curtains, motionless and expressionless.

When Laura got back to the Bedford it was early evening. She had walked from the station, through the quietening town, drawing in the heady salt air, exhilarated not only by that but by the feeling of being free at last. Free from her mother, from the strained family situation, from Fred and his dreary

110

little house and his dreary relations. She noticed how the footsteps of men slowed as they passed her, moving with her long graceful stride. Now that she knew what they wanted she would make them pay for it; that was the only way she could live.

The Bedford was a blaze of light and warmth, the Grecian Hall full of sipping customers and scurrying waiters, the uniformed hall porter ushering guests in and out, touching his tall hat to Laura as she moved towards the metal cage of the elevator, still a wonder to her. There was her room, as splendid as ever, her one evening dress laid out on the bed, with the slippers and gloves that went with it. She bathed, enjoying the still-copious bath powder and Florida Water, and dressed carefully, glad that she could put up her hair in coils and folds without the help of the chambermaid. Obedient hair, her mother had once called it. She shut the thought of her mother out of her mind.

Three evenings of practice had accustomed her to sweep down the grand staircase, graceful and poised enough not to need the help of the glittering brass handrail, and enter the dining-room, aware of admiring eyes upon her. The difference tonight was that she had no escort. The head waiter was quick to notice.

'Mr Broadbent not dining tonight, madam?'

'No. He, er, he had to leave, to attend to business.'

'I see, madam.' It was a situation he had met before. He suavely took her order, made up from dishes she had had with Jim. Because some of the pronunciations defeated her, even in English, she pointed to any doubtful item saying 'That'.

'Madam will take some wine?'

'No, thank you.' She was sure that only fast girls drank alone, and in any case the dry wines Jim had liked rather spoiled the flavour of the food for her.

Other diners noticed that she was solitary. Halfway through her soup a note was placed beside her plate. The writer was sorry to see such a lovely lady on her own, and would consider himself honoured if he might join her. She looked round the tables. An elderly, bald, white-whiskered man smiled and bowed. Laura hesitated, then scribbled 'No thanks' on the note and gave it back to the waiter, watching the old man's face fall as he read it.

She ate hastily, feeling embarrassed, the only woman alone in the room apart from an overpoweringly dignified dowager, and a woman with smooth grey hair and a sweet remote expression whom she had discovered earlier to be the head-mistress of a ladies' college. Even from men accompanied by women she received frank stares, and once a wink. She sensed that the waiters were talking about her amongst themselves; it was the Café Royal all over again, yet now she knew much more about the world – they should treat her as she looked and was behaving, like a lady.

The man with the gardenia in his buttonhole and the bold brown eyes looked at her as though she were anything but that, as without permission he took one of the vacant chairs at her table.

'A liqueur with the coffee, my beautiful?'

Laura could only stammer, taken by surprise. 'What?'

'What's it to be? Brandy, a nice B. and S., Benedictine, crème de menthe? Or a bottle of bubbly for just the two of us to take upstairs, eh? I've had a good day at the races – won a packet on an absolute outsider. What about it, then?'

Laura pulled herself away from the hot eager face now so close to hers.

'No, thank you. I don't want anything.'

'Oh, come on, now! Don't take that line with me. I've been watching you, and I never saw a little girl in more need of a johnnie to take care of her.'

Others had been watching her, too. The head waiter glided across to her table, sympathetic to her imploring glance. 'Everything to your satisfaction, madam?'

'I . . . oh, yes, thank you. I don't want any more,' she said, like the little girl she had just been called. The waiter fixed her admirer with a steely glance, and, saying, 'If you'll excuse me, sir' began to pull the table away from the wall so that she could extract her skirts from underneath it. The man took the hint and left, with an angry mutter.

'Thank you,' she said.

'Nothing at all, madam.' Out of the corner of his eye he could see his employer's wife approaching. Mrs Josie Lam-balle was large, tightly-corseted, rouged, unnaturally golden of hair and given to smoking small cigars, but her views on the behaviour of unaccompanied female guests were strict. She had followed the course of Laura's uneasy meal from her private table, secluded by a screen and a potted palm.

'Ah, Miss Diamond. Hope you've enjoyed your dinner? That's good. I'm afraid I have to tell you that we'll be requiring your room tomorrow morning – at twelve o'clock. Sorry not to let you know before. A rather important client – foreign royalty, as a matter of fact – requires the whole suite at very short notice, and we can't refuse.'

'Oh. But . . .'

'I know, Mr Broadbent provided for you to stay for a week.' The arrangement had been made not with her but her husband, and Charles could always be relied on to be a fool where a pretty girl was concerned. 'Unfortunately there's been a sudden rush of bookings, with the fine weather I expect, and we simply haven't another room vacant. You'll be refunded, of course. In full.' She smiled dazzlingly and swam away, her silk bustle frou-frouing behind her. The old place wasn't going to get a bad name if she could help it, even from an amateur charmer like that one.

Laura watched her go, feeling the colour rising and spreading from her freely displayed bosom to her hairline. No number of amiable excuses could have hidden Mrs Lamballe's real intention in giving her notice – for that was what it was. She rose and left the dining-room hastily, followed by inquisitive eyes, and was glad to find herself in the elevator, with only the attendant to see her blazing cheeks.

That night seemed the longest she had ever spent, as she lay awake, listening to the settling of the hotel into quietness, the boom and swish of the waves beyond the promenade. At one moment she contemplated going to Fred and giving him a full explanation. Surely he'd understand if she told him how bored she had been, how she had not meant to run away from him, exactly, but from the cramping little house and the drabness of Miller Street. But that was not quite true; and the thought of going back to Fred and his tiresome mother and his horrible uncle made her heart sink.

Miss Plum was a friend. But it would be impossible to take refuge with her, in one of the two tiny rooms that she lived in, behind and above the shop. And it would mean Greenwich again, and meeting the family who had cast her off.

So there was only one thing for it. In the morning she must leave, find a cheap lodging, and stay there until she found some sort of work. On that resolution she drifted into sleep, and slept as soundly as even troubled youth can, until morning.

Among the after-breakfast bustle of the hotel foyer one man sat unconcerned by it all, lounging on a velvet banquette away from the hubbub of servants and luggage, the settlement of accounts, the summoning of cabs and carriages. He was young, possibly less than thirty, elegantly dressed in very quiet but very expensive morning clothes, neither handsome nor plain, but something between the two, depending on whether the viewer admired a broad-browed, somewhat intellectual cast of head, and delicate sharp features, grey-blue eyes that missed very little, and light-brown hair waving away from a widow's peak. The bright eyes were at present focused on a girl who was putting her receipted bill into her cheap handbag; and something else, money. Beside her was one small, expensive pigskin case, quite the opposite of the handbag, and a pile of loose, unwrapped clothes.

She paused uncertainly, then moved towards the hall porter in his awesome glass sentry-box. Unobtrusively the watcher rose and followed, listening to what passed between her and the man.

'Excuse me.'

'Yes, madam?'

'I don't know anybody else to ask . . you haven't got a spare case, or a basket or something, that I could put my things in? I . . . I've bought more than I intended, you see, and it's rather awkward.'

'I'm sorry, nothing of that kind, madam.' The tone which had been so obsequious earlier in the week was frosty.

'Oh. Then . . . you don't know of a respectable hotel, or boarding house, I could go to? I've not been to Brighton before, you see.'

The man turned away to attend to another enquiry, keeping her waiting before he turned back to her, answering with satisfaction, 'I'm only concerned with my employers' hotel, madam. You'd better ask in the street.'

She was desperate enough to stay her ground. 'Do you think they want any workers here? Cooks, or chambermaids, or anything?'

'Ask at the kitchens.' No 'madam' this time. He turned his back on her to bow to some departing guest. As she moved away, dejected, the listener went to her side and touched her arm lightly.

'Don't be alarmed. I'm afraid I heard what you said. May I have a word with you?'

She looked up at him in wonder, but after a second's hesitation followed him to the secluded banquette. He had lightly scooped up her luggage, making nothing of the unwieldy bulk of it.

'Please sit down,' he said. His voice was pleasant, cultured without being la-di-dah. 'I know it's dashed bad form to speak to a lady uninvited. But is it true that you have nowhere to go?'

'Yes, sir. I expected to stay here, but last night the manageress said they wanted my room. So I don't know . . . but I shall be all right, really I shall.' She expected the worst from men now, and half-rose, but he gestured her to sit down again.

'It may sound a frightful cheek, and you must forgive me. But I disliked the way that man spoke to you very much, and I should like to make up for it. Will you – would you let me drive you round until you find an hotel you fancy? I know what you must think, and I don't blame you. But believe me, I don't mean to insult you in any way, and I shan't take advantage of you. I just want to help.'

She was surprised to find she did believe him. 'Well. It's very kind of you. I oughtn't to, of course, but I don't know what I shall do by myself.' Gentlemen as grand as he obviously was could stoop to help damsels in distress without demeaning either themselves or the damsels. Jim Broadbent had not been grand, only rich. And it was a chance to get out of the nasty situation she was in. 'Yes, thank you,' she said. 'I'd be very grateful.'

'Good.' At his nod a manservant appeared from nowhere and loaded himself up with her belongings and other luggage obviously belonging to her rescuer. They followed him out to the wrought-iron portico (how long it seemed since she had entered it for the first time) and there in the street waited a neat private carriage whose driver was so discreet that he showed no surprise at his master emerging from the hotel with a lady on his arm. Laura was assisted in, the luggage stowed in the boot, the manservant got up behind and they drove off.

'We'll go eastwards,' said her new friend. 'Hove's expensive.'

'I don't want to take you out of your way, sir . . .'

'Not out of my way at all. In it, as a matter of fact – I'm driving to friends in Rottingdean.' Laura stole a sideways glance at him. He sounded so polite and gentlemanly, but was she being a fool again? There was that song, 'The Gypsy's Warning', 'Do not trust him, gentle lady, though his voice be low and sweet . . .' A pity she hadn't met the gypsy before she made so many awful mistakes.

But, sitting at a firmly respectful distance from her, he produced a visiting card. It told her that he was The Hon. Deryck Hervey-Downes, and owned two addresses, one in London, the other in what Laura assumed was the country. She handed it back, not knowing what to say, except, 'Thank you. I'm Laura Diamond.'

'Laura – Diamond. Pretty names.' They were approaching the hub of Brighton, where the Old Steine joined the seafront road. Even so late in the year it was all life and activity, visitors thronging round the Aquarium. Now the road began to climb up Madeira Drive, a wall-cliff forming below, between it and the stony beach. The tall modern buildings gave place to smaller, more elegant ones, the houses of those fashionables who had come to Brighton half a century and more ago, when the once-dashing Prince Regent had become a tired, bloated king. Stuccoed and graceful, they were reassuring to the eye of one humbly brought up after the grandiose Bedford and its neighbours.

'Just a minute.' He spoke to the driver. 'Next left, Hawkins. Then first house on the left.' To Laura he said, 'There's a little place up here you might like. A young cousin of mine puts up there and finds it very satisfactory. Let's have a look at it.'

Marine Villa was a double-fronted Regency house, cream-washed, with nothing between it and the sea but a long, low-walled front garden. There was no sign of its being in use as a hotel, which Laura liked.

'How does it strike you? Good. Hawkins will go in and see if they have any vacancies, which they almost certainly will have at this time of year.' Hawkins was dispatched inside, and returned with the news that several rooms were available. They went in together. The entrance-hall was modest and attractive, with walls painted a delicate duck-egg blue, touches of gilding on the moulding of the ceiling. On a plinth the marble bust of a girl with long hair and bare shoulders looked down at autumn flowers arranged in a large jug of shining copper. A small plump woman with a guarded smile and a Scots accent apeared between curtains, welcoming them. To her Hervey-Downes explained that his friend was in need of a room for a week or two, until her plans were decided.

'Indeed, sir? I've a nice room on the first floor front.' She led them up a staircase whose woodwork was polished to perfection, along a small landing smelling of lavender and cleanliness, to a bedroom more modest in proportions and furnishings than the one Laura had occupied at the Bedford, and far more homely, all white and soft green. And the sea from the window-view was the same sea, grey now, with streaks of dark emerald where the clouds kept the September sun from it.

'It's beautiful,' Laura said. 'If it's not too . . .' She had visualized something nearer to her memories of Southend.

'Two guineas a week, full board, ma'am. We keep a liberal table and hot baths are provided. And only guests of the highest respectability.' She fixed Laura and Hervey-Downes in turn with a meaningful look.

'Then – thank you, yes, I'll take it.'

Hervey-Downes gave directions for her luggage to be brought up. When the landlady had gone he said, 'There, all settled very easily. Being a person of the highest respectability, may I take tea with you tomorrow?'

'Tea? Oh. Yes, please do.' If he was amused at her surprised reception of this innocent proposal, he showed no sign of it, merely bowed over her hand and took his leave. From the window she watched him enter the carriage and be driven away. She liked him very much: she was afraid to like him too much. Looking at herself in the shield mirror, she told her reflection, 'I wish you were cross-eyed with a turned-up nose and rabbit teeth and rat's-tail hair.' The reflection gazed back at her, serenely lovely, yet a trifle sad at being so ill-wished. Laura gave it a forgiving smile.

'No, I don't. I like you very well as you are, my dear, though you *do* get me into trouble.'

Chapter Nine

ELLIE WISHED VERY MUCH THAT she could have been on holiday in Brighton instead of trudging through its streets in this anxious quest for her sister. It seemed impossible that they could ever find her among so many people. Ellie longed to relax from the scanning of faces, the hopeless task of looking in every direction at once. It would have been nice to stop at the exciting shop windows, to take coffee and buns at the Bun House, and eat shrimps and whelks from a stall. Her boots pinched, and she felt that if she were to take them off her feet would look like red hot flatirons. She and her father had walked down the long street from the station to the seafront then, not knowing their way, a mile or so towards Hove before it came to her that they were going wrong.

'Laura wouldn't be anywhere here, Pa. It's all too grand – she couldn't afford to stay in such places. I mean, look at them. That place – the Bedford Hotel.'

Daniel looked. It was true. He couldn't imagine his Laura in such a setting, even if . . . her mother had said she was with a man, but he put the thought out of his mind as unworthy. She was too good, too innocent; it was all Alice's sour imagination.

'Well, it doesn't look as if it leads to the town,' he said. 'We'd better turn back.'

The town itself baffled them. They could only find their way by using the pinnacled domes of the Pavilion as a landmark, and even so got lost in the winding Lanes and side streets. Daniel was sustained at first by a blind belief that Laura was there, somewhere, and he could not fail to find her. Only in mid-afternoon, when they had tramped over every cobblestone in the town, it seemed, he began to despair.

'We shouldn't have come, Ellie. I ought to have had more

sense. I thought . . . somehow I thought it was a smaller place than this, and we might find her sitting by the sea. You know how she always liked to watch the river. But I never reckoned on all these crowds.' His eyes ranged almost hopelessly now among the strolling, chatting holiday-makers: September was the tradesmen's month, just as October saw the coming of the London fashionables. There was no face like Laura's amongst them.

Ellie squeezed the arm tucked through hers. 'Pa, we can't go on walking. Let's take an omnibus and have a ride. You never know, we might be lucky. She could be doing the same thing.'

The omnibus they took from the Aquarium climbed gently up the slope of Madeira Drive, the well-fed horses nodding, taking their own time to pull the half-full vehicle. Ellie and Daniel, riding on top, held on to their hats against the stiff breeze blowing from the sea, and rested their burning feet on the stretchers below the seats in front, feeling intense relief from the day's weary walking. Ellie admired the white and cream-washed houses, so different from London's grimy bricks and stones, gazing placidly out to sea.

'Look at that one, Pa, with the garden in front. Imagine living there. Marine Villa.'

At that moment, behind the long window looking on to the garden, Laura was taking tea with Deryck Hervey-Downes.

Over thin bread and butter, home-made scones and fancy cakes he told her of his background. Eldest son of Lord Lythe, a landowner in East Sussex, he had grown up aware that his family was under the shadow of local disapproval. 'Papa married into Trade, you see. Brewers, over the Kent border, as big as Whitbread's or Hanbury's. Absolutely not done in our circles, but Mama was a jolly pretty girl and a good deal more suited to be a landed gentleman's wife than Papa's sisters – all of them frankly prune-faced. He adored beauty; so do I.' His gaze lingered on Laura's face. 'A lot of people gave him the cold shoulder after the marriage. But we all grew up happily enough. Then Mama's father died and left her a mint of money. After that my two sisters suddenly became extremely popular, and married well within months

120

of each other. Money talks now, you know – look at the Jews. And I – well, being a lazy fellow by nature I decided to lead a lazy life. As I have done, and do.'

He leaned back, an elegant, relaxed figure, smiling at Laura, who had only the faintest idea what he was talking about, and showed it.

'I travel,' he explained. 'When I'm in England I gamble a bit, play the horses a bit, hunt in the winter, that sort of thing. But I'm not in England more than I can help. I like best to travel – hotel life, rented apartments, villas in Italy – anything but confounded damp English house-parties.' He helped himself to a small iced cake, eating it slowly, thoughtfully, because he was thinking out what to say next that would express his meaning without frightening away this nervous young doe. Her fingers tapped out a compulsive tune on the tablecloth, and he saw that there was a wedding ring on her left hand which he had not seen the day before. That made his path easier.

He had worked out what he should say. 'I like company on my travels – female company, someone to dine with me and dance with me and see the sights of the world. She must be good-tempered and she must be beautiful. Now, I can see your remarkable beauty for myself, and I can guess at the good temper. Would my way of life attract you, do you think? And would you be free to take it?'

'I think you ought to know, sir . . .'

'I don't want to know, at the moment. Let me guess some of it. You're running away – is that it, from something, or someone?'

'It began like that. Now I can't go back, even if I wanted to.'

He glanced at the ring. 'And your husband isn't likely to pursue you with a horsewhip?'

'I don't think he'd know how to use one.' She smiled tremulously. 'Though he *was* brought up on a farm.'

'Good. And your people won't expect you to return to them? Don't cry, my dear. I won't ask you any more questions. Just let me say that if you think you could bear my company, I believe I could make you happy and give you the sort of life you were made for.'

'But you don't know me – and I don't know you.'

'Then we shall have to take each other on trust, if you accept, that is.'

The room was quiet, only the politely hushed voices of the other people taking tea sounding in the pause that followed his words. A more respectable setting for a proposal of illicit love – if that was what it was – could not have been imagined. Laura studied him, the distinguished features, the confident poise of the head, the ineffable air about him of a man used to the best of everything. He was attractive, charming, and would be kind, she thought. She wondered what it would be like to be kissed by that long, decisive mouth, and touched by the strong shapely hands – hands made for holding the reins of a mettlesome horse, or cupping a champagne glass. Or a woman's breasts. The thought made her blush. He saw it, but looked tactfully away out of the window, at an omnibus which had stopped to pick up passengers. When the blush had subsided he said, 'I can't possibly expect you to make up your mind now, Mrs Diamond. I can only say this – that if you agree to become my charming companion I shall take as good care of you as I would of any other precious possession. Now I shall leave you, and when you've made up your mind send a note to me at Rottingdean. Take a day, or several days, but not more than a week – I have engagements in Paris after that. And whatever you decide, please believe I shall understand.' He made her a little bow, and strode out, followed by feminine eyes, Laura's among them.

'Would you care for more tea, madam?' The voice that broke into her thoughts belonged to the husband of the proprietress, Mrs Comfort. He was as mild and self-effacing as his wife was strong-minded, a tall, gangling, ginger-haired man with a stoop. When he had married Ada she had been a handsome black-eyed girl, upper housemaid to a wealthy family in Hove. Somehow the years had changed her into an efficient hotelier and a cold-hearted, sharp-tongued wife. Wistfully he had looked for the girl to return, but she was gone for ever, buried under a mountain of shining silver and scrubbed pans. Lonely, disappointed, ever-romantic, Percy Comfort hung about the establishment registered under his name, doing whatever menial jobs Ada assigned to him. Nothing was too much trouble for him, nothing put him out. He looked into the face of each feminine guest for solace, the

122

soft look and the tender smile which would reassure him that women were angels.

In Laura he had seen an angel from the moment he reverently placed her small case and sprawling mass of clothes in the first floor front room. Her beauty had struck him like a blow, her voice had been gentle and hesitant as she had offered him a poor little sixpence for his pains and he had, almost tearfully, returned it to her with some sort of muttered explanation that he was not the regular porter (though he was). All that day, when she had appeared in the public rooms, he had managed to catch glimpses of her. During teatime it had been easy to hover, carrying in pots of tea, replenishing plates, adding an occasional coal to the fire, glancing without seeming to at the man with her. What could Mr Hervey-Downes have to do with her, so obviously a Londoner and not a lady, remembering the gentleman's cousin Lady Selina, pert and loud-voiced, and given to astounding Brighton with daredevil riding? The Honourable seemed a decent enough character, not the sort to go seducing young women. Perhaps he was merely engaging her as servant to Lady Lythe, his mother. Perhaps he had found her in distressed circumstances and was looking out for a place for her.

Handing dishes, appearing with fresh racks of toast, refilling cream jugs, Percy Comfort stole continual looks at the bent golden head, the troubled face. He noted the nervous beat of fingers on the tablecloth, the blush and the silences. And when Mr Hervey-Downes had left he was at her side.

'Would you care for more tea, madam?'

She started out of a reverie. 'Oh! No, thank you.'

'It's nice and strong,' he urged. Suddenly she realized that she had tasted nothing, neither the fine bread and the butter from a Sussex herd, nor the tea, and now she was feeling almost faint from the impact of what had been said to her. 'Well, perhaps I will, please,' she said, appreciatively drinking the strong homely brew from the large silver teapot Percy Comfort carried. It was how he liked tea, strong and brown and reviving to fainting spirits. Under its influence he saw his angel revive, and basked in her grateful smile. He ventured to linger around her table, a thing strictly forbidden to him, But Ada was lying down with a headache.

'Very changeable weather, madam. Shouldn't wonder if there was a storm by the sea.'

'Do you think so? I think I'd rather like that. I've never seen a storm by the sea.'

'Oh, I don't think you would like it, madam. We get it very rough up here, very noisy.' Her attention had floated away from him; he longed to ask her what Mr Hervey-Downes had said to trouble her so much. If only he could coax her into talking to him, as he sensed she needed to talk to somebody. How like a lily she shone among the other guests in the room, grey, tightly-corseted, buttoned up females: a depressed spinster with an elderly stout mother enjoying the attention her ear-trumpet brought her as she boomed, 'What's that? What's that?' to the poor low-voiced woman. A clergyman's widow sat nearby, accompanied by her slightly hump-backed daughter, then there was a pair of sisters who lived permanently at Marine Villa and were exceedingly High Church, going to service three times every Sunday and early Communion every Thursday. What could this lovely girl have to do with such people?

'Shall you be making use of our card room, madam?' he enquired. 'Some of our ladies like a hand at whist before supper.'

'Oh. No, thank you. I don't play.'

He tried again. 'There are some nice books in the drawing-room bookcase. Novels, and travel stories . . .'

Laura said patiently, 'Thank you.' She wished very much that the tiresome man would go away. The look in his eye was only too recognizable, a blend of infatuation and solicitude. Mr Hervey-Downes had mentioned that Mrs Comfort was a bit of a dragon, which explained why her husband clearly needed female consolation. But Laura was in no mood for supplying it. With a murmured apology she rose and slipped away, conscious that she left a disappointed, lonely man behind her, a man not unlike poor Pa. She needed to think.

Lying on her bed, the spotless counterpane turned down beneath her feet, she watched the sea turn from a dark grey glimmer to no colour at all. Clouds scudded across the sky before a high wind, a scatter of rain flung itself against the windows, and the garden trees tossed their branches, black against the lights on the seafront. The same thoughts went round and round the treadmill in Laura's mind. She could stay in Brighton and find work; perhaps Hannington's would take her as a shopgirl, and there must be cheaper lodgings than Marine Villa. In that way she could keep her respectability (or what was left of it), write home and explain as much as she could. Perhaps they would take her back. Which would mean going back to Fred, and Miller Street. Her mind shuddered away from that.

But to leave England – go away with a man she hardly knew, so far beyond her in wealth, family and education. He had promised to look after her as he would any other precious possession. What a strange way of putting it, as though she were a piece of china or an expensive book . . . He had not even said that he expected to sleep with her, yet that was what men seemed to want, and something told her that she would quite like it, with him, even better than she had liked it with Jim Broadbent. Yet Jim had fooled her . . .

But to have money to spend, to travel in comfort and see the places that had danced in her mind's eye as long as she had known the river and ships. To be still so young, to have the world before her – would this be worth becoming what her family already thought her, a Kept Woman?

The clock on the landing chimed out in its grandmotherly tones. Six, seven, eight. Downstairs supper would be over – the supper she had completely forgotten. Outside the wind was howling and lashing, driving the clouds more hurriedly across the yellow face of a moon that surfaced now and then, like the face of a drowning bather. Laura's disturbed mind echoed the turmoil outside. Her body ached for exercise to get her away from the white enclosed room and the treadmill of her thoughts. Among the clothes Jim had bought her, now neatly hung in a wardrobe, was a hooded cloak of hunter's green velours. It was like nothing she had ever owned, a romantic garment admired on the impulse, a 'cover-all', he had called it. She pulled it on, fastened the drawstrings at the throat, and left the house, looking round cautiously to make sure that her flight was not seen.

The side street was a tunnel of wind, almost taking her off her feet as she struggled down towards the Parade. There were no vehicles or walkers to be seen; only a fool would be out on such a night. No fishermen's lights out at sea, the globes in the gas-standards on the front flickering in the assailing draught. Down to the right, in the town, there were lights. Laura turned towards them and began to walk downhill, struggling to keep on her feet and exulting in the physical challenge of the struggle. The warring thoughts receded as her head cleared. She enjoyed the pressure of the buffeting wind, her own strength overcoming it, stride by stride down the hill. Now she was nearing the Aquarium, and there were people and conveyances, bobbing lights and the steady glow of curtained windows.

She stopped dead as something crashed and splintered only a few yards ahead – a slate blown from a roof. It was not safe to walk near buildings. She turned towards the sea, and made her way down a narrow flight of steps leading to the beach. Now the lights were gone, the shingle crunched under her thin boots. Herself and the tossing waves, herself and the dark shape of the Chain Pier, her thoughts free as the sharp, salt air. A current of wind leaped at her, tearing the hood from her head and dragging down her pinned-up hair so that it whipped about her face, making her laugh involuntarily.

The laugh turned to a scream as two arms came round her in a tight grip. 'Well, strangle me,' said a rough voice, 'where are you bound for, my handsome mort? Thinkin' of takin' a dip, were you?'

Laura gasped and struggled, but the arms were relentless. A breath heavy with spirits puffed in her face as her captor pulled her head round. All she could see of him in the fitful moonlight were gleaming eyes and teeth and a round fur cap such as costers and street-corner haunters wore. Suddenly she became aware that the more she fought to be free the harder she was gripped, and that the man was enjoying her resistance. Against her instinct she made herself relax, and tried to speak calmly.

'Let me go, will you. I don't know you.'

'Crikey, a shakester. Don't know me, don't you, my pretty chy? Well, don't fret, you soon will. What's it to be – a roll on the pebbles, just you and me, or a nice little room I knows of down Edward Street? Come on, let's have a feel. Nice, nice. Don't believe in them starchy stays, do you. Nor drawers neither? Let's see, shall us.'

126

Laura caught at the hand groping at her skirts and fought it off, hearing her own harsh breathing as though it were someone else's, and her inarticulate sounds of angry fear. The hand ceased to wander and came to rest on her shoulder, under her cloak, in horrible intimacy.

'Well, 'specs you're right – don't paw the goods till you've paid for 'em. Tell yer what, in no time at all you'n me can have a nice little business goin'. You works the streets and brings in the customers – you can easy pick up ten or a dozen every night outside the theatre. Then we settles down all by ourselves, wiv enough Old Tom inside us to drown a moke – eh?'

It couldn't be happening; it was a nightmare. But the pain of his grip was real, as well as the sharp bite of the pebbles through her boot-soles. Perhaps he mistook her for somebody else.

'I don't understand you,' she said. 'You've got the wrong person.'

'Oh, no, I 'aven't. I knows a right 'un when I sees it. Come on now, doll. If you don't keep quite and walk alongside o' me nicely I'll slog you one, see?' His fist menaced her chin and she screamed, despairingly aware that the wind would carry her cry out to sea. Then, hardly believing it, she heard the crunch of rapid footsteps coming towards them. Her assailant swore violently, flinging an arm in a foul-smelling sleeve across her mouth to silence her. The footsteps came on, hurrying, sure-footed, the footsteps of a Brightonian who knew that treacherous beach, and a voice said, 'Leave that young lady alone and be off with you!'

'Blast your eyes! What's it to do with you?'

'I'll show you, if you don't clear off.' The form that was almost upon them waved something that might have been a gun. Without waiting to find out, Laura's attacker turned and stumbled away.

'Oh, Mr Comfort!' she said when she could get her breath. 'Oh, thank you. I've never been so frightened in my life. How on earth did you find me?'

'Well, madam, I happened to see you leaving, and as I usually take a little walk about that time I took the liberty of following a little way behind you, to make sure you came to no harm. These gales can be very hazardous. I trust you'll

127

forgive me, madam.'

'Forgive you!' They were back at the steps she had descended, Mr Comfort's hand respectfully beneath her elbow, guiding her. He seemed taller and more manly than he had appeared in the hotel. 'What should I have done without you? It was the silliest thing to do, coming out alone like that, but I wanted to think, and it's easiest when one's walking. That awful man! He said something about Edward Street, and a business, and customers – I didn't know what he was talking about, but he frightened me very much.'

You poor innocent angel, thought Percy Comfort, how could you know, and where would you have been if I hadn't been bold enough to follow you? Aloud he said, 'There are some very bad characters in this town, madam, mostly in a low quarter the council wish to pull down, and good riddance. Houses of ill-repute and nasty drinking dens. I expect that person came from one of them.'

Walking sedately back at his side, things fell into place in Laura's mind. For the second time in her life she had been captured for immoral purposes. Houses of ill-repute, indeed – she had been in one already, long ago in Soho. That such a thing should happen again, to one who had done nothing to invite it! And yet perhaps she had, unthinkingly. It would be stupid to pretend not to know that her looks attracted men powerfully, and to go about unescorted was asking for trouble, the sort of trouble she had just experienced.

In the hall of the hotel, under the reassuring light, she held out her hand.

'Good night, Mr Comfort. Thank you again – very, very much. I don't know what else I can say to you.' She held out her hand, which he shook reverently, as though it were a flower whose petals might fall at a touch.

'Good night, madam. Glad to have been of service.' He replaced the stout heavy ash stick in the umbrella rack, and went downstairs to face a tirade from his wife because he had not been there to answer the bell when a very important guest had rung for brandy in his room. It was all well worth it, to have rescued the angel.

When Deryck Hervey-Downes arrived in response to her

summons the next day, she said nothing to him of the experience which had made up her mind; it only showed her up as a fool. Quietly she told him, 'I've thought carefully about it. And I will come away with you.'

'I'm delighted to hear it.'

'I think I should say that I'm not Mrs Diamond – you called me that. I don't care much for my married name – perhaps I could be Miss Diamond.'

He bent his head. 'Whatever you please.' Disappointment touched her: she had half-expected him to give her a title that sounded as though she were married.

'But I shall call you Laura,' he went on. 'We'll forget formalities from this moment. And you will call me Deryck – the spelling is odd, but I was called after a relative of my mother's, a Dutch great-uncle of impeccable character and immense fortune. By the way, which romantic parent named you after Petrarch's ideal mistress?'

She came to him and put her hands in his. 'I don't know. I don't know who he was, that you just said. I don't know very much at all, and you'll have to teach me.'

'I shall teach you, lovely child – as much as you'll ever need to know.'

Book Two

Chapter Ten

WHEN THE LETTER ARRIVED at the house in Feathers Row it was Alice who picked it up from the mat. For a moment she surveyed, stony-eyed, Laura's round schoolgirlish writing and the French stamp, then she carried it between two fingers into the kitchen and dropped it on the breakfast table beside Daniel's plate. His face changed, brightened; with trembling fingers he opened it.

> *Dear Pa,*
>
> *I am not sure if you want to hear from me but I wanted to tell you that I am quite well. It is very strange being in a foreign country but I like it very much. You would be surprised to hear how many words of French I know already. Paris is very beautiful, much more so than London. I shall not be coming home again so Ma need not worry. With much love to you and Ellie from your loving*
>
> *Laura*

'She's all right,' he said. 'Ellie, she's all right. Here.' He passed the letter over to her. A wave of intense relief swept over Ellie as she read it. When they had failed to find Laura in Brighton it had seemed as though she had died. Now, through the miracle of a piece of thin blue writing paper, she was alive again, and Ellie's world had righted itself. She smiled brilliantly at her father, knowing that he felt the same.

'Paris,' he said, 'that's nice. I've seen pictures – the Exhibition. And she thinks it's beautiful.'

Alice would have liked to ignore the letter, but curiosity was too much for her. She hooked it towards her with a fork, contemptuously scanned it sideways, and sniffed. 'Paris. A wicked place.'

Ellie's rare temper flared. 'You thought Brighton was a

130

wicked place, too, just because Laura was there. You think anywhere she is and anything she does is wicked. You never gave her a chance, and now she says she's not coming home again. It's your fault she didn't stay when she called here, because you told her lies, and us too, I shouldn't wonder. I suppose none of your famous royalties ever went to Paris, did they – or if they did that was all right, because they weren't Laura.'

Alice pushed her chair back and stood behind it, glaring. 'Be quiet!'

'I won't be quiet. And I won't eat your beastly porridge, either, I'll buy a bun on the way to work.' She got up and flung out of the room. They heard her clattering about in the lobby, then the slam of the front door. Daniel stared helplessly at his white-faced wife. He knew that he should comfort her, but he had no heart in it. Since Laura's disappearance a great gap had opened between them, like a crack in volcanic earth.

'Ellie shouldn't have said what she did,' he said. 'It wasn't like her. But it was true, Alice, you know it was. If we've lost Laura, it's your fault.'

Alice watched him get up and leave the room, heard him leave the house. Then, mechanically, she cleared the table, scraped the glutinous remains of porridge from the plates, put the pan to soak, stacked the crockery in the sink and put a kettle on to boil. From the parlour she fetched a large, thin book, bound in gold and green boards; it was her favourite reading, *Royal Treasures*. She spread it out on the table and, while the kettle simmered, sat leafing through it, staring half-aware at ermined robes, draped on dummies, diadems and carcanets whose lustre could only be guessed at from sepia photographs, elaborate carved furniture, statues and pictures. The kettle boiled. She poured hot water on to the dishes in the sink, added a square of coarse soap, and washed each cup and plate, aware of her reddened wrinkling fingers. A woman came in every morning to do the rough work of the house, but today Alice was not leaving the washing-up to her.

She stacked the things on the draining board, removed her apron and hung it up, put on her hat and coat and took up her handbag.

The barmaid at the public house had never seen this

131

customer before, and stared to see such a respectable person entering so early, while the chairs were still stacked on the tables. The woman was taking no notice of her, no greeting, no smile: only a survey of the row of bottles behind the bar.

'Can I get something for you?' the girl asked at last.

'Yes. I want a bottle of something. Which is the strongest?'

'Pardon?'

'The strongest of the drinks,' Alice said. 'I don't know any of them, of course. Which is the strongest?'

'Well, now. Is it for medicine? 'Cause if so, brandy would do you. I've got a nice three-star . . .'

'Gin,' said the curious customer. 'I've heard of that. Plymouth Gin. I'll take a bottle. How much?'

'Two and four, please.' The girl wrapped the bottle up, stealing glances at the pale set face and rigid bearing of this person who looked more like a Sister of Temperance than the sort who'd buy gin. But there, it took all sorts. She gave back twopence change from half a crown and returned to stacking glasses.

Alice put the bottle in her large handbag and took it home. In the kitchen she chose a large tumbler, filled a jug with water, and carried them upstairs, the bottle still in her bag. In her bedroom, the only safe, solitary retreat she had, she settled down in her old place by the window. But this time her hand went out, more and more often, to the glass, and the bottle, and the jug. And there, about noon, the cleaning woman found her, unconscious, snoring, and smelling of gin.

The moment Ellie was out of the house she regretted having spoken so sharply to her mother. What she had said was true, but the saying of it would do no good. She slowed down, half-inclined to go back and apologize, then decided that it would only make matters worse. The apology could wait until evening, when tempers had cooled.

Because she had left the house earlier than usual, there was time to spare before she was due at work. Walking thoughtfully down Church Street, she obeyed a sudden impulse to go into the church, St Alphege's. They attended it regularly, but last Sunday nobody had felt like it, with Laura gone. Hawksmoor's violently weeping cherubs carved on the four

132

great urns had always raised a smile from Ellie. Now the uncomfortable thought crossed her mind that they might be weeping for her sins, hers and others like her who spoke cruelly without thinking. She knelt briefly in the quiet, empty building, shivering a little at the cold, then sat down in a pew and gave herself up to thought.

Under her mother's harshness to Laura there must be some love, some tenderness which felt the loss of her daughter. With kindness and patience Ellie might reach that centre and so help both parents, and Laura; for one day Laura would come back, and she must be welcomed. Ellie shut her eyes and prayed, not repeating the formal phrases that were said on a Sunday, but working her mind to find the right words to use to whoever was listening, far above the painted apse and the organ they said Queen Elizabeth had played. She promised to be very good, better than she had ever been before. Next time her mother resorted to Sitting Up she would go and keep her company, talk to her cheerfully. Perhaps she would give up her work at Ponsford's, though she enjoyed it: that would give her time to . . .

'Excuse me – but can I help you at all?'

The words would have done very well for a voice from Heaven. But, when she opened her eyes, she saw that they came from a human source. In the dim light she saw that he was young and wore a clerical collar, and that his face, like his voice, was kindly and concerned. She blinked up at him.

'Oh – thank you. But I'm quite all right.'

'I'm sorry. I shouldn't have troubled you. But I thought you might be ill, or in some kind of distress. It seemed so early in the morning for anyone to be in church.'

Ellie smiled at him. 'I know it is. But I wanted to think something over before going to work, and this seemed the best place for it. I know one should really pray on one's knees, only it's so uncomfortable.'

'I do beg your pardon for having interrupted you. I'll go away at once.'

'No, don't. Perhaps you *can* help me. If one gives up something important to oneself, because it gets in the way of what one ought to do for another person – do you think God takes that into account?'

'You mean, does He willingly accept a sacrifice?'

133

'I suppose I do.'

'That's very hard to say. It depends on what His plan is for you, and the person concerned, and whether your sacrifice is right in itself. I suppose "sacrifice" might not be quite the proper word, if we think of sacrifices as burnt offerings – which I never have felt can have pleased Him very much.'

'No,' said Ellie, 'I never have, either. Offering up little lambs, and that poor ram in the thicket that Abraham killed instead of Isaac.'

The young man's lips twitched. 'Exactly. Very unfortunate for the ram that it came out at just that moment, though I suppose it spared us a patriarch.'

Ellie wondered whether it was a very wrong thing to laugh in a church, even an empty one, but if the clergyman didn't mind neither did she. They viewed each other with interest. She saw a healthy-complexioned young man, sturdy of figure, brown haired and handsomely whiskered, very unlike the usual ecclesiastical image. Surely he was not old enough to be ordained yet? He saw soft dark eyes that beamed eagerness and – yes, surely, goodness, and a mouth with an attractive eager look not at all spoiled by slightly prominent teeth. He thought her very like Charles the Second's little queen, Catherine of Braganza, a pretty and put-upon lady, as he guessed this one to be. For some reason the cold of the morning quite ceased to trouble him as they talked. He learned that she attended St Alphege's, she discovered that the reason she had not seen him there was that he was merely acting as *locum tenens* for the curate, who had suddenly been taken ill. His regular parish was a rural one, Thimblestone in Essex, which he had regretted leaving just now when the harvest festival was near, and the little Saxon church would be filled with the fruits of the earth. His name was Frank Kenward, his father was the headmaster of a largish boys' school, he was the eldest of six.

'But I'm talking far too much. Tell me about yourself. What work do you do?'

'I'm a clerk – at Ponsford's, the tea-shippers.'

'That's very enterprising for a young lady. Do you enjoy it?'

'Oh, yes. I . . .' Suddenly she remembered where the fascinating conversation had started; with sacrifice. How could she have gone so far away from it, she who was usually shy with strangers? Before she could pull herself together and wish him a polite good morning the clock in the tower above them struck ponderously, eight times. Ellie started. 'Oh! I'm late. I'll have to go.'

'I hope I haven't . . . I should have known . . .' Why did he catch himself stammering, he who was usually outgoing and easy? He could not have said, only that he was disconcerted to find how much he didn't want to part from this girl and lose her in the busy streets outside. It was ridiculous, after an encounter so brief. But he read the same in her face, and said, 'Will you be at matins on Sunday?'

'Yes. Yes, of course.'

'Then I'll see you after service.'

'Oh yes!' She was transformed with relief, and the thought came to him, the rose of Sharon, she is King Solomon's rose of Sharon.

Ellie came home after work with feet that scarcely seemed to touch the ground, after a day of such delirious happiness as she had never known. A deep, sure instinct told her that she had met the one man whom she could love and who could love her. She gave not even the most glancing thought to the wretched Adolphus Duffin and his defection. That had been something childish and quite different, a piece of stupid vanity on her part (but she was just a little glad that Laura was out of the way this time). Over and over again she relived the brief encounter in the church, everything that had been said and not said, wishing she could remember exactly how he looked and spoke. Twice she made a mistake in adding up accounts, causing pained surprise in the counting-house where she was known for efficiency. She corrected them, blushing, but not cast down as she once would have been.

She let herself into a house that was unusually quiet. No sound from the kitchen, where her mother would be preparing supper. When she looked in, it was empty.

Alarmed, she went upstairs, expecting to find Alice in her old place at the window. She was not there, but in bed, a still mound under the eiderdown. The room was full of a rank unpleasant smell Ellie couldn't identify.

'Ma, what's the matter? Are you ill?'

Alice's face, red and heavy-eyed, turned slowly towards her, and her voice, when she spoke, was slow, almost unrecognizable.

'Not well, Ellie. Let me alone.'

'But what is it? Have you been sick? Shall I get the doctor?'

The head was faintly shaken, then subsided on the pillow. Ellie hovered uncertainly, then went downstairs just as her father's key turned in the lock. She gasped out what had happened, while he listened uncomprehendingly. Together they went up and stood by the bedisde. Alice was asleep now, breathing stertorously.

'Drink,' Daniel said. 'She's been drinking spirits.'

'But . . . we don't have such things, Pa. And Ma never drinks. It must be something else.'

He gave her a gentle push. 'Go on down, girl, and make us some tea. Make it good and strong, and I'll waken her.'

Frank Kenward hung up his cassock more hastily than usual and hurried out into the churchyard. She was waiting, but the bright look he remembered was missing from her face, and her greeting was subdued. As they strolled in the churchyard he talked lightly and cheerfully, surprised at her quiet answers after the sparks they had struck from each other at their first meeting. After a few minutes he stopped.

'Shall we sit for a little while? Nobody's likely to object to our using this handsome table-tomb as a seat – least of all the occupant. Are you not glad to see me, Miss Diamond? I had hoped the other day that we were going to be friends, and I was sure you had the same hope. Have you changed your mind?'

Ellie shook her head. 'No. I would like us to to be friends. I'd like to take you home to dinner – knowing you're in lodgings. But I can't.'

Frank had already visualized a pleasant family meal, perhaps with mutton. He had a healthy young man's appetitite, and his landlady was stingy. He concealed his disappointment.

'Don't think about that. I only want to know why you are sad.'

136

Ellie's eyes, darkly melancholy, met his. 'Something awful has happened. My mother's suddenly taken to drink. The day I . . . met you, I went home and found her quite stupid from it. Father and I got her round, but she wouldn't tell us why, or how she got the stuff, and the next day she was the same. Our charwoman came round to Ponsford's to tell us, and we sent for the doctor. He says she'll make herself seriously ill if she goes on like this, and somebody must be with her all the time to make sure she doesn't go out and buy spirits. And so of course I must give up work. It's funny, you know, that was the sacrifice I meant when I was talking to you – but I didn't know it would come about like this.'

'I'm sorry. So very sorry. But surely some other relative could stay with your mother? Someone with time to spare. Why must it be you?'

'There isn't anybody. Father's sister, Aunt Gerti, wouldn't be any use at all, and Aunt Jane is troubled with asthma. No, it has to be me. I mustn't complain, because it's meant. You said accepting sacrifices depended on God's plan. Well, now we know what it is.'

Frank was silent. He had given a lot of thought to Ellie over the past few days, and had prayed that his conviction was right, and that this was the girl he must court and marry. It would be wise, of course, to wait for the slow machinery of Church promotion to provide him with a stipend that would support a wife. But he believed in miracles, in the bringing together of those meant for each other, and he was quite sure he was not being led astray by a rash impulse. But now his chosen one was being snatched away and condemned to the miserable life of a spinster daughter, for years, perhaps.

A robin flew down to the grass near the tomb where they sat, put its head on one side as it regarded them, and sang its short trilling song before flying away. Oddly, Frank was cheered. He laid his hand on Ellie's, cold beneath its glove.

'If the vicar agrees, and if you think it would do any good, may I come and visit your mother?'

She looked up, her mouth trembling. 'Oh, if you would! It would make me so happy.'

Alice received Frank's pastoral visits with polite apathy. It was, he said ruefully to Ellie, like preaching to a congregation who were all asleep. When the regular curate recovered and

Frank reluctantly returned to his parish, Ellie felt utterly abandoned, missing her work and the friendly clerks, shut up in the house to play a never ending game of cat and mouse with her mother.

It was a game Alice almost always managed to win. She quickly became expert at slipping out quietly to buy bottles of the spirit which dulled the pain of thought, gave her a brief illusion of pleasure, then plunged her into oblivion. She would go while Ellie was cooking or bed-making, or out shopping. Locking her in was useless; she had her own keys which were as securely hidden as her hoard of bottles. She enjoyed the game, knowing Ellie to be too soft-hearted to take drastic measures, finding a perverse enjoyment in out-witting both her and Daniel. It all kept her thoughts away from Laura.

Ellie wrote to Frank.

I think there must be a kind of curse on our family. My mother seems to be possessed of a devil, and I wish you were here to drive it away. Pa looks very old and ill – I fear I am not enough to comfort him. It is two months now since Laura went. Sometimes I think we shall never see her again. I expect you will be getting ready for Christmas now. I can imagine your pretty church dressed up with holly, and the carollers going from house to house with lanterns, as you told me; I wish I could be there and see it all.

She put down the pen, sighing. Wherever Laura was, she wished her more happiness than there would ever be again in her old home.

Chapter Eleven

'IF M'SIEUR WILL GO IN.'

Maurice walked past the maid into the drawing-room of Madeline's apartment, a room of elegant opulence in which there was hardly an article of furniture or a picture which had not seen the Revolution, almost a hundred years before. Madeline was there, equally elegant and opulent, in high toilette, bare-shouldered, her neck encircled by the triple pearl choker she had copied from the Princess of Wales, reclining Cleopatra-like on a chaise longue. Beside her, looking equally at home, sat Louis de St Étienne.

'Well, Maurice! What a surprise. You might have telegraphed that you were coming.'

'I didn't know myself until a few hours ago.' He kissed her cheek lightly. 'Suddenly the fogs and the mud became too much for me, and I shut the place up and left. I hope I'm welcome.'

'But of course, always. This is your home as much as mine.' And as much as Louis's, Maurice thought, answering the Frenchman's beaming smile. He sensed that some change had taken place in his mother since their last chilly meeting. The feeling of rapport had gone, along with the special twinkle in the eye that was for him alone. Her letters had been chatty, though rare, amusing accounts of her vacation in the Loire and the social highlights of Paris. There had been no mention in them of a return to England, and he had not pressed it, wanting to make himself independent of her as far as he could, knowing he should have done it much earlier. He had left the house in Greenwich to live in his bachelor apartment and devote himself to painting; but as winter advanced he became disheartened by the constant battle against bad light, even in his Embankment studio high above the river, and a succession of models with streaming colds.

He thought of sunshine in Italy, Spain, anywhere warm and bright, with picturesque peasants happy to pose for him. The south of France, that was it; he would go to Carcassonne or Perpignan and take a place for the winter. And first he would pause in Paris to make his peace with Madeline.

She smiled at him lazily through a cloud of smoke from a Russian cigarette. 'Well, now you're here, what are we to do with you?' We, he noted, not I. 'I hope you're not going to be as cross and humpy as you were before, when I had to run away from you, had I not, Louis?'

Louis shrugged amiably, neither agreeing nor disagreeing. He liked to please, all the time. 'It was my gain, *chèrie*.'

Chèrie. So they were on intimate terms now. Maurice said 'I promise not to be in the least bit humpy, so long as you promise to entertain me for a few days, when you can spare the time. How is the weather, by the way?'

'*Pas si mal*. Mild and warmish. What sort of a crossing did you have?'

'Vile. I thought we should never get as far as Calais. At one point I rather hoped not, it was as bad as that. But here I am, you see.'

Madeline heaved a mock-sigh. 'Well, Louis, here we have this importunate child pulling at his mama's skirts to be amused. So what shall we do with him?'

'I could do justice to a good meal,' Maurice said. 'I lost my last one, as it were, in the Channel.'

'Ah. Then you'll have to wait. We're going to the Opèra, and I do love to get there early and see the belles and the frights arrive, so we shall dine afterwards. Perhaps you could come with us – yes, that's a good idea. Is there room in the box, Louis?'

'Certainly. I haven't invited anyone else. Monsieur Maurice will be most welcome.'

Maurice had been thinking of a leisured meal, with conversation that would put an end to the estrangement between them and start them off on a new relationship. A night at the Opèra was not entirely his idea of his first evening with Madeline, and he had not envisaged Louis being there at all. However, they would certainly not change their plans to suit him, so he could but agree, with the request that first he might change and bathe.

'But of course. In any case I had no intention of being seen with such a rumpled-looking gentleman. Marie will draw your bath and we shall see you looking civilized again in half an hour. Yes?'

'Yes.' It was not until he was relaxing in the very modern bath in the marble-floored bathroom that he realized they had all been speaking French, almost from the moment he had entered the room.

Already it was hot inside the vast theatre, so new still that its crimson, white, and gold had lost none of their freshness. The brilliance of countless lamps shone down on brilliant people, resplendent creatures as anxious to be seen as to see, the perfume of the women blending to make an ineffable fragrant whole. Madeline laughed and chattered with her two men and acquaintances in the next box, blew kisses, made outrageous comments on the toilettes and appearances of the ladies entering, and invited Louis to compare her with them, which he did much to her advantage. Maurice thought her behaviour unbecomingly juvenile and affected; he had never noticed it in her before. His mind wandered off into speculations: if his father had not died, if there had been other children, if she and he had not been so close – woud he now be married, a father himself? Where would he be now, this minute? Presiding at a dinner-party in his Chelsea home – yes, he had always liked Chelsea – philosophizing over the port, agreeing with the editor of a fashionable magazine to receive his reporter and photographer; then, perhaps, when the guests were gone, slipping up to the nurseries to look at the sleeping children: a boy of, say, ten, a girl of, say, eight, a very small individual in a cradle. And, on the other side of each white bed, the figure of their mother; a lay-figure in drapes, with no face.

He sighed, came back to the present and let his gaze roam round the rapidly filling *fauteuils*. The boxes all had spectators in them, coming and going as friends were seen and visited. In a box almost level with Louis's on the opposite side of the theatre Maurice's long-sighted eyes rested on two people, alone and apparently only interested in observing newcomers, the man sitting back, the woman leaning forward, her arms on the velvet rim of the box, her head turning from side to side, her features clearly visible under the bright lights. She was extraordinarily striking at that distance, he thought, though a closer inspection would probably show cosmetics and the use of hair-tint; a symphony in white, snowy tulle clouding about her bare shoulders, no colour about her anywhere but that amazing (if real) pale golden hair.

Studying her, his mind went off to the Blessed Damozel of the artist-poet Rossetti, who had leaned on the bar of Heaven as this damozel was leaning. He, Maurice, could have painted the lady so. 'She had three lilies in her hand, and the stars in her hair were seven.' A scattered glittering moved as her head turned towards the stage, and he saw that there were indeed stars in her hair, points of light that threw off sparks from the rays of the lamps, jewels suspended in the long locks that lay about her shoulders, the rest of the hair being piled up in curls and decorated with another glittering object high above the brow.

He murmured a request for Louis's opera-glasses and focused them on her. She was in full profile, and he gasped. How like she was to his lost Britannia, the Greenwich girl so briefly seen, never to be forgotten. The same lovely line of throat, the same small high-bridged nose and the eager look of a figurehead. Maurice stared and stared. A face one has drawn is imprinted in the memory. He measured the distance across the theatre, the time it would take him to walk round the back of the boxes and look at her more closely, even speak to her, before the rise of the curtain.

Then she turned back to speak to her companion, and smiled, a bright sophisticated smile that made her appear completely French. What a fool he had been to see an English girl in this expensive, bejewelled beauty; he must be faint with hunger, and wandering in his mind. Yet the man with her looked very English, fresh-faced and fine-boned. Maurice would have painted him in hunting pink, a whip in his hand, a hound at his feet. He wondered if the man were her husband or her lover.

'Maurice,' said his mother's voice, 'what *are* you staring at over there? I've asked you twice whether you would like sandwiches brought with the champagne.'

'Sorry. Just someone I thought I knew.'

'A belle or a fright?'

'Oh, a belle, decidedly. But it was a mistake. And I would very much like sandwiches. If I drink champagne on top of this emptiness you'll have to have me carried out.'

'That would be a pity,' Louis said, 'before *Hoffman*. You know *Les Contes de Hoffman*, Maurice?'

'No, I wasn't in Paris when it was first done.'

'You will like it. It is just the piece for an artist.'

Louis was absolutely right, Maurice decided soon after the curtain had risen. Offenbach's romantic, languorous music, and the sensuous fantasy of the tales from the age of Byron, captured his mood completely. He became the poet Hoffman, doomed to fall in love with the wrong woman every time: Stella, the gorgeous prima donna, Olympia, the dancing doll mistaken by the poor fool for a living girl, whom he sees torn limb from limb by her creator: Giulietta, the courtesan of Venice, stealer of souls to the swooning music of the Barcarolle. And Antonia, the sweet singer tricked by a demoniac doctor into singing her life away. Maurice suffered with Hoffman, feeling his pains and frustrations as he had not allowed himself to feel his own before the sight of a French-woman had brought back to him the memory of his lost love.

Louis whispered to Madeline: '*Il est vraiment en ecstase – enivré par la musique.*'

'*Ou par la champagne.*'

'*Peut-être par l'amour?*'

Madeline snorted delicately. 'Maurice? *Quelle blague! Tiens, on commence.*'

Maurice had made up his mind not to look closely again at the woman in white during the intervals, though a sideglance in the second one showed him that neither she nor her companion were in the box. As the opera progressed a change began to steal over him, born of the agitation of seeing her, nursed by the eroticism of the music and action, and by the sexual atmosphere in the box emanating from Madeline and Louis. He was irritated yet excited by it. The forms and faces of the women on the stage began to fascinate him, not so much the magnificent Giulietta and the swan-like Olympia as the chorines who fluttered and swayed, puppets, Venetian revellers, tavern girls, all pretty and all young. A dancer's life could be over at thirty. One girl in particular attracted him;

143

she seemed to be a principal, to the fore in every scene, and her personality shone out like a beacon. Neither tall nor short, she had the compact figure of a Frenchwoman, slightly heavy in the bosom, with beautiful legs amply revealed by her costumes and fluid arms that seemed boneless. She was dark, lively-faced, with a sort of sparkle about her, a vivid aliveness. He trained the opera-glasses on her face and saw huge dark eyes outlined in kohl and full lips painted crimson. He began to be obsessed with her, impatient during the Antonia sequence for the action to return to the tavern where Hoffman had begun to tell his tales.

Yes, there she was, perched on a man's knee, leaping off and running to embrace another one, all bounce and glitter and allure. When the curtain had fallen and the calls were taken she was in the front row of dancers and singers ranged behind the principals. He was oddly relieved to see her, as though she might have flown away. There were sentimental stories of ballet-girls with ailing old mothers in garrets whom they virtuously returned to as soon as the curtain was down – and there were other stories, less sentimental.

He rose as soon as the calls were over and the last rose thrown on to the stage. Madeline said 'You'll join us for dinner, of course? We're going to Antoine's.'

'I'm afraid not. I have an appointment. I may be very late, or not – I don't know.'

Madeline looked at him curiously. 'Do as you please, of course. We shall have to entertain each other, Louis, *chéri*.'

He solicitously put her satin fur-lined cloak around her shoulders. 'That should present no problems.' Maurice knew they were glad to be rid of him.

To reach the stage door he had to push his way through a narrow street filled with chattering people on their way to their carriages, a flurry of top hats and costly cloaks, animated faces and high Parisian voices. Suddenly a uniformed official appeared among them, barring the way of the oncoming throng to allow a couple through from the lighted stairway leading up to the boxes. Maurice, caught behind the man's arm, found himself looking straight at them, only a foot or so away.

He knew them at once. The English aristocrat, lofty of bearing, clean-shaven among so many beards, sharp and sophisticated, and the woman, gold spread hair starred with diamonds not yet hidden by the velvet of her cloak's hood. She looked directly into his eyes; Paris was blotted out for him as he heard the wheeling cries of gulls, saw the trees of Richmond Park in young green, a girl in lilac with a peacock at her side, Solomon in all his glory. He had not been mistaken, even across the theatre, in the proud profile and the moonlight colour of her hair – which, he saw at close quarters, was not dyed, nor her face painted.

Yet the jewels in her hair and on her fingers were real, and her clothing expensive, almost ostentatiously so. So the old woman at the shop had lied to him about her marriage to some workman – or the marriage had been a cover for something else, a liaison perhaps already begun when they had met before. She was a *cocotte*, a *fille de joie*; he had been utterly deceived in her.

And Laura, as their glances crossed like swords, felt a bitter resentment rising in her throat. He had deserted her, caused her so much anguish, driven her into a detested marriage, merely to become a playboy in Paris, a sauntering *flaneur* doubtless on his way to some woman. She hated herself because her heart had lurched when she saw him, hated him for his cruelty and deception, felt tears of anger – if it was anger – stinging behind her eyes.

Their moment of shocked recognition was but a moment, yet long enough for Deryck to be aware of it.

'M'sieur?' His tone was arrogant, as Maurice had known it would be.

'I apologize.' Maurice answered in French, though he was fairly sure the other man was English. 'I thought I had met this lady before.'

Deryck turned to her. 'Is that the case, my dear?' She shook her head, her lips moving soundlessly.

'Then I suggest we move on.' The official carved a way for them to the edge of the pavement, where a carriage waited. Maurice watched the man help Laura into it. Then it was gone, and the brief scene under the lamp might never have happened.

More disturbed than he could have thought possible, he watched the dark shape of the *fiacre* out of sight. All thought of the ballet girl had gone out of his mind. He no longer had any sense of purpose in being away from England. Paris or London, it was all the same, his lost love lost twice over, and in a bitter fashion that turned the knife in the old wound.

Somebody passing was singing Olympia's song from the first act of *Hoffman*. Suddenly Maurice laughed, causing heads to turn in the thinning crowd. He himself was Hoffman; of course he was. Disappointed of Stella, he turns to Olympia – she's only a doll, but what of that? After her there will be a Giulietta, an Antonia . . . how many more, and what did it matter? He made himself remember the dark dancer's legs, her scarlet lips, the excitement she had roused in him as he watched her. Pulling his cloak round him against the chill air of the street, he hurried towards the stage door.

To his surprise – yet why should he be surprised? – he found a dozen or so men already gathered there, opera-hatted and cloaked, some carrying bouquets, some packages tied with ornate ribbons. He hesitated, unused to haunting theatres since his student days, then said to one young man with an amiable foolish face, 'It is possible to visit the young ladies of the ballet?'

'But of course, my friend – what do you think we're here for? Follow me.'

Maurice followed, past the stage doorkeeper in his cubicle, slipping some coins into his hand as he saw the others do. Down a stone corridor they went, then down stone stairs lit by a flickering gas-jet, to another corridor, where laughter and chatter were already coming from a row of dressing-rooms.

'Which particular enchantress do you visit?' his guide enquired.

'I don't know her name, m'sieur. One of the principals – dark, very accomplished.'

'Ah, *la charmante* Fanchette. You'll find her in there – and not alone.'

At first he could see nothing in the dressing-room for the gallants in front of him. Then, peering over their shoulders, he was able to make out four dressing-tables, full-length mirrors along the walls, four girls, each surrounded by a knot of men, laughing and flashing their eyes, delighting in homage. Furthest away was the one he had come to see. She was smaller than he had thought her, perhaps a little plumper, but just as attractive off stage as on it, the dark eyes beaming with life and laughter, the voluptuous mouth alluring under its paint. She was still in her short tarlatan ballet dress, her shoulders bare but for the little cape her dresser had slipped over them, and her arms were full of flowers, a huge bouquet.

The scene delighted Maurice, all colour and movement as it was: the powdered skin and light dresses of the dancers contrasting with the formal darkness of their admirers' cloaks, which showed here and there a flash of blue or scarlet lining, the hanging costumes decorated with sequins and silk flowers, the dresser, small, wizened, black-clad like a starling among tropical birds, smiling and dipping a curtsey to the gentlemen as they bestowed tips on her. He had seen all this before, but long ago, when he was a different person, and the memory had faded. Now its impact on him was like a return to youth and new hope for his desultory life. He wished he had a sketching-pad to jot down impressions of what he saw.

He tried to push forward towards Fanchette, but those before him would not give way. They were arguing who should take her to supper. 'Too late, Edouard! She's promised to me. I have it here in my notebook.' 'Liar. She'll confirm it's my turn. Fanchette, tell him!' The girl twisted about, giving one a cheeky answer, another a come-hither smile. Maurice heard her voice, very Parisian, slightly husky, delightful.

'I said no such thing. I believe I shall not go to supper with any of you *fripons*. I have a severe headache – in my feet. Louise shall see me home and you can all go and . . .'

Suddenly, over the heads of the others, her eyes met Maurice's. She stared full at him, a message passing between them. Then she said loudly 'No, I shall not go with any of you. I shall go with *ce m'sieur serieux qui me regard*. How could I abandon such a plaintive gaze? One moment. Louise!' With a dazzling smile she disappeared behind a screen. A young tawny-haired dancer tapped Maurice on the arm. 'You're very fortunate – she means it. I only hope you have plenty of the ready about you.'

Then, somehow, his rivals were melting away good-naturedly enough, and he was left among the clutter of clothes and frippery, in the heat from the gas-brackets, and the smell of sweat and perfume and cigars, waiting for the woman who would cure his weary celibacy, knowing that he and this place, and others like it, would be often together in the time to come.

'Dégas has finished with the theatre,' he reflected. 'But the theatre goes on, and I shall take up where he laid down his brush. And Fanchette shall be my Muse . . .'

His Muse bounced out from behind the screen, transformed in a street-dress of black enlivened with touches of crimson, eminently chic, emphasizing her tiny waist and small trim bottom, the deeply flounced skirt not over-long, revealing neat ankle-boots. She had taken off her make-up, and Maurice was pleased to see that her skin was unblemished, a delicate olive tint, her mouth a natural red more alluring than paint.

'*Mon Dieu*, what a long face!' she exclaimed. 'Perhaps you already regret your kind invitation – which, by the way, you never made. Well, it's not too late to recall another escort – shall I send after one? I only like to sup with cheerful faces, you know, m'sieur'. Her laughing eyes dared him to accept the escape route. He smiled down into them.

'As if I could be so ungallant – not to mention blackening the reputation of my countrymen.'

'Your countrymen? But are you not then French?'

'Alas, no, mademoiselle. I am English.'

'Then you have a very great talent to deceive, and I shall be most wary of you. Thank you for warning me so soon.'

He slipped his arm through hers. 'I shall try not to deserve your suspicions. Shall we go?' He put some francs into the palm of the hovering Louise, and they left the theatre.

Nothing was said between Maurice and Madeline in the weeks that followed about his frequent absences from the apartment. He was away from it for increasing periods of time during the days, and almost always at nights. The stubs of his tickets for the Opèra were carelessly flung into the wastebasket in his room, to be scrutinized by anyone who cared to do so. He smoked more and drank more. Cigar-smoke hung about his evening clothes; the manservant learned to prepare a blend of oysters, Worcester sauce and champagne, to be served instead of breakfast to a gentleman with an aching head and a very unsettled digestion. A small lace-edged handkerchief heavily scented with Jockey Club

148

was extracted from a coat pocket and passed round among the staff, amid titters. And Madeline, who saw everything, said nothing.

It was Louis who eventually spoke out, at a time when Madeline was visiting friends on the other side of Paris. Louis, boyish, pink with embarrassment, driving himself to the point of breaking silence.

'Maurice, my friend, it is not pleasant for me to have to say this, but Madeline is suffering because of you. Do you think she doesn't notice that you live the life of a *flaneur*, not of a good son any more? I don't like to see her hurt. Tell me, would you wish me to speak to her for you – to tell her, perhaps, that you are going through some crisis?'

Maurice smiled. 'You're a good fellow, Louis. Quite right to speak to me sternly. I've been behaving like a beast – I know it, and I'm thoroughly ashamed of myself. The worst of it is, I've misconducted myself under Madeline's roof – I should have removed myself before. But I suppose I've been too preoccupied. You see, I've been living as I've never lived. It's a bit late, perhaps, but what of that?'

The Frenchman's soft brown eyes were troubled. 'You don't intend to marry her?'

A shake of the head. 'Not the sort.'

'Then, when the affair is over, you might return to Madeline – as you were before?'

'As we were before, Louis, we were precious near to being lovers – platonic, of course, but near enough. Not good to either of us. No, I'm leaving, as soon as the studio I've taken is ready. It's a decent enough place, two floors in the Rue des Écoles – a cut above the usual sort of thing. I've given up my London studio and arranged for all the stuff to be sent here.'

Louis went to the window and stared out at the shifting pattern of traffic. His back to Maurice, he said, 'I have wished to marry your mother for a long time, but I would not ask her until I knew how things lay between you. Oh, I know I have seemed to be always about her, but that is understood, an attractive widow and her cavalier. It need not mean marriage or even courtship. But now I feel I am free to declare myself to her.' He turned. 'I wish it had happened earlier. You have wasted many of her years.'

Maurice laughed shortly. '*Her* years? What about mine?

149

Do you know that she mocked me out of every entanglement I tried to get into – except those that were perfectly safe?'

'You should not have let her. She will not mock me out of anything.'

'No,' said Maurice thoughtfully. 'I don't believe she will. I think I've underestimated you, *mon beau-père*-to-be.'

Madeline took Maurice's congratulations with a social smile behind which he could sense a plea: give up whatever game you're playing, give up this vulgar girl whom I know about, and I'll send Louis away. Everything shall be as it was, just you and me. He hardened his heart and wished her every happiness.

When she became the Comtesse de St Étienne in a small but intensely fashionable church, having taken instruction in Louis's religion in order to do so, Maurice was dutifully present in a morning suit, the picture of English elegance. As soon as the bridal pair had left, he slipped away from the reception and drove back to the Rue des Écoles. Fanchette was doing *pliés* at the barre he had had installed for her along one wall of the studio. She straightened up and ran to him.

'So, the funeral is over. Take off those horrible clothes at once and we will have some wine and a *tarte awx oignons* I very cleverly made for you, and then we will go to bed. *Tu le veux*, Fanchon?'

'*Je le veux*, Fanchette.'

A cold March morning couldn't keep the crowds off the streets of Paris. It was Mardi Gras, the day before Lent began, the day when the carnival procession wound its way through the old city. On a balcony, wrapped in furs, Laura watched with Deryck at her side as the motley cortège went by to the circus-music of brass and drums. Costumes varied from the historical to the ragbag, a Marie Antoinette or a Charlotte Corday marching beside what appeared to be a genuine beggar. Giant papier-mâché heads on human shoulders turned this way and that, mopping and grinning at the onlookers, fantastic dragons made up of three or four men inside a cloth body fell over their own feet and collapsed at other people's. Tableaux on horse-drawn floats were elaborate, grotesque, some beautiful. On one cart, in the setting of a cardboard proscenium arch, Commedia dell' Arte characters postured – a bent whiskered Pantalon, a hugely padded Scaramouche, an Arlequin in a chequered tunic and a cocked hat with a long-nosed black mask. On his knee perched a masked Columbine, her face heavily painted, short skirts, frilling out to show most of a pair of fine sturdy legs in crimson stockings. As the float passed she flung kisses to the spectators, then turned to shower some on Arlequin, laughing.

'Who are they?' Laura asked. 'Actors?'

'How should I know, my dear? Just Parisians. People out to enjoy themselves before a fast they have no intention of keeping. Are you cold? Would you rather go in?'

'No. It's very amusing.' Amusing was one of her new, smart words. Another tableau was passing their window; the one bearing Fanchon and Fanchette had turned the corner of the street, out of sight.

Chapter Twelve

LAURA WAS LEARNING, AND GROWING UP. She had changed a great deal in these last months, since they had been living in the private suite of l'Hotel Mars, in the Champs Elysées. The Mars was expensive, exclusive, impersonal – just the place for a man who disliked fixed residences. It had once been a mansion, and their rooms bore all the signs of past grandeurs. There, among long mirrors, elegant spindly furniture and exotic plants, Deryck had watched Laura turn from a raw, eager, Cockney girl to a young lady, if a rather guarded one. The winter he would otherwise have spent in cold English country houses or extremes of tropic temperature he had devoted to her education.

First of all had come her maid, Nanette. The frivolous name belied that quiet and responsible young person, plain and efficient, who had served a noblewoman for many years and been displaced at her sudden death. Laura at first resented having Nanette at her side day and night, helping her to dress, looking after her wardrobe, laying out evening clothes, even – most delicately – correcting some *faux pas* of hers. But she came to concede that Nanette was always right, and that life would have been very difficult without her. Then there was Madame Aymé, whose name Laura came to regard as a joke, since it was impossible to imagine anyone being bold enough to make amorous suggestions to her. She was tall, pale, and bony, very like the French idea of a typical Englishwoman. Every day she called at precisely the same hour to instruct Laura in etiquette, reminding her pupil just a little of that long-ago teacher who had blamed her for the Valentines and the kissing games.

'*Non, non, non*. How can I make you understand? You encounter a gentleman in the street. You have met him briefly, say, at the house of a mutual friend or at a ball. Do

152

you bow to him?'

'Well, I suppose it would be only polite . . .'

'*Non, non, non*. Unless you have been introduced it would be unconventional, *pas comme il faut* at all. Now, you are invited to a fashionable luncheon party. Do you take off your hat on arriving?'

'I think you keep it on,' Laura ventured hesitantly.

'Ah ha! In France, no. So, the ladies are more at their ease. But you must make quite sure you are *bien coiffée* and will not transform your head into a bird's nest when removing the hat. Now: your parasol.'

'Pardon?' Laura had never owned one.

'*Votre* pa-ra-sol. *Ou peut-être votre parapluie*. When calling upon a friend, you would abandon it in the hall?'

Laura said that she would leave it in the umbrella-stand, only to be sharply corrected. That, said Madame, would be a sign that she intended a long stay. They progressed from the arrival at the house to that fraught thing, the meal, at which, in theory, Laura chose every wrong implement and way of wielding it, and came out of the inquisition with a very low score. She was no more successful when it came to the matter of deportment.

'*Non, non, non*. You slouch, you lounge, you cross your legs, *quelle groissièreté*. Be proud of *la poitrine*, repress *la derrière*. Make the neck very long, *très lo-o-ongue*, so that the head seems small and fragile.'

Laura dreaded Madame's daily arrival, always hoping that Deryck would arrange some appointment which would prevent the lesson. The thought of that voice, that glacial eye, and the sharp cane with which Madame emphasized her statements spoilt the delicious flavour of coffee and croissants served in bed by Nanette, and not shared by Deryck, who rose unfashionably early and went riding in the Bois each morning. But he would never let her off. He saw the slow but gradual improvement in her, the graceful movement and carriage she had always owned refined and perfected, the gauche gestures modified or eradicated altogether.

Then there were the French lessons, also daily, given by a small pince-nez'd person only too glad of a change from the horrors of governessing. At first Laura found them dreadfully difficult, despairing of ever being able to speak the language at all. As for the grammar, she gave it up completely; she had never made any sense of English grammar, after all. But practice worked wonders, and Mademoiselle Perrot was clever enough not to bother her with tenses and participles and all their complexities, so that she soon found herself saying the right thing without thinking. Every morning a French newspaper was brought to her with breakfast, and Deryck would lightly quiz her later about its contents. She found the items in the main either boring or incomprehensible, her efforts to remember them bringing a rueful smile to his face.

'I'm afraid I'm not very clever,' she said helplessly.

'It doesn't matter, *chèrie*. And how would you say that in French?'

'*N'importe pas*. No – *n'importe*.'

'Good girl.' He patted her, as one might an intelligent dog, and she was grateful. So long as she pleased him, nothing mattered, not the rigorous coaching of Madame Aymé nor the columns of almost meaningless print. For she was utterly fascinated by him, only half-alive when he was not there, physically enslaved so that his lightest touch thrilled her.

His love-making was something for which neither the affectionate caresses of Jim Broadbent nor the clumsy lungings of Fred had prepared her. Experienced in the reactions of women of every kind since his first housemaid at the age of fourteen, he knew to a hairsbreadth what to do and when to do it. He was never violent, only now and then giving an exciting hint of strength he would not use. He was not sentimental, yet expressed in words and touch an admiration which flattered and charmed and made Laura feel a thousand times more of a woman than she had ever felt – more beautiful, more alluring, the fire in her burning at his command with a steady flame or a roaring blaze that left her shaken, weak, utterly fulfilled.

Yet he never said 'I love you'.

There were other lessons beside Madame Aymé's and Mademoiselle Perrot's. When Deryck suggested to her that she might learn to sing, she laughed.

'But I can't. I mean, I've no voice. I've never sung.'

'Never?'

'Well. Round the piano, of course. Not ours, because Ma –

my mother never had us taught, but . . .'

'All young people sing. I've heard you – did you think I hadn't? You sing about the hotel. After we've been to the opera, you sing. Olympia's song – Marguerite's jewel song. You have a good, true ear.'

'But what use is it, to sing? Nobody's going to invite me to perform at l'Opèra, are they?'

'No, not that I know of.' He twisted a ringlet that brushed her neck round his finger. 'But music is an accomplishment, and an additional charm.'

So it became about that little Monsieur Jacquelin, grey and bowed, with large watery eyes and a voice so soft that Laura often had to ask him to repeat his words, taught her to sing scales and control her breath, and to memorize frivolous little *bergerettes* and drawing-room *chansons*. After a timid attempt to teach her to read music he abandoned the idea. Within a month she could render 'Maman, dites-mois', 'Rêve d'automne', and 'Le Baiser' to Deryck's satisfaction and the polite applause of the company he invited. So charming, the Parisians, so amiable and sympathetic, beautiful women of all ages and men who might or might not be married to them but squired them most gracefully and paid Laura just the right compliments without in any way giving Deryck the slightest cause for jealousy.

With them she rode, very nervous at first, on the gentle roan Châtaigne to whom Deryck had introduced her very early one morning, when few riders were about in the Bois. To her townie's eyes he had looked the size of an elephant, and once hoisted on to his back she had been very much inclined to scream and demand to be put down. But somehow Deryck's soft words of encouragement had soothed her as well as the horse. The sway of Châtaigne's leisurely walk had been agreeable, and the wind through her hair exhilarating, so high above ground, learning that the least touch on the reins would slow the horse down or stop him altogether. Sooner than she had thought possible, she was enjoying herself, learning the relationship between the horse's movements and her own. When she had ridden out on a few mornings Deryck took her to be measured for a habit, almost as tight-fitting as her own skin, of midnight blue melton cloth with a white cravat at the high-fitting neck, a saucy little hard hat softened

155

by a twisted veil of chiffon, and brown gloves, almost matching Châtaigne's coat, of the finest leather.

'Very seductive,' was Deryck's comment. 'How odd that when a woman dresses like a man she should appear most feminine. Just one of the facts of life. Tomorrow I shall show you off.'

'But I can't ride properly yet!'

'Wearing that, you will. Keep your back straight, ride with a long rein, remember that the horse wants to do what you want him to do. Yes, tomorrow we'll walk and trot, and canter the day after that, and then if the weather holds we'll breakfast at St Cloud.'

The weather held, to give them a fine soft start to the day, Paris veiled in early mists, a legendary city, mysterious and beautiful. On the road to St Cloud they met only farm-carts coming in with produce, drovers, a few workmen. On the outskirts of the forest the others joined them, friends of Deryck's, some already known to Laura, rich sophisticated young people. The sight of them made her nervous again; Châtaigne might not obey her, she might suffer a ridiculous fall. Yet Deryck had been right – the superb habit lent her confidence. Gradually, as they trotted on the springy turf, she began to relax, and when Châtaigne joyfully followed the other horses into a canter, exhilaration flowed into her blood. She was almost sorry when they reached the spot appointed for their picnic breakfast, an open glade between great trees, through which the sunlight filtered. And there, served by footmen who had travelled down in a coach, they drank strong, delicious coffee, and ate croissants and brioches miraculously kept hot, some of the men taking cold meats as well. Laura thought she had never tasted anything so delicious.

As they sat on the grass, carefully protected by groundsheets from the dew, she reflected that they must look like a picture, one of those pastoral scenes in the Louvre, where Deryck occasionally took her for the good of her soul. All young, some noble, short arrogant men, handsome plump women, all dark-eyed, dark-haired, dark-skinned, herself the only blonde. In one of those rare flashes of realization which fix a moment in the memory forever, she knew the dizzy joy of being the focus of all eyes, of admiration, desire and envy, as though the mastery of horsemanship had opened a door, and admitted her to the place where Deryck wanted her to be. She felt his pride in her, as warm as the sun's rays, and threw him a smile of acknowledgment and triumph. Who had once said something to her about begging the passing moment to stay, because it was so beautiful? But she thought in French now, and the words would not come back.

That night Deryck took her to the Comédie Française. They sat, alone, in the Circle box to the left of the stage, framed between two of the great caryatids who carried the ornate roof on their heads. Laura knew that she shone out like a star against the dark of the box. She wore for the first time a wonderful gown Deryck had had designed for her, white chiffon gathered above an under-dress of mingled pastel colours that shifted and changed as she moved, like the facets of a diamond. There were diamonds in her hair, a modest wreath of stones interwoven with flowers which seemed real, though they were of silk. When the lights went up at the interval she saw, without appearing to see, many opera-glasses trained on her. Sometimes Deryck touched her arm, sometimes her hand – little proprietorial gestures that charmed her out of the boredom she had felt during the Molière play. His pride in her was like a tangible thing.

They dined at the Pré Catalan, among wealthy men and glittering women whom Laura knew to be courtesans; contrasted with them, she realized she appeared virginal. But there was nothing virginal in her response when, much later, he dismissed Nanette from her bedroom and himself unhooked the lovely elaborate dress and gently drew it down from her shoulders to lie in a shimmering heap on the floor. He had never possessed her so impatiently or so ardently, even fiercely. When at last he released her she lay still, waiting for him to say the words she wanted to hear. Surely he would say it now: I love you, Laura. I want you for my wife.

But to her disappointment he left her side and slipped into his silk dressing-gown, tying its cord in front of the long mirror, as though even in *deshabillé* his appearance mattered. Then he said, 'Goodnight, my dear. By the way, we leave for London on Friday.'

Laura sat up. 'London? But why? For how long?'

'For as long as the Season lasts. The end of June, perhaps – at least until London gets unbearably hot and people start to drift away. July, I should think.'

'But . . . I was enjoying Paris so much.'

'Paris has seen enough of you for the moment – we mustn't let it become bored. Do you know what they call you? *La Diamantée*, the lady of the diamonds. It's time London found a name for you to match it. Oh, and Laura.' He came back to the bedside and touched the pendant she always wore. 'Don't you think it's time you stopped wearing that rather inadequate little ornament? I'm very proud of you, you know, and it hardly does you justice. What about letting me replace it with something worthier? Another diamond, if you like, or something more original.'

She covered it protectively with her hand. 'But it's a very good one. My father said so, and he knows about jewellery. Besides, I promised him I'd wear it, and . . . and I may never see him again.' Her lip began to tremble and she realized with horror that she was going to cry, something she had never done in Deryck's presence. She sensed that he would dislike it intensely, and hastily turned her face away from him, managing to say, 'I'm very tired, Deryck. Goodnight.'

When he was gone the tears came. Tears of disappointment because he had not said what she had longed for him to say, even on this night when she had pleased him so much. 'I'm very proud of you.' Hardly a declaration of love, yet surely he must love her, to have spent so much time and money on her improvement, never to have looked aside at another woman. Couldn't he see that the only diamond she wanted from him was one set in a ring? 'I wouldn't even ask for that,' she sobbed into her pillow, 'only for a wedding ring . . .'

A sudden thought dried the tears at their source. How could Deryck marry her, when she was already married to Fred? The marriage had been so empty and meaningless that it had gone from her mind, forgotten like the 9-carat ring she had long ago put away. Surely such a union was not strong enough to keep her away from Deryck? He was so wealthy, so clever – he could find a way to end it, if she could only bring herself to speak to him. Tomorrow she would try . . .

But when tomorrow came he was away on business, and the apartment a frenzy of packing. Nanette was to accompany her to England, her tutors were dismissed. She could never have imagined being sorry to see the last of Madame Aymé, yet she was aware of that formidable lady's concealed disappointment at being turned away from a good situation for an uncertain future, teaching spoiled and tyrannical children and young girls who would mock her looks. Even sadder was the parting from Mademoiselle Perrot. 'You have been such a good pupil, madame. I will never have such another. I would like to have continued and make you a perfect Frenchwoman.'

'I'll never be that, mademoiselle, but if anyone could have done it, you would have worked the miracle.' The little woman had been paid off and was dressed for the street; Laura saw that her shabby dress had been turned at the collar and cuffs, and that her gloves were threadbare. Impulsively she pressed a 100-franc note into the governess's hand and refused thanks. When it came to saying goodbye to Monsieur Jacquelin she had another one ready, and was saddened to see the tears spring to his eyes. He had not been well paid, considering the luxury of the suite, and had certainly not expected a present, even from the beautiful girl who would never make a Patti, with her sweet, slight, very English voice, but had taken his instruction patiently and worked at her lessons. He resolved to pray for her, living as she did in a state of mortal sin.

It was a shock to Laura to find that she was not to share a roof with Deryck in London. He was to take up bachelor chambers in Albany, Piccadilly, while she had been assigned a rented house in Mount Street, Mayfair, with Nanette and a colourless woman, Mrs Eager, as housekeeper and chaperon. The house was very small, a mere bandbox squeezed in between two tall ones; after the spaciousness of their Paris home it looked depressingly poky. The furnishings were pleasant enough, not luxurious, showing unmistakable signs of wear. Laura took an immediate dislike to the place.

'I shall miss you so much,' she told Deryck. 'I don't want

159

to live alone, or at any rate with Mrs Eager. Eager, indeed! She looks as if she couldn't say boo to a goose.'

'She won't be required to deal with geese, only with undesirables – people I wouldn't want you to receive. The Mrs Eagers of this world have an unerring eye for them.'

'But if I lived with you, *you* could deal with the undesirables – whoever they may be. Why can't I, Deryck, why?'

He put his hands on her shoulders and looked down at her.

'Because, my dear child, this is London, my home ground. In Paris I'm a foreigner and may do as I please, but here I must be seen to be respectable, whether I am or not. It's a frightful bore but there it is, the mamas will cut me if they think my way of life isn't quite the thing, and one can't afford to offend the mamas.'

Because, of course, they had daughters, and entertained hopes of rich unmarried young men; one didn't have to be worldly-wise to understand that. For a second the question she longed to ask him hovered on her lips: could he not arrange a divorce for her? Then they could be together without reproach, and he would be free of the mamas and their censure. But there was something in his look that told her to keep quiet, something watchful and forbidding. As if he had followed her thoughts, he said, 'You'll be known as Mrs Diamond, of course – nobody will make enquiries about Mr D., you'll find. Mrs Eager will accompany you when you appear in public, and everything will be quite comfortable and easy.'

'And am I ever to see you?' There was a hint of rebellion in her voice.

'See me? But of course, charming idiot. Why do you think I brought you? One doesn't own something priceless without wanting to show it off. Now make yourself at home, and in the morning I'll take you riding.'

When the door had shut behind him she felt very much alone – more alone than she had felt since the morning he rescued her in Brighton. Slowly she went upstairs. In the fussily decorated, rather stuffy main bedroom Nanette was unpacking.

'Nanette, do you like this house?'

'I have not seen enough of it yet to tell, madame.'

'Oh yes, you have – quite enough. Come now, you're so

good at knowing whether things are right or wrong. What do you think a about it?'

The maid folded a garment neatly and added it to a pile of others.

'Since you ask me, madame, for myself I don't like it. *C'est trop usé.*'

'*Usé*, yes. It does feel like that, as though it had been through a lot of hands. Perhaps fashionable London is full of houses like this, but I've never been in one before.'

'It would have been more *convenable* if Monsieur Deryck had put you into a good hotel suite such as we had in Paris. Or even a cottage on the estate of a friend.' Nanette was opening and shutting drawers with unaccustomed noisiness. 'Even the servants' rooms are not good. Two cold attics, one room in the basement next to the kitchen, more suitable for storing food or firewood. One will accommodate oneself, but it is a descent in the world.'

'I'll see what I can do about it. I'm sorry, Nanette. Try to remember we shan't be here long.'

'I hope not, madame.'

Nanette let her mistress's footsteps die away, then opened all the drawers of the dressing-table. One by one she tipped out the things that lurked in them into the tidy-bin: hairpins, a rouge-pad, a little silk bow from a corset, loose powder, a scrap of material. '*Sale putain,*' she said aloud, before lining the drawers with the sheets of clean plain paper she had packed for the purpose. The filthy bitch, to leave her rubbish behind for Madame to find.

Riding in Rotten Row, Hyde Park, was not like riding in Paris. The throng of other riders was bewildering, as was the fact that so many people apparently knew one another, and Deryck, yet none acknowledged her or even looked her straight in the face. It was like riding in a dream, when one is invisible to others; a strange, unfriendly feeling. Laura's mount was a jumpy mare, conscious of her rider's nervousness and doing nothing to soothe it, rolling her eyes and flattening her ears at a loud voice or the near passage of another horse.

'Who are all these people?' Laura asked.

'Everybody,' Deryck said vaguely. 'What one might call the best people. They congregate here, between Albert and Grosvenor Gates. Anywhere else in the park – well, they could be from anywhere, Bayswater, perhaps. This is the choice spot.'

'If they're the best people, I don't think much of their behaviour. The men bow and speak to you, the women don't even look at you, and nobody at all seems to see me.'

'You'll get used to it, my dear. Just Society ways. They may not seem to see you, but they do.'

The mare stumbled, and Laura said, 'Damn.' A passing horsewoman laughed and said something to her companion, who turned his head. Laura flushed with annoyance and tapped the mare with her whip. 'I wish you were Châtaigne, you disagreeable thing. Don't toss your head at me, or I shall get down and lead you, to show you're not fit to be ridden.'

Derek threw her a pained glance. 'Don't talk to your mount, dear girl, it isn't done. Don't want people to think you're eccentric. She'll be more used to you when we ride again this afternoon.'

'This afternoon? You can, if you like. I've something else I want to do – a visit to pay.'

'Really? Do you intend to go far?'

'Greenwich.'

'Ah. In that case, I'll send round the victoria. Hawkins will drive you wherever you want to go.' His tone was cool, and Laura proffered no thanks. They rode toward Park Lane in stiff silence.

At three o'clock that afternoon she stood at the door of her old home.

Chapter Thirteen

DURING THE DRIVE she had been rehearsing what to say when her mother opened the door. The bitter words spoken at their last meeting could never be forgotten, but this time she was prepared, determined to take the offensive, to put her foot in the door if necessary, anything to see her sister and her father. His face had been constantly in her mind since the argument about the pendant, as well as his voice on the day when he gave it to her. Whatever her mother accused her of, she would answer with the truth. She was well-dressed, driving in her own carriage, no longer the shabby creature who had been turned away from the door. Yet her heart beat fast with nervousness as she waited.

But it was Ellie who stood there, staring, only half-recognizing her.

'Ellie! Don't you know me, dear?'

'I . . . Oh, Lorla, is it you?'

Then they were embracing, clinging together, somehow moving into the hall, Ellie crying from shock and joy. Laura drew her into the familiar sitting-room, which now looked so small and humble.

'Come along, sit down, dear. I should have written and not given you such a surprise. But I couldn't wait to see you when I got back to England.'

Ellie was mopping her eyes. 'So you've really been in France? I thought . . . we didn't know what to think. And you never wrote again – why didn't you write? We worried so much. Why, anything might have happened to you, anything.'

'I didn't write because Ma told me, when I called, that you didn't want to have anything to do with me – that you'd finished with me. So I just wrote at first to let you know I was alive, and after that I meant to go my own way and let you forget me. But I had to see you again, Ellie, and it seems you haven't finished with me after all.'

'No! However could you think so? Ma said . . . nasty things.' Ellie looked down at the carpet. 'But we didn't believe them.'

'That I'd gone off with a man? Well, it wasn't quite true, as she meant it, then, but it is now. I have to tell you that. There was nothing else I could do, you see. Do you mind now? Come on, look at me.'

'I don't mind,' Ellie said firmly, 'if it was the best thing for you to do. And Pa won't mind, either, so long as we've got you back. Only tell me all about it, first. Oh, you look so beautiful, and your clothes . . . Princess Alexandra isn't a patch on you.'

'If you'll make me some tea I will.' The strange quietness of the house struck Laura. 'Where's Ma? Why aren't you at work?'

'I haven't been at Ponsford's for a long time. Ma's very ill. At least, it's worse than that. When she turned you away that time Pa was terribly angry. Nobody quite understands what happened, but it seemed that she couldn't face what she'd done, or what she thought you'd done – so she started drinking.'

'*Drinking?* Ma?'

'Yes, I know. When she hardly touched sherry, even at Christmas. She used to go out and buy bottles of gin and brandy, and hide them, and drink herself into a dreadful state. That was why I had to give up work, to look after her. But it was no use, she'd gone too far, and now she's very ill and hardly talks any sense. The doctor says she'll have to go into a – a place, because there's nothing more we can do.'

Laura surveyed Ellie. 'You look as if it was you who was very ill. Have you been nursing her, all the time, night and day – no help? Yes, I can see you have. Your eyes are like black holes in your face and you can't weigh more than a child. It's ridiculous, Ellie. Oh, I'm sorry about Ma, but it's you I care about. Let me think.' If she asked Deryck, surely he would give her some money to pay a nurse, though he had never mentioned her family or invited her to talk about them. It would be the first time she had asked him for money, and it was not for herself. Yet she hesitated. He was so altogether alien from this world, he might not understand or sympathize, or even care. She knew so little about him, even after all their time together; only what pleased him and what offended him.

'I'll see what I can do,' she said. 'We'll work something out. Where is she now – in bed?'

'Yes. The doctor's given me something to dose her with when she gets . . . violent. If she doesn't have it she sometimes hits out and throws things. I've never seen anyone like that. Nobody comes near us any more, Laura, since it started. Nobody but . . .'

'But who?'

Ellie's pale, drawn face flushed. She was not ready to talk about Frank Kenward and the attraction that had sprung up between them in the church, now warmed into love. Every week he came over from Thimblestone to see her, and to sit with the sick woman. He cheerfully overlooked Alice's sometimes outrageous language and behaviour. His very presence seemed to calm her a little, even sometimes to make her smile faintly. He would keep watch beside her, holding her hand when she let him, praying for her in the most unaffected and unparsonical way. Ellie thought that she would have gone mad herself without him. She lived for his visits: the relief from constant nursing and watching, the quiet, contented hour they were sometimes able to snatch, sitting together, her head on his shoulder, as though by their own fireside, Frank talking of parish matters and his parishioners until Ellie felt she had been to Thimblestone and knew everyone there. She would tell Laura about all this, but not yet.

'A clergyman,' she said, 'who very kindly calls on us. Ma's quite good with him. Now tell me what happened to you, Lorla – all of it.'

They were still talking when dusk began to fall and Daniel's key turned in the door. He always came into the house quietly, afraid of what he might find, fearing to rouse his wife and start off one of her scenes.

'Ellie?'

They had not lit the lamp in the sitting-room. In the last rays of a sun now gone behind night-clouds the woman sitting in his own armchair seemed to him like a vision, bright hair, lovely vivid face turned towards him. Paris dress coloured like the heart of a rose.

'Laura. Oh, my darling, is it you?'

As her father's arms went round her Laura knew that whatever he believed she had done, whatever she told him, he would never cast her out.

Deryck was at Mount Street when she returned, and not pleased.

'Where have you been until this hour? I thought you were only making an afternoon call. I'm told you left at three, so what detained you?'

Laura was taken aback. 'Nothing. I went so see my family – there was a lot to talk about. I didn't know you were expecting me earlier.'

'Well, I was, and it was dashed inconsiderate of you to keep me waiting, not to mention putting Hawkins out. Did you imagine he'd drive back to town while you held your precious family conference? A coachman does as he's told, of course, but a four-hour wait in a godforsaken place like Greenwich is going a bit far. I hope the horse didn't catch cold, standing out all that time – he's one of the best in the stable, you know, not just a screw.'

'You'd better go and see for yourself, then. He seemed all right to me – he had a blanket on when I came out to the Victoria.'

'I should jolly well hope he had. Hawkins has been with my family twenty years. Now you can go and get dressed – we're going to a supper party.'

'But you didn't tell me and I've only just come in. I don't want to go out again, Deryck, I'm tired.'

'I said, get dressed. And *pleine toilette*.' He stalked out, and Laura heard him talking to Hawkins in the street. It was obviously no time for telling him about her family situation. During the party, a dull affair given by a middle-aged hostess who addressed her guests with her gaze fixed a foot above their heads, and seemed uncertain who they were, Deryck was his usual social self, introducing Laura to this and that person, bringing her champagne cup and ices. Tired as she was, and still smarting from his anger when she had returned from Greenwich, she showed him nothing but good temper, grateful for his smile; her only friend, even though her family was not after all lost to her. She knew it pleased him that her looks attracted much attention, though the guests seemed rather outside his circle of Society – certainly not so haughty as the riders in the park.

'Who are they?' she was bold enough to ask him, when they were alone for a moment. 'Are they very grand people? You see I only know the French.'

'Oh, they're nothing in particular. The fringe, not altogether *arrivés*. We have to choose our company carefully, you see.'

'I see.' But she was not sure that she did, when in the days and nights that followed she was taken to one function after another at which both hosts and guests were not what contemporary jargon called Quite Quite. There were far more men than women, and such women as were present struck Laura as being what she could only think of as fast. They smoked cigarettes, drank wine freely instead of sticking to the two-glass limit Madame Aymé had imposed on her, and wore rouge and powder. There was a *Punch* joke which had travelled across the Channel and back again, a school-boyish limerick in mock-French:

Il existe une Espinstère à Tours
Un peu vite, et qui porte toujours,
  Un ulster peau-de-phoque,
  Un chapeau bilicoque,
Et des nicrebocqueurs en velours.

Laura had had to have it explained to her, and it had stuck, as had the drawing of a very casual young lady lounging on a gate, the *nicrebocqueurs* which Madame Aymé would have found so shocking, dreadfully evident. But at least she had looked amiable, and so were these ladies and the men who were so free with their compliments, yet never made Deryck jealous. She would have liked him to be a little jealous.

They were always caught up in a whirl of activity: the hated Rotten Row parade every morning, and then whatever Deryck had planned. They were seldom alone together except at night, and not always then. He had his male friends and his clubs. She was taken to two of them, after the theatre, the Bachelors' and the New. Only a few women were present, all actresses. Laura smiled dutifully, accepted the men's compliments gracefully, as she had learned to do, and appeared to be amused at their jokes. Why did Deryck like them, with their loud voices and braying laughs? His own manners were impeccable. Laura had a growing suspicion that she was shut out from a great part of his life – that there was a social world he moved in to which she was not admitted. Because she feared to be pushed farther away from its doors, she put off asking him for help for days. Then, one evening when they were dining at home, she plucked up courage.

'When I went to see my family, Deryck – I didn't tell you then, but my mother was very ill. She's had a sort of breakdown.'

'Yes?' His tone was uninterested.

'My sister has to stay at home and nurse her.'

'That's usual.'

'Yes. But my mother's a very trying patient. It's wearing my sister out. She needs help, someone to take turns with her, so that she can rest sometimes.'

'You're not suggesting that you should oblige?'

'Oh no, of course not. That wouldn't do, and . . .' She was beginning to run out of words. 'I wondered – you give me money for clothes and . . . and things. But it goes very quickly, and I wondered – could you give me some for my sister – to pay a nurse?'

There was a silence in which Deryck took a cigar from a silver case, meticulously prepared, lit it, drew on it, and met her pleading eyes with a cool stare.

'Let's get something straight, shall we? When I took you up I made no promise to provide for your family. They have nothing to do with me and I don't wish to know about them. In fact, I'd prefer you to keep clear of them altogether. They've managed without you so far, very nicely, I'd say. Very well, let that continue. I've spent a great deal of time, trouble and money on you, Laura, and I don't propose to let it go to waste. Do you understand me?'

'Yes,' she half-whispered. With a sinking of the heart she knew that she was beginning to understand him, at last. Behind the handsome face and the suave voice there was coldness and emptiness, and the discovery was more than she could bear. She slipped to the floor beside his chair and laid her head on his knee, her face hidden. He gently turned it towards him.

'Look at me, Laura. You and I aren't going to quarrel, are we? There are things that must be said sometimes, that's all.' He began to take out the hairpins that kept up the elaborately draped and curled pile of her coiffure, releasing it into a golden shower about her shoulders, and she knew that he would not return to his Albany chambers that night.

'Happy now?' he asked.

'Yes.' But it was not true.

Very soon after that she began to sell things. A tortoiseshell comb set with brilliants, an ivory fan, a pair of unworn gloves, a petticoat she seldom wore. He would not miss them, when he had given her so much. Nanette, with French practicality, found a shop in Curzon Market which offered fair prices for high-class goods, and asked no questions. A satisfactory pile of money accumulated in a locked drawer of Laura's desk.

And Mrs Eager, who had her own reasons for keeping an eye on the contents of Laura's wardrobe, watched and noted.

When the heap of coins was large enough Laura waited for her opportunity. It came when Deryck went down to Sussex to visit one of his sisters and the Lythe stud. Laura was expected to remain behind quietly in Mount Street, taking a little gentle exercise in the company of Mrs Eager, attending morning service on Sunday at St Mark's, North Audley Street, sitting discreetly in the park to watch the fashionable promenade. Instead, alone, dressed as plainly as she could, she took the train to Greenwich.

Ellie's face lit up at the sight of her. 'I'm so glad to see you, Lorla. It's made all the difference, knowing you were coming back. Oh, you do look beautiful.'

'Too beautiful for the passengers from London Bridge to Greenwich and all stations to Abbey Wood and goodness knows where, judging by the way they stared. I thought I was going to have my jacket ripped off my back. How are you, dear? And how's Ma?'

'You wouldn't believe it – so much better. She's been almost like herself the last few days. We think it's because the

169

doctor changed her medicine, but whatever it is I'm so glad of it. Oh, it's lovely that you're here. Take your hat off and we'll have something to eat – what have I got now?'

'It really doesn't matter, dear, I eat far too much as it is. Der . . . I don't want to get fat.' She had mentioned Deryck's name in their last conversation, but something stopped her from saying it aloud now. She would keep the present of money to herself until later. It was as though she wanted to keep Deryck and Ellie as far away from each other as possible. Only after they had eaten and talked as though both had been under vows of silence since their last meeting, was the house in Mount Street mentioned. Laura impulsively asked, 'Do you mind, Ellie? About me living there with . . . my friend? Do you thing it's wrong of me to be what they call kept?'

Ellie shook her head. 'Why should I? It's a better way of living than you'd ever have had if you'd stayed here. Some people would call it wrong, but I know you don't live like that out of wickedness. I only wish you could marry him.'

'I wish it, too. At least I think I do, though there are things . . . I can't explain about them. I liked it all better in Paris. Here it's stuffier, and snobbish, and I have tiresome Mrs Eager watching me all the time. And anyway, I *am* married. How is Fred?'

'We never see him. Pa thinks it was because of him you ran away. If they ever meet at Ponsford's Pa pretends he hasn't seen him. I suppose he's still living with his mother and that awful uncle. If only you hadn't insisted on marrying him. But there, what's the use?'

'What, indeed?' Laura sighed. 'I try not to think too much – it doesn't do.'

Ellie glanced up at the ceiling. 'I think I hear Ma moving about. I wonder . . . she's been so different lately. Why don't you come and see her, just for a minute? It might make everything all right between you again.'

'Or it might not. You didn't hear what she said to me last time we met.'

'But she's been so ill since – she must feel different now. Oh, do come up, Lorla. If it seems to upset her you can always come down again. And I don't think it will, truly.'

'You always hope for the best, don't you? Well, all right.'

170

There were sounds behind the closed bedroom door. Ellie tapped and opened it. 'Ma? I've got a surprise for you – you'll never guess.'

Laura faced a caricature of the mother she had not seen for almost a year. Haggard, livid-complexioned, baggy-eyed, her wispy hair quite grey now, hanging loose over a shabby dressing-gown, Alice Diamond stared at her, a slow stare ranging from her head to her feet.

'What – are you – doing here?'

'I've come to see you, Ma. I'm sorry you've been ill.'

'Ill. Yes. I told you – not to come here again.'

'I know, but that was a long time ago.' The air of the room was heavy with something that was not medicine. On the dressing-table stood a green bottle, its stopper off. Ellie saw it, and said gently, 'Oh, Ma, where did you get that? You promised, you know. Let me have it.' She moved towards Alice, who backed away, her eyes on Laura.

'Look at her,' she said in her slow deadly voice. 'Tricked out. In gauds and frippery. The Woman on the Beast. The scarlet-coloured Beast, full of names of blasphemy. And the Woman was arrayed in purple and scarlet, and decked with gold and precious stones and pearls. Having in her hand a golden cup full of abominations, even the unclean things of her fornication.' Suddenly she turned and drank deeply from the bottle, a swift practised swig. Laura whispered to Ellie, 'She's mad. What can we do?'

'I don't know. I've never seen her like this before.' And to Alice, 'Ma, dear, you don't know what you're saying. Laura's just going. Come back to bed, now.' But Alice followed the retreating Laura to the door and through it, lurching and swaying, a dreadful figure, one hand behind her back, her eyes fixed in a glare. 'Harlot!' she shouted. 'Whore! Filthy Jezebel!'

'Go down, Laura, hurry!' Ellie cried. But as Laura turned and began to descend the stairs her mother's hand came out from concealment and flung the wine glass she had been clutching straight at Laura's face. It caught her on the forehead, breaking the skin with its jagged rim. Laura screamed and ran, blood streaming down her face. Before Ellie could reach Alice she had leapt after Laura, overshot the top of the staircase and toppled down the straight steep flight

171

to lie at its foot, unmoving.

Ellie, gasping and sobbing, ran to the bottom after her. Laura stood in the hall, transfixed, her hand to her bleeding face, staring at the distorted figure, its legs doubled under it and the arms flung out.

'Oh, my God,' Laura said. 'Oh, Ellie.' Ellie was on her knees, turning her mother over, gently straightening the limbs, holding up the limp head.

'She's alive. But she's badly hurt. We must get the doctor.'

'I'll go,' Laura said. She dreaded the thought of being alone with the woman who had tried to destroy her.

'You can't – you're bleeding. Let me see.' She mopped the wound with her handkerchief. 'I don't think it's deep but it looks very nasty.'

'Then the doctor can deal with it. He's only two streets away. Don't worry, I'll get there.' She gently pushed Ellie, who was white and trembling, into the spiky hall chair. Ellie caught at her hand.

'There's something . . . will you do something for me?'

'Anything, dear.'

'Well, can you use the telephone? I can't – I've only seen one, Mr Ponsford's, but Doctor Miles has one, I know.'

Laura had, not without difficulty, learned to approach the instrument on the wall which Deryck insisted on her using both in Paris and London. She still shouted into it, unable to realize that the person at the other end could hear normal tones, but at least she was no longer frightened of the new invention. She assured Ellie that she could use one.

'Could you telephone someone? It's my clergyman friend, Mr Kenward. I know there's a telephone at the vicarage – it's Thimblestone in Essex. He doesn't live there but the vicar would get him for me, I mean for you. He made me take the number in case we needed him. I need him now, oh, Laura!' Ellie subsided into uncontrollable tears, kneeling by her mother's body and holding one limp hand. At Laura's urging, she sobbed out the number.

Doctor Miles, elderly and taciturn, was called from his dinner to see Laura. Before she could tell him her errand he has whisked her into the surgery and was bathing the cut on her forehead, dabbing it painfully with iodine, applying a cross of sticking-plaster.

172

'There, that looks worse than it is. What have you been doing to yourself?' He knew of her disappearance, but asked no questions.

'It was a wine glass – Mother threw it at me.' Baldly, she told him what had happened.

'I see. Well, I've been attending your mother, doing what I could, which wasn't much. I'm not surprised she turned violent. Right, I'll come back with you. Funny how these things happen the day there's rabbit pie.' As he reached for his coat Laura, who had been nervously eyeing the telephone, asked if she might use it.

'You mean to say you know how to? You've learned a lot, young lady, wherever you've been hiding yourself. Carry on, there it is.' He checked the implements and medicines in his bag while Laura turned the handle and stammered into the mouthpiece. It still seemed like a miracle to her that human voices answered; the local operator, a far-away country postmistress, a vicar who was slightly deaf but able to comprehend what she wanted. Yes, he would send to Mr Kenward with her message. He was sure that Mr Kenward would be with her as soon as possible. He pronounced a blessing and rang off.

Dr Miles examined Alice Diamond where she lay, then got creakily to his feet. 'Can't tell yet what the damage is. One leg broken, but the neck's all right. Dangerous to move her. Cover her up with blankets, make her as comfortable as you can, don't try to give her anything while she's unconscious. I'm off to get splints for the leg. As for you two girls – I don't want any hysterics.' He was looking at Ellie, who was still shaking and hardly able to speak. 'I always though you were the strong one, the rock, Miss Ellie, but you look to me as though you need some of this.' He produced a bottle of *sal volatile*, and administered a dose of the pungent stuff. 'And one for you, Miss Laura. Shock's a nasty thing. Don't trouble, I'll let myself out.'

Four hours later Alice still lay motionless, deeply unconscious, breathing stertorously, the broken leg now in splints. Her two daughters were watching beside her, Ellie in a kitchen chair, Laura sitting on the stairs, her chin in her hands.

'It was all my fault,' she said. 'If I'd behaved better – if I'd

173

not married Fred, or not run away. Her brain was unbalanced – I ought to have known. She was probably right about me when she said I was wicked. I never bothered to understand her, and now there's nothing I can do for her. Perhaps nothing anyone can do.'

The doorbell rang. With a cry, Ellie flew to answer it, and fell into the arms of Frank Kenward.

Alice Diamond died that night without recovering consciousness. It was Frank who carried the limp body to its bed, went for the doctor, made tea for the shocked family, talked cheerfully and sensibly as though the comforting of relatives were a normal part of his life (which it was), made sure that Laura was accommodated with a bed, himself slept without complaint in front of the kitchen fire. Next morning he persuaded Laura that she must return to her home, about which he asked no questions, and escorted her to the station. Parting from him, she held his hand in both of hers.

'Thank you,' she said. She would have liked to talk to him, of herself and the way she was going and her confused feelings for Deryck, for there was only friendship and kindness in his eyes, without the speculative desire she was used to seeing. But she only said, 'Please look after Ellie for me.'

'I promise you I will.' As the whistle blew and the train began to move he called to her, 'Take care.'

When Deryck returned two days later the cut on Laura's forehead was healing but still obviously a fresh wound. He saw it at once.

'Good God, what's that?'

'I cut myself on a piece of glass. It's nothing.'

'It's enough to spoil your face. I hope you haven't been showing yourself like that?'

So he cared nothing for the hurt, only that people might have seen her looking less than perfect. 'I've been to church, and the shops,' she said.

'I see. Well, I suggest you don't appear in public again until that ugly mark has disappeared – if it does disappear.'

'I shall have to go to Greenwich on Wednesday. My mother has died, and the funeral's that day.'

He looked sullenly angry. 'So you've been there again. Well, go if you must, but you'll wear a veil. And I won't have any more of this family visiting, Laura, do you hear? You know my views on it.'

She came to him and clasped his arm. 'Don't be angry, dearest. I'm sorry I vexed you, but they were in such trouble. They won't need me any more now.'

'Well.' He kissed her perfunctorily, not looking at the scar. 'I was going to take you to Verrey's tonight, but we'll dine here instead.'

'Oh, yes. I'd rather not go out, so soon after poor Mother . . .'

She had said the wrong thing. His eyes narrowed. 'You're not, by any chance, thinking of going into black for a year? Because if so, you can forget it at once. I won't have you turning yourself into a fright and a frump for the sake of a ridiculous custom.'

'But . . . I can't *not* go into mourning, for my mother!'

'And who do you suppose is going to know or care about your mother, in Mayfair? You haven't been boring people with chatter about your distinguished family, have you? So you can keep quiet about it. Damn it, I'm hungry. My sister's cook ought to be put on to feeding chickens.' He pulled the bellrope. 'Now go and put on something pretty and wear these with it.' He produced a pair of long earrings from a jeweller's box, tiny coloured stones set in pinchbeck. Laura thanked him dutifully, full of silent resentment. She had not loved her mother, and her guilt was going to be magnified by Deryck's refusal to let her wear mourning. He was being hateful, and it hurt her to find that he could be so. But to quarrel with him would only bring more insecurity to the shifting sands she felt under her feet. And so she came down to dinner, the earrings swinging, glinting in the lamplight, wearing the dress Deryck liked best, figured silk of dull gold, and smiled and listened to accounts of the hunter that had cost almost a thousand guineas, and the new foal that promised greatness. She had combed a few strands of hair down into a light fringe; if he couldn't see the scar he would forget it.

But deeper and more treacherous sands lay ahead.

Chapter Fourteen

Mrs eager was dissatisfied with her situation. She had got along nicely for many years, by way of introductions and chaperoning young women who were in need of a respectable-looking female as a social watchdog. By and large it had been an easy life with plenty of perks. A flaccid person of low vitality, she enjoyed the stimuli of the fast life led by her ladies, the ornaments and articles of dress she acquired from them one way or another. She did not wear these things, merely collected and admired them from time to time, making up to herself for the few possessions she owned as against her ladies' wages of sin.

But life at Mount Street was dull. Mrs Diamond had no men friends except her protector, and the actresses and demi-mondaines who were the only women she was allowed to know never called on her. She was fond of walking in the streets and the park, but Mrs Eager's limbs were stiffening with middle-age; when they walked she fell behind and suffered silently.

Even more to be resented was the lack of perks. She had been used to pocketing a brooch here, a piece of lace there, from what she found in the drawers and cupboards when she was alone in the house. At Mount Street the sharp-eyed Nanette kept a strict watch over her mistress's possessions; she knew Mrs Eager's type. Everything that had a lock was locked, and the keys were kept on the Frenchwoman's *châtelaine*, swinging beside her neat apron. Things with no lock proved infuriatingly to hold nothing desirable. Yet Mrs Eager knew perfectly well there were pickings to be had if she could only be left alone with them.

She was intrigued to see objects she fancied disappear, one by one. An ivory fan, a comb, a locket, gloves. By pausing strategically on a landing one day she managed to overhear

Mrs Diamond telling Nanette that she felt sure something would fetch a high price – 'the stones aren't real, but very good imitations'. Then Nanette went out, alone. When she came back she went straight to her mistress's parlour, hastily followed by Mrs Eager, who knocked against a chair in her hurry. Nanette was speaking in English: 'He was pleased to buy it, and the petticoat.' Then she paused, and switched to French, baffling the listener. But Mrs Eager had learned what she wanted to know. Things were being sold, presents from Mr Hervey-Downes. He certainly knew nothing of the furtive sales, and wouldn't be pleased. If he were told, it might turn him so much against Mrs Diamond that he would give her her marching orders, in which case the household at Mount Street would be broken up. But Mrs Eager would be praised for her vigilance and recommended to another place, a more amusing one. And she would have got her own back on the doll-faced girl whom she envied as only a very plain woman can. Perhaps he would even claim back his presents and give her something as a reward. Which should she ask for – the garnet brooch, the amber beads?

She chose her moment, and her words, carefully. 'Sir, it's none of my business, but there is something you should know.'

Deryck looked up from the accounts he was checking: Mrs Eager functioned as housekeeper as well as chaperon. 'Yes?'

Mrs Eager coughed genteely. 'It's that things have been . . . going. Personal things of Madam's. I keep an eye on them, though, as I say, it's not my place to do so; but to be quite frank with you I don't entirely trust that Frenchwoman. And sure enough, I've seen her take things out of the house.'

Deryck frowned. 'What kind of things?'

'Small items. Some of them I know you'd given Madam.'

He went straight to Laura. 'What's all this about? I can't believe that Nanette steals. Is Eager making it up, or has something been going on?'

A deep flush coloured Laura's face and throat. 'Yes. But only that I asked Nanette to sell a few things for me. I've got so much – you've been so generous . . . and I needed money. I know what you said. But they needed it so, at home, then.

177

There won't be any more, I promise. Please, Deryck, don't look like that – don't be angry with me.'

For a long moment he stared her down, grim-faced, his pride and his authority flouted. Laura sensed the unmistakable scent of danger. A hair's breadth either way, and she might find herself out in the street, penniless and homeless, rejected without remorse by this man who was not used to having his will crossed.

Then, without a word, he turned on his heel and left the room and, a moment later, the house. She had been reprieved.

But he let her see that a shadow had crept over their relationship. When he returned to Mount Street, after a pointed absence of a week, his manner was coldly casual. He deliberately left it to her to woo him back to good humour, which he bestowed on her like a present to an undeserving child.

Mrs Eager, to her disappointment, heard no more of the episode and received no reward. More than ever, she wished for another place.

The scar on Laura's brow faded to pink, almost invisible, but she kept the becoming fringe, and Deryck began to escort her again. Hot summer days had come now. The Season was in full swing, a pageant of wonderful dresses and hats gracing Ascot Week, gourmet picnics, always with champagne, the glossy horses running their noble hearts out almost ignored in favour of social pleasures, just as the actual cricket played at the Eton and Harrow match at Lord's took second place to massive luncheons consumed in carriages. Laura began to feel that she never wanted to see cold chicken or hear the pop of a champagne cork again. She preferred the evening events: late parties at houses where the hostess was not Quite Quite, laughing, flirting guests on the lawns of villas in St John's Wood, fairy lamps of all colours strung between the trees, iced wine and music, dancing to a Blue Hungarian band, the arrival from their theatres of actors and actresses, a little larger and more highly-coloured than life. At these parties Deryck was in the same world as herself, not separated from her by a social barrier. He laughed, and was charming, and showed her off as his *Diamantée*. Hope sprang up in her again. The shadows of the year had passed, she felt that he

178

was happy in her company, happier than he would have been with one of the starchy young daughters of distinguished mamas who were paraded before him in drawing-rooms where Laura was not welcome.

On a Thursday evening of July he arrived unexpectedly at Mount Street. Laura jumped up to meet him. 'What a surprise, darling! Are we going out?'

'Not tonight. But tomorrow we're going away to the country for the weekend.'

'Oh, how marvellous.' They had never spent a weekend out of London before. She dared to hope that it would be in Sussex, even at Lythe. At last he might be about to introduce her to his family. But to her disappointment he said that it was at a country house near Ascot, with friends of his who took it yearly for the racing season, and were staying on for an extra month. 'You'll enjoy it. The Darringtons are both good sorts and they've some interesting people coming.'

'Interesting? You're looking very secretive. What sort of interesting?'

'Wait and see.' He was smiling, teasing.

'Let me guess. Ellen Terry? Madame Bernhardt?'

'Wrong. Never mind. You're to wear your prettiest frocks – the lace, I think, and the white over blue. You'll need your habit, they ride a lot. And I say, Laura, take your music. They're very musical, they like their guests to sing.'

'*Sing*? But I haven't sung since Paris. I mean, Monsieur Jacquelin would be ashamed of me, I'm so rusty. I couldn't possibly sing in public – please don't ask me, Deryck.'

'I am asking you. There's a piano in the other room, isn't there?'

She laughed. 'Yes, but I can't play it.'

'Then pick the tunes out with one finger. Anything, so long as you can make a respectable noise – or possibly not so respectable. I wish old Jacquelin had provided you with a livelier repertoire. Now, get Nanette busy with packing.'

'Is she to come with me?'

'Of course. Do you imagine any lady arrives at a house party without a maid? I'll be here for you at three o'clock tomorrow – we're going by train, by the way.'

The Darringtons were very much what Laura had grown to expect Deryck's friends to be. Sir Ronald was young, amiable, with a loud laugh and a vacant stare disconcerting to the newly-introduced guest; his wife Doria a pretty creature with a nest of blonde curls, quite obviously recruited from the ballet or the chorus. Deryck told Laura that Sir Ronald's family had refused to meet either of them since the marriage, but Ronald had already come into an inheritance from his grandfather, and in any case could have supported himself easily on his winnings on the racecourse and at the gaming-tables, where his only accomplishment showed itself. But he was genial, and Doria friendly in a patronizing way. Laura enjoyed herself more than usual at the lavish dinner, not following the sporting chatter of the gentlemen on either side of her, but then all they expected of her were smiles and murmurs.

The English country house breakfast was new to her. The dining-room of the lavishly furnished mansion was lined on one side with massive sideboards, loaded with dishes, each one with a silver cover over it. Under the covers were to be found porridge, scrambled eggs, fried bacon, kedgeree, sausages, smoked haddock, devilled kidneys: after that Laura lost track, merely helping herself to eggs and bacon. She was horrified to see how much the young men of the party ate – surely they could never ride, as they proposed to do, after stuffing themselves so outrageously, and swilling the food down with large cups of tea or coffee.

Food, food. It seemed impossible that the human body could absorb a hearty lunch after such a breakfast, and a solid tea with cakes and sandwiches. Heavy rain set in early, imprisoning the ladies in the house, though the gentlemen and their horses braved it. Laura, knowing nobody, felt lonely and out of place. She had hardly seen Deryck since they arrived. As convention decreed, they had been given separate bedrooms on the same corridor, but he had not visited her room. When he came back from riding after tea he disappeared to the billiard-room with Sir Ronald, leaving her to her own devices. She found one of the few comfortable chairs in the huge drawing-room, and sat leafing through illustrated magazines, conscious of the conversation going on round her. At the far end of the room two bridge tables were in full swing, the rest of the ladies content to chatter in discreetly lowered voices. Laura's attention wandered from her magazine as she caught snatches of what was being said on a sofa behind her chair, where a dark head and a brown one were close together.

'Positive, my dear. Gerald bet me a pair of gloves that it wasn't so, but I told him he'd lose.'

'Well, well. It's quite the most extraordinary thing that . . .' Whisper, whisper. 'But if we're not supposed to know, how are we to behave?'

'Oh,' Giggles. 'Charmed surprise, I expect.'

'I do think it's too bad of Doria not to tell.'

'You know what she is – fond of her little joke.'

'Misplaced sense of humour sometimes. What do you suppose . . .' The tones were lowered, but Laura was aware of the two heads turning fractionally in her direction, and knew that she was being talked about.

Doria Darrington was approaching her, a three-cornered catlike smile on her piquant face.

'Quite happy, Mrs Diamond? You wouldn't care for a hand at bridge?' Her voice had the ultra-refinement of the stage, which slipped very occasionally into something like her native Cockney.

'No, thank you. I'm quite happy.' Not true: she was uneasy in the atmosphere of something which pervaded the room like a fog. What was it? Conspiracy, or malice?

'Going to wear something charming tonight?' Doria's eyes were teasing her. 'Whatever it is, I'm sure you'll outshine us all.'

Laura had learned that compliments from women were usually suspect. 'I've brought two gowns. I'm not sure which I shall wear,' she said briefly.

'Oh, do choose the one you like best. I always think one feels so much more ravishing in one's favourite things, don't you?' Doria drifted away, the perfect hostess making sure her guests were not bored. She sat down between the two on the sofa, and more hushed conversation began.

'But it's an open secret, Doria,' said the dark girl.

'In that case I don't need to tell, do I? Anyway, Ronnie would kill me if I did. He's promised . . .'

Laura gave up trying to listen. Whatever the open secret was, she would find out in time.

She chose the cream dress, an exquisite French creation

which subtly complemented the tone of her skin, the plunging bodice revealing her shoulders edged with vivid cyclamen ribbon. As Nanette was putting the finishing touches to her hair Deryck entered, after a cursory knock.

'Aren't you ready yet?' Hurry up, my dear girl. Bad form to keep your hosts waiting. Good, I'm glad you chose that one – less *ingenué* than the other. Must you wear that trinket?' He indicated the small diamond, in its usual place, on her bosom. 'It hasn't even any fire to it.'

Laura looked down. It was, indeed, dull against her skin, a mere lump of glass. For an instant she thought of replacing it with something else, perhaps the necklace of rose quartz that echoed the edging ribbon. Then, with startling reality, a vision of her father's face rose in her mind, seen at the moment of their reunion, and she heard his voice. 'Laura. Oh, my darling, is it you?'

'I'll keep it on,' she said. 'At least it isn't showy, and from the look of them these ladies will be wearing everything but the Crown Jewels.'

A spasm of amusement crossed Deryck's face as he said, 'You think so? Well, perhaps somebody will. Come along, now, or the gong will have sounded before we're downstairs.'

Nanette stood back, her task finished. Her eyes met Laura's in the mirror in a long, grave look. '*Amusez-vous bien*, madame.'

'*Merci*, Nanette.'

The guests were already assembled in the drawing room. As Laura had guessed, they were dressed in the height of fashion, the women sparking in jewels and jewel-colours, the men immaculate penguins. Much wine would be drunk at table, but the aperitif had yet to be invented, though some gentlemen indulged in a furtive morale-stiffener of brandy in their rooms. Again Laura walked into the almost palpable atmosphere of expectation which she had sensed in the drawing-room. Conversations were bright and nervous, laughter shrill, eyes darting towards the door near which the Darringtons were standing with an air of expecting a cry of 'Fire!' to come from it.

But it was a footman in powder and knee-breeches who appeared unobtrusively at Sir Ronald's side and murmured in his ear. Instantly the pair were gone. Couples turned to each other, whispering; Deryck's hand fastened on Laura's arm in a sudden painful grip. As she pulled it away the footman reappeared.

'Baron Renfrew,' he announced portentously to a room which had become uncannily quiet.

Baron Renfrew was not a tall man, yet still gave the impression of being tall. He was broad, even stout, wide-shouldered and thick-waisted. The light brown hair receding from his expanse of brow was compensated by a thick growth of beard, trimmed to a point on his jutting chin, and joined with a sweeping moustache. His heavy-lidded blue eyes, mere slits between pouches, seemed to take in the entire assembly at one glance. Behind him hovered the Darringtons.

An agonized female voice was heard to whisper '*Do we curtsey?*' But almost before the words were out all the women of the party had sunk gracefully to the ground, their skirts spread wide. Deryck gave Laura an urgent push, and she too curtseyed, wondering, in the split second that it took her to copy the others, whether Madame Aymé could have envisaged her pupil in such a situation. For the man framed in the doorway, though he might call himself Baron Renfrew, was unmistakably Edward, Prince of Wales.

As though a herd instinct of hypocrisy had taken them over, the guests surged forward and behaved towards the newcomer exactly as they would have done had he been proclaimed as Royalty. His alias would be respected, that was all. More curtseys were made by the ladies, the men bowed over his hand. Everybody called him 'sir', the statutory first address of Your Royal Highness tacitly dropped. Deryck made his way through the crowd, drawing Laura after him.

'Ah, my boy.' The voice was deep and guttural, slightly German-accented.

'Delighted to see you here, sir. May I present Mrs Diamond?'

The blue slits surveyed Laura from head to foot. The word '*diablerie*' came into her mind; so all-confident, all-conquering might Satan look.

'Charmed,' said Queen Victoria's son. '*La Diamantée*, I presume?'

Deryck smiled. 'You have a remarkable memory, sir.'

'And a remarkable information system. News travels from

183

Paris . . .'

He turned away to speak to someone else. Out of his hearing Laura said, 'Why didn't you tell me? Everybody else knew, I heard them talking. It wasn't fair, Deryck, indeed it wasn't.'

'Nonsense. If I'd told you, you'd have been twittering with nerves. I wanted you to be yourself and make a good impression.'

'Why?'

'Because, my dear, it pays to please one's future sovereign. Come along, they're going in to dinner.' He linked his arm in hers.

The party filed into the dining-room two by two, in order of the ladies' precedence, Laura the lowest in rank among these countesses, wives of knights and lords. Then followed the hostess on the arm of the Prince, whose appointed seat was at her right hand at the head of the long table, clothed in snowy lace, glittering with cutlery of real silver and strewn with fresh flowers. Laura was relieved to be placed too far from the Prince to be in danger of having to talk to him throughout the nine-course meal. She glanced at him often with curiosity, noting that his manner seemed cool towards the lady on his left, and that when she talked to him at any length the heavy lids drooped and the red mouth became sulky. She murmured as much to Deryck.

'That's because he hasn't brought his current charmer.'

'Who's that?'

'Daisy Brooke. Going to be Countess of Warwick when Brooke inherits. A raving beauty and a holy terror. There's some trouble going on at the moment, so – Baron Renfrew – has temporarily left the field. He's evidently bored with the lady next to him. Doria's having to work hard. And you're neglecting your neighbour – don't talk to me so much.'

Laura obediently turned to the man at her side. She had only exchanged a few words with him so far; he seemed to be as shy as herself. He had introduced himself as Otto von Schlager, 'a business man', he modestly said, who had travelled down in the company of Baron Renfrew. In early middle-age, he was clearly Jewish, dark-haired with a neat Imperial beard. His brown eyes were melancholy and his voice almost too soft to be heard through the chatter. Turning to him quickly, she surprised a look of something like wonder on his face as she smiled at him. Smiles were like gold, they won you instant attention.

'Why do they have to give us so much to eat?' she asked, for something to say. 'We don't need it, and the servants seem to take most of it away.'

'I expect they are glad of that, since they eat it themselves downstairs.' His voice also was faintly German accented.

'Oh. Yes, they would. Do you know what that dish is, approaching us?'

'Since this is July, I would guess it to be lark pie.'

'*Lark* pie? You mean they shoot larks?'

'Trap them, I think. They are easy birds to catch.'

'How horrible. Ugh. Poor things.'

'You are not a young lady of the country, I take it, or you would not be so concerned for birds.'

'No, I'm not – I'm from East London, Greenwich.' She was finding this gentle person surprisingly easy to talk to. 'This is the first country house party I've been to.'

'And do you like it?'

'Not very much, so far. I don't know anybody, except Mr Hervey-Downes.'

'Nor I, except Baron Renfrew.'

'Do you know him well?'

The shoulders lifted. 'Not intimately. He is good enough to use me sometimes as a business adviser.' He might have added, as an obliging low interest moneylender. 'He was kind enough to invite me to accompany him here, so that I may enjoy a little fresh air before I return home.'

'Home?'

'To Austria. I go always at this time of year to the Salzkammergut, for my health. I suffer sometimes, you see, here.' He tapped his chest.

'I'm sorry. And does the – what you said – do you a lot of good?'

His eyes glowed. 'So much. It is very beautiful, lakes, mountains, castles, the little houses of the people, the great forests. You would enjoy it, Mrs Diamond.'

'Yes, I think I would. I love Paris and the country round it, – when we were there I used to dream of travelling beyond it, to see what other places were like and if I'd love them as much

185

– but we came back to England . . .'

'You should live on a mountain, I think, in one of our fairy castles, with a lake to sail on and a white horse to ride in your own forests. That is the right life for a fairy princess. And you must be one – *eine Prinzessin des Märchen*.'

She laughed. 'I've never been called that before.'

'Ah, you think I am flattering. You are so often called beautiful, when yet another man tells you so you are bored, you yawn. I can see I have displeased you.'

'No, you haven't, Herr von Schlager. I believe you mean it more than most of them do.' Her glance met his frankly. A waiter loomed over them with the dish of lark pie, which they both waved away. Deryck took the opportunity to say, 'And now may I have the privilege of a word? You seem to be getting on extremely well with your Hebrew friend.' His voice was mocking, and she resented it. He had often spoken before with contempt of the Prince's Jewish friends, but now she knew one, and liked him. He reminded her a little of her father, and of her own Jewish blood. Stung, she replied, 'You can talk to me any time. Had you anything particular to say?'

In fact, he had not. He was watching Baron Renfrew, as they all were, without seeming to do so. He ate of everything hugely, from the bisque soup, through fish, entrées, removes, game and sweets, to ices and fruit. There was a magnum of champagne by his plate; they watched it go down and be replaced by another. Deryck laughed.

'He's having family troubles. His eldest son, Eddy, Prince Collars-and-Cuffs, isn't exactly papa's joy and pride.'

'Girls?' suggested Laura.

'No such luck – boys.'

Laura looked blank. 'What do you mean?'

'Never mind, never mind. But that's why he stuffs himself. The more he has on his mind, the more he eats. The Queen's worse, she employs a shovel, not a spoon. Not pretty manners.'

They certainly were not pretty to watch. Laura was, at a distance, developing a disloyal revulsion for the principal guest. Even without his presence the evening would have been a strain. Deryck's manner towards her was strange, as though she were a child to be watched and chided, not a treasured mistress brought to impress company. Not once since they arrived had she felt cherished, protected, or even admired, until von Schlager had paid her his gentle, hesitant compliments.

The meal was over at last, the gentlemen left to their port and cigars, while the ladies retired to the drawing-room for coffee and tea. The men were not long absent – Baron Renfrew was known to prefer female company. Laura saw von Schlager alone, and set off to join him, but Deryck intercepted her.

'Where are you going? You promised to sing, if you remember.'

'*Sing*? Before – before – the Baron? I couldn't possibly. I told you before we came here. Now it's even more impossible, don't you see?'

He propelled her into a quiet corner, away from the others, and spoke low and dangerously. 'If I asked you to get up on the table and dance, you'd do it, or I'd know why. You must attract attention somehow, so you will sing. You're going to tell me you have no music. But you have – I asked for it to be brought down. The governess has been sent for to play for you.' He snapped his fingers, and a timid-looking young woman in a mouse-coloured dress came forward and seated herself at the open grand piano. Doria appeared, as if on cue.

'How delightful – Mrs Diamond is going to sing for us. Now quiet, everybody, while we choose.'

'But I can't . . .' Laura began. Unheeding, Doria was going through the small pile of sheet music brought from Paris. 'Perfect!' she cried. 'A dear little German song. That should please . . . everybody.' Her eye was on Baron Renfrew, ensconced in a wing chair surrounded by ladies, with yet another magnum of champagne on a table beside him. 'I hope you can hear from there, sir' she called, and with a wave of her arms created a clear space in front of the piano.

Fear filled Laura as though she stood on the edge of a precipice with snakes at the foot of it. She felt her knees shaking and her lips trembling; she would never be able to get a note out. She wished the floor would open and swallow her. Anything, even the end of the world, would be better than having to sing.

Suddenly von Schlager was at her side, very close and speaking very low. 'I long to hear your voice. Don't be afraid. But keep the song very short.'

'All right,' she whispered. 'Thank you.' Her breathing grew easier. The governess played a little prelude, and Laura shut herself off from all of them but von Schlager. The song was an old one, simple, even childish: a lover promising a wayside violet that he would pluck it to give to his Lotte, who would put it in her breast and kiss it.

Blühe, liebes Veilchen, das ich selbst erzog,
Blühe noch ein Weilchen, werde schöner noch.
Weisst du, was ich denke? Lotten zum Geschenke
Pflück ich ehstens dich – Blümchen, freue dich!

Out of the corner of her eye she was aware, with horror, of the royal guest's face, heavy and sullen. Von Schlager, under the pretence of turning a page, whispered, 'He dislikes the German. Quickly, the last verse.' To the evident surprise of the accompanist Laura skipped to it, getting through it in record time.

. . . Bald will ich dich pflücken, ihre Brust zu schmücken.
O dann küsst sie dich, und vielleicht such mich!

There was a polite sprinkling of applause – as much as her school-girlish performance warranted. Doria's face was alight with happy malice. She knew all about the Prince's anti-German prejudice, the result of his mother's passion for everything Teutonic. Laura was poised for escape, but von Schlager had another piece of music in his hands and was putting it in place. 'This,' he murmured. 'Very short and light. He will like it. Quickly.'

It was a French *chansonette*, a cheerful trifle about *bergères* and lambs and love. She knew that she made a better thing of it than of the German song, and was rewarded by the sight of a faint smile on the royal features. Hastily she left the piano and the baffled accompanist. Doria stood in her way, obviously displeased.

'The Baron would like to speak to you.'

Laura stood in front of him, feeling smaller than in her first year at school. But he said amiably, 'Charming. You speak French?'

'Quite well, sir.'

'Good. I like that. It is a civilized language to sing in. Tell me about yourself and France.' He patted a small chair at his side. Laura took it, and nervously answered his questions, aware that she was being mentally undressed, garment by garment, until she sat there without a stitch on above her shoes. Or perhaps he was visualizing her in can-can costume – frothing skirts, black stockings and frilly knickers. Suddenly the interview, or audition, ended. With a snap of his turtle's eyelids she was dismissed, able at last to efface herself.

But not ready to do it. Now that fear had receded, anger took its place. She confronted Doria.

'Lady Darrington, why did you ask me to sing a German song?'

'What on earth do you mean?'

'I mean that you deliberately picked out a song the P . . . Baron Renfrew wouldn't like. It was bad enough having to sing at all, without that. I think it was very cruel of you.'

The fine eyes flashed. 'Really! I find that a very impertinent remark – especially from a person lucky to be here at all.'

'It was not my choice to come here. If it were up to me I'd leave.'

'Delighted if you would, I'm sure!' Doria snapped, her voice for once frankly Cockney.

If she had known it, that delight was in store for her.

Chapter Fifteen

DERYCK STAYED POINTEDLY AWAY from Laura for the rest of that long, tedious evening, ignoring her glances in his direction. He joined a bridge table, leaving her to the attentions of gentlemen who were not so engaged and were getting steadily drunker. It was clear they all belonged to that raffish fringe-world that was all Deryck allowed her. She accepted their often risqué compliments and heavy attempts at flirtation with practised ease, increasingly bored, suppressing yawns behind her fan. Von Schlager had retired. The royal guest was playing baccarat for high stakes, taking no notice of anything else and seemingly unaffected by the champagne.

At last one or two of the older women went to bed, and Laura seized the chance to follow them. She half-hoped Deryck would follow her, though she was so tired that she was relieved when he made no appearance. As soon as Nanette had left she put out the beside lamp and fell instantly asleep.

The opening and closing of the door woke her. In the pitch-dark room the flame of a candle flickered and wavered.

'Deryck . . .' she said, 'how late you are – I thought you weren't coming.'

'It is not Deryck,' said a voice from the darkness behind the candle, a voice that she recognized. Before she had lit her lamp she knew whom she would see. He stood watching her, the ample figure clad in a rich silk dressing-gown of purple figured with gold, the beard jutting out arrogantly above a white stock, and Laura, sitting bolt upright with the sheets clutched to her, stared back, tongue-tied with shock.

'Enchanting, the Prince said at last, 'delightful. Not so much a diamond as a pearl, I should have thought. Tell me, madame, are you about to set a fashion for negligées that reveal the arms and bosom? If so, I shall undoubtedly recommend you for so valuable a service to mankind.' His gaze strayed appreciatively over the flesh revealed by her scanty nightdress, low-cut and sleeveless, small frills of ribbon-threaded broderie anglaise just covering her shoulders. She pulled her two heavy plaits forward over them, conscious of rising anger and resentment. It was bad enough to be wakened from a deep sleep, and by a perfect stranger, however exalted; let alone to be looked over like a prize cow in a pen. He had set down the candlestick and was casually loosening the knot of his dressing-gown cord. In a moment she would be treated to a sight of the royal nightshirt.

'I bought this in Paris, sir,' she said coolly. 'No doubt many ladies wear the same sort of thing in this weather. I'm glad you approve of it. And now perhaps you will leave me. I hope you find the room you were looking for.'

'But this is the room I was looking for.'

'I don't think so, sir.'

His thick eyebrows were drawn together, and the candle-light made sinister shadows under the heavy bags beneath his eyes. 'The slippers were outside the door. I was told I would be welcome.'

'Not by me, sir.' An odious suspicion had flashed into her mind. 'Would you be kind enough to tell me who said such a thing to you?'

'I think you know the gentleman's name very well.' There was no mistaking the anger in his voice, matching her own mounting fury. 'He assured me that you would be *complaisante*, even delighted. Otherwise I should not be here. Come, madame, shall we have a little less coyness?'

'Whoever the – gentleman – was, sir, he had no right to tell you any such thing. Your visit is a complete surprise to me, and not a welcome one, I must say. Would you be kind enough to go now?'

'I see. Evidently a mistake has been made.' He was fastening the dressing-gown cord. 'I apologize for my intrusion. It is not my habit to pursue unwilling ladies. You will perhaps forget the incident.' His tone was as icy as her own.

'Certainly, sir. Goodnight.'

He made no answer, but turned on his heel and left the room, closing the door with practised stealth.

Rage and shock are bad soporifics. Laura lay awake, tossing, for two hours and more. So Deryck had betrayed her, sold her, as he thought, to the royal woman-fancier without even sounding out her own views. She had been brought down to Surrey, paraded, made to sing her silly little songs in order that the Prince would have no excuse for not noticing her; it had all been a masquerade, a pantomime, with herself as the Fool. She felt humiliated, soiled, and above all furious. The birds were beginning to sing and the sky to lighten before she fell into an uneasy sleep.

Nanette seemed to see nothing, but saw everything: the pillow tossed to the ground, her mistress's weary face. 'Something has happened,' she stated, folding and tidying.

'Yes. *Quelqu'chose d'horrible*. I shan't go down to breakfast. Bring me a tray here, please.'

Deryck appeared before she had finished the last of the coffee, grim-faced, standing over her like a boxing referee surveying a fallen fighter. But Laura was by no means quelled. She looked up at him steadily, saying, 'I'm glad you're here. I was going to send for you.'

'*You* were going to send for *me*! That's rich. It should be the other way round, I think. What did you mean by it, tell me that?'

'By what? Do sit down. You look so uncomfortable standing in the middle of the floor.'

'Don't quibble. I know how you behaved last night, and I want to know why.'

Laura arranged herself on the pillows. She was quite calm now, very certain of her ground. 'You mean, why did I send away the gentleman you so kindly invited to my room. I saw the slippers outside – I suppose you took them from my wardrobe in Mount Street, since I don't recall packing them. I sent him away because I didn't like him, Baron or Prince, whatever you care to call him. It was a dirty, sneaking thing to set him on me, Deryck. Fortunately he behaved well, or I'd have screamed the place down and told them all why. Why did you do it? No, don't bother to think of an excuse. You've tired of me, haven't you, and you thought this would be a profitable way of getting rid of me.'

'Profitable!' he spat at her. 'It's been my ruin, that's all, you bitch. He's furious – called me a liar and a cheat.'

'Well – aren't you?'

'Shut your mouth. You ought to have been bloody grateful, a little nothing like you, offered the highest honour in the kingdom.'

'Honour? Not quite the word, surely. Dishonour's more what I'd call it.'

'Dishonour, you! A kept woman, a Cockney tart from nowhere, dependent on me for every piece of bread that goes into your mouth, for the roof you live under, and not even able to satisfy a man in bed. I wasn't doing him a favour, but I was doing you a big one, and you throw it back in my face.'

She was pale and trembling now. 'I'm sorry. I didn't know I was so . . . unsatisfactory.'

'Didn't you? No, you wouldn't, you don't know the time of day. Shall I tell what you're like? A Frenchman I know adores women, can't stand live ones, wilts if they come near him. So he had a Jumeau doll made – life-size, soft and pliable, with certain details that I needn't explain added to make it suitable to his purposes. It doesn't respond but it gives him what he needs, and its face is so pretty that he keeps it in his drawing-room *en pleine toilette* to receive guests and act as hostess. Do you see the likeness?'

'You're very cruel. Now don't say any more.'

'Oh, but I will. Sometimes he amuses his guests – his male guests – by undressing her and letting any who choose sample her charms. Do you know what they do? They . . .'

Laura's hands were over her ears. 'I don't want to hear. I understand perfectly. You just wanted me as a showpiece, and now you're tired of me. Very well, I accept that. But you needn't have humiliated me as you did.'

He laughed sharply. 'There's nothing you can tell me about humiliation. This morning, *before* breakfast, I was sent for and given a sermon that wouldn't have disgraced the Queen. I'm out of favour there, and no mistake.'

'You deserve it! You told lies about me.'

'How should I know it was lies? I don't know you, any more than you know me.'

They stared at each other. Laura knew that it was true. They had travelled together, shared an apartment and a bed, yet she knew nothing of his inner soul and he had never encouraged her to talk about herself. What was between them had suddenly crumbled into ashes, because it had never had any substance. Now there were only two strangers where there had seemed to be two lovers; or perhaps a master and a slave, Laura thought bitterly.

'I shall leave here this morning,' he said. 'The Darringtons have been told I've been recalled to town. They'll know what that means, particularly as every servant in the place will have contrived to find out what happened last night. Don't look so shocked. You haven't found out the ways of an English country house yet, and you'll never have the chance again.'

She sighed. 'When do we leave?'

'*I* leave in half an hour. You may please yourself, of course. They'll hardly wish you to remain under the same roof as the Prince.'

'But – where can I go?'

He shrugged. 'Where you like. But not back to Mount Street, in case you had that in mind. And by the way, you may keep the clothes and trinkets you brought with you. Everything else stays where it is.'

'Ready for the next occupant, I suppose?'

'Naturally.'

Laura got out of bed and went to the dressing-table drawer where she kept her jewellery. From it she took two necklaces, two pairs of pendant earrings, a jewelled hair-comb and a bracelet. For a moment she stood with them in her hands, then flung them down at Deryck's feet.

He laughed, without mirth. 'Which melodrama did you copy that from? Pick them up, and don't be an hysterical fool. Look on them as the wages of sin, if you like.' He stirred the glittering heap with his foot.

'I'm not in the least hysterical – just disgusted. I used to think you were a gentleman.'

'And I, my dear, did my best to make you into a passable imitation of a lady. I didn't realize how much alloy there was left under the silver plating. I thought I was educating you for the life of a successful *poule*, but I failed – because I was dealing with a stupid, prudish little peasant with an eye to matrimony. Oh, don't think I missed that. Well, let me tell you that I hope to go through life without wearing that particular chain; but if I'm ever forced into it I shall choose somebody very different from you, Mrs. Diamond. I should put a wrapper on, by the way – like that you look shameless – hardly your style.' Abruptly he turned and went out, leaving

194

the jewels where they lay.

Laura sat down on the bed, her mind very clear. She had known subconsciously that some such scene would one day happen between them, though she could not have imagined that it would take such an ugly form. There must be something about her which made men abandon her. Here she was, just as she had been when Jim Broadbent had left her in Brighton, with what she stood up in. Now she had a walking dress, a tea-gown, a riding habit, several evening dresses, lingerie, shoes and stockings. And nothing else in the world. Deryck had not even had the grace to let her leave the house with him, but had left her to make what lame excuses she could. Already she saw Doria Darrington's mocking face, and heard the malicious whispers. Somehow she would survive it, and then – what?

She rang for Nanette. The maid looked uncomprehendingly at her, still clad only in the flimsy nightdress, then at the jewels on the floor.

'Will you pick those up, Nanette? They will have to be sold to pay your wages and keep you until you find another place.'

'But . . . Madame?'

'Mr Hervey-Downes and I have had a quarrel. A final quarrel. Now I must make my own way in the world, and I can't afford to keep you on. If you speak to Lady Darrington I'm sure she will recommend you. I shall be very sorry to part with you, but it can't be helped.'

For the first time in her service with Laura Nanette became emotional, her cool blue eyes filling with tears and her sensible face contorting like a child's. She broke into French. It was not possible, M'sieur could not desert Madame like this. Such a beautiful lady, so kind, so amiable! Surely it was just a *petite brouille*, a very small disagreement that would pass, a misunderstanding. The temper of gentlemen was not always easy to understand. In half an hour, perhaps less, M'sieur would return and apologize.

Laura explained that it was not so. 'M'sieur is tired of me, Nanette. He will not return in half an hour, or ever. I must do the best I can. Will you pack for me, please?'

Doria Darrington was engaged with menu-planning when Laura was shown in to her. She waved away her housekeeper and turned on a social smile.

'And what can I do for you, Mrs Diamond?'

'I came to say that I must unfortunately leave this morning, and to thank you for your hospitality.'

'Ah. Called away, too? I thought we should have the pleasure of keeping you, even though Deryck has had to leave us. How curious, he didn't mention it.' The black-fringed eyes snapped amusement. Already tales had been told in the servants' hall and had miraculously filtered upstairs. 'Baron Renfrew will be most disappointed. I hear he was very taken with your singing.' But not so taken with the way you turned him out of your bedroom and made a fool of him, the eyes remarked. Aloud Doria said, 'Will you be travelling by carriage?'

'No, by train. I wondered if you would kindly tell me how I can get a cab to take me to the station.'

'Goodness, I wouldn't dream of it. Porter shall drive you in the dog-cart, if you haven't *too* much luggage.' She pressed the bell.

Laura quickly worked out that she had enough money to tip the man as well as buying her railway ticket. After that . . .

'That's very kind. Thank you.' She held out her hand and felt it briefly touched by the hostess to whom she had been a joke, the object of a little conspiracy which had failed.

Ascot station was almost deserted. Laura, in her finery, was openly stared at by a straggle of passengers and railway officials. She was glad of the company of Nanette, who had refused to ask for Lady Darrington's help. 'I will stay with Madame, as far as London, at least. Then we shall see.' The next train was not due for twelve minutes. The two women stood on the platform, out of the soft driving drizzle. For the first time since her scene with Deryck Laura began to feel the loneliness and peril of her situation. If he had appeared and asked her to go back to him, she would have refused, knowing him as she now did in all his emptiness and cruelty. Yet he had been a protection, an anchor, and now she was a boat adrift.

A porter emerged from the booking hall pushing a trolley of luggage. Behind him, lost in the *Financial Times*, came Otto von Schlager. At her involuntary exclamation he looked up, his lined melancholy face transformed with pleasure.

'Mrs Diamond! You are travelling, too? May I join you?'

'Please do.' She was oddly glad to see him, as glad as if they

196

had known each other for years, as if he were a familiar friend instead of someone to whom she had spoken only a few words at a party. Once in the carriage they sat in opposite corners, Nanette in a third corner, working at the piece of embroidery she carried everywhere.

'I had no idea you were leaving,' he said.

'Nor had I, until this morning.'

'And your companion, Mr Hervey-Downes – he is not with you? Excuse me, I sound too curious. I should not ask questions.'

'It doesn't matter. Mr Hervey-Downes has gone. I shall never see him again,' she added to her own surprise, for one didn't say such things to strangers. Yet she had the odd feeling that in the stuffy, dusty atmosphere of the carriage a bubble of clear air enclosed herself and him, in which they were able to communicate as people do in dreams, with no conventions or restrictions.

'I am sorry,' he said gently. 'Or perhaps I should not be sorry.'

'No.' Suddenly she heard herself telling him the story, from Deryck's first speaking to her in the hotel foyer in Brighton, up to the episode of the night before and the morning's conversation. He listened, nodding occasionally, as attentively as a confessor or a doctor. Nanette appeared to hear nothing of the quietly-told tale, frowning abstractedly over her work.

'That's all,' Laura said suddenly. 'I suppose you think I'm no lady, telling you all this. Well, I'm not – my father's a clerk and my grandfather was a jeweller, and Ma's was a grocer.' She heard her carefully-acquired high-society accent fading away. 'So I'm nobody special, and you'll have to excuse me.'

He nodded gravely. 'It is of no consequence. Only the truth is of consequence. And you are going home to your people?'

'I can't. I couldn't, you see, go back like this.' She indicated her elegant travelling-dress. 'But I shall go back to Greenwich, I never thought I would, but my mother's dead and it won't be so bad. I shall sell these things and be ordinary again. I shall quite enjoy that – being ordinary again.'

He was gazing out of the splash-grimed window, at the flat

fields of Surrey gliding by: grazing sheep, little churches, cottages and handsome villas, trim back gardens, small huddled towns, then country again. At last he said, 'I think you don't know why you have told me your story, Mrs Diamond. It was not for pity – it was not for help.'

'Oh no!'

'I think perhaps that you were telling it not to me, but to yourself. To understand better what has happened to you by saying it aloud, openly. Do you think this is so?'

'I don't know . . . yes, perhaps. It made me see how silly I've been. Not just this time, but before. Because there was another man, the one I ran away with. Does that surprise you – shock you?'

He shook his head. 'It has left no mark on you. You have not been . . . I am sorry, I cannot find the word.'

'You mean you think I still look virginal?' Her laugh was brittle.

'To be cynical does not become you,' he said gravely. 'No, I did not mean that. You appear no less and no more virginal than Botticelli's Venus, who is as pure as the crystal sea that bears her. I mean that your mind is as untouched as your beautiful face.'

'How can you tell?'

'I have studied a little in these things. In Vienna there is a great and new interest in the things of the mind, the dark secret country few men have explored. Some day much more will be known. I have a young friend, a doctor, Sigmund Freud, who has already discovered much . . . Let me tell you what I feel is true, from what you have said to me. I think you seek not for a lover but for a father. It may be that this search is bad, since it has not led you to happiness.'

'A father? What a strange thing to say. One doesn't marry one's father.'

'But perhaps, without knowing it, one may wish to, until one grows up. You seek for somebody, that is certain. Just as I do – but I can never find her again.' From an inner pocket of his coat he produced a leather wallet, wadded with silk, inside it a slender oval case. At a touch it flew open, to reveal a miniature on ivory: the head and shoulders of a young girl wearing the piled curls and high neckline of years ago. The hair was pale gold, the fine-boned face pale too, a faint smile on the lips. Laura said 'She's charming. Your daughter?'

'My wife.'

'I'm sorry. A stupid mistake.'

'To be forgiven. She is very young, and I am so old now. Or I feel it. Does she not look familiar to you?'

Laura studied the portrait. 'No, I don't think so.'

He smiled. 'They say we never recognize ourselves.'

'Oh. You see a likeness to me?'

'A strong likeness. The nose, the dark eyes.'

'My father's Jewish,' Laura said. 'I've been told I don't look English.'

'So was my Minna a Jewess. She has been dead many years. but to me she is not dead, no. Sometimes I glimpse her in a passing face. Images of her, shadows of her. When I look at you, I cannot take my eyes away.'

Laura said impulsively, 'I don't mind how much you look at me. It's not the way other men look, as if I were on sale in a shop window. I'm sorry about your wife.'

The train drew into a battlemented station. 'Windsor,' called the guard, 'alight here for the castle. The train now standing at this platform will call at Datchet, Staines, Ashford, Feltham and all stations to Waterloo.' Laura eyed the bulk of the Round Tower and the airy pinnacles of St George's Chapel without favour. It would be a long time before she would be able to think of the royal family without a shudder. The fat bed-hopping Edward, the cruel Tudor monarchs her mother had so admired, seemed to move in a stiff procession before her, glittering with jewels which merged into one great heap, a monstrous magnification of those she had thrown down before Deryck. The broken night was telling on her, the rocking of the train sending her to sleep. 'Only one diamond left now,' she said, half-aloud, and drew from where it nestled under the collar of her dress the single jewel on its thin chain.

It blazed up at her in a shimmer of colours, rays and points of brilliance that dazzled her heavy eyes. The man in the opposite seat watched fondly as she let it drop and leaned back in her corner, instantly asleep like a child.

Three days later they were in the highlands of Austria.

Chapter Sixteen

THE ATMOSPHERE OF THE STUDIO met Maurice like a palpable thing after the rainy freshness of the street. Cigarette smoke, paint, onions, garlic, dust, Jockey Club perfume. Even when Fanchette was out the essence of her remained. Judging by the silence, she was out now. Maurice had left her in bed that morning, setting out early for a journey to Clichy, on the other side of Paris, to sketch a picturesque ruined chapel as a background to a new painting. Intended for the English market, it was to show a young fugitive nun taking refuge from Henry VIII's despoilers. He had found a model, a pretty, undernourished girl with the eyes of a startled hare. But rain had set in before he reached Clichy, growing heavier until it was impossible for him to work in comfort.

He took off his wet overcoat and hat and unpacked his sketching things, swearing softly at the ruin of perfectly good paper. The rain had got into his shoes, and he set off upstairs to fetch his slippers.

Six shallow steps led up to the curtained-off alcove bedroom. At the foot of them he halted, struck by something unusual in the silence: as though his footsteps were being listened to, hidden from. Thieves? Very quietly he approached the alcove and pulled aside the curtain.

On the wide, low divan bed Fanchette was half-lying, half-sitting. She was completely naked, as was the man beside her, a short, muscular fellow who might have been a coal-heaver or a porter from Les Halles. Maurice thought, dispassionate in the first moment of shock, that he had never seen so much black hair in his life as the two of them displayed. Fanchette's huge eyes blazed alarm and defiance.

'What are you doing back here?' she demanded. 'I thought you'd be out for the day.'

'Evidently. So you decided to spend it profitably. I don't

think I know your friend, do I?'

The man growled and reached for a blanket to cover himself. He was not remarkably clean, Maurice noticed, still calm, just as he noticed the classic beauty of Fanchette's round breasts, the great dark aureolae, more splendid than those of any other woman he had known.

'What's it to you if I amuse myself?' she said. 'The way you're always drawing and painting, I don't get all that much attention. Not doing you any harm, am I?'

'Only cuckolding me. But perhaps you consider that some kind of benefit. May I remind you that I pay the rent here, and that every stitch of the clothes you don't happen to be wearing were paid for by me?'

'Well. I give you plenty back for it all, don't I?'

'"Plenty" isn't enough, Fanchette. When I keep a mistress, I expect to own all of her, while she's mine. It isn't the first time you've handed out a share to somebody else, is it? I knew that, but I've never seen it in action before, and I don't like what I see.' Rage was rising in him, flooding his veins. 'I should beat you, Fanchette, and kick your friend from here to the Châtelet, and from there into the river. In a minute or two I might do exactly that, so I advise you to get up, dress yourself, and clear off.'

The man was already scrambling into his clothes. Fanchette had turned pale. 'Clear off?'

'That's what I said. Get out. Pack your things and leave my studio, and don't bother to come back because you won't be admitted. I'll give you half an hour, and if you're not gone by then I'll chuck you both out myself. I've had enough, do you understand? Now get on with it.'

He ran down the stairs and out into the street, oblivious of the rain and the stares of the passers-by at his hatless, coatless state. Let them think him a maniac; he had never felt closer to the edge of madness. He walked and walked, not caring where, down the Avenue des Gobelins, as far as Ivry, then back along the Quai de la Gare to the Pont Bercy and across it to Vincennes, carried along by rage and self-disgust and the smart of betrayal.

Back towards Paris, he leaned on the parapet of the bridge and looked down into the grey, slow-moving river. Slow-moving like his life, which was creeping towards his thirty-fifth year, and had so far brought him – where? To a certain reputation for conventional portraiture in England, a higher one in France for capturing the ephemeral life of the ballet, the theatre, the circus. To freedom from the mother-sister who had kept him in her power from childhood; to entanglement with a lovely, luscious, amoral dancer, who had never loved him any more than he had loved her. Was he, in fact, another Hoffman, always in love with the wrong woman, always doomed to disappointment? There had been a girl once who had seemed like a light to him: but he had let her go, and she was the plaything of men, perhaps on the streets by now. Lost, like his youth. Words came back to him, sung often, unthinkingly, in his school chapel: 'Turn back, O man, forswear thy foolish ways.' If only it were not too late to turn back. But he knew that it was.

More than two hours had passed when he let himself into the studio. Now it was truly empty, no listeners behind the curtain. Fanchette was gone – her chaos of clothes, her twenty pairs of shoes, her Pierrot doll with the white face of the dead mime Deburau, her boxes of powder and pots of paint. All that remained of her was the heavy perfume on the air, and the mess. Cigarette-ends scattered everywhere, unwashed pots in a tin basin, a month's store of empty wine bottles, a knot of hair-combings by the mirror. He went upstairs, reluctantly, and stood by what had been their bed. Impossible to sleep in it again, even to touch it. He would leave a note for the *blanchisseuse* to wash everything and leave it clean and folded for the next owner of the studio. Downstairs, he wrote a letter to the landlord giving up his tenancy, then began to pack up his paintings and equipment. Next day they could be collected. It was evening before he had finished. Those who saw him in the street, waiting for a cab, swaying on his feet, thought him drunk – but he had touched neither food nor drink since breakfast. As the cab took him towards the hotel where he would spend the night, he was conscious of light-headedness. And of another sort of lightness, as though he had cast off something which had been weighing heavily upon his heart.

A week later he joined up with the Cirque Cossu, a small travelling circus which he had found performing on the southern outskirts of Paris. It toured a few animal acts, but its speciality was a quantity of accomplished tumblers, clowns, conjurers and puppeteers. They accepted Maurice readily, happy to pose for him for the price of a bottle of wine or a pie. All day he drew and painted, and at night slept soundly in the caravan he shared with one of the animal trainers, a boy from Spain who spoke almost no French, impervious to the strong scent of bear which hung about Pedrillo's clothing.

And so, travelling always south-eastwards, they came to the snows of Switzerland, and as autumn began to touch the trees they entered Italy.

At Mantua he said goodbye to them all, for they were bound for Rome and he for Verona. They wished him well, embraced him, kissed him on both cheeks and accepted with grateful tears the sketches he gave them as presents. Emilie, wife of the Strong Man, was particularly languishing; he thanked his new knowledge of himself that he had not yielded to the temptation of her mature charms, or to the twin prettiness of Janine and Janette, the proprietor's daughters, or the sloe eyes and inscrutable smile of Zoë the fortune-teller. On parting she drew one long finger down his cheek.

'So brown and handsome now. With such a look and such a fine beard you can't fail to win many Italian ladies' hearts. And yet I don't know . . . let me see your hand.' She held it tenderly in hers. 'Beware of steel. Yes, I see steel, endangering you.'

Maurice laughed. 'Oh, come, Zoë, we're not living in the fourteenth century, you know.'

'I know nothing about centuries. I only see what I see, and it is that. You seek for something. What is it? A green leaf, leaves? These things come to me in symbols and pictures, and I don't know what they mean . . . Little red fruits, so pretty. And only just out of reach of your hand, if you were to stretch it out. Don't you understand?'

He shook his head. 'It sounds like holly-gathering at Christmas. No, meaningless. Anything else?'

'Venice. You will find what you seek in Venice. I see the name written in letters of gold.'

'But I'm not going to Venice.'

'Then you will – believe what Zoë says. Now give me a kiss

for my prophecy.'

He kissed her, not having to pretend warmth. He felt great affection for these simple, clever people who had given him friendship without complication and experience without regret. Even Bruno, the meek odorous little bear in Pedrillo's charge, seemed to know that he was going, and leaned over the gate of the stall to offer the paw-wave that passed for a handshake.

And so Maurice left the courtyard of the Leone d'Oro, where the circus had been permitted to give a small performance, and Mantua herself, city of *campaniles* rising from the mists of her lakes and swamps, and set out for Verona.

He hardly knew what drew him towards the place, when he might have made his way to Rome, or Florence, or Venice, since according to Zoë it promised him so much. He still saw himself as a kind of Hoffman, chasing the deluding marshlights of women. Hoffman's Giulietta had been of Venice. Yet it was not Giulietta but Juliet whom he sought. From the travelling life of the road he had decided to turn back to the theatre; not the theatre of Paris or of London, but the theatre of Shakespeare. Here he was in Italy, where Shakespeare had surely travelled and found so many of his people. Here he would search for a girl who could be the living, breathing Juliet Capulet of Verona, and he would paint her in her own city, while other artists were wasting paint on the English Ellen Terry, in her forties, and the American Mary Anderson, in her thirties, stiffly robed, posed against stage trappings. Wherever she was, he would find her, the girl whose innocent beauty would cure the sickness Fanchette had left in his soul.

He told the *padrona* of the *pensione* to which he had been recommended that he was in search of the scenes of Juliet's life. A talkative, earthy woman, she was only too pleased to enlighten him. 'So you are here to visit *Romeo e Giulietta*, signore. They all come for that, our guests from all over the world. Sometimes they go away happy, sometimes shaking their heads, depending how much *credenza* they have.'

'I am extremely credulous,' Maurice said.

'That is fortunate, for then you will not be disappointed to find that the house of the Capulets is now an inn, and that the tomb of Juliet is empty. After all, it was many years ago – I forget how long . . .'

'The twelfth century, some say.'

'So long? Well, places grow old, like people, and change. But you must see what there is to be seen, and my Tomaso will be your guide'. A shrill call brought a small boy from the kitchen. 'Round the corner is the Via del Pontiere, where he will show you the *monasterio* where the poor young things were married. It is not very far. Nothing in Verona is very far.'

Even for a short distance Maurice could have done without the presence of Tomaso, who talked very little because he spoke only parrot-phrases of English, but his short legs kept up easily with Maurice's strides. It would have been pleasant to absorb the look, scent and feeling of Verona alone – old *palazzi* and churches, towers of pink and grey and faded ochre against a shot-silk evening sky, a glimpse of medieval ramparts, the spun-sugar gleam of the distant Alps, the River Adige rushing swiftly under the Ponte Aleardi, dark cypresses and bright gardens. Verona might be old, as the *padrona* had said; to English eyes dulled by Victorian building it seemed like a city untouched for at least five centuries. To Maurice, in his mood of longing, it was immensely romantic, the setting for some charming unwritten play that concerned himself, not the long-dead lovers.

Yet when they reached the remains of the monastery, a cloister of Roman arches set round a garden where flowers grew among orange trees and vines wreathed above, excitement possessed him to see what the woman curator who had swiftly deposed Tomaso was about to show him. Down steps, in a little vaulted crypt, she pointed triumphantly to the stone shell, rather like a small horse-trough. *'Ecco la tomba di Giulietta la sfortunata.'* He gazed at it, wanting to ask where Romeo's coffin was ("As rich shall Romeo by his lady lie") and if the statues in pure gold had ever been made. But his Italian was not good enough, and he could only listen while she gabbled on, perhaps telling him that this was the very vault where Juliet imagined herself frenzied among her ancestors' bones. He looked intently into the coffin, trying to see in his mind what had once lain there. A haze of fine gold hair, a fair, imperious young face, still in death . . . The vault struck a sudden chill in him. He thanked the curator, tipped her, and followed Tomaso back into the street, and then to the Casa dei Capelli, Juliet's supposed house.

The orchard and its walls had gone, if they had ever been there; there was only a front courtyard, and the position of the balcony suggested that the most famous love-scene in the world must have taken place in distressingly public circumstances. Tomaso stretched a small arm to point out the sign over the gateway, a hat – *uno cappello*, token of the Capelli family.

On an impulse Maurice went inside the taverna. It was full, noisy and hot. He ordered Valpolicello, dry red wine from the valley beside Lake Garda. Nothing around him suggested that he was in the halls of the Capulets, where Juliet once had taught the torches to burn bright. He was tired and heavy-hearted, telling himself that he had come to Verona on a fool's errand.

But the next day he found her. As though the Fates had intended it, he walked out beyond the old town to where the river wound among meadows and scattered cottages. In the garden of one of these a girl was hanging out washing between two apple trees, still burdened with ripe fruit. The slenderness of her figure and the grace of her movements caught his attention, and he paused to watch. Then she turned, and he saw his Juliet: an oval face of heavenly beauty, dark-eyed and dark-browed, the mouth full-lipped yet pure and childish, the complexion so faint an olive as to seem almost pale. Her hair hung virtually to her waist, straight and shining and dark red, the colour Maurice had imagined to be Rossetti's invention. Yet here it was, living hair, and she a living picture, waiting to be translated into paint.

He advanced and spoke to her in halting Italian. She paused in her work, startled, not understanding his words. He tried again. '*Buon' giorno, signorina. Sono pittore, e io volo, molto, molto faro una pittura di . . .*' Heavens, what a mess he was making of it. The girl smiled hesitantly, showing perfect white teeth, then called towards the cottage, 'Mamma!'

The woman who waddled out was short, dumpy, and looked nearer fifty than thirty-four, her actual age. Her lined face was heavily whiskered about the mouth and chin, and the small amount of hair showing under the handkerchief round her head was coarse and black. It was impossible to imagine

206

her giving birth to the exquisite creature at her side.

She evidently knew as little as her daughter what Maurice meant. He tried sign-language, elaborate pantomime with pencil and paper. Both women seemed baffled, and the mother seemed to be ordering the girl, Maria, inside. Maurice's frantic and incoherent appeals to her attracted the attention of an elderly priest making his slow way past the cottage. The mother hailed him, and in a rapid stream of words explained the situation. To Maurice's relief, the old man nodded.

'*Danese? Francese?*' he asked.

'*Inglese, Padre.*'

'Ah, I speak . . . small English.' His attempts to do so proved this to be only too true, but between them the situation was cleared up, and the priest explained to Maria's mother that the English gentleman was a respectable artist who wished to paint her daughter in a classical character. No, it was not a personage from the Bible, but Giulietta of Verona. This, for some reason, caused the lady to laugh uproariously; Maurice supposed it would be the same if he went to Elsinore and requested to paint someone as Hamlet. But all was well, it seemed. Permission was granted provided that money changed hands and that Maria's mamma was always present to maintain the proprieties. Maurice was not exhilarated by the prospect, but had to agree. He was to return the following day with his painting materials to make the preliminary sketch. But where? The cottage interior proved to be poky, dark, and half-filled with young children who were, incredibly, Maria's brothers and sisters.

The priest offered a solution. The signor was welcome to paint at his presbytery, where his housekeeper would serve as a chaperon (and where, Maurice guessed, any contributions to expenses would also be welcome). Grateful, and even able to find a few Italian words, he took his leave, dazzled by Maria's parting smile.

Back in the town he set out to find the perfect background. The Capulet house was impossible. He might search all the *palazzi* for the right room, and in any case a room was not what he wanted, for Juliet must be alone, and the only scene in the play to fit that condition was the Potion Scene. He fancied her mother would not be enthusiastic about any portrait of Maria featuring a bed; and he wanted to show the girl in her unspoilt beauty and happiness, not transfixed by terror. A church would be the place. Not the little *monasterio*, for that was a ruin. He would look for something better.

A few streets from the pension he found it, an ancient church, rich in Romanesque carvings and paintings. He sat down and worked out the exact place where he would position the figure: by the south doorway, as though she had just entered, on her way to meet Romeo for their wedding. One hand should be on the carved marble of a pillar, the other touching her breast, her face joyful, an excited child's yet something in her eyes speaking of apprehension or doubt. Her cloak should barely conceal the white dress, its hood thrown back to show the full glory of her hair. Against darkness and shadows, the outlines of tomb-figures and the distant glow of votive candles, she would shine out as Romeo pictured her, like a rich jewel in an Ethiop's ear; youth and hope among death-symbols, making the vaulted place a feasting-presence full of light.

When she came for the first sitting Maria was wearing her confirmation dress, white, certainly, but all frills and trimmed with artificial roses, as well as wide gold hoop-earrings. He had not the heart to tell her the outfit was quite wrong, and sketched outlines, ignoring it. The more he looked at her the more he rejoiced in her, and her rightness for his Juliet. She was very slight, her figure hardly developed. When he asked how old she was she replied, '*Quindici anni*'; only a year older than Shakespeare's girl, still a child untouched. He was enthralled by her, fascinated, never having her out of his mind day or night. It was hardly love, for he knew nothing of her, her character or her mind. But neither had he known Fanchette, or Lady Kitty long before her, or beautiful Mrs Hugh-Jones, his first mistress. During those happy sessions at the presbytery, Maria standing so still and patient, every fluid line of her an artist's dream, he thought of carrying her away to England, having her educated and moulded into the likeness of the ideal wife, as some eighteenth-century man had done with a hopeful orphan. She was a peasant, ignorant, of course. But there had been another girl of humble birth, in England, whom he could have taken up and made his Galatea, and he had failed her. Perhaps he might do better with Maria.

The days passed. He sketched first, then began to paint. From the theatre in Verona he hired a white velvet dress of medieval style, trimmed with imitation pearls, which Maria's mother took in to fit the reed-slim body. The result was breathtaking, an awesome realization of his vision of Juliet. To the quiet cackling of the priest's hens in the yard outside, the picture took shape; every evening Maria stole up to inspect it. 'Bella, bellissima,' she breathed; he had never known sweeter praise. He tried to tell her that she was more beautiful than her picture; the priest's housekeeper flashed suspicious looks over the socks she was mending.

But from where she sat she could not see the model's face and the betraying look in her eyes, which was not for Romeo but for Maurice. Maurizio, he had taught her to call him; she murmured it over and over to herself when she was alone. He was so unlike any man she had ever met. The village boys now looked ugly to her, awkward and coarse-featured. They were peasants, and he was a gentleman, un' nobile signore: tall and graceful and yet manly, with such deep, expressive eyes, dark as night yet without the bovine look of her countrymen, and a mouth that could be tender as well as passionate – she knew that instinctively, longing for the moment when she might find out for herself, away from the sharp gaze of the old dragon. And then, he was so strongly-built, yet not thickset like Goffredo and the others.

Everyone expected her to marry Goffredo. Before the coming of the Englishman she had not very much cared whether she did or not. Then she had been a child, and now she was a woman. She could not read, but the priest had told her the story of Romeo e Giulietta, after she had said that to know it would help her to pose better for the picture. And, hearing it, she knew that Giulietta's growing-up had been the same as hers; the moment when she had turned from hanging up the washing, and seen Maurizio there, had been not a bit different from the meeting of Romeo e Giulietta at the Capulets' ball. If only her own story might end more happily! She knew that he admired her – already loved her, perhaps. One day, when the picture was finished, he might ask her father for her hand in marriage, and take her away to the unimaginably wonderful land of Inghilterra, where she would live like a lady, like a queen, and never again have to wash linen or feed goats and milk them. And Maurizio would say proudly to people, 'This is my wife, and also the Giulietta of my famous picture.'

It was almost finished. She was to meet him at the church, and stand in the right place, wearing the dress and cloak, so that every detail might be exact. Maurice walked on air towards Verona from the last sitting at the presbytery, remembering over and over again the promise he had read in Maria's eyes, and the thrilling touch of her little work-coarsened hand as he had helped her to take off the cloak. Surely something·had flowered between them, near-strangers as they were, different as were their places in life. Ah, Juliet, if the measure of thy joy be heaped like mine . . . then sweeten with thy breath this neighbour air, and let rich music's tongue unfold the imagined happiness . . .

He was taken utterly by surprise when he was jumped on as he turned a corner. The assailant was young and strong, so savage and ruthless that Maurice's own strength and old experience of boxing at school, where he had been something of a champion, stood him in very little stead. For a few moments he wrestled desperately, the boy cursing in Italian, Maurice fighting to keep his feet and get a forcing grip on the other. Suddenly he felt a foot hooked round his ankle – that old wrestling trick – and fell heavily, his head crashing against cobblestones with a sickening impact, yet he was still conscious enough to try to rise. But the youth had a knee planted in his chest, hard enough to crack the ribs, and the dark face was fiercely triumphant. Maurice felt a sharp pain at his throat, then burning agony and a rush of blood; and the onset of darkness.

When they found him he was unconscious and bleeding freely, white-faced as a corpse. They carried him to the convent hospital nearby, where for two days the nuns nursed and prayed for him. Then they saw, with thanks to God, that the ugly gash in his neck was beginning to close, and that the windpipe was not severed. The blow had been aimed for the carotid artery, which would have meant his death; but the clumsy angry haste of his assailant had caused the knife to miss its mark.

Word got to the old priest, who came to visit him. Maurice

could hardly speak, but somehow managed to ask if the good father had any idea why he had been attacked, since robbery had not been the motive.

'Ah, my son, I know too well. It was Goffredo, the *sponso* of Maria. I have told him myself that the painting was innocent, mere art, that there was no wooing. But he said that she has often spoken too kindly of you; he was jealous. He is a passionate boy, his father's despair. Now he has run away and he will not return until you are gone.'

Which might be quite some time, Maurice thought, hardly daring to touch his bandaged throat. He was sick of the convent, the calm unworldly faces of the nuns, the distant roofs and towers glimpsed through the window. He felt drained of more than blood – of the last of his youth, perhaps the last of his dreams. Another of Hoffman's Tales was over, and the girl vanished, the curtain down on the act.

As soon as he was judged fit to leave he sent a messenger to collect the painting, and had it packed so securely that there was no temptation to look at it. Gazing in the mirror as he dressed for departure, he thought himself much changed, the sideburns and every vestige of beard gone, his face thin and pale, the suntan faded, grey streaks in the hair at his temples. Yet he looked in some way younger, more vulnerable, as though the wound had been deeper than it was.

Zoë's prophecy had been true – steel had endangered him. He toyed with the idea of trying out her second one and going to Venice, But if romantic adventure awaited him there, he was not ready for it. On a late autumn day he took the train that ran over the Brenner Pass to Innsbruck.

Chapter Seventeen

LAURA SAW OTTO COMING TOWARDS HER and waved. It was growing cold in the gardens of the Kurhaus, and she was becoming tired of the admiring stares she was getting even from the polite residents of this most polite little spa town, Bad Ischl, where she and Otto had been staying for three months before moving on to Vienna. Otto came here every year to drink its famous waters and take the curative sulphur baths at the Kurhaus, a palatial building set like a country manor house in gardens which blazed with colour, even in October, and were always immaculately trim and tidy.

Austria was the tidiest country Laura had seen, and the cleanest. Compared with it, France and England were squalid. Nobody threw litter down, or scribbled on walls, or left rubbish about in piles. Buildings shone with cleanliness, park benches like the one she was sitting on always seemed to be freshly painted; the air was as clear and exhilarating as it must be at the summit of the glimmering alps.

Laura loved it, and the quiet of life after the hectic round of London. Otto disliked large parties and social occasions: Laura learnt that he suffered from a slight heart condition, and was recommended by his doctor to avoid over-excitement, which suited him perfectly. He had many friends in Ischl, mostly people of his own age, sedate and as respectable as Deryck's friends had been raffish. At first Laura had been overawed by them, but as she began to pick up German under Otto's patient tuition her confidence grew. The language was so easy if one forgot about grammar and didn't bother about the gender of nouns, and she already had the feeling of it from the German songs she had learned, without properly understanding the words.

'It is because your family roots are in Germany,' Otto told her. 'The blood remembers as well as the brain. You have a good ear and soon you will have a good accent. At present you have an Austrian one picked up from the servants.'

'Well, that's something. How funny that I can speak French and German now, when I was so stupid at school.'

'That is because at your school they thought you were so beautiful that you had no need to be clever also.'

'Quite wrong,' Laura said. 'If one is beautiful one ought to be *very* clever, so as not to get into scrapes. I've been getting into scrapes all my life. This is about the first time I haven't been in one – thanks to you.'

'If you wish to thank me, *liebchen*, you must practice the Schubert songs. I would like to hear you sing them in Vienna, where he lived and wrote. I hear they have taken him from his grave and re-buried him in the Central Cemetery. Poor Schubert. He will not rest there, it's a bleak place he never knew.'

Otto's life, apart from his work, was music. In the suite at the hotel near the Kurhaus he had a fine Steinway piano, which he played, in Laura's judgment, as well as any professional. He taught her songs: the songs of Schubert and Johannes Brahms, the big genial man who was his near neighbour in Vienna, and the songs of Handel, 'since the English have adopted him, though he came from Hallé'. Laura worked at the songs, not always because she liked them, but to please Otto; she preferred the operettas performed at Ischl's pretty opera house, light pieces full of catchy tunes, Viennese waltzes, Hungarian czardas, passionate gypsy music that stirred the blood. They were like the Sullivan tunes everybody hummed in England, and yet not like them, more sugared, determinedly gay.

He had almost reached the bench where she sat, walking today at a brisk pace, she was glad to see.

'So, here you are, *liebchen*. It was not hard to find you – I went by the backward looks people were casting at you.'

'Yes, and I do wish they wouldn't! I shall take to wearing a veil, I think.'

'And deprive so many of such pleasure? That would be cruel. Come – where shall we take coffee? I'm a little tired of the taste of sulphur.'

'Oh – the usual place. The one near the church.'

It was their special favourite, a small café warmed by a

213

great stove decorated in blue and white, with a cheerful stout proprietor who bade them *Grüss Gott* as he showed them to one of the coveted tables near it. Otto ordered coffee, piping hot, rich with thick cream and sugar, and cakes, the *torten* and *kuchen* that were as much cream and chocolate as pastry. Laura adored them. She supposed they would make her fat in time, but all Austrian women seemed to be fat, unless they were spectrally thin as they sometimes became in old age – which seemed a very long way off.

They would sit at the café table an hour or more, talking quietly, sometimes in English, sometimes, when Laura felt bold, in German, or glancing at the thoughtfully provided local newspaper. Then they would walk back to their hotel through the neat, friendly streets, past shops that sold every kind of chocolate – chocolates shaped like flowers, like pigs or cats, like little people, chocolates decorated with sugar icing or tinsel, chocolates contained in huge boxes whose lids were coloured portraits of ladies as luscious as the contents. There were *lederhosen* for sale in the clothes shops, the short leather trousers worn by young men, the dashing hats with a feather in the hatband which both men and women wore. There were music-shops, where one could buy all the fashionable songs and scores; a photographer who was proud to proclaim himself By Royal Appointment, and to display portraits of Austria's royal family. They had their summer palace only just outside the town, the Kaiservilla. They were there now, the Emperor Franz Joseph, with his bald head, expressionless eyes and sweeping white moustache and side-whiskers; the Empress Elisabeth, at fifty still one of the beauties of the world, with the figure of a nymph and the loveliest face in Austria – though *was* she in Austria, or on one of her safaris round Europe, in search of something, escaping from something? Nobody knew what motivated the strange, sad empress, a gypsy soul at that most formal Court.

Laura always lingered in front of the wood-carver's shop near the church, to look at the images. She was no more religious than she ever had been, but there was something curiously fascinating and touching about the Madonnas and Children who filled the shelves. All were different, Mary sometimes seen as a peasant girl, sometimes a Queen of Heaven, yet always carved with faultless skill and delicacy,

214

expressing in their grace and gently smiling looks the quality of motherhood at its highest. Laura wondered if she would ever be a mother herself. It seemed unlikely, and she could not wish for it in her present circumstances.

Sometimes, when Otto had no morning treatments, they would walk outside the town, along the road that wound beside the dark-green hurrying waters of the Traun, through the meadows to the woods where nightingales sang, towards the dark bulk of the Dachstein that loomed above the little town. Or they would take the steep way that led upwards, among little country dwellings as neat as dolls' houses; or to the tiny cemetery where even the gravestones looked spruce and cheerful, and coffins on their way to burial were attended by small bands of musicians in Tyrolean costume. There were always pleasant things to do in Ischl.

When evening came they either attended the opera or took supper in the sitting-room of the hotel suite, supplied as comfortably as a private house with ornately carved furniture and a great number of pictures, mostly religious and all valuable. 'Art has no religion,' Otto said when Laura asked why he, a Jew, collected Christian paintings, 'and taste no definable limits. If I were to confine my collection to the Old Testament we should be surrounded by blood-sacrifices, battles, and variations on the story of Adam and Eve. Don't you think these are pleasanter? A good deal pleasanter to me than those that festoon your English walls, packs of hounds chasing hares and foxes, or tearing them to pieces, and glassy-eyed personages in silks and satins.'

'I never really looked at pictures. At least . . .' A vivid image flashed into her mind of herself walking through a gallery of naval portraits, and the man who had talked about Lord Nelson, and said that one day he would tell her a story. But the story had never been told and the man had gone away without saying goodbye; why should that matter now, when she was no longer the girl of that spring morning, but quite a different person – and why should a stab of pain still go through her at that small betrayal, when she had been twice betrayed, and more cruelly, since?

She said quickly. 'Play for me. Or I'll sing for you, if you'd like that better. '*Heindenröslein*', or '*Lindenbaum*'?'

At the piano, Otto shook his head, turned the pages of the

Schubert album, and went into the solemn, boding prelude to 'Der Tod und das Mädchen'. Reluctantly Laura began to sing the maiden's plea to the grim spectre of Death to let her be, for she was so young; then Death's answer:

> Gib mir deine hand, du schön und zart gibild,
> Bin freund, und komme nicht zu strafen;
> Sei gutes mut, ich bin nicht wild,
> Sollst sanft in meinem armen schlafen.

The music, funereal and dark, echoed him in a few chords, then died into silence. Laura saw that there were tears in Otto's eyes.

'Oh, why did you make me sing that horrible song? Now you're upset. I won't sing it again, I promise you. I don't even sing it well, it's too low for me. Dear Otto, please don't. Cheer up, just to please me.'

He was smiling again. 'Yes, I know, in England men are not supposed to weep. But we Austrians are an emotional people – sometimes we enjoy being sad. And, *liebchen*, it is not really a sad song. Death tells the maiden he is her friend, not come to hurt her, and she shall sleep softly in his arms. He knows, you see, what he is saving her from – all the pains and sorrows of life, and the cruelty of old age. He comes in kindness . . .'

He was looking at Laura, but she knew that he was seeing someone else; someone whom death had taken, young and fair. Minna. She longed to comfort him, but he seemed not to feel the hand she laid on his. There was no warmer comfort she could offer. In their three months together he had not asked her to sleep with him, or spoken to her in any way but as an affectionate father. She was puzzled and a little piqued, but it was not for her to approach him. And at least here was one man who thought of her as something other than a beautiful face and body. When they parted for the night she kissed his cheek, and he both of hers, in the Continental fashion. She lay awake, wondering, haunted by the song.

At the end of September they left Ischl for Vienna. Otto could no longer neglect his business interests. Laura was sorry to leave the place where she had been happy and at peace, though excited to be going to the great city in its high season. From the train, as it gathered speed, she thought of sleepy, gentle Ischl, and wished urgently that she could stop the train and go back to their dear hotel and unpack, and all be as before.

But it was too late. The train was speeding eastwards, past woods, lakes and mountains, through meadows still gold and green where neat toytown cattle grazed, past the twin towers of the monastery of Melk, ever faster towards Vienna. Then it was slowing down, goods-yards and sidings and the outskirts of a city appeared; they were sliding into a great station, and the porters were calling: 'Wien – West-Bahnhof!'

'Good heavens,' Laura exclaimed, 'they can't have put up Union Jacks for *us*? I mean me?' It could well have been some delicate compliment or a joke arranged by Otto. But he disillusioned her. 'Alas no, though a pretty thought. The flags are for an acquaintance of yours and mine, at present a guest of the Emperor.'

'Not . . .?'

'The Prince of Wales, yes. Don't worry, *liebchen*. I shall see him, but you will not, unless you catch sight of him in procession, which I think not likely – he prefers informality abroad. And my house is hardly next door to the Hofburg Palace.'

His house was in Karlgasse, which ran beside the stately City Museum. It was tall, five storeys high, built of stone and plain-faced, its windows secretive with shutters. Inside Laura was reminded so vividly of the hotel furnishings at Ischl that she realized Otto must carry his decorative scheme around with him. There were the same pictures, or others very like them, the Steinway, cabinets carved with figures and patterns: sombre, moneyed comfort everywhere. The servants were quiet and courteous, needing no orders, it seemed. A maid, Adela, was produced for Laura, who had left Nanette in Paris when they were passing through. She was amazingly efficient and unbelievably swift for a young woman of portly figure. Laura wondered what her own status in the household was supposed to be, but guessed that she would never hear it from Adela, who smiled benignly but scarcely spoke. The food at dinner was perfectly cooked and impeccably served. Otto was only content with the best of everything.

Next day he took her driving. 'Vienna is a temperamental

lady – one must be properly introduced to her or she sulks. She is quite small and tidy, you see, unlike sprawling London or rabbit-warren Paris. Her outer garment is the Ringstrasse, this wide boulevard which the Emperor had built where the old city ramparts stood. It was a grandiose scheme, and don't you think it a grandiose road? Theatres, municipal buildings, museums, and of course cafés, circling the city like a great horseshoe, each tip of the shoe resting on the banks of the Danube.'

'It's very handsome, I suppose,' Laura said. 'but really rather like Paris, whatever you may say, Otto.'

'Ah. If you think so, we will leave the Ring and you shall see that Wien is only herself, and that there is no other like her.' He turned the horse towards a street bordering a park; and at the other end of the street everything was different.

Laura could not have said, to Otto or anyone else, what it was about the old city that overpowered her senses at first sight. It was something like meeting a tremendous personality in a small drawing-room, someone you might dislike or fear or find alluring but never ignore, someone who would change your life. Narrow twisting streets held tall houses of every century from medieval times onwards, except for the present one, crowding conspiratorially together as though whispering about the stranger. Great baroque churches loomed everywhere, named for more saints than Laura had ever heard of; buildings that had been convents or monasteries bore paintings and carvings of still other saints, of the Virgin and Christ. Houses seeming humble enough until one reached them suddenly revealed a glimpse of an ancient garden courtyard. 'The British Consulate,' Otto said of one of them. 'And now I am going to show you something superb.'

From the shadowy tunnel of a street they emerged into an open space. 'The Michaelerplatz,' he said. 'And there is Michael himself.' Laura gasped. Over the portico of the church a drama was taking place in stone. St Michael was hurling Lucifer and his minions out of Heaven, and they were all larger than life and twice as terrifying. At any moment, it seemed, the great falling figure might crash through the fragile roof beneath him and flatten the passers-by. Yet, miraculously poised, he held the position he had held for two centuries.

'You like it?' Otto asked.

'It's frightening. No, fascinating. I don't want to look at it, but I can't look away. I shall keep coming here to see it again.'

He nodded. 'That is how strangers always feel. Now I shall show you more great stone people, the guardians of the gate of the Hofburg.'

From the huge, sprawling medieval palace that was home of the living royal family, he took her to the place that housed the dead ones. The small church of the Capuchin friars in the Neumarkt was plain and modest by Vienna's standards. It was dark inside, with a chill atmosphere sharper than the wintry air of the street. The friar who admitted them to the crypt, watching keenly the money that went into the offertory box, seemed to know Otto well. In the crypt it was colder and darker still, poorly lit by lamps and small lunette windows. Laura was immediately conscious of an overpowering sensation of the presence of death, something far beyond the melancholy of a graveyard.

'They are all here, our rulers from the farthest times,' Otto said. 'In the caskets on the shelves there are the oldest remains, only dust and fragments now. The later ones are properly interred. Don't you think this one beautiful?' He indicated a stone sarcophagus richly carved, emblems, garlands, flowers surrounding the scroll bearing the titles of the dead man. At each corner, almost life-size, was a carven skull, wearing a wreath of roses. Otto saw Laura eyeing them with distaste.

'Don't be afraid of them. They are like Vienna herself. We celebrate Love and Death together, you see: to us they are very close. The skull and the roses, the worm and the crown. Look here, and here, at the beauty of sepulchres.' Laura realized why this place felt like no ordinary cemetery. The dead were not buried, but all above ground, their bones only the thickness of a piece of stone or metal away from the living. Gruesome thoughts and images began to assail her, not normally nervous about such things. A few other sightseers wandered among the tombs; she wished that there were more, and that the light was brighter.

Otto led her through another row of arches to what he called the masterwork of the place. 'The tomb of the Empress

Maria Theresia, mother of kings and queens. Here, you see, she wakes from the sleep of death at the same moment as her husband, the Grand Duke of Tuscany, after fifteen years had separated them.'

The table-tomb was imposingly high, but every detail of the wonderfully vivid sculpture could be seen. Husband and wife, in full Court dress, were half-rising from their stony pillows, their hands going out to clasp each other, their faces alight with surprise and joy, reunited lovers, watched from above by a benevolent airily-clad cherub. Laura was unable to look away; as with the sculpture in the Michaelerplatz, attracted and fascinated as though under the influence of some drug. Suddenly she shivered violently, not from cold.

'Can we go, please, Otto? It's very cold and I should like some tea.'

'But of course. I'm sorry, *liebchen*. I am so used to this place.'

Evidently, thought Laura; too used. Over tea and rich cakes at Sacher's he was cheerful and talkative, enjoying, she knew, introducing her to his beloved city. But he was not the man she had met in England nor the companion of her travels, as though this mysterious, beautiful, sinister city had claimed him back.

In the sunshine of the next morning her tenuous fears vanished; the stone lovers on the tomb faded from her mind. Otto explained that for much of the daytime he would be engaged in business, but that his carriage would be available to take her wherever she liked to go – he had written out a list of interesting places. Laura, scanning it, was relieved to see that no churches were included. 'It would be desolate for you to travel alone,' he said, 'so I have spoken to a friend, Frau Valerie Tisza, who would accompany you with pleasure. But I know that women don't always get on with each other. If you find her not agreeable to you, she will understand perfectly if your first expedition is also your last. You have only to tell me.'

'How kind you are, Otto. Very few men would have thought of such a thing. I hope we shall like each other.'

Fortunately they did, and on sight. Frau Tisza was one of those ageless women who might have been anything from thirty-five to fifty; plump yet shapely, with a round, blunt-featured face, heavy dark eyebrows and eyes more black than brown, and a sweet expression. Laura discovered that she was slightly deaf, more so on some days than others, so that it was advisable to talk to her slowly and clearly. She was a widow, Hungarian born, rich, with plenty of time to spare and an encyclopaedic knowledge of Vienna and its surroundings. With her Laura was to discover the lovely Vienna Woods and the wine-growing villages north of the city, the pretty house at Heiligenstadt where Beethoven had written the sad short testament of his life of frustration – 'he was deaf like me, you see,' said Valerie, 'but quite deaf, so that he could only hear music in his own head. Poor fellow, he saw the church clock, there across the garden, but couldn't hear it strike. How sad an affliction!'

On another day they explored Schönbrunn Palace, to the south of the city, where Maria Theresia had held court in splendid state. The majestic figure awakening on the tomb became a living woman in her portraits, handsome and rosy, powdered hair looped with pearls, sometimes a matron, sometimes a young mother with children round her knees, one a tiny girl who would become Marie Antoinette, the martyred queen of France. The presence that still lingered in her apartments was as strong and impressive as the rooms themselves. 'What grandeur,' Laura said. 'I shouldn't think Austria's royalty today comes up to this.'

'You will know tonight,' said Valerie. 'The Crown Prince is to attend the theatre.'

The Theater an der Wien was packed that night. Royalty was expected, and Johann Strauss himself had agreed to conduct his own operetta, *The Gypsy Baron*. The whisper was that the Emperor might for once condescend to attend. Long years ago Strauss had offended him by publicly conducting 'La Marseillaise', the republican rabble-rousing hymn of which Franz Josef so sternly disapproved, and the Emperor was not of a forgiving nature. The audience chattered and rustled, all eyes on the royal box. In the stalls, Valerie wielded her fan excitedly. 'Soon you will see,' she told Laura.

But when the orchestra struck up the first notes of 'God preserve our gracious Kaiser' the personage who entered with

221

the Crown Prince Rudolf was not his father, but someone at the sight of whom Laura gasped. The Prince of Wales stood to attention beside his cousin until the anthem ended, then bowed and smiled to the audience, who cheered and clapped him. "Wales" was a popular figure.

'You said I wouldn't see him,' Laura whispered to Otto, who shrugged.

'So long as he doesn't see you, *liebchen* – and if he does he may not recall you, though I think it unlikely.

'How stout and elderly your English prince is,' Valerie said. 'But what do you think of ours?'

They were close enough to see him clearly. A young man with a broad head and a disproportionately narrow face, a curiously anxious expression, a huge drooping moustache above a weak mouth and chin. Beside Edward he looked painfully thin, and the elaborate uniform he wore seemed to weigh down his narrow shoulders.

'I don't think him at all handsome. Is he ill? He looks very sickly.'

'But how strange of you! All the ladies here are dying of love for him. He is so charming, so stylish, so . . . ah, dear Frau Diamond, are you sure you don't need spectacles?'

Johann Strauss raised a white-gloved hand. At the summons of his baton the orchestra sprang into life, into the sparkling music which had made him the idol of Vienna. Laura had heard *The Gypsy Baron* before; her mind was only partly on the stage, her eyes constantly straying to the royal box. Would the Prince recognize her? Yet why should he, among so many ladies? When the lights went up for the first interval she held her fan before her face, but after a moment Otto murmured to her, 'The Prince has seen me. He is beckoning me to join him. I must go.'

When he returned just in time for the second act she looked enquiringly at him, but he only smiled. 'I will tell you afterwards.'

At home, over supper, he said that Edward had been most amiable, speaking of his pleasure at being in Vienna, of the splendid hunting he had enjoyed in Croatia and the excellence of the Grand Hotel, where he was staying. There was some discussion of business matters – a loan, in fact. That was all.

What he did not tell Laura was that the Prince's keen-sighted eyes had not missed her. 'So, you rescued the beautiful lady who vanished so suddenly from the houseparty. You were more fortunate than I, my friend. I congratulate you. Is she as delightful as she appears, and don't you admire her Parisian lingerie?'

'I have not seen it, sir. Our friendship is entirely platonic.'

Edward gave his celebrated roar of laughter. 'If I didn't know you for a serious fellow I should think that a very good joke. What's the matter with you – or her? Now I come to think of it, she gave me the very cold shoulder. Have you not succeeded yet?' His voice was loud: Rudolf, talking to friends, turned round with an enquiring glance, and Otto said quickly, 'Things are not quite as they seem, sir. Mrs Diamond is a most virtuous lady.'

'Indeed? Then I can't congratulate you after all. By the way, she might be interested to know that Hervey-Downes, who misled me about her, is laid up. Fell off his mount at the first meet of the season, I hear – broke both his legs. Retribution, eh?'

'Yes, sir.'

Though Laura was not told any of this, she noticed a sadness in Otto's eyes and a quietness in his manner. Something had happened – something had been said to lower his spirits. She didn't believe so little had been said between him and the Prince, in that long interval. Just before the lights had gone down again she had seen the royal gaze rest momentarily on her. He had recognized her, and had said something about her to Otto. She knew men well enough to guess what it had been.

She leaned across the table and put her hand on Otto's.

'You're sad tonight. Why, after that jolly evening? Is it something to do with me?'

'No, *liebchen*.'

'That's not true. Is there anything – *anything*, Otto – that I can do to help?'

'Nothing, *liebchen*. It is I who . . . never mind. So you don't admire our Crown Prince?'

'I think he looks like a skinned rabbit.' They talked casually of things that were not concerned with themselves; then Otto kissed her cheek and went off to his bedroom on the second floor. She had not been inside it, but wondered why he didn't occupy what was obviously a much larger one, judging by its long windows, on the floor below. On her way to bed she was tempted to turn the door handle.

The room was locked.

Chapter Eighteen

Laura read the letter again.

'. . . I wished so much that you could have been at our wedding, but the letter I sent to your Mount Street address was returned, with 'Gone Away' on the envelope. Frank and I thought we should not wait for a year to be married, even though Mother died so recently. The wedding was in Frank's church, and was very quiet indeed, as you may imagine, just Pa and Frank's family, who have been very kind to me. Pa is not to live in Feathers Row any more, and the house is let. He has joined us in Thimblestone in this dear little house, which is home to us already. Oh, Lorla, we are so happy. And what is best, I am to have a baby in the New Year . . .'

She put the letter down, sighing, It seemed that Ellie, the plain sister, was far more blest in life than she, the beauty. Aroused by Deryck to full consciousness of her own sexuality, she found herself now at the height of her looks, leading the life of a nun. Otto, kind affectionate Otto, adored her with his eyes, but hardly touched her and said nothing of love. She felt that he never would. Was he like Deryck, merely one who wanted a beautiful woman beside him to show off to society? It seemed unlike him; and they lived so quietly. Perhaps he was impotent and feared to disappoint her and shame himself.

Or the secret might lie in his marriage. She put guarded questions to Valerie Tisza, who looked uncomfortable and said only that poor Minna's sudden death had been a terrible blow to him. So young and lovely, to die so soon. Valerie looked round nervously, as though somebody might be listening to her next revelation. 'Poor Otto, he was so distracted that he spent some time in the Leidesdorf Clinic. That was where he met Doctor Freud, of course. It's a wonderful place for nervous complaints – all sorts of fashionable people go there. They treat you with electricity, I believe. I shouldn't fancy it myself, but it must have done Otto good, since he's quite well now.'

Or is he, Laura wondered. Is he still just a little mad? She knew Dr Sigmund Freud, that solemn black-bearded young man who sometimes called on Otto just before teatime (Otto kept English customs.) Laura thought that Dr Freud possibly didn't get enough to eat, since he disposed of such a quantity of food, and was slightly shabby. Otto said that he had left Professor Leidesdorf and was now in private practice. The two men shut themselves away, sometimes for as long as two hours, when tea was over. What did they talk about?

Well, brooding on the question would do her no good. As Christmas approached Vienna grew more and more delightful. A thick snowfall early in December cast a dazzling veil over buildings and statues, low ancient roofs and the towering pinnacles of the Stefanskirche. Christmas trees appeared in the streets and in the windows of houses, making a fairyland; children skipped along by their mothers' sides on the way to toyshops. Laura bought a ball of glass that held an exquisite tiny castle; when it was shaken, snow fell in a most realistic manner. It was not perhaps the gift for a new-born baby, but when the eyes of her niece or nephew began to focus it might enjoy the falling of the mimic snow . . .

She went skating at the new Ice Palace with Adela in attendance and tempted the maid out on the ice, amused to see that staid young person become her real age, shrieking and giggling as she scuttered about and lurched into people. Partners appeared from all quarters to take their hands and steady them, often needlessly, and to display their own skill for the benefit of bright eyes. It was impossible not to flirt a little, or to refuse the refreshment offered when one left the rink, impossible not to feel gratified to see, in the daily newspaper, polite appeals.

Will the enchanting blonde lady wearing a grey fur hat and muff, who was gracious enough to accept the hand of a gentleman in brown in partnership on the ice yesterday,

226

and afterwards to take coffee with him, kindly signify to him by way of box – –, this newspaper, when he might be privileged to bestow on her a gift of winter violets.

Otto looked up at her laugh. 'Something amusing?'

'Just a newspaper item.'

'I am glad to hear you laugh. Sometimes I think you are like a caged bird, living here with me.'

'A bird that has plenty of liberty to spread its wings.'

Otto shook his head. 'It is selfish to keep birds in cages. You'd tell me if you wanted more feedom, *liebchen*?'

'Of course. But I don't.' Not freedom . . .

At Christmas the doors of all the churches stood open, despite the cold, their interiors a blaze of lighted candles, joyously golden, and bells rang in the steeples. Then, with the New Year, came in Vienna's carnival season, the *Fasching* which had begun as a round of gaieties which would end when Lent began. Waltzes, masked balls, fancy costumes, laughter and delicious nonsense filled the streets and the houses; but not the quiet house in Karlsgasse. There had been no Christmas tree in the drawing-room, no festal flowers under the great Florentine painting of the Christ Child and His mother. The only visitors had been Otto's brother, Max, and his wife, who lived in a northern suburb. Max was older than Otto, and looked it; a balding swarthy man who seemed to have little in common with his brother. His wife was stout, formidable and silent. Laura sensed their disapproval of her presence in the household. So uncomfortable was the atmosphere that she excused herself early and went to her own room. Much later, she heard sounds of departure, and was drawn by curiosity to open her door enough to hear the voices. Max's wife was speaking.

'. . . an insult to the family to have her here. We've always had a good name, and now this.'

Otto's answer was barely audible. '. . . not what you think, I've told you already. *Es ist ganz unschuldig.*'

A shrill laugh from Luisa, and a growled comment from her husband. Laura shut her door. The situation was all quite innocent, he had told them, and Luisa had laughed. As well she might; on the face of it few people would believe that she was there merely as a friend. She could hardly believe it

227

herself.

The next time Dr Freud called she waylaid him as he left Otto's study.

'Dr Freud, there is something I so much want to ask you – can you spare me a moment?'

He looked surprised, but answered, 'Certainly, madame.' She led him into a small parlour and shut the door. Otto must not overhear.

'I should be so grateful if you would tell me something about Otto – you must know him well.'

'If it is not a breach of confidence.' Freud was guarded.

'No, no, I don't want any details. But he *is* ill, isn't he – in the mind? Unhappy, seriously troubled. There is something very wrong with him. I know this, you see. *I cannot help but know it.*'

She met the dark, probing eyes, which seemed to draw knowledge from hers in the silence that followed. Then he said, 'I believe I see your meaning, madame. It is something you would find difficult to say in words?'

'Very difficult, even in English. In German, more so, I don't speak it well. But . . . is he a full . . . *voll, besetzt* . . . man? For I feel I am being made a fool of. You understand?'

He nodded, slowly. 'I understand. He treats you as an object of beauty. As we all must do.' He bowed stiffly. 'But that is all. There is no question of man and woman.'

'None. A long time ago he called me *eine Prinzessin des Märchen.* That is what I still am to him, a fairy-tale princess, no more. What is the matter with me, or with him?'

The doctor strolled to the window, and back again. 'Shall we sit, madame? I will try to explain to you. Herr von Schlager is my patient, and has been for some years. He was once under my care in the Leidesdorf Clinic, in a distraught state after the death of his wife. The treatments helped him, and he was discharged. But then a relapse came and he asked me to help him. I am a poor man, madame, my practice is hardly enough to pay our rent, and I have a wife and a young child. So I come often to see him, though I knew that my time with him was wasted. I practise, you see, *hypnotismus.* The patient is told that he will sleep, yet his senses will be awake to take in what I suggest to him. If I say that he will no longer think in a certain way when he awakes, then he will not –

perhaps. It is a most interesting system, I have had some remarkable results – complete cures in some cases. But with Herr von Schlager there is an obstacle. What is it?' He shrugged. 'Who knows? I think it is a kind of – *wehmut*. You don't understand me. Well, then, it is a love of death, a fondness for what is past . . . I have the very word in French, *mélancolie*.'

'Melancholy. Yes, I understand that.' Laura's mind went back to the crypt of the Capuchiners, the rose-crowned skulls and dead lovers. 'That is true of him.'

'He is, you see, in love with these things. It is a Viennese trait. He clings to the dead one, and so he cannot give himself to life. He hoards relics . . .'

'So, what must be done?'

'The relics should be destroyed.'

Laura had no idea what they were talking about, but she sensed that he was being as frank as he dared. 'What are they, and how should we destroy them?' she asked.

A guarded glance. 'I cannot tell you. You must find out for yourself.' Their eyes locked, and Laura could not look away from his. She knew that she was being told something insistently, something that could not be said in words. There were points of light in his eyes, perhaps reflection from the street-lamp outside. She stared at them, riveted, suspended in time, until he moved his head, and they were gone.

'I must find the key,' she said, as though the words had been said to her.

'That is right – the key. You are a good subject.' For the first time she saw him smile. She found herself thanking him, bidding him good day, showing him out. Then she went upstairs, thinking hard. What he had put into her mind tied up with what was there already, if she had only remembered it: the locked room that should be the best bedroom, that Otto should have occupied instead of his own, a floor higher. It had always seemed strange, a room that was nobody's, in a house which was very well accommodated to those who used it, every room having a purpose.

She stood in front of it. A solid, panelled door, with a fingerplate and an ornate gilt knob. The two long windows looking on to the street were shuttered, she knew. A determination to get past the door possessed her. Impossible now, while Otto was in the house. Tomorrow she would try.

She made her question to Adela deliberately casual. 'There must be many keys to so many doors.'

'Yes, madame.'

'I have mine, of course. But where are all the others?'

'Frau Grünberg keeps them in the kitchen, by the big cupboard.'

Laura waited for two days for her opportunity, the moment when the housekeeper was at the market and the kitchen empty. Like a practised thief she whipped the heavy bunch of keys off its ring and into her pocket and hurried upstairs. Disappointment awaited her: not one would fit the locked door. But of course. If the room was so secret, Otto would keep the key himself. And it was impossible to ask him for it.

Almost a week passed before the plan she had formulated could be carried out. Otto was away for the day at a conference of bankers. The maids had carried out their daily duties of sweeping, dusting, fire-lighting; *mittagessen* would not be on the table for another two hours. Laura slipped out through the January damp to a shop she had carefully noted in a back street. The locksmith listened courteously to her account of a door that would not open because the key was lost, and of her husband's dislike of seeing tradesmen in the house. The job must be done quickly.

'But of course, madame. It will take only a few moments. I will do it for you myself while my son minds the shop.' He trotted along behind her, a small bowed figure, a gnome in the wake of a princess. Together they slipped into the house and up the first flight of stairs. From his bag of tools he took two or three, knelt and worked silently, as he had promised, for only a few moments. The lock was off, the door free to open. Laura thanked him and paid him. No, he should not remain to replace it, that would do another time.

When he was gone she went in. The room was all in darkness. By the light from the landing she made her way to the windows and pulled back the curtains. The shutters were outside; she opened one window and pushed them apart. Grey light and dank air came into the stuffy room.

Laura drew in her breath sharply, for she was surrounded by people. Three were standing, another seated in a chair. When her eyes grew accustomed to the poor light she saw

230

that there was someone in the bed. Fear took hold of her, prickling the hair on the back of her neck and stopping her breath. She wanted to run out of the room, anywhere, away from the silent presences. With an effort she controlled herself, made herself look.

They were all women. All the same woman, the same pale delicate face and long neck under blonde curls dressed in a fashion some years out of date. The clothes, too, were out of date, their shape subtly different: panniered skirts, swelling hips and tightly-draped knees, giving a fishtail look, no hint of today's padded squareness; all romantic fluidity and grace. One posed in a walking costume of soft blue, with a tiny flowered bonnet perched forward on her chignon. Another was in evening dress, low-cut to show white shoulders and bosom, heavily bejewelled. A third wore fancy costume, the dirndl skirt and laced bodice of an Alpine girl. The woman in the chair wore a simple house-frock, youthfully pretty, in dairymaid style, hair in ringlets on her shoulders.

Laura made herself approach one and look closer. The white skin was wax, delicately tinted, even the fingernails of soft pink. The dark eyes were of glass, the hair from a wig-maker's. She could not bring herself to touch what would be cold and dry to feel.

What lay in the bed she examined last of all. Relics, Dr Freud had said. It was not impossible . . . The still figure covered bosom-high by bedclothes lay as though she had fallen asleep softly and easily, head half-turned to one side, one hand curled on the pillow, the beautiful hair plaited as Laura plaited hers at nights. With a great effort she bent down, fearing almost to breathe.

But the sleeper was another girl of wax. There was dust on her cheek and her white arm. At the edge of the lace wool counterpane that covered her moths had begun their depredations. A faint, sweet, stuffy scent hung about her. Laura straightened up, immensely relieved not to have found a mummified corpse.

She looked round the room ignoring its motionless inhabitants. A large, stately room, the marital bedchamber. A great carved double wardrobe; before looking inside it Laura knew what it would hold, racks of clothes, just as the bow-fronted marquetry chest held delicate lingerie. There were rows of shoes, slippers, a pair of smart riding boots. The dressing-table held creams, powders and perfumes, not arranged in any order, but as though their owner had just turned away from using them. In the dusty mirror Laura caught sight of her reflection, and started from it, so like it was to Minna's waxen face.

Very quietly, as though the sleeper might waken, she went out, pulling the door to behind her. The servants would not be likely to pass the door for some hours, and there was a good chance that they would not notice the missing lock.

When Otto came in, late in the afternoon, she was reading in the salon. She put down the book and waited. He went upstairs. Long moments after, she heard him approaching. There was shock on his face. It was impossible to tell if anger were there as well, since she had never seen him angry.

'Why did you do it?' he said.

'I did it for you, Otto. For us both, perhaps. It was time to break the spell.'

'And if I did not want it broken?'

'The time has come when it must be. Will you come upstairs with me, and we'll look at it together?'

Silently he followed her. On the landing she took the lighted lamp from a table and carried it into the room. It threw flickering shadows on the wax faces, lit sparkles in the blonde curls, and lent an awesome look to the five dummies.

'They are only waxworks, Otto. They are not Minna. In time they will fade and lose their shape and become no more than ugly, out-of-date fashion dolls. Why do you keep them?'

'To have her still with me. Still beautiful, still alive.'

'But she is not alive, Otto,' Laura said gently. 'Where is she buried?'

'In the Jewish cemetery.'

'But you don't believe that she herself is there. What do you believe – that she's in Heaven?'

'We have no Heaven. I don't know what I believe . . . now. Why did you disturb me, and her?' His voice was trembling, as were his hands.

'Because I had to, my dear. You see, you had made a wax doll of me in Minna's likeness, just as unreal as these things. Now, I am alive, and she is not, and you must accept that if

232

we're to have any happiness. You've been living on the dead. What was that you said in the Hapsburg vault? Something about celebrating love and death together, wasn't it? But they're very far apart, you know. Don't you think that all this would frighten Minna – that she wouldn't like it?'

'She wanted to stay alive,' Otto said dully. 'She loved life, and I killed her.'

Laura was shocked into silence. Then she said, 'I don't believe that. You loved her too much.'

'I killed her with love. Our child could not be born, and so after three days and nights Minna died.'

'And the child?'

'The child too.'

Laura went over to the bed and touched the hand on the pillow. 'So cold,' she said, 'and not at all real to the touch. Do you know what I think, Otto? If Minna were alive now she wouldn't look at all like this. She'd be plump and matronly, like so many Viennese women, and her hair would have changed colour a little. And she'd want to wear modern clothes, not these old-fashioned ones. These figures are not at all like her, really, are they?'

He was looking from one to another, as though seeing them for the first time. 'No,' he said in an almost normal voice. 'No, they are nothing. Dolls.'

'Then shall we get rid of them?'

'Yes, Anything you like.' Abruptly he turned and left the room. Laura heard his footsteps going up to the next floor.

She summoned Elena to her own room. 'Elena, I want you to help me with something. I know you're very discreet, and there's nobody else I can trust not to talk about this. Come with me.'

The maid gasped at the sight of the figures, and crossed herself. Laura said briskly 'These are waxworks, of no further use. We are going to take off their clothes and then dispose of them. You start on that one.'

'Yes, madame.' Laura heard her murmur a prayer under her breath as she began to unhook the fastenings of the walking costume. She herself removed the evening dress, relieved to find no lingerie underneath, took off the jewels and laid them aside. One by one the figures were denuded, until they stood in ghostly paleness. Laura intensely disliked handling them, particularly the seated and prone ones, which had to be lifted bodily. At last the task was finished.

'What do we do now, madame?'

'We carry them down the back stairs, separately, each wrapped in something. This will do.' She picked up the motheaten coverlet. 'They are not heavy, and we're both strong. We carry them to the end of the garden and there we burn them. A *freudenfeuer* won't surprise anybody on a winter evening in *Fasching*.'

The task took less time than Laura had imagined, and they only met one servant on the stairs, the houseboy. 'Clearing out rubbish,' she told him; he stared, but said nothing. The pile of pale limbs and tumbled hair looked ghastly by the light of the storm-lantern. Feeling like a murderess, Laura struck a match and put it to one of the wigs. It ignited at once, dry with age. The flames crept along the face, which began to melt. Quickly she went from one point to another, applying matches. The wax flesh lost shape, liquified, one moulded limb running into another. Where it remained stubborn she stuck a lighted candle to hasten the process.

It was done. Nothing remained but a pool of hot liquid, with here and there some glass eyes and unmelted pieces, and a rank smell of wax and burnt hair. 'Go in,' she told Elena 'and parcel up the clothes. Josef can take them to one of the convents near the Ottakring, for distribution to poor people. I'll see to this mess in the morning. And thank you, Elena.'

Otto did not appear at dinner. The manservant said he had gone out. Laura sat up until late at night, waiting for him, wondering if the destruction of his sacred relics had unbalanced him and driven him to frenzy. Only a short walk away was the Donaukanal, its waters anything but beautiful and blue. Then there was the constant carriage traffic in the Ring, hooves rising and falling, wheels rolling relentlessly along. She had interfered with strong emotions, which might lead to catastrophe.

But about eleven o'clock she heard his key in the door and went into the hall. He looked tired, but spoke calmly enough; he had been walking, he was sleepy. He bade her goodnight and went upstairs. Until then she hadn't realized how exhausted she was, worn out with physical effort, nervously drained.

Next morning she took her breakfast in bed. When she came downstairs Otto was gone. She summoned Elena and Gretel the housemaid. 'One of the bedrooms has been shut up and neglected. We are going to put it to rights.' Together they transformed the waxwork room. The windows were opened, carpet, curtains and furniture dusted and cleaned, the bedclothes changed. From the wardrobe and chest of drawers all the garments were removed. 'Take what you like,' Laura told the two girls. 'They are old-fashioned and may not fit you, but some of them may be worth having. Only, don't wear them in this house. The lady they belonged to is dead, and the sight of them might distress Herr von Schlager. Anything you don't need is to go to the convent.'

When they had finished Laura looked round with satisfaction. The room was hardly recognizable. Even the cosmetics from the dressing-table had gone, and the faint perfume with them. A new coverlet of rose-pink on the bed gave a changed tone to the furnishings. Only one detail remained. On Laura's orders the pictures were taken down and exchanged for those from her own room. It was done, the wax wraiths banished. If only it didn't turn Otto against her . . .

But when she led him into it he said nothing at first, only took in the changes, and she knew that he missed none of them. Then he smiled and said, 'It is good. Thank you, *liebchen*.'

'And you're not angry?'

'I am not angry.'

That evening he asked her to wear her best dress. It was low-cut and moulded to the figure, with a small train, grand enough for Court wear. In her hair she wore a jewelled spray, her father's diamond round her neck. The dining-room was ablaze with candles, the table set with silver and bright with the fresh flowers so expensive in January. Otto was immaculate in evening dress, looking younger than she had ever seen him. The meal was sumptuous, champagne served throughout it; at the Hofburg she had tasted nothing better. Then, when it was over, they retired to the salon for coffee. Otto sat down at the piano and played, straying from one air to another, from Schubert to Brahms, then into tunes Laura didn't recognize, lyrical and flowing, waltzes and *zigeunerlieder* and rhapsodies. Perhaps he had never played them to

235

her before, or they had never sounded as they did now.

He shut the piano-lid, came over to her and took her hand. 'Shall we go to bed, *liebchen?*'

On that night, she would never forget, the gentle, melancholy Otto turned to a creature of fire and passion, a passion almost savage that roused her to heights she had not known before. Both deprived, both starved, they took from each other life and joy and refreshment, until they were satisfied.

Otto lit the lamp and surveyed her, propped on one elbow. Gently he touched her mouth. 'Your lip is bleeding. I am nothing but a wild man.'

She held his hand against the cut. 'As if I cared.'

'Most beautiful one. I love you. *"Dein is mein herz, und sollst es ewig bleiben."* Will you sing that to me tonight?'

'Of course.' Schubert's rapturous song of impatience for the beloved. Thine is my heart, and shall be thine for ever. It was not true of herself, she knew, now that their transports had subsided and she was calm. Something had not been there, the touch of the god Eros that alighted only on true lovers. But she was deeply fond of Otto, happy for him and herself; it would have to be enough.

'Free at last,' he said. 'Freed by you from my dearest Minna, as she would wish, and her spirit is free of the sepulchre I made for her. Who told you about it – was it Doctor Freud?'

'Well – he hinted. But I'd guessed something already.'

'He knew, of course. He talked a lot of jargon about traumas and hysterical symptoms, the need to get rid of symbols. He was right, I see that now. But I was deaf and stupid, until you showed me the truth.'

'I'm glad.' She rubbed her head against his shoulder like a cat. 'Glad to have done something for you.'

'I owe you so much, everything. There is one way I can repay you. Will you marry me, *liebchen?*'

Laura sat upright. 'But, Otto – how can I? I'm married already. It means nothing, but there it is.'

'There are ways. Money will do anything, and I know powerful people. In Austria we lose our citizenship if we divorce, but England is not so pious. Leave it to me.' He picked up her left hand. 'And now will you take off that ring, which also means nothing, and never wear it again.' He slipped it off her finger and put it aside. 'You shall have another ring tomorrow . . . today, that is. Would you like diamonds, to match your – what do you call it – *gahänge*?'

'Pendant. No, Otto. I would rather not be *La Diamantée* any more – only Frau von Schlager.' To be safe, to have a place in society, not to be a wanderer through the world . . . When the lamp was out she slept almost instantly.

She woke to hear the sounds that meant the house was awake, and reproached herself for not wakening earlier. Now she would have to await the chance to slip out unnoticed, or there would be talk. She touched Otto's shoulder, whispering, 'Good morning. I must go now, my dear.' Getting no answer, she dropped a light kiss on his cheek, half-turned away from her, but his body was heavy, begining to stiffen. She crawled over him and looked into his face. The eyes were staring open; he was dead, and had been for some hours.

The need for caution was forgotten. She began to scream, running to the door and throwing it open. Within a minute servants were there, clustering round, exclaiming and crying.

Somehow, in the hours that followed, she managed to dress and compose herself. Elena brought her a cup of hot, reviving coffee. A doctor arrived, and asked her questions that ashamed her to answer, but she told him boldly, 'We were to have been married', aware of the disbelief on his face.

'You know that Herr von Schlager had a weakness of the heart? He should not have been allowed to indulge in violent sexual activity.'

There was no reply she could make, no explanation for Otto's years of abstinence and sudden return to virility. Pointedly the doctor turned away to discuss practical arrangements with Frau Grünberg the housekeeper, who made no secret of her enmity towards Laura. She had always suspected this foreign woman of living off her master, and now he was dead, killed by the woman's wicked behaviour. The story of the waxworks had filtered through to her in a garbled way. She would spare no effort to lay the blame where it was due.

Since there was nothing she could usefully do in the tragic house, Laura went out and wandered about the streets, hardly aware of where she went or of the curious glances at her shocked face. The day was cold, grey and wet. Tired of walking, she turned back from the Ring and went into the Karlskirche, the beautiful ornate church of Karlsgasse. A pyramid of candles burnt in front of a painted statue of the Mother and Child. Laura, feeling self-conscious, bought a candle and placed it in its socket, then knelt to watch its steady flame. A Protestant, burning a candle for the soul of a Jew in a Catholic church: what a farce. But it was all she could think of to do for him.

She became conscious that her feet were cold and damp from the rainy streets. It would be as well to change her shoes. Stiffly she rose from the floor and made her way back to the house.

The bell clanged inside the hall without an answer. She pulled it again. This time the door opened. Max von Schlager stood there, lowering down at her.

'So,' he said, 'what are you here for?'

'I . . . I've come back to change my shoes.' He still stood between the hall and her. 'May I come past, please?'

'No. Not now, or at any time. This house is closed to you.'

'But . . . why, what . . .?' She was shocked into stammering. 'I live here.'

'While my brother was alive. Now he is gone and the house is mine. There is no place for foreign adventuresses in it.'

'But . . . we were to be married.'

He smiled grimly. 'Prove it, madame.'

'I can't, naturally . . .'

'Naturally. My wife and I came here as soon as Frau Grünberg telephoned us. We at once made a search for Otto's Will and Testament, and found it where one would have expected it to be, in his desk. There is no mention of you in it. My brother was a very rich man, he could have spared you some trinket if he had cared for you – if only as payment for your services. So be off, before I call the police.' He started to close the door.

'At least let me come in and get my things! All my clothes are there, everything I have . . .' Desperately she tried to push past him, but he caught her arm in an iron grip and flung her away, so that she had to grasp at the handrail to save herself from falling.

'Anything you call yours was bought with my brother's money, and reverts to me. Be off now.' The door was

238

slammed in her face.

Laura stood in the street, staring at the blank face of the door, at the windows shuttered against her. A few hours ago she had been happy, betrothed, her future safe. Now she had nothing, only the clothes she wore, a winter dress and coat and a hat that didn't protect her hair from the rain. In her handbag were a few notes, perhaps enough to buy two meals. Even her wedding ring was gone, taken off by Otto and left on his bedside table. In a stupor she began to walk back towards the church. At least it was warm there.

Chapter Nineteen

THE HOURS OF DAYLIGHT WERE NOT SO BAD. She stayed in the church a long time, looking at monuments, sculptures and pictures, finding a sort of security in the place. Catholics were fortunate, to believe in the power of these smiling statues to help and comfort. A candle, and someone's soul was saved. A contribution to St Antony's box and your lost treasure was found. Pick the right saint and your limp or squint or whatever complaint you had would be healed. Enough supplications to the Virgin, and a barren woman might find her arms filled. Laura thought about that. If her one night with Otto resulted in a child then she was ruined indeed. But surely she would know, some change of feeling would tell her. She put one of the smallest of her precious coins in Mary's box, hoping.

When, outside, the light began to change, she went in search of cheap food. In a cellar *speisehaus* there was a great stove sending out heat, a generous helping of soup and *leberwurst*, appetite-appeasing liver-sausage, for a smaller price than she had known could be paid for food. There were the usual glances at her face and hair, now wet and untidy. She ignored them, staring hard at the print of Prince Eugene doing something sensational at the siege of Vienna, and a list of prices. The time came when she couldn't decently stay any longer.

It was cold out in the street. She thought intently of what she might do, whom she knew. Otto had so few friends, and none of their addresses were known to her. The great Johannes Brahms lived at Karlsgasse 4, as everybody knew, and was a familiar, revered sight. His music, drifting out through the window, was listened to with awe. Otto had had only the slightest acquaintance with him. Doctor Freud lived on the Mariatheresienstrasse; but he was well-known to be very poor. There was an old countess who was some sort of pensioner of the Empress, and lived near the Hofburg, or possibly in it. She had sometimes been to dine and listen to Otto's playing, though obviously as deaf as a post. There Laura's acquaintances ended. Valerie Tisza had gone back to Hungary.

She walked slowly through the rain along street after street, her shoes now in danger of giving out; they were the first she had found in the panic of the morning, not the sensible boots she should be wearing. The streets gave way to trees and lawns – she had reached the Burggarten, so pleasant in the sunshine, now a place of wet grass and bare dripping branches. She sat on a bench and shut her eyes. It must be rather like this, knowing you were going to die and waiting for it. Otto had been lucky.

A voice roused her. 'Now, now, *meine Schätze*. What d'you think you're doing there, darling?' She opened her eyes. A tall young policeman was looming over her, hands on hips.

'I've nowhere else to go.'

'Oho, a foreigner. This isn't a place for naughty ladies, you know. Hadn't you better get going? Up, now.'

'Tell me where, then, officer.' She turned her face towards him, a face of mournful beauty, ashen under the light from a street-lamp. Raindrops bespangled her hair, glittering in the fine threads, making a diamond halo. This was no strayed city prostitute, thought the young officer. A religious man, he furtively crossed himself. He had been brought up on legends of Our Blessed Lady appearing in most humble guise; this might well be another example of Her testing of poor humanity.

He sat down carefully by Laura's side. 'Are you lost, madame?'

'In a way. The only friend I had has died. I have no home, nowhere at all to go. And no money, only a few marks left after buying a meal. It's all been so unexpected, you see.' At the sight of the sympathetic young face her control suddenly broke, and she burst into violent weeping.

'There, there. Now, now. Madame, don't.' He was mopping her face with a large clean handkerchief, trying not to put his arm round her shoulders (though by now he was fairly

241

sure she was human, not divine). 'If you'll trust yourself with me I can take you to a place where you can lodge for the night. It's not grand, but quite respectable. Can you walk?'

'Oh yes, thank you.' She mopped up her tears; after all she was English, and it didn't do to behave like a Viennese. The walk was a long one, into increasingly drab surroundings, but the young man kept up a stream of questions, genuinely interested in the beautiful waif, and determined to turn her mind from desperate thoughts. Vienna had quite enough suicides as it was. She gave him a guarded version of the facts, leaving out her real relationship with Otto. He whistled. 'What you want's a good lawyer. I'd see about getting one in the morning if I were you, madame. There's Herr Frank, just off the Graben, he's well spoken of. Here we are. Not too bad, is it?'

The tall thin house was almost indistinguishable from its neighbours in the badly-lighted, shabby street on the north side of the city. Laura's friend knocked with assurance, went in and spoke to the old woman who answered the door, then drew Laura inside. To her shame, she saw money change hands, and remonstrated.

'I have enough to pay, truly. For tonight, that is. Please let me.'

'No, no, no, it's my pleasure. When you hear talk of our brutal police remember they *can* be helpful. This place isn't on my beat, but I'll look in tomorrow night to see how you are.' He saluted and left, glancing back. If not an angel in disguise, she must surely be a princess . . .

The basement room to which the old woman conducted her was not inviting. There were several pallet-beds made up on the floor, all inhabited bar one, farthest from the stove. Her guide showed her to it.

'That's yours. Put your clothes under your pillow if you take 'em off, then you might just find 'em still there in the morning. All out at six, and a mug of coffee for a bit extra if you want it.'

Laura said 'Are they – these people – all female?'

''Course they are. What d'you think I keep – a brothel? Good night to you.' She took the candle with her. Laura decided to take nothing off but her coat, hat and shoes, and made a damp bundle of them which she jammed between the bag of sacking which was her pillow and the wall. The pallet was hard and lumpy, the atmosphere so rank and stale that holding one's breath seemed preferable to inhaling it, and the stove gave off almost no heat. Yet exhaustion befriended her, and she slept heavily, beset by hideous dreams.

In the morning she rose, stiff and aching, surrounded by yawning, muttering women clambering into their outer clothes. Her coat was still there, though crumpled and damp, her shoes sodden, uncomfortable to wear. But she had had a night's sleep to act as a bastion between her and the events of the previous night and day. She went out into a morning of pale steady sunshine and rain-washed air, and set off walking briskly away from the street of the lodging house. It was kind of the policeman to think of calling on her, but she had no intention of being there for another night. As she walked her circulation began to return, and with it an unexpected lifting of the spirits, an exhilaration she hadn't felt for a long time. The grave house in Karlsgasse, Otto's melancholy, the middle-aged life she had been leading, were all behind her, and she was starting again – with nothing to call her own but youth, and herself.

She knew now that she had not loved Otto. There had been gratitude, and affection, and something of the father and daughter in their relationship, and finally a physical longing not for Otto, but for anybody. By her rash action in destroying the waxworks she had brought him brief happiness and herself brief appeasement, and now the episode was over. Max and Luisa von Schlager were welcome to her clothes and possessions; they were no more than a snake's cast skin.

She went into a coffee-house and read a morning paper over a cup that was strong and fragrant, unlike the swill she had been served with earlier. There were the usual columns of classified advertisements: for servants, children's nurses, housekeepers, clerks, all useless to her who had only earned money serving in a shop. Then her eyes were caught by another heading: *Theatrical and Musical*.

Wanted, violinists for the State Opera, a wind-player for the Theater an der Wien, and a flautist. Accomplished musician wanted to teach the son of a nobleman. Master carpenter required. Gentleman experienced in theatrical management. And, almost at the end of the column, Chorus members, male and female, wanted for a new production of *Der Bettelstudent* at the Theater Elisabeth. Applicants auditioned now.

Laura put down the paper. She had seen the operetta in Ischl. The music was light and easy – she had sung more difficult stuff to please Otto. Her voice was not trained, but it had improved with practice recently. It was worth a try.

The Theater Elisabeth was in an unfashionable district outside the Ring, near the Votivkirche. It was a long walk in shoes badly out of shape, but she reached it not much after eight o'clock, when people were still going to work. There was no sign of life about the place. She hesitated, tried various doors, all locked. Perhaps she was too early, after all.

Then an aproned man appeared from the foyer, carrying a bucket and a mop, which he wrung out on the steps, Laura called to him. 'Anyone about?'

He jerked his thumb. 'Round the back. You'll see.'

Round the back was the stage door, where she should have gone in the first place, and outside it a few people huddled together like birds. Several girls, three very young men, an older man and woman. 'Waiting for the auditions?' Laura asked cheerfully.

One of the girls said 'They've started. They'll let us in in a minute.'

'About time, too,' said the man. As they waited, Laura knew herself to be the target of eyes, measuring, judging, envying. The women were all shorter than she was and, by ordinary standards, less attractive. But they probably sang like nightingales.

The door was opened to them; an attendant ushered them to a corridor with two benches set against the wall. Gallantly the men gestured the women to be seated. From a room at the end came sounds of piano-accompanied singing. Laura was seized by nervous apprehension. If this failed, what happened next?

Yet the nervousness dropped from her when she entered the audition room. The *kapellmeister*, a middle-aged man of anxious appearance, was highly susceptible. After so many plump little Viennese partridges he found Laura's looks enchanting. She, the practised flirt, saw it, and responded.

244

They exercised mutual charm on each other. It was fortunate that the accompanist's prelude reminded her of the popular tune she was asked to sing, for her musical memory was considerably better than her sight-reading, and she got through the piece reasonably well. 'Very good,' said Herr Vogel, taking the opportunity to pat her arm. 'Not a strong voice, but true. When you find yourself singing with others you will show us what a good loud sound you can produce – yes?'

'Yes,' said Laura, with a seraphic smile.

It was done; she was engaged for the duration of the piece. 'It is St Hilary's Day,' Herr Vogel told her, 'a good day to begin enterprises. You will be lucky. We must celebrate, *nicht wahr*? As it happens, there is an excellent little *speisehaus* just round the corner. Perhaps we may eat there together?'

Offered a free dinner; whoever St Hilary might be, Laura felt obliged to him. And even further obliged by the end of the day, when she had been offered a lodging with one of the girls who had also been taken on. Marta's mother let off rooms, cheap and clean. How strange were the workings of Fate: yesterday tragedy and despair, today a bright future.

On a freezing January night, a week afer rehearsals had begun at the Theater Elisabeth, Crown Prince Rudolf shot his mistress, Countess Mary Vetsera, and then himself, at his hunting lodge of Mayerling.

Maurice Reide stood at the window of his hotel sitting-room, overlooking the Kärntnergasse, the long street that ran between the Opera and St Stefan's Square. Even at that early hour it hummed with life. A party of revellers was passing, still in carnival costumes, laughing and singing on their way to breakfast at the coffee-house. The shops were opening, shutters coming down, window displays being rearranged to tempt passers-by, people on their way to work stopping to glance at them. Maurice was seeing none of this, for a picture filled his mind – the picture he had come to Vienna to paint.

He had grown tired of idling in the mountains of Carinthia,

recovering his strength and finishing *Juliet in the Church*. Late in November he had decided to winter in Vienna, at an hotel which had been recommended to him as comfortable. On its excellent food he had put back some of the flesh lost after his wounding. He had been to theatres and concerts, had attended a ball, had seen the Emperor and Empress, and Johannes Brahms, had made sketches of the great statues. People had been kind, welcoming, courteously overlooking his poor German. He liked the Viennese, he liked Vienna, but he was restless, unable to give himself up entirely to the gaiety around him. It was sad to be alone in such a place, where pleasure should be shared. He looked into the eyes of women – eyes sparkling behind a carnival mask, bold eyes of strolling prostitutes, innocent eyes of young girls walking with their families; but no look answered his with the promise of love. She was somewhere, the one he longed for, who was only a misty shape in his mind. He would search the world for her if he must. Yet a fear was growing in him that he would never find her, for Madeline had taken the years of youth and courtship, and he was paying for them with loneliness.

At least there was his painting. He decided to change his style to suit his surroundings. The spirit of Vienna was music, the music of the time was operetta. He would cover a canvas with its charming silly extravaganzas, just a little caricatured – dashing princes and noblemen disguised, pretty girls of the village in short skirts and frilly aprons, highborn ladies wearing Magyar costume, gypsies and merry drinkers, comic serving-men and saucy maids. And the colours should be of the theatre: sugar-pink and sky-blue, military red and primrose yellow, the colours a child would choose from its paint-box. He would design a scrolled white frame flecked with gold for the finished canvas. The Royal Academy might not accept it, but he would have very much enjoyed painting it.

His memory of details needed refreshing, and he wanted live models. The hotel receptionist, who appeared to know everything there was to be known about her city, and loved to give information, told him that a new operetta production of an old favourite was being rehearsed at *Die Sisi*.

'Die . . .'

'The Theater Elisabeth, *mein herr*. Sisi is the little name of

246

our Empress, not quite so grand as Elisabeth. It is not in a very smart district, but a good theatre. All the cab-drivers know it.'

Maurice waited until the day had warmed up before he set off for the theatre, arriving there just after noon. His request to see the manager was not understood at first. When at last it was comprehended he was shown into a dingy office in the corridor leading from the stage door. He waited, conscious of a hubbub of voices nearby, excited chattering, a woman noisily weeping. Then the man he had come to see entered. Herr Vogel's face was a study in harassment. 'I'm sorry to have kept you waiting. Exceptional circumstances . . . if I can help?' While Maurice was explaining slowly in his halting German the man's eyes kept straying to the wall behind which the noise was going on.

'I regret very much, *mein herr*, I don't understand altogether what it is that you want. But it will be impossible for you to work here at your drawing. The theatre is closing.'

'Closing? But I understood . . . *Der Bettelstudent* – is it not in rehearsal now?'

Vogel's face was tragic. 'It was. But a telegram has just been received. There has been a terrible event – our Crown Prince is dead. All public performances are cancelled. There is nothing for it but for our singers to go home.'

'But – dead? Rudolf? How, what happened?'

Vogel shrugged gloomily. He didn't know, nobody knew yet, but rumours were flying about. Some said a stroke, some said violence, poison, perhaps. Whatever it was it would mean the end of *Fasching*; all Austria would go into mourning. Perhaps it would be the end of the Austrian Empire, who could tell? 'Now if you will excuse me, *mein herr*, I must go and talk to my poor singers . . .'

He left the door open behind him. Maurice sat on, stunned. He saw people begin to drift past, down the corridor, grim-faced men and sobbing women. They had lost their jobs as well as their crown prince. Two girls were clinging together in noisy grief, a tall young woman was tying a scarf round her fair hair; he could not see her face.

The city was in panic, rumours everywhere, but no facts. The Hofburg was surrounded by agitated crowds, newspaper offices were besieged. At Maurice's hotel the charming receptionist was crying; the tea he ordered was cold when it arrived, an unheard-of thing.

Next morning, oppressed in spirit by the changed atmosphere, he suddenly cancelled the rest of his stay. He had made up his mind to challenge the fortune-teller's prediction: he would go to Venice.

Laura searched the recesses of her handbag. No, there was not a single coin left; all gone, the last of the salary advance Herr Vogel had given her, hoping for favours in return. For three days it had kept her at the lodging house she had stayed in before going to the Sisi. Now even the squalor of that would have been welcome; anything rather than the February streets. Desperate ideas chased through her brain as she trailed along them. Herr Vogel might help, but her pride could not face the thought of asking a man to become her protector. The two previous ones had only led to disaster, and Vogel had a jealous wife. Yet, if she had not travelled so far from the Sisi's neighbourhood, she would have been tempted to go back.

Time passed slowly when one was petrified with cold and aching with hunger. For most of the day she had sat in one church or another, getting a little warmth from the glowing candles. Now night had come down; the curator of the Stefanskirche had spoken sharply to her as she tried to hide in the shadows at the back of the vast building, telling her that it wasn't a hostel for the down-and-out. She was in the street again, walking to keep herself from freezing, though her shoes were broken and her feet badly blistered. Two women, standing under a street-lamp, stared at her. As she passed by them one grabbed her arm.

'Here, what game d'you think you're playing at? This is our beat, you know, we don't want no strangers on it. Get out of it if you want to keep your hair on your head.' A vicious tug at her hair accompanied the threat.

'But I'm not,' she said. 'I mean, I've nowhere to go.'

A coarse laugh and a stream of obscene advice followed her as she walked away as quickly as she could. Only to hear a kind word, to see a friendly face . . . She would have cried with pleasure to see the young policeman who had taken her to the lodging house, but the face beneath the helmet was never his, and she was afraid to attract the attention of any other officer. It was hard to remember what he looked like; her thoughts were becoming addled with cold and exhaustion: Otto and Deryck turning into people she didn't recognize, faces that grew large as they came nearer and nearer to her, then receded or turned into other faces, the wax faces of Minna, melting away into a viscous liquid with glass eyes floating in it.

Waxworks. She tried to remember something, something that might help. The clothes had gone to a convent. If only she could recall its name, or where it was, but her mind was a blank. They were a charitable order, they might take her in. At the next church she would ask.

But her knees suddenly buckled and she clutched at a wall to steady herself. It was a shop, two steps leading up to its door. Laura sank down on them. Perhaps there was no warmth anywhere in Vienna; perhaps everyone was cold in death, like its Crown Prince. Down the sewers, they said, it was warm; the city cats spent a lot of time there, enjoying the heat as well as the fat rats. In the siege of Paris people had eaten rats. Once that had been a revolting thought, now it was bearable. *Rattenzuppe, rattenwurst. Rattenkuchen* at Sacher's. One coffee with cream and a rat-cake, please . . .

Someone was speaking to her.

'Had a bit too much, *liebchen*? So've I. Let's have a little rest together, so?' The speaker was a young man in evening dress, very much the worse for drink. As he slumped down beside her the fumes of wine were overpowering on the frost-laden night air. Laura wondered if it was possible to feel sick when one hadn't eaten for a day and a night.

'No, I haven't had too much,' she said with an attempt at hauteur. 'I've had exactly nothing to eat or drink, and I feel very weak.'

He seemed not to take in what she said, being occupied with running his hands over her and mouthing her neck. With one hand he pulled the scarf off her head and caught at her hair, loosening the pins.

'Don't!' She tried to push him off, but her strength was no match for his, drunk as he was. Wildly she looked round for help, but the street was deserted. Suddenly he struggled to his feet and dragged her up, pulling her against him and tearing at the fastenings of her coat. 'Pretty,' he mumbled, 'very nice girl. Let's have a good time. Come on, come on. Don't be shy.'

'Leave me alone. Get away. You're drunk.' But it came to her that she was going to be overpowered, however desperately she tried to fight him off with numbed hands. Her coat-buttons had been ripped off and her skirt dragged up round her waist. Suddenly she thought of a delaying tactic. If he thought her a whore, she must behave like one.

'Here, wait, I want some money first!' she cried. The trick worked.

'All right, all right. Greedy little girl. How much?'

While he was fumbling in his pockets she drew away from him and held out her hand. 'Whatever you've got.' Waveringly he found the hand and put some coins into it, others falling on the ground and rolling in all directions. She clutched them, backed away and began to run, her feet winged by fear, not looking back; though she heard his shouts even when she had turned a corner into a wider street. She crossed it and stood in a doorway, listening. The shouts had ceased, there were no running footsteps. She had escaped, and she had money.

Still walking fast, she struck off to the left, completely lost now in a street of small, mean houses. Between two of them ran a narrow alley; from a building three doors down came a strong, unbearably fragrant smell of coffee. Laura twisted her dishevelled hair up as well as she could, dragged her coat round her, and made for the door. They could only turn her away.

But in the dingy, shabby old coffee-house there were others who looked like vagrants, ragged men and women huddled over cups and bowls. Alongside them were people presentable enough but dressed in a motley fashion; flowing neckties and velvet jackets abounded, a girl was dressed like a gypsy, some men wore shoulder-length hair. The Café Linder was a democracy where the homeless poor mixed with artists and writers and those who fancied night-life and unconventional talk. Laura found herself a stool at a table where five people were already sitting, and sank down on it, weak with reaction. The buxom young waitress looked curiously at her, but took her order without comment. There was enough money to pay for a decent meal. But when it came she could hardly touch it, and sat looking at the steaming cup and laden plate.

'*Sind sie krank?*' asked a voice beside her. A youngish man wearing a wide black hat and a dashing black cloak lined with blue was the speaker.

'No,' she answered. 'Not ill. Only too hungry to eat.'

'Here,' said the other briskly. 'Take it a little at a time. Come on, now. A spoonful. That's better. Now a bit of bread.' Laura obeyed, and began to feel more normal, aware of a pair of very sharp dark eyes watching every morsel.

'Been in trouble?' he enquired.

'Quite a lot,' Laura replied with her mouth full.

'All right, don't talk till you've finished.'

At last Laura pushed away the cleared plate. She would have preferred not to talk, but her companion seemed determined, asking her questions about herself which she answered more or less evasively. She was a singer out of a job because of the tragedy of the Crown Prince; down on her luck. Something about the timbre of the man's voice puzzled her. Suddenly he said, 'But you're English.'

'Yes.'

'Well, that's a laugh – so am I. Shake hands.' A long thin hand took hers in a painfully strong grip.

'What an extraordinary thing,' he said, 'I congratulate you on your idiomatic German. Have you lived here long?'

'Only a few months.'

'Then I congratulate you even more warmly. Our race hasn't a great reputation for its ear for languages. I've lived here ten years, myself.' The piercing eyes were searching her face disconcertingly. Laura flinched as he stroked her hair back from her brow, the fingers touching, pressing.

'Excuse me,' she said, with the courage of desperation, 'but if you're by any chance thinking of making love to me, please forget about it. I don't think I ever want to hear about love-making again. I'm worn out, and until I had this food I was starving. I've just got away from a drunken beast who tried to rape me in the street, somewhere back there. I made him give me this money, or I wouldn't even have been able to buy coffee. So, you see, I'm not interested in men, only in finding somewhere to sleep for the night. Alone.'

The man in the wide hat stared, then laughed abruptly. 'Well said. As it happens, I was going to offer you that very thing. I have a studio in the Fleischmarkt – you may have guessed I'm a painter – and there's a spare bed. A *spare* bed, I said, you note. You're welcome to it.'

'I see. Thank you. I'll accept – if I can trust you.'

Again the sharp laugh, like a bark. 'Oh, you can trust me, certainly. Shall we leave?'

Laura, still uneasy, said, 'If it isn't far. I don't think I can walk any more – my shoes are worn through.'

'No question of walking. I'll call a *drosshke*. You haven't told me your name.'

'Laure.' For some reason she used the German form.

'Laure. Charming. You may call me Johnny – most people do.' At the door, he flung back a flashing smile that did nothing to allay Laura's doubts.

Chapter Twenty

JOHNNY'S ROOMS WERE IN A BUILDING bowed and leaning with age, seeming almost too old to be inhabited. The small room provided for Laura had grotesque carvings at each corner of its ceiling, and over the door: the outlines of bodies of animals and human faces could just be made out. Johnny said it had once been a cell, and the house a medieval chapel – 'but don't worry, the old priests won't bother you.' Matter-of-factly he produced a slipper-bath from an alcove and heated water for it. 'You'll want some night-clothes, I suppose. As it happens, I have some here. Left behind,' he added with a wry smile. The nightdress and negligée were of the most delicate lawn finely embroidered, a little short for Laura, but not a bad fit. She wondered who had worn them – a defaulting wife, a mistress? It didn't matter. She was only concerned with getting clean and warm. Johnny, who seemed to think of everything, found some ointment for her sore feet and chapped hands, and put a mug of steaming tisane by the side of the narrow bed. When she had finished her bath and thankfully climbed into the bed he knocked perfunctorily and walked in.

'All right?'

'Yes, thank you.' There was something unfathomable in the way he looked at her, a sort of calculation. But she was too exhausted to worry about it, and he showed no sign of breaking his promise.

'Good night, then.'

'Good night.' There was a bolt on the door. Laura eyed it, then decided against repaying his hospitality with suspicion. She drank the spiced draught and fell into a sleep that was more like unconsciousness.

When she woke, it was to the scent of coffee. A tray was by her side bearing a coffee-pot, hot croissants, butter and jam,

253

neatly laid out. Johnny strolled in as she was finishing the last of it. Without his hat he looked younger; not handsome, but arresting in a dark arrogant way. He was dressed like a peasant, in rough frieze trousers and a loose smock, splashed with paint. He surveyed her.

'So, you've breakfasted.'

'Yes, and it was delicious. I don't know how to begin to thank you.'

'Oh, you'll find a way.'

'I hope so. When I think of the awful state I was in last night – and now I've had a wonderful sleep and a good breakfast. I'd better get up now. Perhaps I can make myself useful somehow.'

'I wonder. Were you thinking of housework? Because I doubt if you're very used to it, by the look of your hands, even chapped as they are at present. But you're not a lady, are you? When you speak English it comes out quite surprisingly, whereas in German you can get away with it. Educated in a fashion, but essentially bourgeois.'

Laura was outraged out of her gratitude. 'What an impertinent thing to say! It's no business of yours what I am. I should have thought living in Vienna would have taught you a bit more politeness than that. Yes, I *have* been educated – I'm glad you noticed it.'

But, ignoring both indignation and sarcasm, his gaze was wandering over her exposed arms and bosom. She pulled up the coverlet and held it round her neck.

'Don't bother to do that,' he said, 'I've very sharp eyes. No, my dear, I'd rather you didn't get up yet. I'm going to draw you.'

'But . . . not in bed, like this, please!'

Johnny perched himself negligently on the edge of the bed.

'Yes, just like that. You see, in that wispy garment your bones show, and your face and neck are thin, refined, attenuated. Perfect. When you get fattened up you won't be half so interesting.'

'But I don't want to look interesting in that way – how horrid. You make me sound like a skeleton.'

'You'd make a charming one, *liebe* Laure.'

Laura sat upright, the duvet pulled tightly round her for warmth. 'Now listen, Johnny, and I'm sorry I don't know your other name yet, because I'd prefer to stay on formal terms. I know all about this Viennese *morbidismus* or whatever they call it, and how fond they are of skulls and graves and dead *mädchen*. I don't understand it, because I'm English, and I don't want to understand it or have anything to do with it – see? So don't you go drawing me in my bones.'

He laughed, a long light laugh, and patted the outline of her knee beneath the bedclothes. 'What a girl of spirit you are. I like that. But don't imagine it will stop me, for one moment, doing what I intend to do. See.' From nowhere he produced a sketching-pad and pencil. 'So, stay like that, angry, wrapped up in a cocoon, with your beautiful cross face peering over the top of it. Or jump out of bed and show yourself to me in your borrowed plumes. You wouldn't like that, no? Then stay as you are.'

Laura, frustrated, stayed as she was. There seemed nothing else to do. He said, his eye on his work, 'You clutch at your throat as though you were protecting something. Not merely your virtue. What is it?'

'Very clever,' she said coldly. 'There is something I miss. A small diamond pendant my father gave me. I had to pawn it – it was the very last valuable thing I had, and it fetched very little.'

'We'll get it back, then, if you value it so much.'

'*I'll* get it back. With my own efforts.'

'Such as . . .?' What a curious conversation it was, more like the sort of squabble she had occasionally had with Ellie. She subsided into silence, turning her head when he asked her. There were sounds from the studio outside, a broom and scrubbing brush wielded to the accompaniment of a tuneless humming.

'My cleaning woman,' Johnny said. 'Our valued chaperon. There, that's enough, you may get up.'

'If you'll kindly leave the room.'

He laughed. 'Don't be so coy. As though it mattered!'

'It does matter to me.'

'Very well. But are you going to drift about in those little bits of lawn? Charming, but chilly.'

Laura sighed heavily, knowing that she was being teased, unwilling to play whatever game was in the mind of her strange benefactor. 'Very well, so I must dress. What do you suggest?'

He pulled aside a curtain which hid a hanging wardrobe. Dresses drooped from their pegs, a soft brown woollen robe, a maroon skirt and top. Laura took it down. 'This will do. But my underclothes . . .'

'Washed and dried on the stove, my dear. Here. All ready to put on. May I help you?'

'Certainly not!' Laura flashed at him. 'I'm quite used to doing without a maid.' But he lingered, until her adamant stare drove him out.

Dressed and washed, she left her room and mounted the stone steps which led to the rest of the apartment. The old cleaner rose stiffly from her knees in the corridor, and, with a terse greeting, went off with her bucket, broom and duster towards the spare room. No doubt she was used to seeing strange ladies come and go. Laura pushed open a heavy oak door and found herself in what was obviously Johnny's studio. The window had been much enlarged to let in as much light as possible. An easel was set up, an almost blank canvas on it. Suddenly Laura was back in time, in another artist's studio, a peacock peering inquisitively in at them. If his mother had not come in just then; if they had got to know each other better, would he have gone away? She saw him vividly, just as he had been then, heard him quote the German phrase she hadn't understood, sat by his side in Greenwich Park as he talked of foreign places . . .

Why did she think of Maurice Reide, known so briefly, when the other men in her life were only shadows, even poor Otto? Something had sprung up between them at the first meeting which had demanded fulfilment and had not received it; and then everything had gone wrong.

With a sigh, she went to inspect the canvases round the walls, some hanging, some stacked. As she moved from one to the other curiosity gave way to astonishment, then revulsion. She was in a gallery of nightmares. Monsters, human and animal, inhabited them. The long necks of swans, floating on waters in which drowned heads bobbed, became hands reaching up to clutch at other victims; snakes writhed and hissed round limbs and necks, winged women of fabulous, evil beauty rode upon bulls and huge fish; voluptuous sphinx-women crouched over their prey, lovely Medusa

256

heads dripped blood on the bodies of slain suitors.

'Admiring my enchantresses?' Johnny had come in silently, and was standing behind her.

Politeness struggling with truth, Laura said, 'They seem very well painted – so far as I can tell.'

'Thank you. And you like them – they fascinate you?' His hand was on her shoulder.

'No, I'm afraid they don't, at all. I think they're horrible. Why are they all women, those . . . things?'

'I always paint women. I adore them.'

'I should have guessed you hated them.'

'That, too, perhaps. Blood and kisses, smiles and talons, Andromeda changing places with the dragon, the slain at the feet of the goddess – can't you see the theme, in all its wonderful variations? One loves, one hates, one possesses, one surrenders; how can you resist this? We are a school of Art and of Thought, we Decadents, we the *Verfallen*. We are here in Vienna, in Munich and Berlin, Paris and London. We are the new Message. Don't you hear it in Swinburne's lines?' Standing very close behind her, he murmured in her ear:

> *Was it myrtle or poppy thy garland was woven with, O my*
> *Dolores?*
> *Was it pallor of slumber, or blush as of bood, that I found in*
> *thee fair?*
> *For desire is a respite from love, and the flesh, not the heart,*
> *is her fuel,*
> *She was sweet to me once, who am fled and escaped from*
> *the rage of her reign;*
> *Who behold as of old time at hand as I turn, with her*
> *mouth growing cruel,*
> *And flushed as with wine with the blood of her lovers, Our*
> *Lady of Pain.*

Laura eyed the window, wondered what depth of drop there was under it, and whether she would be heard if she ran to it and screamed.

'Won't you be . . . sweet, my Dolores?' His mouth was against her neck; he was pressing her closely to him. Suddenly, with a thrill of shock, the truth dawned on her and the whole bizarre situation fell into place. She was still for a moment, then turned to face Johnny.

'You're a woman,' she said.

Johnny pulled the loose smock tight against unmistakable outlines.

'I wondered when you'd guess. Now you're not frightened of me any more.'

'Yes, I am.' Laura backed away. 'Are you mad? What do you want with me?'

'Everything, your beauty, your soft sweetness, your delicious sins.'

'But what use would I be to you? Anyway, I haven't any delicious sins, just the ordinary kind.'

Johnny laughed incredulously. 'Come, *liebchen*, don't tell me you're as much of an innocent as all that – you've knocked about the world a bit, I know. Don't pretend you're a prude. I can tell a worldly lady when I see one.'

Laura was by now quite convinced that she was in the presence of a lunatic. Johnny, or Joan or Jane, was certainly not alarming to view, rather like an amateur drawing of Lord Byron, with straight hair and a nose too big for the face. There was even something pathetic in the droop of the mouth and the eagerness in the dark eyes. 'You ought to see a doctor,' she said more kindly. 'I know a very good one for, er, troubles like yours – his name's Freud and he lives at Maria Theresiastrasse 8. I believe he's rather expensive, but he gets remarkable results.' She chose to forget that the good doctor's treatment of Otto by way of herself had produced results that were cetainly remarkable – but hardly in the way intended. Perhaps if she talked reasonably this strange creature would become more normal.

'But I knew as soon as I saw you that you were my type,' Johnny said. 'I was going to paint you as a beautiful thin Chimera riding a goat through the water, with yards and yards of pale hair tangling round three drowned knights. It would have been a wonderful success. Won't you at least let me sketch it out?'

Laura felt a strong dislike of the idea that a version of herself might join the gallery of monsters. 'I wouldn't care for that,' she said, 'but if you want to make a sketch of me, just like this, you can.'

'Very gracious,' Johnny muttered. 'Sit there, then, with

your head half-turned to the window. My God, how beautiful . . .' A few minutes later she ripped the top sheet from the sketching-pad and handed it to Laura. It was a perfectly conventional portrait, a young woman with a slightly severe expression and no suggestion of the Chimera about her. 'There you are,' Johnny said, 'portrait of an English Miss abroad and not approving of it. I suppose you *are* a Miss, by the way?'

'*Nein, ich bin verheiratet*,' Laura said primly, wondering if such a grand description really applied to Fred, 'and I'd really rather not talk about myself, if you don't mind.'

'As you please. Keep the drawing, I don't want it – it's not the Laure I imagined. I've enough souvenirs as it is,' she added bitterly.

'Of others?' Laura remembered the clothes behind the curtain.

'Yes, the others who left me alone. "*Liebe ohne Gegenliebe ist wie eine Frage ohne Antwort*." A question without an answer, that's love unreturned.'

Laura had begun to feel sorry for the strange creature. 'I'm sure you'll find a friend some day,' she said, 'and I hope it will be somebody who'll make a nice Chimera.'

Johnny threw back her head, laughing hysterically. 'I can't wait for the day. A cosy lady friend and a nice respectable Chimera in a boned collar and a hobble skirt. Thank you. Now get out. You're no use to me.'

'So you helped me last night just because my face attracted you, not because you pitied me?'

Johnny shrugged. 'I suppose so. There are plenty of ugly vagrants around the streets.'

'I see,' Laura said thoughtfully. 'You know, I've learned one thing at least in my travels. It's only my face that matters to people – they don't want me for anything else. I rather wish I could catch smallpox or something, then I might find out what it's like to be a person.'

'You'll find out soon enough – women do. Now go on, I'm sick of the sight of you. You can keep the clothes, by the way.'

'They all say that – how odd.'

'What? Well, I can hardly send you out naked, can I, though I'd like to, just to be able to paint you so afterwards.

There are your coat and shoes – get them out of my sight.'

Laura was only too glad to be leaving, but made a last bid for practical help. 'Do you know anyone who might take me in, or give me some work? I don't mind what I do, so long as I can live on it.'

'Find work for yourself, it's no business of mine.' As Laura went down the stairs Johnny shouted after her 'I had an Englishman here the other week, looking for models. You'd better ask around for him – he seemed the respectable kind, just your sort. His name was . . .' But the door had shut behind Laura.

As though Otto himself spoke to Laura, the thought came insistently into her mind that he had once told her something that would help her. It was on the day when he had first shown her Vienna, she was certain of that. What had they seen? The Michaelerkirche, the Hofburg, the Chapel of the Capuchins, the Opera, Sacher's . . . and they had driven round narrow streets where he had pointed out interesting buildings. There had been a tall old house with a courtyard before it and a familiar flag flying: the British Consulate, Otto had said.

She could remember the street it was in, even now. In her cracked, still damp shoes she hurried towards it.

They were polite at the Consulate, but sceptical. As it was impossible to tell the whole of her story she confined herself to Otto's part in it: an invalid gentleman with whom she had been travelling had died, and his relatives had asked her to leave and refused to let her have her property. An official ordered tea for her and asked her to be prepared to wait for an hour or two. She knew that they would go round to the house in Karlsgasse to investigate.

In less then two hours the suave man with shrewd eyes was back, carrying a valise. 'It appears there was a misunderstanding,' he told her. 'Frau von Schlager believed that you would be sending for your belongings, but had heard nothing from you. She was, of course, quite willing to let us convey them to you.'

'I'm very grateful,' Laura said, knowing the story to be a diplomatic fiction. 'Very. If I may be taken somewhere to change into other clothes, I'd be most obliged.'

Of course it could be arranged. A brisk young woman marshalled her to a vacant room where she put on the most suitable garments in the valise, feeling a deep sense of luxury at wearing them again. Her ragged coat and shoes she bundled up and jammed in the waste-paper basket. Then she was led back to the office where she had waited. The Consul's deputy proceeded to go over all the ground they had covered already, make endless notes and ask endless questions. Asked to give references in England, Laura could only think of Frank Kenward and Miss Plum. Neither sounded very imposing. But he seemed to accept them, and after another long wait, reading old copies of the *Illustrated London News*, Laura was informed that she would be given sufficient money to return to London at the lowest rates, and travelling arrangements made.

On a cold grey morning, after a night in a lodging arranged by the Consulate, she set off on the long journey by train and boat. Her last errand in Vienna was to call at the back-street pawnbroker's to reclaim her diamond with some of the money given to her for extra expenses. It went obediently to its home round her neck, and she sighed with relief, touching it again and again as she sat back in the crowded railway carriage, watching telegraph poles and meadows fly past, taking her ever nearer to England.

Ellie fell into her arms. An Ellie plumper, rounder than she had been, with a great air of busyness and responsibility about her.

'Oh, Lorla, is it truly you? Why haven't you written, and what *have* you been doing, and why are you so thin? And you must see Thomas, this minute, though I haven't had time to dress him in his best, because your telegram only got here just before you did, and Frank's out at a meeting and the spare bed hasn't been aired, but never mind, because you're here.'

It was wonderful to see Frank's simple pleasure in his wife's joy at being reunited with her sister, wonderful to be at the heart of their welcome, to be in an English home again, the four-square cottage in Thimblestone. A comfortable fire burnt in the grate before which Ellie nursed the very new, plump, precocious Thomas. Outside, a wintry moon shone on the little garden, but already hazel catkins were showing above the stream that ran through it, and snowdrops bloomed under the apple trees. It was wonderful to Laura to sit by her father's side, his hand in hers, seeing him so much smaller and older than she remembered, yet knowing that the link between them was strengthened with absence.

She told them only an outline of her adventures; it seemed she was never to tell the full story. Frank was a clergyman, her father had feelings to be hurt, they were all innocents. They seemed to understand what she told them, but she knew they only took in a part of it. What pleased them was to hear of the countries she had been in, the manners and customs and looks of the people. They listened incredulously as she recited to them scraps of French and German.

'That's right, that's right!' exclaimed Pa. 'Just how I remember my grandfather talking. And to think you should speak it like a native, after such a little time. Dear me, what a clever daughter I've got. No, two clever daughters, one a born mother.' He looked fondly at Ellie, her dark shining head bent over Thomas. Next year Thomas would have a brother or a sister, and for years after that there would always be a child in the cradle.

Frank took his pipe out of his mouth. On him, too, maturity had descended; already he had the air of a vicar, yet he was none the less boyish. Laura wondered how much of her story he had read between the lines, but if he guessed more than she had told, he would never let it be known to others.

'Of course you'll stay,' he said. 'We can't let you go again, Laura. You can be a great help to Ellie, and to me, in the parish, now that Thomas takes up so much of her time. Even in a little place like this there is so much to do. You're needed, believe me.'

'Frank, I can't. I can't live off you. If you were an archbishop I might think about it, but as it is I must try to make my own living.'

'In London? Oh, no,' Ellie said. 'Whatever could you do there?'

'Well, I've served in a shop . . .'

'The shops in London, my dear,' said Frank, 'are either family businesses or large stores where the assistants live in, with strict rules and low wages. I cant see that independent spirit of yours putting up with the conditions of a boys' boarding school. You've very little experience. Who would be likely to employ you?'

'I don't know, but I can find out.' Laura tried not to sound daunted by this probably true forecast of her future.

Next morning Frank asked her to accompany him on his parish rounds. There was the church to be visited, church notices checked, a chat with the verger and the gravedigger, then calls on parishioners. 'Poor ones,' Frank said, 'the vicar takes the others.' From cottage to cottage they went, Laura increasingly surprised to find the want and squalor that lay behind the picturesque village street with its pink-washed and pargetted houses. In side streets and isolated cottages poor old women, or couples, huddled over miserable fires with what bedclothes they owned round their shoulders. Large families lived in one room; mothers nursed babies, or prepared to give birth to them, surrounded by watchers. Consumptives coughed their lives away with children around them, in foetid little dwellings where pigs and hens walked as freely as people. To each dweller Frank spoke kindly, asked what their particular need was and noted it down in his parish book. Some looked at Laura sullenly, resenting her good clothes, but they all responded to Frank. Laura thought him the most likeable and good person she had ever met.

'So this is the country,' she said when their errands were done. 'I thought such things were only to be found in towns.'

'Alas, I wish they were, though that would be bad enough. Poverty is no respecter of green fields and bird-songs. At least our community is small enough for us to keep an eye on everyone, though helping them practically is another matter. We do have generous people who give freely, but that's the only source we have. Charitable societies don't want to hear about villages where everything is supposed to be sweetness and merriment. I believe they think we spend the year crowning the May Queen or gathering in holly. Ah, well. You see now, dear Laura, how much there is to do?'

'Only too well.'

He smiled his boyish, beguiling smile. 'and so, you'll stay

and help us – just for a few days?'

'Oh, Frank. You're a serpent. You only brought me out to talk me into staying.'

'Not at all. You want to stay, I know, even though your very proper spirit of independence insists that you leave us eventually. Why not promise to stay a week? Then you will have time to talk to Ellie for as long as you both want, and get to know your fascinating nephew, and let your father get used to the idea that you are still on this earth. I think he hardly believes it yet.'

'Very well – yes. Because you ask me so persuasively, and because I really do want to. But I must go after that. You do understand?'

He stopped and faced her, leaning against a stile.

'Yes, I understand, and I think it very brave of you. Perhaps . . . perhaps because of what I've seen of people's troubles, I can guess at some of yours – things that you very rightly don't wish Ellie and your father to hear about because they might be puzzled, or alarmed, or saddened, or all three.'

'All three, Frank, believe me. But please don't think of me as one of life's victims, like the poor people we've seen this morning. I've had every chance – money, and education, and all that and made the most terrible muddle of things. When I go to London to make my own way I shall *try* not to make the same mistakes. I hope I shall be strong enough not to. I can sing, you know – I'll easily find theatre engagements.'

'I shall pray for you; and I don't mean to sound pious.'

In the days that followed, Laura found a peace and contentment she had never known before. She had felt something of it at Ischl, but then she had not been with her family, who gave her such happiness, or in her own land, this gentle countryside struggling out of winter into the greenness and the flowering time that were to come. The things she regretted and was ashamed of in the past began to seem like ugly dreams. She was not unhappy, frustrated Mrs Mares, or *La Diamantée*, or Otto's uneasy companion, but Miss Laura, the curate's sister-in-law, who visited people with food and medicines and was good with sick people and babies, now that she had had so much experience of handling the strong-willed Thomas. 'Time she was wed,' the wives said, 'a pretty-looking maid like her. Maybe she'll take up with some gentleman hereabouts, and settle down – and won't that be a comfort to Mrs Kenward, now.'

The week Frank had asked for was nearly over. On Sunday she would go to church with the family for the first time, and forget the candles of the Stefanskirche that had kept her from freezing, and the statues and holy groups, and know herself truly back in England.

The church was familiar to her now in its grey-stoned simplicity. She sat by Ellie's side, rose and sat and knelt in the old rituals, sang the hymns, and watched Frank, grave and handsome in what he called his canonicals. Less than half-way through the service she was aware of a growing headache, a nagging pain that grew worse, however hard she tried to concentrate on what was going on. Her back was stiff, too, and the pew was hard. She shifted about, trying not to distract others by her restlessness, but felt no better. In the hymn that preceded the sermon she whispered to Ellie, 'I'm afraid I don't feel very well, dear. I think I'll go home – you stay, don't bother about me.'

The air in the churchyard was fresh and sweet, making the pain seem less. But it seemed best to go back to the house. Her back was definitely aching now, and an oppressive feeling of malaise coming over her. In the house she made tea for herself, but it tasted musty, and she left it. Suddenly she was violently sick. When the family returned she had crawled into bed.

'It's nothing,' she told Ellie, trying to smile. 'Just a cold, or something.'

But downstairs Ellie met Frank coming in, with a face of alarm. 'Doctor Trenchard says the Wiles boy has smallpox. Is Laura all right? I saw her go out of church.'

Ellie told him. 'Oh, dear Lord,' he said. 'They were almost the first family I took her to visit. Has she had it?'

'No – neither of us has . . . Oh, Frank, if it's that!'

By evening they knew that it was.

Chapter Twenty-One

NOBODY KNEW HOW THE DISEASE had come to Thimblestone. In winter or very early spring it seldom visited the countryside. But the whole Wiles family contracted it, and neighbours of theirs; two children died. A few days after Laura had been stricken, Ellie developed the symptoms. 'Thank God they took him,' she kept saying, 'thank God.' For when Laura's illness had been diagnosed Frank had telegraphed to his mother, at the headmaster's house by the school near Colchester, begging to be allowed to bring Thomas to her. There had been an outbreak of smallpox at the school only two years earlier, he had had it himself as a child – surely, if the baby were not already infected, he would be safer there.

'Certainly, at once,' came the answer. Frank, accompanied by a neighbour, drove over with Thomas, protesting loudly at being separated from his mother. They arrived to find that Mrs Kenward had already found a wet-nurse of good health and character, and was perfectly happy to look after her grandson. 'He looks very well to me, Frank,' she said. 'Babies are far stronger things than they seem. Tell Ellie that, and look as cheerful as you can.'

But Ellie was beyond such assurances. She raved in a high fever, her body and face covered with pustules that ran together in terrible patches almost hiding her skin. The doctor had never seen anybody so ill with smallpox, and said so gravely to Frank. 'Your sister-in-law is only lightly affected, but your wife . . . You must be prepared for anything.'

Three weeks passed, and Ellie still lived, while Laura was almost recovered. Another few days, and she was pronounced out of danger. Laura begged to be allowed to see her. But they made her wait until she began to fear some dreadful injury or mutilation had happened to Ellie. Her own face she looked at as little as possible in the mirror. It was thin and pale, even sallow, and depressed pits here and there showed where the pustules had been: a few on the brow and the side of her cheek, and more on her neck. The doctor told her she had escaped lightly, but to her own eyes she seemed a different person.

When at last she was allowed to see Ellie she understood him. The face on the pillow was ruined. A mass of scars, still livid, covered it. Ellie's hair had been cropped short, and stuck up in bristles. From the wreck of her face two beautiful dark eyes looked out, and the untouched mouth curved in a smile, as she stretched out a hand to Laura.

'Lorla. I kept asking to see you, but they wouldn't bring you to me.'

Laura was speechless from shock. She took the proffered hand and kissed it, then sat down by the bed, not looking at Ellie.

'It's very bad, isn't it.' Ellie said quietly. 'I know, though the nurse won't let me have a mirror. I can feel it for myself. But it will get better with time, the doctor says. And it's so wonderful not to be itching and burning any more, and able to talk sensibly again. I believe I was quite out of my mind for some of the time, you know. I saw faces sometimes – the nurse, and Frank, and Pa – but I didn't really understand what was happening or where I was. Only somebody kept saying to me that Thomas was all right, and I understood that. But you've been through it all too, dear – I don't need to tell you.'

Laura had gained control of herself. 'No,' she said. 'I wasn't really very ill at all, though it was horrible while it lasted. I was lucky. But why? I was the one who went to the Wiles's cottage, not you – and yet you . . . oh, I wish I'd never come here. If only I'd waited – but I was so anxious to see you all. Anyone might have known I'd do the wrong thing. All that time away from you, and then I come back and bring you .. . such misfortune.'

'You're not to worry about it, dear. It's over, we're both alive, and yours is the face that matters, not mine. I never was much to look at, you must admit.'

'My face! If you knew all the trouble . . .' but Laura stopped. She had been told not to distress Ellie in any way.

She talked instead of the good news of Thomas, thriving with his grandparents, already growing his first tooth and trying hard to make his babbling conversation understood. Ellie smiled, serene and happy. Laura marvelled at her spirit and endurance, and, when she was allowed to get up and come downstairs, at Frank's reaction to his wife's altered looks. He accepted them as completely as she did, never referred to them, and treated her with the tenderness of a lover, letting no chance pass of touching or kissing her. Not long before it had seemed that he would lose her. Now his Eurydice had come back from the gate of Death, and he could not do enough to show his thankfulness and love. In time the dreadful marks paled; they would never vanish, but the sight of Ellie's smiling eyes and mouth made people forget them. The cropped hair grew again, thick and wavy; Frank told her that she looked like a pretty little boy.

One morning in May, when Laura was setting out for a walk, she encountered Ellie alone by the little stream, gathering cowslips. As Laura approached, she looked up with a face so radiant that the scars were for a moment invisible.

'What is it, dear?' Laura asked. 'Was there good news in the post?'

'Not in the post but good news – the best. Another baby, a snowdrop baby, in January.'

For an instant a pang shot through Laura that was quite new to her, and acutely painful: a pang of envy. It was something she had never felt for any other woman before, least of all her sister, the plain one, the one looked upon as a natural spinster. Now the plain one had lost what looks she had ever possessed. Yet she was loved even more than before, a wife, a mother and mother-to-be.

She kissed Ellie. 'I'm so glad, dear, so very glad for you.'

The time had come to go. There would be another mouth to feed in the Kenward household, and food was scarce enough already. Frank's salary was pitifully small. Daniel Diamond no longer worked at Ponsford's, the journey to Greenwich too much for him now. He got himself the occasional job of clerking in nearby Colesford, but the payment was poor. A substantial doctor's bill had arrived after the long illnesses of Ellie and Laura; Doctor Trenchard was no philanthropist, even to the families of impoverished curates. Laura had not missed Frank's many-times-turned cuffs, and the shine of wear on his black suit, or the repairs to Ellie's few dresses and skirts. She could live off the Kenwards no longer.

They protested, but not as strongly as when she had first arrived. Only her father would have kept her by him if he could have done. Wistfully he watched her packing.

'The little diamond,' he said. 'I'm glad you still have it.'

'I'll never part with it, Pa.' He must not know that she had parted with it once, in a bad time, and might again if her luck failed.

'Did it do as I said it would – tell you when you were making the right choice?' he asked.

'I'm not sure. I think so, perhaps.' It had been bright when Otto came into her life, yet what danger he had innocently led her into. Perhaps that was because he himself had been good, well-meaning towards her. 'I shall watch it, and take care,' she said.

'Yes, take care. I think it'd kill me to lose you again.'

She put her arms round him. 'Now you're not to worry. I shall turn up like a bad penny. Don't I always?'

Daniel sighed. 'I thought some young fellow round here might just take your fancy – then you'd have stayed. But you wouldn't go out like a young girl should, to dances and such . . .'

'Oh, Pa. Round Thimblestone? What dances? You wouldn't expect the gentry to invite me, now would you?' How it would hurt him, poor innocent Pa, to know that she had put herself outside the pale of respectable marriage, even if Fred had not existed. The family had heard nothing of him since the separation, but undoubtedly they would have done so if he had prematurely but fortuitously died; and why should he, young and strong as he was? The mere thought was wicked. Laura no longer thought it, or wished for Fred's removal from her life. He made no difference now.

It was hard to leave them all – lonely to embark on the train to London and an unknown future. Frank had found a respectable lodging for her with a woman who had a relative in the parish. The street led down from the Strand to the river, and was quiet enough, but for the noise of the trains at Charing Cross. The room was clean and cheap. Laura had sold some clothes to provide herself with money in hand. She would soon have more from her earnings.

But the days came and went, and at the end of each one she came back to the small room with no work. Plenty of interviews, but no engagements. 'Sorry, dear, no vacancies.' Managers raised eyebrows: it was girls they had advertised for, they pointed out. When she gave her age they smiled unbelievingly and nodded dismissal. One took her to the window of his office, stared at her face, turning it this way and that, then pulled down her collar to examine the marks on her neck.

'What's this, then?'

'The smallpox. But I only had it lightly.'

'Not lightly enough, dear.'

'But grease-paint . . . wouldn't they be hidden?'

'Sorry, can't take the risk. There's plenty of girls with a whole skin about.'

And I wished for it, she thought bitterly, I wished once that I could take smallpox and find out what it was like to be valued for myself, not my face. Now she knew only too well what it was like. There seemed to be hope when she auditioned for the chorus of a new musical play. Her face was hardly glanced at, as a sheet of music was thrust into her hand, and the jaded accompanist sat with hands poised. The music was impossible to sight-read. Laura tried, faltered, then stopped.

'If I could just hear a bar or two first . . .'

The chorus-master laughed sharply. 'We could be here all day and all night if they all wanted that. Can you sing or can't you, miss?'

'Oh, yes, I can sing, but . . .'

'All right, let's hear you.'

She cleared her throat and plunged raggedly into the first song that came to her, Yum-Yum's 'The Sun Whose Rays'. After two lines the man banged on his desk.

'That'll do. Voice like a penny-whistle, no training. Sing in the church choir, do you, and think that gives you the right to come wasting my time? A very good afternoon to you.'

The money in the box she kept in her room was almost gone, the little store in her purse down to a few pence a day for food. When she looked in the glass she saw a face growing thinnner, a lankness about her once bright hair. Time was running out. One hope remained – a revival of Offenbach's *La Belle Hèléne*. Laura had seen it at Ischl. She remembered the large chorus, the sparkle of the music; surely this time she would be lucky.

Many others had thought so, women and men assorted in age and looks, from comely youth to shabby middle-age. Surely here she would stand a chance. As they waited, silent or murmuring amongst themselves, a man emerged from a side room and stood surveying them. Then he began to move among them, separating them out. 'Over here, you, and you – stand in line.' When he had selected about thirty he turned to the ones he had pushed aside, including Laura, and said, 'Right, thank you. You can all go home.'

They did not argue; they were too used to rejection. But Laura stood still, almost stunned. She had hoped so much, this time.

'Well, what are you waiting for?' he asked, seeing her linger after the others.

'I thought . . . I know the piece, you see – at least I've heard it . . .' Her voice died away, seeing his glance flicker up and down her figure and across her face. He patted her arm, not unkindly. 'Sorry, dear, too old.'

Moving mechanically out into the street, she heard a voice at her side. 'Down on yer luck, are yer?'

Laura nodded. The speaker was a diminutive young woman who might have been anything between twenty and thirty, with a good-natured, sharp-eyed look to her.

'So'm I. Name's Polly, Polly Martins. Don't give us much of a chance, do they? Tell you what – I'm off to try another place, down Holborn. I been there before, see, worked there, but I thought I'd have a go at something classier. You might suit them, 'cause you're tall and they likes that. 'Ow about it?'

'Thank you. That's very kind. Polly Martins shot a knowing look at her and drew her aside towards the public house on the corner.

''Ere, 'ow about a drop o' something to perk us up? It's on me, mind, I've got the odd bob just for once. Don't neglect this re-markable hopportunity, what may never occur again. Come on – 's all right, they know Polly, they won't take us for tarts. Now, what's it to be?'

They crowded each other for room on the walls, the Royal Academy's chosen canvases. Fishing boats came in and went out, against backgrounds varying from golden sunsets to impending storms, Lord Mayors posed in crimson and the chains of office. Next to a famous beauty, pensive in a foam of black lace, a nude lady managed to display all her charms in an entirely blameless manner. Two cardinals shared a joke over the remains of a large supper in a room lavishly furnished enough to suggest a high standard of monastic living, oblivious to the distress of the lady hung beside them, wringing her hands on the edge of a precipice. One of Sir John Millais's angelic children, dressed as Little Miss Muffet, gazed limpidly out at cooing beholders, while Miss Ellen Terry, improbably charming as Lady Macbeth, rivalled her partner, Henry Irving, in the public's attention.

But the largest gathering stood in front of the slender girl with the flowing hair the colour of beech-leaves, and all the wonder of young love in her eyes. *Juliet in the Church* was the success of the season. Maurice answered the same questions over and over. 'Where did you find her?' 'Why did you choose a model with red hair?' 'Are you going to paint her again?' 'Does this mean that you have returned to classical subjects, after making a reputation as a painter of actors and performers?'

'I'd say that Juliet is a theatrical subject,' he replied patiently. 'I may decide to paint other Shakespearian characters – probably will, if I find the right models. No, I shall not ask Miss Terry or Miss Anderson to sit for me; I prefer to work with unknown models. My Juliet was a peasant girl, not a professional model, and I shall certainly not be using her again. The colour of hair seemed exactly right. One can't make dark hair interesting against a dark hood and a dark background. I'm glad you admire the expression. No, I didn't have any trouble in getting her to look like that – the merest hint was enough. She was a natural actress, and completely without self-consciousness.'

The woman at his side laughed softly. 'Are you sure that's entirely true, Maurice? I can tell you two things about that picture which nobody else seems to have mentioned.'

'Please do. Surprise me.'

'Well, then. The man who painted it was in love with the model, and she was beginning to be in love with him.'

Maurice, taken aback, paused as they moved towards the edge of the crowd. 'What an extraordinary theory, Cecily. You've succeeded in surprising me; congratulations.'

'But it's true, though, isn't it?'

'Well . . . that's hard to answer. I was immensely struck by her beauty, and the . . . the Juliet quality she had. Yes, I suppose I was infatuated. As for her – I think she liked me. I was English, and a novelty to her, and she thought me rich because I could afford to pay her. The family was very poor.'

'What utter nonsense. I'd no idea you were such a bad liar. Now I want some tea. Take me to Brown's, please.'

In the elegant, quiet restaurant of the famous old hotel they chatted easily of other things. Cecily Hugh-Jones was not anxious to re-open the subject of love; she was not ready to do so yet. Years before, she had been Maurice's mistress. The affair had ended when her husband found out. Maurice had been prepared to face it out and risk the scandal of a divorce if she wished it, but she had preferred to break off the connection. Cecily liked peace, and security, and comfort, all of which her husband could give her; about Maurice's ability to provide them she was not so sure, with that odious young mother of his no doubt waiting to make the life of any daughter-in-law a misery.

Now, on his return from the Continent, they had met again, and the old attraction had been rekindled. To her he was infinitely more attractive than he had been – older, experienced, self-assured, yet with that tinge of romantic melancholy which women of Cecily's lively sort find irresistible. Handsomer, too, in the newly popular clean-shaven fashion. Her husband had died two years before – a nice convenient period for her to emerge from mourning and get back into the social whirl. It was sad about George, of course, but one soon got over these things. A sadder thought than George, beneath his expensive headstone in Kensal Green, was the comparatively small amount of money he had left her. Enough to keep up the Mayfair house, with fewer servants and no carriage, but not as much as she had hoped

273

for, and wanted.

Maurice had money; that was another of his charms. The new picture set the seal on his reputation – it was fairly sure that he would be elected an R.A. before long, and with some careful manipulation from her (he was too modest himself) a knighthood might follow. 'Lady Reide' would sound well . . . Besides, he was such a dear and she didn't mind a bit about the Juliet episode.

But he was still sore from it, or from something, not ready yet to give her all his attention, and she wanted that. A few more weeks together, more pleasant social occasions in this pleasant London Season, and the moment would come to prompt him, as she well knew how to do, into a proposal. They had suited each other very well in the past, on those stolen afternoons with the parlour door locked, and in his rooms by the river. She remembered those times so vividly: Maurice's youth and strength, and a touching eagerness, a gratitude for her beauty, and an urgency, as though he sought to find something hidden in her. If only she had known what it was. Perhaps now she would find out.

He watched her across the table, dainty hands busy with the silver teapot and hot-water jug, hands as delicate as Brown's china. She looked as decorative in her trim dove-grey afternoon dress and wide blue feathered hat as she did dressed for a ball. Her features were as finely formed as her limbs, an oval face with bright hazel eyes and a clever mouth, dark hair just winged at the temples with grey. Perhaps she was a little, a very little, like Madeline. He put that thought away. Cecily, familiar, a good companion, an enthusiastic lover. His mind, like hers, dwelt on prudent delay and the right moment.

'How was Venice?' she asked him.

'Wet. Everywhere, all the time. The rain came down incessantly and the canals somehow got into the streets. I was astonished that the pigeons in St Mark's Square hadn't turned into ducks. The city's sinking under a weight of water; such loveliness, to be condemned to death by drowning.'

'You didn't find it romantic?'

'Infinitely. Lovely muted colours, and such an air to it; the Bride of the Sea. I stayed in a palace, no less, with a dear old *contessa* who didn't seem to notice that her house was

274

crumbling. All the English seemed to be elderly and single.'

Her eyes quizzed him. 'So you didn't find another Juliet there? Or should it be Desdemona?'

'Sometimes you're too clever. No. Although . . .' he hovered on the brink of telling her of Zoë's prophecy, and of his blank disappointment when it was not fulfilled. He went on, 'Couples drift about the Gran' Canal in gondolas, of course. I suspect they take their partners with them.' The Barcarolle from *The Tales of Hoffman* was running through his head; once again he was at L'Opèra in Paris, watching the bejewelled figure of the stealer of hearts and souls, and the helpless Hoffman – himself, as he fancied – and, somewhere round the corner of his vision, a woman glittering in white and diamonds, a woman like a swan. He wanted to talk about these things, perhaps to unload them from his memory. But Cecily was very daintily and pointedly handing him a plate of sandwiches, cut exquisitely thin.

He took one, switching his mind to a time when he might sit just as now, but at his own tea-table, with the same smiling woman opposite. Once he had dreamed or fantasized about a home in Chelsea, where he would live with his wife and children . . . children? Would Cecily want children, or even be young enough to have them? He knew little about such things, only that the small brown children of Italy had charmed him; there had been a baby in a cradle in the cottage where Maria lived with her family, her infant brother, a tiny thing with a head of curls the colour of her own, and the same melting eyes. He would like to have painted her and the child as Mary with the baby Christ.

Cecily was smiling at him, challenging him to tell her his thoughts. But now was not the time. He put out a hand and laid it over hers, the pretty hand with the polished shell-pink nails, noticing idly that she still wore George's wedding ring, but not the sapphire engagement ring that had been above it. In the obtuse way of men, he wondered why.

She was talking about a fancy-dress ball at Devonshire House to which they were both invited. 'I may count on you as partner? Oh, what fun – what shall we go as? I fancy being the gorgeous Georgiana, in hoops and powder – though I expect every other lady will have the same idea. What shall we do with you? Something romantic – it must be romantic.

Childe Harold, perhaps, since you're such a wanderer. Black velvet and knee-breeches, and an open shirt-neck. I can see it all.'

Playing up to her, Maurice recited solemnly:

'And dost thou ask what secret woe
I bear, corroding joy and youth?
And wilt thou vainly seek to know
A pang e'en thou must fail to soothe?'

Cecily clapped her hands. 'Bravo! He even knows the right sort of poetry. What a distinguished pair we shall make.' She leaned across the table, smiling into his eyes, and the waiter, passing them, thought what a distinguished pair they made then. Mrs Hugh-Jones was a very sharp lady; she knew how to pick 'em, and very likely it would be a match before too long.

Chapter Twenty-Two

MADELINE HAD DECIDED TO SELL the Greenwich house. It was to sign some papers on her behalf that Maurice went to Bedford Row, where her solicitors had their offices. The day was warm and bright, and after almost two hours in dark, stuffy confinement he decided to get some air by walking back to his studio; and so found himself in High Holborn.

Because he had nothing better to do he read shop-signs and hoardings, taking in the character of a street unfamiliar to him. Outside a dilapidated building with an ornate portico and an air of having seen better days he stopped, arrested by the poster pasted on its door. "Grand Bal Masqué," it announced, and the date, that day's. "Full cabaret, excellent band specially engaged. Sensational Poses Plastiques! A Feast of Beauty and Wit! Dancing in the Famous Marble Ballroom! Come early and avoid disappointment! Admission two shillings."

Maurice smiled. Difficult to imagine such a façade hiding a marble ballroom, or much beauty and wit. He was seized with a sudden curiosity about the place. There would be professional performers, perhaps unlike any he had drawn lately; since his return to England he had visited only a few low-class music halls. His costume had come from the theatrical suppliers. He would try it out at a ball very different from the Duchess of Devonshire's.

He hesitated whether to ask Cecily to go with him. She would think it a lark, but he knew nothing about the place – things might well get rough, and though he was not afraid for himself it might be no place for a lady. He would go alone, with not too much money on him and no valuables. Amused at the prospect of an unconventional adventure, he walked briskly home.

The evening was clear and starry, an evening made for

romance. A curious excitement possessed Maurice as the cab took him towards the place. When the cabbie had asked him, 'Where to, sir?' his mind had been a blank; he remembered the site of the building, but not the name. Now, paying the man off, he glanced up and saw above the door 'Casino De Venise' in large gold letters.

Inside, his excitement faded. The foyer bore signs of one-time grandeur, but it had been allowed to deteriorate. Chipped plaster had not been renewed, faded paintings of Venetian scenes had been painted over in crude colours, pillars had been scrawled on and the scrawls only partially erased. The Casino de Venise was not flourishing, as it had done twenty years before.

A painted, bored-seeming woman took the money and directed him to the ballroom, where the cabaret was to take place. It had, indeed, a great deal of marble in it, and must at one time have been handsome. Crystal chandeliers lit it, but not so well as they once had done, for many of their drops had vanished, and some had not even been converted to gas, and remained unlit. In front of the stage at one end of the room a small orchestra was tuning up, surrounded by potted palms; they may have been specially engaged, but their appearance suggested that they were out-of-work theatre musicians.

They were evidently under instructions to play until enough people had come in to make the entertainment worth going on with. While they plodded through selections from musical comedies Maurice passed the time by sketching them: thin little men, stout men purple-faced from beer and gin, sombre dark foreign men, and, at the harp, a sharp-faced middle-aged woman in a black ball-gown. At last sufficient revellers had arrived for the money-taker, who seemed to be in charge of the proceedings, to give the signal for the cabaret to start. The red curtains parted, revealing a man in a baggy loud-checked suit and a grotesque clown's make-up. Maurice was disappointed. He had drawn such characters often, and found them more sinister them amusing. The man's patter was predictable, a string of increasingly bawdy stories followed by a crudely suggestive song and dance. Maurice began to be glad he had not brought Cecily.

Next came a conjuror, a slick performer with an American

accent Maurice suspected not to be genuine. With his per-
petually smiling partner, a robust young woman in spangled
tights, he ran through a succession of familiar tricks, to the
accompaniment of remarks from the audience growing increasingly restless. 'Get on with it,' they shouted. 'We want
the girls.' It became a steady chant. 'We – want – the – girls.'
The conjuror hurried to the end of his act, grinning nervously. As the curtains closed on him a cheer went up.

The orchestra broke into a languorous, Eastern-sounding
number. Now silent and excited, the audience seemed to hold
its collective breath as the curtains parted again. Maurice
glanced at his programme. 'The Bath of Venus' it proclaimed.

Against a backcloth of badly-painted rose trees, the girls
for whom the audience had waited so impatiently were posed,
quite still, hardly seeming to breathe, kneeling, standing or
lying around a large marble basin on which artificial doves
perched. In centre-stage, one foot advanced as though she
were about to step into the basin, stood a large blonde young
woman, draped in a white veil, which completely covered
her. Her attendants were not draped at all. They were so
cunningly posed that it was impossible to tell whether they
wore all-over fleshings, or flesh-coloured tights, or neither.
Some had long hair cascading over their shoulders, some
necklaces of bright-coloured beads that hung forward to
conceal their bosoms. Maurice, used to female nudity, decided that they were probably wearing nothing; and that the
audience knew it and had come to the Casino for that reason.
The girls were heavily made up, with rouged cheeks and
blue-shadowed eyelids; it was impossible to tell whether they
were naturally pretty, but none of them were as plump as
fashionable taste dictated, apart from one small girl well to
the front, and Venus herself. It was not hard to guess that this
was their passport to food, and that they were unemployed
actresses and dancers, or possibly prostitutes.

The music rose towards its climax, the moment eagerly
waited for, Venus raised her arms, and in one lightning
movement unveiled herself, in naked magnificence, her
breasts lightly rouged and a pink jewel lodged in her navel.
Before the eye could fully take in the vision, the gas floats
went down to a glimmer and the curtains closed rapidly. A
groan of disappointment went up as the orchestra changed to

a frisky number. Maurice hastily made a rough sketch of the figures as he remembered them and the unveiled Venus. The woman who had taken the money approached him with menace in her eye.

"'Ere, you ain't a rozzer, are yer?'

'No, an artist.'

'Ho yes?' She beckoned to a huge burly man leaning against the wall. 'Bert 'ere'll sort you out if you are, see.'

'I assure you there's no need. Do I look like a rozzer?'

They eyed him up and down, a slim black velvet-clad figure most unsuggestive of the police force. Maurice in return summed up the potential fighting ability of Bert, who was immensely overweight and flabby. Strong as he looked, he might be baffled by some neat footwork and well-placed blows; Maurice had been a considerable boxer at school. But he would prefer it not to come to the test. He opened his sketch-book, flipping over the pages so that they could see it had been well-used.

'The drawing I've just done is only one of many – look. I really am an artist, you know, and I thought the, er, tableau too amazing to miss.'

They glanced at one another, and the woman nodded to Bert, who retreated to his wall. 'All right, if you ses so. But don't let me see you gettin' up to anythin'.'

Maurice wondered what she had in mind: there seemed to be plenty of possibilities at the Casino de Venise. The orchestra had temporarily stopped, and drinks were being handed round. He decided to refresh himself from the bar with a pint of beer, but it was as warm as the atmosphere. The bar was crowded; he realized that the majority of those present were men, and that among the few women there seemed not to be one with an unpainted face. Pierrettes, nuns, powder-and-patch ladies, harem girls, looked equally raffish. He made rough sketches of them, as unobtrusively as possible. Drawing was evidently looked on as a suspicious activity. He was enjoying himself, looking forward to what might happen next.

Laura pulled the satin evening dress over her head and began to hook it up. It felt acutely uncomfortable, tight and awkward over her sweaty skin. There was no time to wash after the tableau, even if there had been any facilities beyond the basin of used water on the washstand. The crowded dressing-room smelt rankly of sweat and cheap perfume. The twelve girls crammed into it frequently lost their tempers with each other, herded as they were like cattle in a pen. Nude posing was not an enjoyable business. Even on a hot night they were chilled on the stone staircase down to the stage, and the effort of keeping still tried their nerves.

Laura craned over Polly's shoulder for a glimpse of the communal mirror, adjusting her eye-mask.

'Dunno why they gives us these things,' Polly grumbled, "less it's to make us look mysterious. Or cover up a bit o' the old physog. And some of us could do with it,' she added gloomily. 'Not so easy to keep yer girlish beauty on two-pence-farthing a week, which is about all yer get after *they*'ve taken their cut from what the gentlemen gives us. 'Ere, how'd you make out with that old geezer last night? He looked good for 'alf a quid to me.'

Laura shuddered, wincing away from the memory of the old man with whom she had agreed to go out into the dark street, for the money he would give her. 'Not as much as that,' she said, 'just about enough to buy a bit of meat with.'

'That's just about what *we* are, bits o' meat. Yer might call this place the meat-market. Cor, though, wouldn't I just like to get my pearlies into a slab o' nice beefsteak.' Polly sighed. 'At least I stays fat. Now you don't look no thicker than a hairpin. You watch you don't fade right away one of these fine days.' Laura didn't need the warning. She knew that if she lost much more weight her job would go with it.

'Come on, you two,' shouted the manageress from the doorway. 'Goin' to 'ang about all night, are yer?'

The dancing had begun when they entered the ballroom, and prospective partners were waiting for them to emerge. It was not wise to refuse anyone, however unappealing; he might turn rough or report a girl to the management. A weedy young man in a costume that might have represented any period of history offered his arm to Laura, and she accepted it with a mechanical smile. Polly was not immediately snapped up; Laura saw her waiting forlornly, as she and the weedy youth stepped on to the dance-floor.

Several dances later she had still not been propositioned by any of her partners, though she had had to submit to various familiarities. They were always mean early in the evening, before they'd had enough to drink; and it was still not dark outside. Suddenly all the strength went out of her. She sank into one of the chairs ranged round the walls. 'I'm sorry,' she told the man who had been just about to lead her out, 'I must rest for a few minutes.' He shrugged and walked away.

In all the days of her poverty she had never felt so weak, so utterly drained of energy, of hope, even. She wondered if it might not be easier to let herself die than to go on trying to keep body and soul together in such a degrading way. Death, with no violence about it – just the going back to her bare basement room and lying down, not to get up again. The landlord would find her at last, and there would be a pauper's funeral. Uncontrollable tears of weakness began to trickle down her cheeks, smudging the rouge and falling on to her almost bared bosom, where the diamond no longer rested.

Someone was speaking to her. 'What is it? Can I help you?' The voice was deep and musical, not the sort of voice usually heard in the Casino. She lifted drowned eyes to see a tall, slim man, dressed very plainly in black velvet knee-breeches and jacket, his white shirt poetically open at the neck to show a brown throat. His dark hair looked clean, and what she could see of his masked face was brown too, the mouth well-shaped and kind-looking. To her embarrassment she found she was too full of tears to speak to him.

'Come on,' he said. Raising her to her feet, he led her firmly through the outer fringe of dancers to a comparatively empty corner of the room, and sat her down on a small gilded sofa. 'Stay there, don't move. I'll be back in a second.' It seemed little more than that before he returned, a wine glass in his hand. 'Drink this – it's brandy and water. It will do you good.'

She sipped, then drained the glass. Underfed as she was, the liquor took immediate effect; the tears stopped and she managed a wincing smile.

'Thank you. You're very kind. I'm not ill, just . . .'

He was staring at her, not with the rude assessing stare she was used to, but a close, intent inspection of her face, from hair to throat and back again. Then he said, quietly, 'Take off

282

your mask. I know the rule is masks off at midnight, but never mind.'

Thankful to be rid of it, she unhooked it and let it drop. He drew a sharp breath.

'My God,' he said, 'it *is* you. Britannia. Laura.'

She started. 'What? Who are you? I don't know you –'

For answer he took off his own mask. 'Don't you know me now?'

'Yes, oh yes! At least . . . I think . . .'

'Ah, I used to have a beard. Otherwise I'm just the same. Laura, this is a miracle, To find you here, of all places, after looking for you so long – for it *was* you I was looking for, I know that now – after remembering you, and regretting that I ever left you, and wishing I could find you again. And now I have. I can't believe it.' He was looking at her as though he would never look away.

'I remembered you, too,' she said softly. 'And regretted, and wished. But it's too late now.'

'Too late?'

'You see what I've come to, Mr Reide. Go away now, and leave me. I wasn't worth finding.' Tears pricked her eyes again, tears of bitterness, now, for the futility of life and the ironies of fate. Maurice stood up.

'Yes, I will go away now, as you suggest. But you're coming with me, if I have to carry you out – I daresay a few screams would go unnoticed in this place. However, if you prefer to come quietly, run along to your dressing-room and get that stuff off your face and something over your shoulders. And just to make sure you don't give me the slip, I'm coming to the door with you. Ready?'

When she came back to him, a shabby cloak covering her dress, her face was clean of paint, and deathly pale. Maurice took her arm, feeling the trembling of her body. 'Now we'll find a cab,' he said cheerfully, as though what had happened was the most ordinary thing in the world, though he felt as though his voice must betray the agitation that shook him. In the cab he took her hand and held it, till it grew warm, and she leaned back with a sigh.

The air in the sitting-room of Maurice's studio was sweet

with wood-smoke from the small fire burning in the grate and freshness blowing in from the river. Outside the night sky was star-sprinkled, the stars seeming reflected and magnified in the lights along the Embankment and on the south bank. There was silence and peace and comfort. Maurice watched Laura, stretched out in a deep chair, her feet on a stool, as motionless and limp as a broken doll, asleep.

With aching pity he had watched her eat the meal his manservant had prepared for them, avid, hardly tasting the food for her need to eat it quickly, then suddenly pushing it away, sated. He saw the young roundness gone from her face, in which only the bones now were beautiful, the brightness from her complexion, the pock-marks on brow and neck, the hair somehow dimmed and faded from its old fairness. He saw the faint lines of experience and trouble at the side of her mouth, and the shadows round the eyes that were not made by paint. Suddenly the eyes opened, and met his.

'What were you thinking?' she asked sleepily.

'That it was your nose I recognized you by; the sweet little Roman nose, like Frances Stewart's, the first Britannia.'

Laura shook her head. 'I'm too stupid just now to understand that. How could you possibly admire my nose? I've always thought it was just a beak.'

'Her Majesty's is very similar.'

She laughed weakly. 'What ridiculous things you do say.' She struggled to sit up. 'Mr Reide – no, Maurice – you must let me go. I . . . I'm dirty.'

'I have a splendid bathroom. People come for miles to see it.'

'I don't mean that. I mean – the men. At that place. The worst part of it. It's too horrible to tell you.'

Maurice leaned forward, his face serious. 'Laura, my dear, I would rather you didn't try to tell me, because there's no need. I've travelled a long way, and seen many things, among them night-houses. I know girls who dance, and pose in them are sometimes obliged to take money from men in return for favours, to pad out the wretched payment they get. That's what you mean, isn't it?'

'Yes,' she said, relieved. 'But – they were only favours. Nothing else. I'd only just decided I must do the same as the others, if I wasn't to starve, you see.'

'I see, and I'm glad for you. And now you've told me the worst, tell me the rest, if you want to.'

'I do want to. I want to tell you everything that's happened to me – about Fred, and why I married him (that was because of you, you know) and why I was at the Paris Opéra with Der . . . with the man you saw, and all the silly, mad things I did after that. And then you can turn me out, if you like, and shut the door on me.'

'I shall never do that,' Maurice said. 'After I saw you in Paris I did think badly of you, I must admit. I thought . . . I don't know what I thought. I'd been told you were married, and to see you as I did was something of a shock. I put you out of my mind, or imagined I had. But of course you were there all the time, and I've searched for you – without knowing it, I suppose, because I thought you weren't for me. I know now that it was you I looked for in other women.'

'Were there many – other women?' Laura was not looking at him. He laughed suddenly.

'No – now I come to think of it. They were only shadows – shadows of you. A lovely young girl in Verona; I nearly got my throat cut on her account, but that was as far as it went.' At her horrified look he took her hand and held it tight. 'Don't worry, I'm hard to kill. And in Vienna – now there's a romantic city, full of beautiful women, yet I saw none like you.'

'But . . . I was in Vienna! I was to have been in an operetta at the Theater Elisabeth, and then the Crown Prince died and I was out of work and nearly starving – and a very strange . . . person took me home and wanted to paint me as a female monster – why are you looking like that?'

Maurice shook his head. A great sense of wonder possessed him at the realization of their nearness to each other in distant places, and how closely they must have missed each other. He gripped the pretty, soiled hand so tightly that she winced.

'Were you ever in Venice?'

'No. Why?'

'A fortune-teller told me I should find you there. And I did – at the poor old shabby Casino de Venise. We must always take soothsayers seriously in future, my love.' He lifted her out of the deep winged chair, lifted her out of it, and sitting down himself set her on his knee.

'Your love? Even though I've lost my best looks, and voice, and innocence, if that's what they call it? All that, Maurice?'

'All that, Laura. I see in you what I always saw, though what it is I can't tell you, because love has its own reasons which even lovers don't understand. Whatever makes you Laura, and nobody else.'

'So it wasn't just my face,' she murmured, against his shoulder.

'What, my love?'

'Nothing – only that I used to be rather jealous of my face, because that was all people seemed to like me for.'

For answer he held her close and kissed her many times, vowing to himself that in his care she should have her beauty back, and her health and her peace of mind, and that the bad times and mistakes of their search for each other should be forgotten like unhappy dreams.

A vow which he kept, far beyond his highest hopes, and hers. And the diamond, reclaimed from the pawnshop, never again lost its brilliance.